Also by Stephen Swartz

Contemporary Literary Fiction

After Ilium

Aiko

A Beautiful Chill

A Girl Called Wolf

Fantasy & Science Fiction

The Stefan Székely Vampire Trilogy

I. A Dry Patch of Skin

II. Sunrise

III. Sunset

Epic Fantasy *With Dragons

The Dream Land Trilogy

I. Long Distance Voyager

II. Dreams of Future's Past

III. Diaspora

EXCHANGE

A Novel

Stephen Swartz

EXCHANGE

Stephen Swartz

MYRDDIN PUBLISHING GROUP

UNITED STATES · UNITED KINGDOM · AUSTRALIA

ISBN-13: 978-1-68063-057-2

ISBN-10: 1-68063-057-1

www.myrddinpublishing.com

Cover Design by Iris Schaeffer

Whoever fights monsters should see that in the process he does not become a monster.

—Nietzsche, *Beyond Good and Evil*

1

BILL MASTERS AWOKE WITH A START, realized the damn phone was buzzing again. Why couldn't they leave him alone? He had no more comments to give. It's done, isn't it? Finished. Nothing more to say. Hell, what more could anyone say? Only questions too big to answer. Why? How? Why couldn't it have gone a different way? He'd already considered those questions, couldn't stop thinking of them, and the answers, any answers—any *other* answers. Something different.

He pushed himself up from the bed enough to reach for the phone on the nightstand. Fumbling with the device, he pushed his thumb on the green circle to answer it.

"Hello?" he spoke, holding the phone in front of his face, wrist resting on the crumpled pillow. His voice was gruff, full of the night's phlegm. Maybe whoever was calling—some damn reporter probably, a newspaper writer, or, worse, somebody with words of comfort—would be put off by his bluntness, his weary tone.

He couldn't hear the caller, pushed the button for the speaker.

"Hello...?" came the voice on the other end, light and feminine. He replayed the word through his mind, wondering who it could be. Sounded like a kid. Prank call?

"Yeah?" he demanded in a stronger voice.

"Uh...hello." It wasn't a question this time but a statement. "Are you...Mister Masters?"

He grumbled, cleared his throat. "Yeah, what do you want?"

"Sorry."

The pause gave them both time to adjust their expectations. This was not the usual way they spoke when calling. He hated how they tried to be so professional, so positive, upbeat even, like nothing had happened, one more quirky human interest story. But he'd had enough of that. He didn't need even one more—especially someone who didn't know how to get right to it and ask the same damn questions the others asked. How's he doing? How's he getting by? What's next for him?

"Shit, say something," he shouted as gruffly as he could, holding back his anger a little. He couldn't put enough wind behind his words.

"I...I'm here," the girl's voice declared. He could tell the voice was scared now. Maybe not a kid. But definitely not a reporter.

He still wasn't having any of their games. "Here...?"

"Airport," she spoke, her voice hopeful.

He rubbed his forehead, squinting at the phone, still seeking the darkness behind his eyelids, the only place where he could find any peace. Taking a long breath, he let it out slowly.

"What about the airport?"

"I'm here."

"So you're at the airport?" He shook his head, feeling all his anger and frustration returning. Anger at the whole world. Frustration at the situation he was forced into. "What's that supposed to mean?"

He had enough, pushed the button to hang up.

Why couldn't they leave him alone? He rolled back on the bed, stared at the ceiling, blinking. Yes, he was still here, still alive, in his house. It was probably Monday or Tuesday by now. He had lost his lost weekend. How long had he been in bed? He felt his face, a good growth of beard there. Hair oily, matted. He gave himself a sniff. It had to be at least three days. Bad smell under his arms. His breath tasted terrible. Maybe it was time to get up.

He'd only pulled himself out of bed to pee and drink more beer from a case in the fridge. He would try to stay up, but a few minutes staring out the windows of the kitchen, seeing the patio furniture, the abandoned swingset, was enough to send him back to bed, where he could forget. He took pills the first night, he remembered. The second night? He'd forgotten. He was waking from the third night—

The phone was buzzing again.

As he stared, the buzzing seemed to intensify, becoming insistent.

He reached for the phone, his hand hovering over it. Answer? Get it over with? Or press his finger to the red circle to hang up? Let it go to voicemail? The options were many these days. Other things, well, not so many options. The people in that store weren't given any options. They were just there, in the way.

"Yeah?" he growled, picking up the phone.

"Hello. Sorry. I'm still here—"

"Yeah, I figured."

"—at airport. May I please speak to Missus Masters? No answer on her phone."

He held the phone away from his face, loading a string of profanity to fire back at the caller. But something stopped him. The tone of her voice. A girl, sweet tone, nervous, afraid. He was rude before, so of course she was afraid.

"I'm sorry," he spoke in as plain a voice as he could conjure. He had to start dealing with the world again. Might as well start with a simple phone call. He cleared his throat. "She's not...available."

"Oh." A pause, car noises in the background. "May I please speak to Becky Masters?"

Hearing his daughter's name stung his ear. Must be one of her friends calling. Sounds like she doesn't know.

"She's also not available."

"Oh."

The silence seemed like an hour.

"May I help you?" he spoke at last, resigned.

"Yes, please," said the tiny voice, a shade of accent lingering.

He shook his head. Too much to deal with. He wasn't ready.

"I'm Bill Masters," he practically shouted. "You're the one calling me. Don't you know who you're calling? You should know who the hell you're calling if you're doing the calling, right?"

He heard sobbing on the other end.

"Okay. Hey. I'm sorry. I didn't mean to be...mean. It's just that...."

The crying got louder.

"Hey, now," he said in a calmer voice. "I'm sorry. Really. I guess you don't know." He found himself breathing hard. "Who are you?"

Sniffles. "My name is Wendy."

"Wendy?" He dug in his brain. Some school friend of his daughter?

That was the only possibility. He thought he knew all of them. "I'm sorry, but things have been...crazy around here. Is there something I can do for you? Why are you calling?"

He heard some irregular breathing as she calmed herself.

"I come for exchange program," she said, sniffling.

His eyes closed tight. Something Barb had told him but he had dismissed. Like so many moments. She would tell him something and he would assume it was nothing important, give her a nod and uh-huh and go on with whatever he was doing—grading papers, planning a lesson, typing his stories. Now he recalled her mentioning an exchange program. His school had an exchange program.

"Exchange program?" he asked hesitantly.

"Yes. I come for exchange program. I'm going to live with Masters family," and she gave the complete address of his house.

He threw his feet off the bed, pressed them to the floor and sat up, feeling his head move farther than he expected. The room seemed to fold in on him and he ducked.

"That's my address," he muttered. "What's your name again?"

There was a relieved giggle. "Wendy. My Chinese name is Wang Wu Ting. Please call me Wendy."

Shaking his head, he felt the pain swirl inside his skull. He did recall—now. Barb said a girl would stay with them for the school year, sharing Becky's room. He had nodded his approval. He hadn't thought any more about it. Barb would handle that business. Barb would pick up the girl. Barb and Becky would greet her at the airport and bring her home. To this house. She likely had called Becky first and gotten no answer. Then tried Barb.

"Yeah, okay, I got it now." He breathed deeply. There really was a world out there full of things happening. He had been taking a break from it, but it was always there, ready to pounce on him. "Listen, uh, Wendy. Things are, uh...everything's changed now."

"But I got school starting...."

"I know, but...." Taking a big breath, he knew he couldn't explain everything over the phone. And she needed to be picked up from the airport regardless. That was the right thing to do. Who else could do that? Just go, he ordered himself. Sort it out later.

He tried to laugh, an ironic utterance that would keep the devil at bay. This situation certainly was irony: a good example for his class. He would need to call someone. But in the morning; after all, it was.... He looked at the phone: past ten p.m., oh my god. How long had she been waiting? How long had he lain in bed, trying to forget everything? Could it ever be forgotten? Arrangements could be made. Had to be made. Then he could get back to his endless sleep, drink his beer and take his pills and hope that when he finally awoke nothing would be the same.

"Listen, Wendy. I'll pick you up. Let me get myself together. Maybe take me thirty minutes, then thirty minutes to drive down there. So sit tight for another hour. Sorry about the wait. But I will pick you up. I'm on it."

"Thank you," replied Wendy. "I can't wait to meet everyone." She added something about Becky, plans they had made through email. And a compliment for Barb, who'd been so generous and promised they would go to special places and do special things.

He frowned, pursing his lips, hating the taste in his mouth. He thought of something to say, something neutral, but he couldn't. He blinked, returning to a reality he hated.

"Yeah," he mumbled, more like an exhale than a reply. "See you soon. Hold tight."

Bill didn't bother shaving but did take a shower, shampooed, put on fresh clothes, like what he'd wear to school, slacks and a button shirt, argyle socks, and his comfortable brown sneakers that looked close to leather shoes but were more comfortable. Had to make a good first impression. His wife always harped on how he dressed: casual sloppy, she called it. And Becky teased how old-fashioned his style was.

Sitting in his blue Ford Escape felt strange, like he hadn't driven the SUV in a month. Barb's jacket still lay on the passenger seat, his daughter's school bag in the back seat. He took time to remove them, setting them on chairs in the kitchen. Returning to the vehicle, he pulled the seatbelt across himself and started the engine. It groaned to life. It sounded different; everything was different.

He started to go but stopped before hitting the garage door.

"Geez," he grumbled, slamming his foot on the brake. Rubbing his forehead, he took several deep breaths.

He pushed the button on the clicker and the garage door rose with its usual clangs. Once up, he rolled out and paused on the driveway to make sure the door closed. Then he remembered to push the button again. The door slid down. He backed out of the driveway into the dark residential street, the house centered between two streetlights.

Rolling along under the speed limit, he wondered how much beer he had drank. He stopped at the main avenue, Broadway, checked cross traffic, turned. So far, so good. The street was the same. For late night, on a...what day was it? He started to count back, then stopped. His eyes became wet. Rubbing them, he knew he shouldn't count back. It would only hurt.

But he wanted to hurt. He wanted to feel the pain he'd felt in that first moment of shock—and the hours after. He wanted to experience it again and again, like he deserved it.

Red and blue lights lit up the night behind him and he cursed, pulling the Escape over to the shoulder in front of the Whataburger.

"License and registration," said the officer.

Bill handed them over.

After a moment examining the documents: "Oh, Mister Masters. You were on the news. I'm sorry." He leaned in, holding his flashlight, studied the man driving the SUV. "You okay? I mean to drive."

Facing forward, Bill spoke calmly: "I'm just tired."

"I'm gonna give you a warning. Drive carefully. You were weaving across the lanes. I thought you were a drunk driver."

"I've only had three beers in three days," he muttered.

"Maybe get some coffee," the officer suggested. He pointed to the Whataburger. "Theirs is all right. Wake you up anyway."

Bill stretched over, took a look. He was already late. "I'll go through the drive-thru."

Sitting behind a pickup truck in the drive-thru lane, he pondered what he was doing. Driving drunk in the middle of the night to pick up a girl he didn't know. And then what?

"Large coffee," he spoke. "Cream and sugar."

He drove slowly, focusing on maintaining his lane and not going too fast. Broadway became a highway as he continued south into Oklahoma City from the suburb. Other travelers came up to him, sped ahead. He watched for signs directing him to the airport. He hadn't been there for a couple years, when he'd flown to a conference. He knew there was a jog in the highway at the place he was supposed to exit to get on the road leading to the airport. He had missed it last time and had to circle around.

And there it is!—*was*. Again, he cursed. They needed some neon lights on that sign. He got off at the next exit, circled around, tried the airport exit again.

The road leading to the terminal was dark but the terminal itself was lit up ahead. Arrivals on the lower level. Taxi lane, bus lane, hotel shuttles this way, cars that way. He got the right lane, slowing.

There she was. A girl standing alone beside a large pink suitcase. Had to be her. Nobody else around. The last passenger to arrive.

He rolled to the curb in front of her, shut off the engine, glancing out the passenger-side window at her. She didn't seem to register that he was the one arriving to pick her up, not curious about the vehicle, gazing to her left down the sidewalk.

He got out of the Escape, walked slowly around the vehicle, stepped onto the curb.

"Hi," he said, forcing a smile. "You're Wendy?"

She wiped her face like she had been crying. "I'm Wendy."

"Hi," he repeated, extending his hand.

She timidly shook it. "Hello."

"I'm Bill Masters. Sorry about the phone before." He started to grab her suitcase, stopped. Digging out his wallet, he flipped it open, slid out his driver's license, handed it to her. "Here. My license. To prove I'm me. Bill Masters. See my address there? You don't want to get into a car with a stranger, do you?"

She grinned at that courtesy, gave her eyes one last wipe.

"Thank you, Mister Masters."

She handed back the license and he put it away.

"You can call me Bill."

He grabbed the pink hardside suitcase and opened the rear door of the Escape. Moving some gear around to make room for the suitcase, he mumbled how big the suitcase was, asked if she had everything she needed in it, listening to her way of speaking, like a child or cartoon character, light in tone, high in pitch.

He shut the rear hatch and opened the passenger door for her, waved his hand for her to climb in.

She grinned as she slid past him.

Going to the driver's side, he shook his head, leaning against the SUV a moment, then got in and buckled his seatbelt. She didn't seem to know about seatbelts. He leaned over to snap it for her.

"Not used to driving?" he asked, making a joke.

"I usually ride subway or bicycle."

"Ah, I see."

He started the engine and they drove away, following the circuitous route out to the highway.

Once they were on the main highway heading north, he glanced at the girl. Standing on the sidewalk, she looked short and thin. Her hair hung long and straight, dark brown in the lamplight at the airport, full on her shoulders and down her back. An oval face, with a bigger nose than he expected on an Asian girl, chin a little more prominent than expected. She wore a dark blue blazer, too much for the late summer heat of Oklahoma, he thought. Maybe part of a school uniform. Under her blazer was a white knit pullover. He took a quick look down: light blue slacks, casual yet stylish, with an embroidered fish on one knee. Her shoes were white sneakers, flawlessly clean.

"I'm sorry for the delay picking you up," he began absently. "Things have been a mess around here. Everything's disrupted. You'll see. First, though, are you hungry? It must've been a long trip."

"No, thank you," she replied with a polite smile.

"I'm serious. If you're hungry, we should stop someplace. There's nothing to eat at the house."

He saw a row of restaurants along the highway. Two were still open at that hour. Before she could answer, he exited.

"I'm hungry, too. Let's stop over there." He pointed to the brightly lit House of Pancakes. "You know what pancakes are?"

"Pan...cakes...?"

"Yes, like for breakfast. Even though it's night now. I think that may just hit the spot." He almost bit his tongue at his words. *Hit the spot.* He meant his stomach, of course. The right food for what his stomach craved. "They also have sandwiches and salads, if that's a better choice for you."

She really had no choice, he realized. Whatever he wanted to do, she was his captive. The thought made him wince. Captive. Hostage. He wasn't a criminal. He wouldn't hurt her.

"Just a stack of pancakes," Bill told the waitress, an older woman with her blonde hair put up with a clip, "and coffee."

"And you, hon?" asked the waitress.

Bill could see the way the woman looked the girl over. And what she must've been thinking. What's this middle-aged white guy doing out late with this Asian teen? How much did she cost? He frowned, waiting for her to leave.

"Please, I want a...what did you say? ...stack? ...of pancakes," said the girl. "And coffee." She smiled like she'd won a recitation contest.

"You sure you want coffee? This late? You probably want to go on to sleep, don't you? But me, I need to drive. Maybe try O.J.?"

"O.J.?"

"Orange juice."

"Oh." She grinned like she'd learned something important. "Yes, I want O.J., please."

"That'll be fine, hon," said the waitress, making a note on her pad.

When she stepped away from the booth, Bill leaned across the table. "Excuse me for a minute. Gotta go to the restroom. Be right back. Sit tight."

Once inside the men's room, he let out a big exhale, like he had been too afraid to breathe. He'd been holding himself in check for an hour. Was it a panic attack? He'd read about those. Or what he'd felt last week. Were those also nothing more than panic attacks?

He stared into the mirror, saw a gaunt figure staring back at him. Should've shaved. It had been a week. Last week? No, the same week. Same damn week. Going to look like a fool if he can't remember what day it is. Saturday night. Almost Sunday morning.

He blinked, staring at himself. Then something wet popped out of one eye, ran down his cheek. The other eye followed. He wiped his face. *Stop it. Just stop already.* He ran some water, washed his face.

What the hell am I doing? He knew how it looked. He saw it in the waitress's expression. Maybe she was calling the police to report this sex trafficker, this desperate pervert. Got to rescue the poor girl.

Too much to deal with. His world was upside-down. Maybe it was a good idea when he and Barb agreed. Becky liked the idea. They could be sisters, sharing the same room, going to classes together, learning from each other. That's the point. International exchange. Supposed to be a good thing. But now everything was ruined.

The food had been served when he returned to the table. Wendy sat patiently, waiting for him, not touching the pancakes.

"All right," he said in a grateful voice. "Let's eat."

He slathered the butter between the cakes and on top. He chose the blueberry syrup and let a thin line drizzle the top of the stack, let some run over the side. She watched him like a scientist.

"I don't like a lot of syrup. Too sweet." He sat down the syrup and she followed suit: butter, syrup, just as he had done. "You never had pancakes before?"

"Pancakes. More thin. Put vegetables and meat inside." She flashed a smile. "Chinese style."

"Oh, right. I've been to Chinese restaurants where they served these thin uh—they're like tortillas—and we rolled up the meat—pork, I think it was—and veggies, bean sprouts?—with a dark sauce."

She giggled, a pleasant sound.

"So...Wendy...." He paused to chew, swallow. "I didn't get to know very much about you or, in fact, this whole situation. How about you tell me about yourself? Where are you from in China?"

She sat down her fork and rolled her eyes up as though she had to recall her canned self-introduction speech.

"My name is Wang Wu Ting. Wang is family name. I come from a small city near Beijing. Name is Langfang. In Hebei province." She spent several minutes reciting what the city was famous for and what its leading products were. She seemed proud.

He forced a grin. "But what about you?"

A moment of confusion, her set script interrupted, then: "I am seventeen years old. I like playing tennis, playing swim, and anime. I like to cook. I don't have any brother or sister. I have a little dog. Name is Chu-Chu—"

"Like a train, huh?"

She froze, puzzled.

"Trains go *choo choo*." He waved her to continue.

"I want to be engineer. I will study engineer in university."

"*An* engineer," Bill automatically corrected. "And it's engineer*ing* you want to study."

She frowned, like she had made serious errors.

"Hey, don't worry about it." He forced a smile. "That's why you're here, isn't it? To learn English *gooder*—better? Yep, to get the whole American experience. Right? Sure isn't to see Oklahoma, I'll bet...."

He watched for a reaction.

She had resumed eating the stack of pancakes, not making much of a dent in it. Her forkfuls were tiny and delivered with precision to her little mouth. A bit of syrup blotted her chin and she dabbed it with her napkin, displaying the embarrassment of committing a major faux pas.

"Wendy, relax." He regarded her as she took another bite, chewing as though trying to hide the fact she was chewing. "Don't think this is the normal way things are done here. This isn't a normal situation. What I mean is...like me picking you up late at night like this, and then...uh...."

He became aware of two police officers sitting behind him.

"What I mean is...we're not going to be doing this again." That didn't sound any better. He knew how it looked. The waitress had confirmed how suspicious they appeared. "I expect us to settle into a regular schedule, one that fits your school hours. And then we can...."

He felt the police officers were listening to him.

"You're an exchange student. You came to America for one year. You will live with us and go to school with my daughter, Becky."

Wendy nodded at each statement. "Yes, Mister Masters."

"I'm just picking you up from the airport. Sorry it's so late. My fault. It was going to be my wife, Barbara, who picked you up, but she...."

His face became red and he threw up a hand to cover his face. He felt a flush come over him. He heaved and a sob slipped out.

"Miss? Are you okay?" asked one of the officers, getting up from his seat and standing there to address her and Bill, the creep who had picked her up for late-night fun. "This man bothering you?"

Wendy shook her head, giggled. "He is my daddy."

The officer narrowed his eyes at him. "Daddy, huh?"

"Host father," Bill corrected, staring soberly across at her. "She's our exchange student. She'll be living with us for the coming year."

"Oh, I get it," said the officer.

As Bill lowered his hand, it was obvious he had been crying.

"Are you okay, sir?" asked the officer.

"No," said Bill.

"No?"

"Things are not how they're supposed to be." He looked up.

"Oh, hey—you're that guy." The officer turned to his partner. "Jim, this is the guy on TV. The Quail Run guy."

Officer Jim craned his head to see over the booth wall. "Oh, yeah. Real sorry for what happened, sir. Your interview showed real courage. I'd blow the bastard away, too. But you didn't hear me say that."

"Yes, very brave. Especially at a time like that," the first officer added. He glanced at the girl, back at Bill. "Well, I'll leave you two. Enjoy your dinner."

The officer sat down in his booth and Bill leaned forward against the table, rubbing his eyes. "I gave an interview, that's all."

"Are you okay?" asked Wendy, her face showing concern.

"No, I'm not." He hid his eyes from her, fingers poking the tear ducts, trying to stop the flow. "You see...."

"What is the matter, Mister Masters?" the girl asked so innocently.

Bill dropped his hands on the table, let his teary face be revealed. He saw the shock on her face. Yes, who is this creep the police seem to know? That's what she was thinking. And where is the woman and the girl who are supposed to welcome her to America?

He took a long breath, thinking through his checklist. "Do you need to call someone? To let them know you arrived safely?"

"I called Mama." She sat still as stone.

"Good."

"I called at airport."

Bill gazed a moment at the wall behind her, a Western landscape painting hanging there.

"Listen, Wendy.... The reason my wife is unable to pick you up tonight is.... And my daughter, Becky, too...." He couldn't finish the sentence, took a breath. "You two had some correspondence?"

"We exchange emails. And we are on WeChat."

"WeChat.... Some other online thing, huh?"

She nodded happily, an endorsement.

"Yes, well, uh.... There's no easy way to say this, so I'm just going to say it out. First, let me remind you that we *will* make some kind of arrangement for you. Don't worry. I'm sure you can still have a good year here."

Her worried expression returned. "Arrangement? What is it?"

He held his breath, let it out slowly.

"The reason my wife and daughter couldn't pick you up tonight is because...because...they are dead."

Her face registered shock, but more like she was checking whether she had heard the word clearly. "Dead?"

"There was a shooting about two weeks ago. Several people were killed. My wife, Barbara, and my daughter, Becky, were among the victims."

2

BILL STARED AT THE WALL behind Wendy. A painting of a Western scene hung there: desert landscape, a rickety covered wagon and horses. He tried to imagine himself in that scene, riding away, going to a new place, forgetting everything.

His eyes were drawn to an old man with a cane, shuffling back to the restrooms, opening the women's door then pausing, realizing his error and going instead to the men's room.

Bill looked away from the restrooms but couldn't face his guest yet. He turned to his right, avoiding her. He could hear her sniffling, upset at the news. There were diners in booths along the opposite wall, at 2 and 4 o'clock. At 2 sat two beefy men, beards and tough faces, denim jackets, probably bikers. He watched as one man lay his gnarly hand over the other's hand on the table, beside their empty plates. Bill looked away. At 4 he saw a young couple, dad on one side, mother and infant on the other. Only a large glass of iced tea on the table, like they had no place to go, no money for anything but tea. The infant was getting fussy. When the mother grabbed a towel and positioned the infant for nursing, he looked away. Behind him, the police officers had finished and left.

"I'm sorry," he mumbled, intending how he ignored her just then, but it could have been for the world itself, Oklahoma, or this restaurant. "I know it's a lot to digest. I mean all at once. I've had a week. Since the funeral." He thought a moment, shaking his head. "Not that a week's long enough. It's just that, well, sorry I forgot you were coming." He felt his eyes wet again. "It's all been too much. And now.... I don't know what to do with you."

She dug in her tiny purse, hanging from a strap around her neck and shoulder, and retrieved a travel packet of tissues. She pulled out one and handed it to him. Another she kept for herself, dabbing at the corners of her eyes, then pinching it around her nose. Sniffles.

"Barb planned for you and Becky to share a room. Like sisters, you know? We got another bed for you to sleep on." He stabbed his fork into the pancakes, no longer warm, saturated with syrup. He decided he was done. "Anyway...for tonight you can sleep there. Unless it seems weird...being in her room. Tomorrow we'll figure out what to do."

"What to do?" Her eyebrows colluded. "I come for high school. Can I go to school?"

"Yes, of course. I meant as far as your accommodations."

Her eyes were dark, warm, innocent. Did she not understand? There was no way a teenage girl could stay with him. He wasn't any kind of creep, but how would it look? He had to teach. Students these days could be merciless teasing about anything that seemed irregular. Moreover, he was too distraught. It all seemed like a bad dream. He hadn't even begun the stage of grief where you pack up things. And George Griffin, principal at the high school, told him he should take time off after dealing with the funeral.

He looked over their plates. "Finished?"

"Yes." She nodded, pursed her lips. "Thank you."

"You're welcome."

He waved for the check, which the waitress brought over.

"I thought I recognized you," said the woman like she was now a good friend, setting the check on the table. "From the TV, ya know. But you got a beard now."

"Yes. I need to get myself together."

She lingered, staring at Wendy. "Couldn't help overhearing y'all talkin. Just wanna say 'Welcome to America'. Welcome to Oklahoma City, hon."

"Thank you," said Wendy with a dip of her head.

Bill rose from the booth, followed the waitress to the cashier stand, paid the check, Wendy right behind him.

The highway was dark as they drove. They waited at a stoplight in the suburb of Edmond. Bill stared ahead. He sensed the girl getting tired. She repressed a yawn. He turned the Escape at the next avenue, went east, pointing to the university entrance. Another stoplight, green left-turn arrow. The residential street was quiet, everyone asleep. He pulled into the driveway and pushed the button on the remote to open the garage door.

Barb's silver Lexus sedan was not parked there, he saw, and for a moment he forgot that something had happened. It must still be in the parking lot, he thought. He would need to go and find it, arrange to tow it home. Then what? Sell it? Drive it once in a while? Barb only drove it to work, a couple miles each way. And to the mall.

He pulled into the garage, shut off the engine, pressed the button to close the garage door.

There was such weight pressing on him that Bill couldn't move. A moment became a couple minutes.

The garage light went off.

"Mister Masters?" called Wendy in the darkness. "Are you okay?"

The sounds of sobbing filled the vehicle. He laid his head against the steering wheel. The honk echoed a long time. He sucked air, sniffling loudly, groaning his pain.

Suddenly he opened the door and stepped out. The motion made the light click on. He went to the rear of the Escape, opened the door, and retrieved her pink suitcase. Meanwhile, Wendy had opened her door and climbed out. She stood there as Bill took the suitcase around the driver's side, up to the door leading into the kitchen and entered, closing the door behind him.

The garage light clicked off.

A second later, the kitchen door opened and a hand switched on the garage light.

"I'm sorry," Bill called out. "I'm not thinking. I thought you already went inside."

He waved her around the rear of the Escape and over to the steps.

"I'm sorry," he reminded her as she passed him.

Her narrow, delicate shoulders brushed against his chest, some of her long brown hair flying up and tickling his nose, the scent of lilacs or some other flower curling into his stuffy head.

"And we should stop by the mall, get some bedding," Barbara had called out to their daughter and him. "We want her to feel comfortable the first night. Do you know her favorite colors?"

"Definitely it's pink," his daughter Becky had replied loudly from her room. "She's always decorating her pages with pink characters."

He remembered the conversation from that morning. He stood in the hallway between the rooms, Barb in their bedroom, Becky in hers. Caught between them, they had expected him to hear and remember, he supposed, but not be part of their conversation. It was girl talk, nothing for him to be concerned with.

So they would drive down to the mall that Saturday afternoon.

The door to Becky's room was closed. She had started closing it at age twelve whenever she was inside. Keeping the door closed made him believe she was still there, doing her thing. And he would not disturb her.

His hand felt uncomfortable on the doorknob.

Wendy stood close, ready to enter once he performed the breach. Her pink suitcase sat nearby.

"This is Becky's room," he said, repeating it for the second time, and she nodded. But her face registered fear. There was too much mystery to his efforts, like something terrible was hidden inside.

He went ahead and turned the knob, pushed the door open, flicked on the light. A frilly, girly room decorated in white and pink, exactly as she wanted at age eight. The room was neat and well-ordered, not the usual mess of tossed clothes and scattered objects like in a lot of teenagers' rooms. She had always been conscientious. She liked her privacy but never used that privacy for nefarious activities. The twin bed against the outside wall where she slept had been made up, the white comforter folded neatly on the foot of the bed, the pink blanket stretched tight and tucked. The pillow in its pink case was set perfectly between each side of the bed, tilted at just the right angle against the headboard.

Opposite the perfect bed, which Becky had used since they moved in, was the new twin bed. They had already taken off the plastic around the mattress and the gray rectangle lay so plainly on the bare wooden frame. The pillow was still in its wrapper.

He stared at the bed, sensing Wendy stepping into the room behind him and moving to Becky's side, pulling her pink suitcase along.

"This was supposed to be your bed," said Bill, embarrassed that it wasn't ready. "They didn't get any bedding.... I mean, they, uh, didn't return with any...." He took a breath. "There's probably another sheet in the closet. I'll find a pillowcase and blanket. You might get cold. I keep the air conditioning rather cool. Barb always complains and sets it higher but I need it low to fall asleep. And stay asleep. Whenever I wake at night, I know she raised it. I know when the temperature goes above seventy-two. I wake up. How about you?"

Her pout was something between sadness and thoughtfulness.

"We don't have air-con."

"Oh." He wasn't sure why he was surprised. Wasn't China a modern country? But she lived in a small town, she said. "Anyway, I'll get you a blanket."

When he returned with bedding in his arms, Wendy sat upon the new mattress, staring across at Becky's perfect bed.

"She looks so organized," said Wendy, her voice cheery, glancing around. "I love this room." She pointed to posters of anime characters on the walls and commented on them, knowing each one's name and background. "We talk a lot about these stories."

"I'm glad to hear that."

"She said we can play video games."

"I guess she keeps the controls in the cabinet." He pointed his chin at the TV on top of the cabinet. "I'm not sure how they work."

When he set the bedding down beside her, she popped up. He started to unfold the white sheet with a pattern of pink flowers on it and the white blanket, then fixed them to the mattress. She tore off the plastic from the pillow, then held it while he worked the pillowcase over it. He stood back to admire their work.

"There you go," said Bill. "I hope it will serve."

"Thank you," said the girl. "It looks so comfortable."

With a weary sigh, he stepped away, paused in the doorway.

"My room's across the hall. At the end of the hall is the bathroom." He pointed through the bedroom wall. "Sorry, it's a modest house, so only one. Well, there's a tiny bathroom off the master bedroom, just a shower stall, but it would be a hassle to use. I mean, always coming through the bedroom. I hope that's not a problem." He pointed down the hall again. "Just close the door. Nobody will bother you. It locks, too, if you prefer, but if you should slip and fall, how is anyone going to help you? Well, even if it's locked, if you need help, I'd break the door down to get to you. But I swear nobody will bother you when the door is closed. Same with the bedroom door here. It's a house rule."

"Thank you," she spoke, flashing a smile. "I like to know rules."

"You know the kitchen. Nothing there, really. I'll go shopping in the morning—later today. You can come with me and we'll get whatever you want. And need. Anything at all. Like, if you need, umm, you know, feminine hygiene products. Whatever you want, we'll get."

Standing between the two beds, hands clasped, arms twisting back and forth, she turned away to hide a yawn. He pulled his phone from his back pocket, looked at the time.

"It's really late now, so I'll leave you to get yourself to bed." He pointed back over his shoulder at the master bedroom. "I'll be over there. I'll close the door to give you more privacy but just knock if you need anything. It's no problem. Okay?"

"Okay," she repeated. "Thank you."

He regarded her: this short, thin girl with the long, dark hair and the pure face. If she was seventeen, she sure didn't look it. A little girl, too innocent to come to America. Definitely not in violent America.

"Well," he said, feigning a smile, "goodnight."

She fought a yawn. "Goodnight, Mister Masters."

Good night. Was there such a thing? The quiet calm of the darkness, the comforting warmth or the refreshing coolness depending on the season, the distant din of cricket chorus, or the tintinnabulation of a light shower as white noise. The peace of repose, when nothing but idle thoughts danced in the vacant rooms of the mind.

He backed out of Becky's room, reaching for and closing the door as he exited. When the door caught, his hand lingered, hesitant to let go, to give up the room to a stranger. He felt he was already forgetting his daughter, letting this new girl take over the room.

Stepping away from the door, he let the sensations and memories wash over him—and cut through him. His chest was tight. He realized he hadn't had a proper breath since they arrived home. He was too busy playing the good host, holding it all in, keeping his emotions in check so they wouldn't overwhelm this visitor who had nothing to do with what happened.

He pushed himself down the hallway to the kitchen, opened the fridge and reached for the open can there, the beer he started just before he left for the airport. It tasted awful but he finished what was left. He let out a big sigh. A belch followed. He took deep breaths.

As he leaned back against the counter, he heard a door open and a few seconds later another door close. Then water running.

A tingling warmth rolled through him, soothing his belly, knocking his heart back into proper rhythm. The sounds of someone at home again. He wasn't alone. Only a couple weeks ago, they had been talking about this girl coming, staying with them, sharing Becky's room, and going to school with her—at his school. She might be in one of his classes. And here she was, washing up before sleep.

The water noise ended. Later the door opened and then another door closed.

Perfect, he thought. The house felt better already. He could pretend it was the same. Like nothing had happened. The sounds of the night would soothe him, let him sleep, let him escape for a while.

Sitting on the edge of his bed, Bill realized he had broken house rule 2. He had worn his outdoor shoes indoors. They usually took off their shoes at the front door. Barb had slippers to wear around the house. Becky usually went barefoot. So did he in summer, socks in winter. There was a small shoe stand by the door for everyday shoes. But he'd been distracted.

He pulled off his shoes and tossed them toward the bedroom door, which he closed as soon as he entered. There was a stranger in the house now and he wasn't sure how to act, what to wear or not wear. For sleeping, usually he would strip to his shorts, add sweatpants and t-shirt if it was cold. Barb wore a nightgown, short and frilly in summer or long and thick for winter. Becky, he wasn't sure, but in the mornings she wore a silk robe to breakfast. He recalled the Chinese dragon design down the front of that red robe. She had an interest in Asian culture. But he'd slept in his clothes for three days and nights, and managed to rip a button off his shirt.

He stood beside the bed, taking off the fresh shirt he put on to pick up the girl. He unbuckled his trousers and slid them off, pulled off his socks and sat again on the bed. Somehow wearing just shorts didn't feel right. He went to the chest, opened a drawer and retrieved a t-shirt, whatever was on top. A light gray shirt with a shark on it he'd gotten in Port Aransas, Texas a few summers back.

The bed felt different. He glanced over his shoulder at the other side, where Barb slept. He remembered the day the mattress was delivered and how she claimed that side immediately, closer to the master bath. Fine, he relinquished. The bed was empty. Her pillow remained. He lay back and pulled the pillow to his face, breathed in the scent of her, still there. He rolled over and sniffed the sheet. It hadn't been changed for a week; she insisted on that Saturday morning chore prior to doing the laundry. He had promised to take care of it while they went to the mall.

With a grunt, he got up and padded around the bed to her side, stared down at the space where his wife once slept. Never again, he realized. Tears came to his eyes. For a week he'd been too busy to let out his grief. Then he was in a stupor, numb to everything that had happened, going through the motions of proper etiquette, a show for the mourners. Now this girl had arrived and forced him to awaken from his trance. Her arrival seemed to give him permission to finally let it out. So he sobbed. Tears spotted the sheet. His throat clenched, his chest tightened. He threw himself down on the bed and cried into Barb's pillow.

After a while, when he'd run out of tears, he stared up at the ceiling, wondering what he was going to do. He was sweating, partly from nervousness and the crying, partly from the summer heat on a muggy August night making a run to the airport.

"A shower," he mumbled, getting up.

He checked that the bedroom door was fully closed, then stripped and entered the master bathroom. Barb's bra still hung on the towel rack, her towel there, too, her sponge and loofa, her curvy bottle of bodywash and shampoo and conditioner in one caddy. His bottle of liquid soap stood in the corner of the shower cubicle.

As he turned on the water, he recalled the times they had showered together, just for fun. Saving water, he said. Or she said. He waited until the shower warmed before stepping in, then with little thought he grabbed Barb's bottle of bodywash.

He wondered as he dried off, what things belonging to Becky might still be in the hall bathroom and that he should remove them for his guest. It was late and she had gone to sleep, so he stepped lightly down the hallway in his sleeping shorts, once used for jogging. In the bathroom were only Becky's soap products. In the cabinet under the sink a box of tampons, toilet paper, air freshener. In the cabinet behind the mirror, a razor and various lotions. No stray clothing. Good. It was awkward enough to have her sleep in Becky's room.

Returning to the master bedroom, Bill heard talking. He paused outside Becky's room, listening. It was Chinese. The girl was probably on the phone. He listened, not knowing the language, but heard the emotion in her voice. He shook his head, none of his business, and turned into his room, swung the door closed.

He pulled on the gray t-shirt again and reclined on the bed under the sheet and a thin blanket, the air conditioning running. The lamp on the nightstand provided a golden glow over a stack of books he would read from before turning out the light. Barb's side had a similar stack of magazines. But he hadn't read his books for a while. He forgave himself, like reading them was a task he swore to complete no matter the distractions.

He selected one and held it in his lap, opening it to the bookmark and finding where he left off. Anything to clear his mind, even if it was prancing through a fantasy tale of elves and wizards.

Two pages in, he heard a light tapping on the door. He thought it was part of the story at first, then realized it was Wendy.

"Come in," he called softly.

The door swung open carefully, eventually revealing the hands and face of the girl.

"I'm sorry waking you," she said, her voice barely two notches above a whisper. "I saw light on so I think you awake."

"Yes, just reading a bit. Not ready to sleep yet." He curled his hand to draw her in. "What's up? Anything wrong?"

"I talk with my mama." She paused demurely, as though that was enough to say, the full story. Standing at the foot of the bed, her lavender pajamas thin, lacey around the edges, cut off at the elbows and knees, she resembled Becky at age ten. "I told her what you said. About Missus Masters and Becky. I'm sorry. My mama is sorry, too."

"Thank you," Bill said with a sniffle.

"My mama say too dangerous in America. She is afraid. I told her it's done already so no worry. But she want me come home."

The silence between them was exactly what Bill would have wished for a pleasant night's sleep, that kind of calm. But he knew there was a wrench tossed into the calm.

"I get it. Probably it's all anyone hears about the U.S.—the violence. Guns. Damn guns. Always the crazy ones." He stopped himself before he could launch into the same rant that had made him famous on TV. "Do you want to go home? Back to China?"

She stared at the floor, her hair hanging down, blocking his view of her face. A few sniffles filled the silence.

"Come here," he called. "Sit here."

She moved to the edge of the bed, near the hump of his knee under the blanket. When she lowered her hand, fresh tears dropped.

"I know you didn't expect this," he spoke in a quiet, soothing voice, and was surprised that he could. "I didn't expect this, either. Any of it. I'm sorry, too. This is not an ideal situation. You expected to come to America and experience the life here. Not the violent life. Of course your mother is worried. We cannot know when something bad will happen." He waited for a reaction, wondering if he was going down the right road, but she continued dabbing her eyes. "I'm sure there's a way to exchange your ticket for a flight home. Maybe pay a change fee. I'll cover that. I mean, if that's what you want to do. I know it's not fair for you to be in this situation, the way things are now."

She wiped her face, swept her hair back. Her face was finally red and wet. She sniffled back tears.

"I—I want to go to school in America," the words spilled out. "I'm here now. I—I want to stay. I want to be with Becky. But Mama want me come home." Tears ran.

"Hey...." Bill reached for her hand, patted it. "I know. I understand. If I sent Becky over to China, I'd worry, too. I'm her dad. I've got to be protective. Probably it's safer there than here. Actually, until...until this incident...nothing bad ever happened here."

Here meant in little Edmond, a comfortable suburban community on the north side of Oklahoma City. But even Edmond had the first post office shooting years before they moved to the town. Also the Murrah Building bombing down in the city. Those were unusual, rare. He reviewed the daily news reports in his mind. In truth, not a night went by without a rape, a burglary, a road rage incident, or a shooting reported on the TV news. It was a violent place. Why didn't he see more of it himself? No, he had to wait for it to happen to the people he loved. Then it was real. When it was on the news. National news. The 'blow the bastard away' guy. But he never got that chance.

"I can't apologize for this." He wiped his eyes, then pushed his legs out from under the blanket, pulling himself up beside her. "It's still not real to me. I look at this bed and see my wife sleeping there. I hear you in the next room and think it's my daughter staying up late to play video games. I go to my school and teach my classes and think that's my life. My fucking life. Every day. Then, in a flash, it's gone. Some crazy person who doesn't know anyone, doesn't have a gripe with any particular person, just wants to cry out at the world and make a statement. Look at me! Listen to me! I matter! See what I can do? See what power I have? The power of life or death over you—all you pitiful, ignorant fools, you stupid wretches of society, who don't matter, who don't notice me, who never submit to my innate superiority! And the world erupts in violence. Small scale and we call it a crime—large scale and we call it war."

She was bawling by then and he knew he'd gone too far.

He lifted an arm, wrapped it around her shoulders. It felt odd. But the girl leaned in, tears wetting his shoulder.

"I'm sorry. I'm sorry. I lost my temper. I'm still angry. Not at you, no. I hate what happened. I wish it didn't happen. But I can't undo it. Nothing can undo it. Nothing can make it like it never happened."

Her arm rose, stretched across his chest to his other shoulder, latched on there, a half-hug, and her sobbing continued.

"And you just happened to arrive." He raised his hand, patted her back. "It's not your fault. Tomorrow will be another day. A better day. Don't worry, Wendy. We'll make things right for you, I promise."

3

BILL SLEPT DEEPLY WITHOUT ANY PILLS. He awoke at the first
noise in the kitchen, a clinking of dishes, the running of a faucet. For a
moment he had to orient himself, remembering why he was in the bed
alone, why the house should be so quiet, and everything he had to do.
Then, with a great exhale, he pushed himself up from the bed, rubbing
his eyes like he had seen too much.

"Barb, I...." He frowned, catching himself. She wasn't there. It
would take a while to get used to that.

More noise compelled him to stand. He went to the chest and dug
out a pair of lounging pants to put on. When he trudged out to the
living room, he found Wendy standing before the wall of pictures. A
dozen framed photos hung there, images marking events in the
Masters family history. She held a coffee cup and studied each picture.

Bill noticed she'd gotten herself up, gotten dressed, and gone in
search of something to drink. Already at home, he mused. She had
dressed in cute blue jeans that stopped short of her ankles, tapered
with a rounded cuff and flowery embroidery. She wore a clingy pink
top with thin straps that seemed better for gymnastics, her shoulders
bare. That top accentuated her figure.

She reached for an upper picture, straightening it, flashing the
shadow of armpit hair. The long, dark hair on her head had been
combed out: a rich brown shade, he saw in the light of morning. She
applied a plastic clip to the back of her head, a white butterfly which

seemed to want to launch into flight, to fly away from this place.

He came up behind her, his hand lifted to identify the picture.

"That's Becky," he said and she startled.

She nodded as she gazed at the image of the teenaged girl, smiling in her track uniform, holding a prize ribbon. He remembered that day, just a year before, the spring meet. He never would have believed his daughter could jump over hurdles like a gazelle.

"I see her already," said Wendy. "We exchange many pictures. On WeChat. And email. She is beautiful."

"Thank you." He inhaled. "She *is* beautiful." He gazed at the picture a while. "You said you play...tennis?"

"Yes, tennis. And I'm also in swimming team at my school."

"Swimming, huh?" He pointed to another picture. "This is Barbara, my wife. She loved to swim, too. We were at a lake near here in that picture." He pursed his lips. "She never liked having a picture of herself in a swimsuit up on the wall. You know, for visitors to see." He nodded. "But she does look good."

The woman in the blue one-piece suit squinted at the camera, the sun in her eyes. Around her face her dark brown hair lay full on her shoulders. Her face radiated confidence. Her regal nose and serious lips made her appear strong, determined. But she could be wonderfully passionate, even silly sometimes, he knew.

A twinge in his chest made him stop reminiscing. He placed his hand over his heart. He had no history of cardiac problems. Just emotions, he decided. His throat was also tight.

"Better get some coffee going." He went to the kitchen. "You drink coffee?" That was a stupid question, he knew. "I mean, how about tea? Would you like tea?" He opened the cabinet, saw the dozen boxes of different flavors his wife had collected, using half a box before growing tired of one variety and getting another. "We have Chamomile, English, Cinnamon, Chai, Indian, Ceylon, Earl Grey.... Plenty of choices. Just add water, right?"

When he turned to get her response, she was right beside him.

"I got water," she said, raising the coffee cup.

They bantered about coffee versus tea and debated which tea to drink before settling on the Earl Grey. He put the coffeemaker on, just boiling water, and prepared two cups and saucers. He laid out the tea bags. Fetched the bottle of cream from the fridge. Sniffed—not too old. He made sure everything was ready, then sat at the kitchen table.

He noticed he was barefoot, felt embarrassed. His guest wore gray slippers, a bunny's face over the toes. She had come prepared. Maybe Becky had told her they didn't wear slippers at home, so she brought her own.

"Nice slippers," said Bill, pointing at her feet as she sat at the table, facing out toward the boiling water on the countertop.

"It's gift from Mama," she said shyly, like she was hesitant to have to explain. "We wear slippers in the house."

"I get that. A good idea." He took a moment to collect his thoughts, organize his memories. "You know, I spent a year in Japan back when I was right out of college. I went there to teach English." He shook his head like he regretted it. "Sure was a long time ago. But I learned the customs. Barb, well, she didn't see any reason for the slippers thing, so I gradually lost that custom, too. But I walk around mostly barefoot anyway, especially during hot weather."

She watched him and he felt flashes of happiness cross his face as he told her some anecdotes of living in Japan.

"You probably saw pictures in Becky's room, too." He chuckled. "And all her stuffed animals. What do you think of her collection? She started to want those when she was two. Got one for each birthday, for Christmas, for summer vacation trips. Like the black bear when we visited the Rockies. The dolphin when we went to the Texas coast. The mascot of my university. The panda from...I guess, that's from you. I remember her saying it was from her pen-pal in China. She never would give them up. She always...."

Again his own words condemned him to be sucked back to the event. He tried so hard to forget what happened. The arrival of this girl from China had served as sufficient distraction. The hug she had given him when he cried the previous night was welcomed. He needed that hug. No one had hugged him at the funeral. Maybe they didn't think it was proper. Maybe they didn't think a man would want to be hugged. Sure, a few ladies tried to give him a shoulder squeeze or a half-hug. The men shook his hand, clapped his shoulder, slapped his back. That was enough for public display. He really needed a deep, bone-crushing embrace that would squeeze out the stress from his body.

"Thank you," he said, standing and going over to prepare the tea.

"You're welcome," Wendy responded automatically.

"You don't know what for, do you?"

He poured water into the cups.

"No? What for?" She was puzzled.

"I really needed that hug last night."

She seemed too serious. "You were crying."

"Yes, I was. And so were you." He paused, tea bags in his hand. "It's a process. That's what they say. Stages to go through." He plopped a bag into each cup, added a spoon to each. "I'm too stressed to check them off as I go through them."

He carried the cups on saucers to the table, set them down, slid one to Wendy. He sat, adjusting his cup, using the spoon to press on the tea bag. Then he popped up to retrieve the bottle of cream.

"No, she would never give them up." He stared out the kitchen window into the backyard. Wendy's eyes followed. "That swingset's been there for years. Set it up for Becky, but after the first weekend—a birthday gift; we had her friends over for a party—after that weekend she hardly ever used it. Now it's all rusted. Probably should take it down now."

He felt a hand over his wrist. He tilted his head. Regarding Wendy, he sensed a tear about to fall. He sniffed it back.

"I'm sorry," she spoke solemnly, gazing into his face to be sure he heard her and understood what she was saying. "I know you are sad, Mister Masters. I'm sad, too. I miss Becky so much. She's my American friend. And I want to meet Missus Masters so much. She send me many gifts. Becky is my sister." She gave his wrist a squeeze. "I miss them, too."

He let his head slip, his chin going to his chest, as tears fell.

"Thanks."

He tried to catch his breath. To hide his emotions, he lifted the cup and took a sip. Too hot. He set it down, spilling some.

Wendy jumped up to get a towel, returned to clean the spill.

"My father...he also gone." She wiped the table, took the towel to the counter. "He died from accident. Construction of building."

His face went blank. "Oh, I'm sorry. I had no idea." That pulled him out of his own grief. "How old were you?"

She looked up, counting. "Seven?"

"Wow. So young. Then it's been just you and your mother?"

"Yes. She want me to learn everything and get good job, and make big career so I can take care her."

"Yes, yes, I understand." He drank more of the tea, finished the small cup. "Sorry to hear that. It must've been hard for you."

Wendy crossed her legs, one foot balanced over the opposite knee, the gray bunny slipper dangling off her foot, the motion making its eyes blink. His gaze was drawn to it. His eyes walked up her leg to where her two hands held her cup, raising it to her lips, elbows bent. Her eyes were a little red from crying. Like his.

She lowered the cup to her lap.

"They went to the mall to get the bedding for you," he muttered, then found some strength to put behind his voice. "Some crazy guy with a gun started shooting. Right inside the mall. Everybody ran—naturally. I guess they ran, too. I don't know all the details. Supposedly the shooter cornered some shoppers in a store. Police tried to negotiate the release of the hostages. Didn't work. The shooter just wanted to make a statement. How powerful he was, I guess. What other reason could there be?"

He stopped, not expecting to tell her what happened. It had just come out. He gazed at her. She put a finger to her eye.

"Eventually, they tossed a smoke grenade in and stormed the place. They shot him. But they found some of the hostages dead, too. He shot them. Each of them. One at a time. What could they have ever done to deserve that?"

He couldn't catch his breath, had to stop. Wendy's face was stone.

"America is a violent place. You never see it. Most days everything is good, everything is peaceful. Then some piece of shit crawls out of the sludge trying to make his mark."

He focused his gaze on Wendy.

"I rushed to the mall when I heard what was happening. A TV crew caught me, asked me for my thoughts. I let them have it. I ranted. That's why I'm famous. But...I didn't know, not at that time, if they were all right or...if they were dead. I waited. And waited. Until they brought out the bodies. Seven people—bodies. I tried to say good-bye there, them covered in cloths, but they made me wait, go down to the morgue later and identify them. Barbara Masters. Becky Masters. I cried all night."

He got up and opened the fridge, seeking distraction. The shelves were filled with casserole dishes and Tupperware. The food that well-wishers had brought over in the first days after the incident. And after the funeral.

"You see this? All this food? Who can eat at a time like this?"

He shut the door hard and stood there, arms out, feeling ashamed of his rant, of his ineptitude. He should have been there. He didn't know what he could've done, but he would gladly take the bullets that killed Barbara and Becky. He gladly would.

"Excuse me," he said to Wendy and left the kitchen.

The drive was silent, just ten minutes before turning into the parking lot of the Homeland.

"And this is our local grocery," said Bill, getting out of the Escape and coming around like a gentleman to open the door for Wendy.

She slipped out like an athlete, lithe and fluid, landing on her pristine white sneakers.

"We have grocery in China," she said.

"Well, uh, it's not really a tourist spot. We're just getting food. You saw what we had at home. Nothing I want to eat."

Inside, she halted as her eyes took in the many aisles of products. The endless fruit and vegetables impressed her the most and Bill urged her to get whatever she wanted. She carefully selected several items and placed them in the huge shopping cart. He told her to get more so she picked out a couple more items.

Down through the aisles of boxes and bottles, cans and jars they went, pausing to put a few in the cart. The meat department made Wendy stare in awe again. She admitted her grocery was small, but had different foods. The refrigerated aisle with case after case of frozen items made her look closer to see what food could be returned to life in a microwave.

Back to the aisles of boxes for some forgotten items.

Two guys in their twenties were there, bickering over what snacks to get. It was their lucky day, as Wendy stepped around the end of the shelves and started up the aisle. The boys' eyes focused on the Asian beauty approaching.

"Hey, babe," said one, as Bill started up the aisle, pushing the cart.

Wendy regarded them, blinking. "Hello."

"How you doing?" said the second boy with a leering grin.

"I'm fine, thank you," Wendy replied in textbook fashion.

The boys were hooked. The pink top she wore, tight over her figure, her bare shoulders pale, made the view enticing. They didn't hesitate tossing compliments at her until she blushed.

"Excuse me," said Bill in an authoritarian voice. "My daughter...?"

The boys smiled sheepishly. "She's your daughter?" asked one. The other chuckled at the proposition.

"Yes," Bill insisted.

"But you don't even look alike."

"Ever hear of adoption?" Bill retorted.

Wendy had selected a snack, some kind of healthy granola bars, and put the box in the cart.

"Thanks, Daddy," she said, giggling.

The boys moved on.

"You have to be careful here," said Bill. "You're very attractive. The boys will be hounding you, I'm afraid. Maybe you should dress a little less, umm, maybe more plain. I used to tell Becky the same thing, but she complained and her mother always scolded me. We're supposed to tell the boys not to harass, not the girls to cover up. And I believe that. But the reality is.... I had to mind my own business, let her dress as she liked. She said I was being a chauvinist."

"Show-vin-ist? What's it?"

"Well, in that case, a man who tells women how to dress." He shook his head, resigned. "I was only trying to protect my daughter. Protect her from boys who want nothing more than...well, sex, eventually. I was a boy once, so I know what they're thinking." He tried to grin. "But now I'm a father so I'm protecting my daughter."

He froze a moment. His words stuck in his throat. Protecting.... Yet he hadn't. He felt the store engulfing him, everyone judging him.

"Thank you, Mister Masters." Wendy had a bright smile. "Boys in China, mostly they are shy. They afraid talk to girls."

"I wish that were true here. More respect on both sides, I say." He pushed the cart on. She followed. "More respect for everyone. Respect for life. The sanctity of human life. For all life." He stared at the packs of meat in the cart.

"Mister Masters?" Wendy called when he'd paused long enough in the aisle.

He wiped his eyes. "I'm sorry, Wendy. Everything reminds me they're not here anymore."

She placed her hand on his back, gave it a couple pats.

"Okay," he said, taking a big breath. "I think we have enough. Let's go home."

Being a Sunday, the store was crowded and the check-out busy. It took a while. Wendy showed him a few pictures of Becky on her phone. He had never seen them. Wendy promised to send them to his phone. Then she showed him the app on her phone which she used to pay for everything. But you had to have a bank account in China to use it, she said. He laughed, whipped out his credit card.

"This is what we use over here. Plastic money."

They took the long way home, Bill showing her points of interest, keeping the air conditioning running cold until Wendy shivered. He turned it down. They went through the university campus, then by the high school she would be attending—if she stayed. The same school where he taught English. There was a tea shop run by a Korean family. There were strange metallic statues as public art. Here was the library. A church. The elementary school Becky had attended. A big statue of an Indian chief. A couple banks, nail salons, vitamin shops, clothing stores, a dentist's office, and plenty of fast food restaurants. There was a lot to unpack for her and he did his best as they arrived back at the house.

"Are you okay?" asked the Chinese girl beside him, her legs extended, ankles crossed.

Lost in thought, he had pushed the button to raise the garage door and rolled the SUV inside, then absently pushed the button again to lower the door. But the engine remained running as he stared ahead through the windshield at the wall. Wendy politely waited, afraid to disturb him. Then she coughed.

"Mister Masters?" Her voice was sharper.

He broke from his trance, shaking his head, and turned off the motor as though nothing had been wrong. Realizing the exhaust in the garage, he pushed the clicker to raise the door.

"I'm sorry," he said with a shrug. "Spaced out a moment."

They carried in the groceries as the garage aired out, putting everything away. Bill directed where each item should go in cabinets or refrigerator or countertop. She seemed to like the regimentation of the exercise, learning the system of the Masters household.

Finished unloading, Bill went to the garage, lowered the door.

"This kitchen so big," Wendy complained, or was she pleased?

The doorbell sounded, which caught Bill by surprise. They always used the garage door and kitchen entrance, so it had to be a stranger. Wendy offered to check the front door.

"Ah—hello," said an older woman as Wendy swung open the door.

She tried to push the door open to talk to the woman but there were so many flowers wrapped up as bouquets that had collected on the front stoop, she couldn't.

The woman held up a large dish in her two hands. "I brought this for Bill. I know he needs to eat, but he's probably too tired, and in mourning, to cook. The ladies at the church thought to give him this casserole."

Wendy, in her tight pink tanktop with bare shoulders, reached for the dish, still warm in her hands.

"Thank you," she said with a pleasant smile. "I give to him."

The woman, dressed elegantly as though she'd just come from the church, grimaced like she felt a pain. "That's kind of you, Miss...?"

"My name is Wendy," she replied in a bright tone.

"Wendy...." The woman thought over the pronunciation.

"Yes. I come here yesterday."

"Oh. Yesterday?" Then, under her breath, muttered: "That's quick."

"You want talk to Mister Masters?"

The woman froze. "I suppose it's not necessary. You can say I stopped by. Missus Garver. From the church."

"Yes, Missus Garver. I tell him."

"Thank you." The woman turned to go, mumbling as she stepped off the stoop.

Bill arrived at the door as Mrs. Garver reached the end of the driveway, a car waiting there, her husband sitting in the driver's seat. Bill gave a wave to the husband as she got into the car and they drove away.

"Ignore her," said Bill. "She's a busybody."

"She brought food for you." She stepped around him with the dish in her hands.

"Let me." He took the dish from her, returned to the kitchen.

"So many flowers," she called from the front door.

He heard the sounds of the door squeaking open, the rustle of papers and leaves. When he went to help, she had gathered most of them and set them inside the door, on the square of tile.

Bill kicked off his shoes at the edge of the kitchen floor, walked in socks across the carpet.

"So many flowers," he echoed. "Well-wishers."

"Well-wishers," she repeated, adding the term to her vocabulary list. "They wish you well."

"Yes, like that." He stared down at the pile of flowers. Some had little cards attached. A few crosses. "Barb was a member of the church. I never went—seldom went. A few special days. Becky went when she was young, then she got busy with school and extracurricular activities, so she preferred to sleep in on Sundays. But...now...."

He paused, then knelt and plucked a card from one bouquet, opened it.

"*So sorry for your loss,*" he read. "Sorry for your loss, yeah."

Wendy stood at the end of the L-shaped chestnut couch in the living room. It was positioned so one open side faced the TV that sat on a long entertainment center stuffed with DVD cases. A low table sat to one side of the couch, a wide vase with drooping flowers occupying the center.

"Well-wishers.... Well-wishes.... Lots of wishes," he muttered as he went through the cards. "Lots of sympathy. Yeah, thanks. Glad it didn't happen to them, to their families. That's what they mean."

She helped him gather up the flowers and followed him to dispose of them in the trash bin in the garage.

"Well," said Bill with a big sigh. "Sunday."

4

"USUALLY I HAVE LUNCH READY when they come home from church," explained Bill. "What would you like? A sandwich? Or maybe Missus Garver's casserole?"

"What is casserole?" she asked, raising her eyebrows.

"It's something church women put together. Whatever you want to put in it. Meat, veggies, and cheese. Usually lots of cheese."

Wendy seemed intrigued, so they agreed to try the casserole. It still felt warm, but Bill gave it a reheating in the oven. Ham and broccoli, noodles, and lots of cheese. Not bad. She liked 'casserole'.

"You might as well watch TV," he suggested after they ate. "I want to make some calls. I need to find you a better place to stay for this school year."

"But I want to stay here," she responded, surprised. "It's Becky's house. She sent pictures."

"Yes, I know, but...." He already at his cell up to his ear. "Hey, Gary. Bill Masters here. Is Sandy available? Need to ask a favor."

She listened to him, even after he went down the hallway to gain some privacy.

"Yeah, she's fine, but with everything that's happened, I don't think I can manage it. Besides, it's rather awkward.... You know, middle-aged guy and.... It's better if she stayed with you and your daughters. ...Of course. Yes, certainly. I understand. I just thought.... Okay. Thanks."

She flipped through the TV channels, found a tennis match and stopped to watch it. Bill made another call which went the same way. And another.

He shuffled into the living room, dropped onto the opposite end of the couch from Wendy. He seemed exhausted, let out several sighs and threw his arms up on the back of the couch.

"I tried. I'll try again tomorrow. There's got to be a family with room for you."

He regarded the girl: sitting with her legs bent up, her feet tucked under herself on the couch, so demure, so innocent. So sexy, he found himself admitting. Maybe she doesn't realize it, maybe she does. He shook off the thought.

"You should be staying with a family that has daughters. Like we planned to do. But now...now it's not a good idea. You heard Missus Garver. People will talk—are talking. It's not considered proper...for a young lady, such as yourself, and a man of my age. And a widow...-er, besides, to, umm...to live together. If there's another family, it would be better if you live with them."

She studied him, the tennis match going on beside her. He kept talking, making the case for her to go someplace else. The more he talked, the more he didn't make sense. He was doing the right thing. Yes, as though that mattered at all. What did people think? Who cared? It was a week since the funeral already and nothing mattered. He was operating on auto-pilot.

His eyes shifted to the tennis match. She was a good distraction; if not for her arrival, he would probably still be drunk, in a stupor, or sitting in his Ford Escape with the motor running, garage door closed, sucking exhaust, trying to forget everything, trying to find them, his Barb and his Becky, somewhere in a happier place than where he was.

"I'm going to lie down a while," he announced, getting up. "Call if you need anything."

"Okay," she called after him. "Have good sleep."

Wendy heard the phone buzzing in the next room, the bedroom where Bill was napping.

"Yes, I'm fine." His voice was shaking, the new normal. "As fine as anyone could be after their wife and daughter are murdered."

She turned the volume down on the TV to listen better.

"I intend to come in tomorrow," he continued. "No, I don't want someone else teaching my classes and then I come in and have to figure out how to switch them back to my lesson plans." Pause, then grumbling. "We can talk tomorrow. Oh, and I'll be bringing in our exchange student."

She put the TV on mute and got up from the couch, stepped around the end of it and stood in the hallway. The door to the master bedroom was open.

"Yes, she came anyway." He tried to chuckle. "Nobody told her. What's she supposed to do? Assume there would be a tragedy? That her plans would be, I don't know, ruined?" More grumbling. "No, no trouble at all. She's a lovely girl. Speaks English well. Wants to study engineering, so I'm sure she's good at math. Maybe put her in the AP class." Pause. "I guess so. I'll take her. Might be good if she's in my class, some kind of continuity through the day. Sure.... Okay, see you tomorrow."

Then, before she could retreat to the living room, Bill came out from the bedroom.

He winced. "So...you heard that?"

Wendy nodded, her eyes sad.

"I'm sorry if I said anything that upset you. I'm only thinking of your well-being."

She pondered a new word. "Well-being...."

"Being well. In good spirits. Healthy in body and mind."

Again she gave a nod. "I'm sorry."

"Don't say that. You don't have anything to be sorry for. You didn't know. You arrived right on schedule. It's everything else that's fucked up." He shook his head. "Sorry, I shouldn't say that. Everything is *messed* up."

"Fucked up...?" She pondered the phrase.

"You don't need to learn that."

"It's in pop songs," she said with a giggle. "Did you sleep?"

"Not really."

He stepped up to her. She moved against the wall to let him pass into the living room and followed.

"I keep getting calls. From people giving me their condolences. My voicemail is full. I just delete them now. I stopped answering the phone so they leave messages. I don't know what else to do."

He flopped down on the couch, wearing shorts and t-shirt, in the corner of the L, put his bare feet up on the corner of the coffee table.

He stared at his feet. "Barb never let me do that."

Grinning, Wendy pulled her feet out of the bunny slippers, set them on the edge of the coffee table and wiggled her tiny toes. Bill smiled, amused. Rules were made so people could break them, he explained to Wendy. Then, deciding how ugly his feet looked, he pulled them down. Wendy did too.

"I miss her. I miss her telling me not to put my feet on the table." He sucked in air, let it out slowly. "I don't know what to do now."

The tennis match continued silently on the TV.

"We go to school tomorrow?" she asked cautiously.

"Yes, that's the plan."

He studied her a moment. Just as pretty as in the grocery store. But troubled. She seemed on edge, wary, ready to run. Well, no doubt because he was being a jerk—although he had a right to be. All the more reason she should stay with another family. Everybody trying to show their sympathy. It was irritating now.

"I don't know what to do," he mumbled to himself.

Bill knocked on the open door of Becky's room, gazing at Wendy reclined on the new bed, wearing pink pajamas and propped on her elbows with a paperback open before her. She looked up, blinking, a faint smile on her face.

"Wendy, I want to go out," he said, watching her expression. "I want to drive down to the mall and check the car. Barb's car. I know it's late, but all the doors are locked. I'll come in from the garage. I have keys. Be about an hour. Are you okay to stay here by yourself?"

She frowned, which slipped to a pout. "I think so. I will sleep soon. After read one more chapter."

He squinted. "What are you reading?"

"It's called 'Red Letter'." She held up the book to show him the cover. Puritans in a forest. But the title was in Chinese characters. "*Hóngsè zìmǔ*," she pronounced for him.

"Oh, that one." He laughed. "We call it *The Scarlet Letter*. Not one of my favorites. That Hester Prynne is quite a lush."

"It's very exciting," she said, adding a smirk. "I learn about America from this book. It's history, right?"

"Well, it's fiction, so...." He straightened up. "Enjoy it. I'll be back in about an hour. I'll leave the living room light on."

"Okay, thanks."

He returned to the master bedroom and opened the top drawer of the chest, the one he didn't use much because it was a bit high and difficult to see into easily. It matched the suite of furniture, however. He felt for the second set of keys for Barb's car. He never drove her precious Lexus but, if he needed to, he knew where the keys were. The sedan was supposed to become Becky's once she got her license but she hadn't taken the test yet.

His hand felt something else as he flipped through the clothing there. Something metallic. He remembered the pistol was kept there, the gun he inherited from his father, something he'd accepted out of politeness. Bill had never fired it. There was a clip of bullets in the bottom drawer, he knew. But that drawer had his winter socks and, in Oklahoma, he seldom needed to get into it.

He thought of the pistol, a Glock, he recalled, and had the urge to examine it. He wondered if he should take it with him to the crime scene. In his TV interview he declared that the shooter should be blown away by law enforcement. Then, learning that Barb and Becky were among the victims, he wished he'd had the opportunity himself. The car would be parked in the mall's huge parking lot, without crime scene tape. If he showed up with a firearm and there were any police around, it might not be good. So he covered the metal with a sweatshirt and closed the drawer, keys in hand.

The drive down Broadway, stopping at every major intersection, seemed to take forever. In the dark, time was unmeasurable. Could be Sunday night or Saturday night, when he drove down to the airport, or any other night.

Lights illuminated the parking lot although the stores were closed. A few cars remained, likely employees finishing up their work before heading home. He knew where Barb and Becky were going so he drove to that side of the mall, where the entrance closest to the store was located. He immediately spied the Lexus and pulled up beside it. He examined the silver sedan from inside his SUV before shutting off the engine and getting out.

No reason it should be harmed. But it had been parked for more than a week. The mall's security patrol might have noted it. Thieves could have tried to break in. But there was nothing of value visible inside. The car was a few years old, chosen to get Barb to work and back in style. And to the mall.

"To the mall," he mumbled, unlocking the driver's side door.

Inside was his wife's sunglasses; she was obsessed with wearing them whenever she was outdoors. On the passenger seat, crumpled against the seatback, was Becky's light blue sweater, which she wore in cars that had too much A/C, like when she rode in his Escape. In the back seat was a sack of prior purchases. He reached for the sack, pulled it up front. Some bath items, cosmetics, hygiene products, girly things. Were they still good after sitting in a hot car? He wasn't sure if they were intended for their international guest or the two of them.

Then they had gone into the mall to get a set of sheets and blanket. The entrance closest to the car remained blocked off with sawhorses and yellow tape. Inside, probably more restriction. He heard the mall had reopened but that wing was off-limits. The store would be blocked off longer, he guessed. Cleaning the blood. Twenty-four hostages. Eleven wounded. And seven killed.

He adjusted the driver's seat and sat, his head against the headrest, hurting, his eyes tearing up.

"I don't know what to do," he confessed, just above a whisper. "Better that I came here than let her see me...being so pathetic. The dad. Man of the house. Couldn't protect my family. Couldn't prevent this stupid...senseless crime." He sat back, sniffling. "I mean, who *does* that kind of thing? What does it prove?" He slammed his hand against the steering wheel.

He was breathing hard, thoughts racing through his head, wanting so much to be violent. He could be violent, if pushed far enough, he knew. Besides a few years playing soldier in the National Guard during his college days, he had punched that guy in Japan, the one molesting the high school girl on the train. He felt good about his role. Then he returned to America—violent America—and got soft. He settled down.

He went back to college and earned his Master's degree, and met Barbara Fletcher in the library. He never considered any reason to stay strong, to be ready to fight when needed, when the time was right. They married and had Becky and life was good.

"If I had gone with them...."

He took several deep breaths, trying to calm himself.

"If I had that gun with me...."

He stared at the blocked-off entrance to the mall.

"If I was with them, armed and alert, then...maybe I could've blown the bastard away and saved everyone. Saved my ladies. Yes. Saved myself."

He turned the key and started the engine, ran it ten minutes, then shut it off. He would rent a trailer and hitch it to the Escape, and bring the Lexus home. It could sit in the driveway and every day when he returned, he would think they were still alive. Or park it in the garage and have the same experience when he raised the garage door. Or maybe sell it, get it out of his life.

Climbing out and locking the door, he stood staring a while at the mall entrance. The mall's security jeep came around on its patrol, detoured to check on him but left when Bill waved him off.

The girl was asleep when he returned. He didn't want to awaken her but the garage door raising and lowering made noise.

Poor girl, thought Bill, arriving in a strange country in the middle of a tragedy and having to make do with a forlorn man with a broken heart as her so-called host family. He had to make things better for her. That would be his new goal, starting the next morning when they went to the school.

He looked in on her, door open, room dark, faint light filtering in from the living room. A peaceful angel. Purring in the bed. So sweet. Like Becky when she was little—so active when awake, so darling when asleep. He had the urge to pat Wendy's head, to kiss her brow.

Stepping away from her room, he realized that despite everything else, there just might be some good in the world and sometimes it came without warning, just like the bad.

5

WENDY CAME OUT TO THE KITCHEN dressed for school in a dark green dress with white polka-dots. The dress went to her knees. Very lady-like, thought Bill. She wore brown sandals that raised her two inches higher. Her dark hair fell straight down her back.

He looked up from his tablet, reading the morning paper online.

"Lovely dress. Perfect for the first day of school. Of course, classes don't start until next Monday. It's just teachers this week. We have to 'go prepare' our classrooms. I left mine ready to go, hah. But you look great. You'll make a good impression. We'll get you enrolled and I'll give you a tour."

"Thank you, Mister Masters," said the girl with a wide smile that seemed more pretty in the morning light, less cute like a little girl's. Her dream was coming true.

"I said you can call me Bill outside of school."

"Okay...Bill."

He wasn't dressed for school yet, sitting at the kitchen table in shorts and t-shirt, barefoot, hair tussled. He'd just rolled out of bed, of course. That was a Masters house rule: you could come to breakfast straight from bed. He explained the rule to Wendy. Except there was no breakfast ready.

"We can grab breakfast on the way. It'll be easier," he explained.

When he got himself together, dressed in a white shirt with thin blue stripes and brown dress slacks, his hair combed, face shaven—

taking longer for his week-old growth—he finally resembled a teacher. He stood in the living room for inspection. Wendy gave her approval.

"You look like handsome man now," she said, grinning.

"Thank you. I don't hear that enough."

He grabbed his school bag from a side table, a well-worn tan leather satchel already stuffed with papers and books. It looked heavy. He saw her staring at the bag.

"I haven't cleaned it out since March. Give me something to do today," he said. "I have eight hours to k—to spend at school. After the meetings. So many meetings, just to tell us what we already know."

He drove them to a bagel shop, ushered her inside for breakfast, saying he was too tired to cook in the mornings. Barb took care of breakfast; she was a morning person. He handled dinner since he came home before her. More Masters protocols, he chuckled.

They sat at a table and ate bagels. The bagel halves sandwiched ham and egg with cheese. He drank coffee, English tea for her. On the way out, she grabbed an apple from a basket, holding it up as a reminder to eat healthy food. He chose one for himself and paid for both.

"You have any American money?" he asked, walking out the door.

"I got some money from bank in China." She climbed into the Escape and he started the engine. "Is two thousand dollars enough?"

"Oh, geez. Enough for what? You want to buy a car?"

"International Exchange office said I must pay for myself."

"Well, that's a nice gesture." He turned onto the main avenue. "But we expect to cover everything for you during the year. Of course, if you want to buy something special, souvenirs, or go out with friends, then, well, it's good to have some cash in your purse, I suppose."

"It isn't expensive here?" She looked at the stores along the avenue.

"No, reasonable. Mortgage is the most." He glanced at her during a red light. "You put the money away somewhere? In Becky's room?"

"Lock in suitcase."

The school was not much farther away than the bagel shop. He rolled up the drive and parked in one of the spaces in front of the building, the ones for visitors. Three were marked reserved.

"You're a visitor, so it's appropriate, right?"

Wendy looked out the window at the school. "Yes, I'm visitor."

"We're going to have to work on those articles." He smiled, ready to open the door and get out. "I'm *a* visitor."

"Me, too." She laughed.

Bill gave a smirk as he got out. She had a sense of humor.

The front of the building was one floor but beyond it the school rose to a second floor, the taller gym to the left, auditorium on the right. Further to the left were sports fields and the stadium. It was quite a large campus. He saw her eyes widen.

"You'll find your way around," said Bill, standing beside her.

"My school is one building. It is five floors. And one gym—a bubble tent over tennis court."

"Well, it's crowded over there, isn't it?"

She nodded, then seemed to get emotional, like she missed her school in China or she was apprehensive of this new one, so large and confusing.

"Don't worry. I'll introduce you around. You'll make friends. This is your new home. Come on."

They stopped first at the office, a suite just inside the doors.

"Hi, Margaret," called Bill, holding the door for his guest.

The 50-ish woman at the first desk was surprised to see him, and asked how he was doing, asked why he was coming in. He acted like nothing was amiss. He was expected to attend meetings, wasn't he?

He waved Wendy forward.

"And this is our exchange student, Miss Wang."

"Wu Ting Wang," she said at Bill's prompting. "Please call me Wendy."

"Wendy Wang. She just arrived Saturday night. She would be a senior this year. Same as Becky. Need to get her enrolled—"

Everyone in the office froze at his daughter's name.

"It's true," he said to break the tension. "We need to get a schedule of classes for her. She's excited to start her senior year. Same as Becky. They are supposed to be like sisters."

Margaret seemed offended he would talk that way.

Out from a back office came a chunky man with a short salt-n-pepper goatee but balding on top. He wore a tie in the school colors of blue and orange with a wildcat logo, already loosened, over a wrinkled white shirt and blue slacks.

"Bill!" He also was surprised. "How you doing? Good to see you."

"Building seems the same. Didn't wreck it over the summer, I see."

"No, we didn't." The beefy man frowned. "Why'd you come in today? You can take the week off, you know. I know you're ready for classes. But...maybe you need more time to...you know, take care of things."

Bill ignored him, introduced the new girl.

"Nice to meet you," said George Griffin—the 'Griff', as Bill teased, a famous football player in his high school and college days but never went pro. He was tall and broad-shouldered but no longer athletic.

Wendy dipped her head and smiled. "Nice to meet you, too."

"He actually went to this school," Bill explained to Wendy. "But it was a different building. Over there." He pointed over to the football stadium, visible through the bank of windows in the lobby. "They tore it down ten years ago and built this one."

"Yessir, once a student, now principal. The apple doesn't fall far from the tree, yeah?"

"Apple...? Tree...?" Wendy was puzzled. "Where?"

"Can we get her enrolled?" asked Bill. "Probably AP Math, whatever variety fits. She wants to go into engineering. And you can put her in one of my classes for English. I promise to be gentle. Maybe Advanced Composition."

"Do you have literature class?" she spoke up.

"Literature? Are you sure?" He turned to George. "Well, I did catch her reading *The Scarlet Letter* yesterday. That's high-brow enough." He gazed at Wendy. "Okay, lit it is. Put her in my American Lit."

George made a face. "Bill, can we talk? In private?" He called over to Margaret: "Can you give our new student a tour of the school? And take your time."

He ushered Bill into his office, the loose PRINCIPAL plate rattling on the door as he closed it.

"Have a seat," he offered, and Bill sat, pulling a worried mask over his face. These were the chairs where people got a talking-to. Angry parents, surly students, the odd Board member or two. The Griff was good at that kind of talking. "Bill," the principal began, "I'm surprised to see you back so quick. You really need to take time off. Now, I'm no counselor but I think you could do with some counselling. You know?

You've gone through a heckuva lot. The shock phase is just ending but there's a long way to go to get you—"

"I'm ready to get back to my schedule. Keeping busy is the best thing, I think. I need distraction."

"Are you sure?" They stared at each other. "Actually I've managed to cover your classes already. I figured you needed time. So I wasn't expecting you in this semester. Not after, you know, everything that's happened. I mean...geez, it's hard to talk about it." He refocused. "We're all so sorry for you, Bill." Another moment of thought. "We've planned a memorial for Becky once the school year begins. Some of her friends've been asking for it. She was loved by a lot of us here. Great student, superb athlete, all-around decent person, a credit to you and Barb, and our school. She was someone who was going to do great things in the world."

Bill felt emotion welling inside him, fought to keep it in check.

"Thank you for saying that."

He took a big breath, let it out.

"Actually, staying at home, all the silence, is worse for me. Ever since I got the call—funny story—from Wendy, that she was at the airport, waiting since forever to be picked up.... Well, I...I've had to pull myself together to seem like a real person. For her. Don't want her to feel unwelcomed, you know. She—her presence, even in a day and a half—kind of forces me to get past what happened. It's not her fault, but she arrived at a bad time, in a bad situation. Of course she can fulfill her dream of spending a year in the U.S., going to an American high school, but as for staying with me.... With Barb and Becky not here, it's not very appropriate that she stay with me. With just me."

George was grinning, nodding.

"I'm not kicking her out, mind you. But you see the situation. Right? I called Sandy. They have two daughters, so I thought it could work, but no. And Debbie Kent, too. No go. They don't have any spare bed. Fred Lang's wife said 'no', too. Do you know any others? They don't have to be faculty, just a family with kids going here."

George waved him off. "What's the matter? Don't trust yourself?"

Bill gave him a sour face. "It isn't appropriate. I'm sure neighbors are talking already. They don't know who she is, only that she showed up right after the funeral." He made a disgusted face. "Like I need comforting."

"Well, she is gorgeous." George raised his eyebrows. "I mean, wow, what a hottie."

"Shhh!" Bill glanced back over his shoulder at the closed door, making sure it was closed. "That's what I mean."

"Bill, I understand what you're saying. You're a teacher. We have standards, morals, whatever you call'em. Just teach your classes and at home she's your daughter. Treat her like your daughter. I mean, not a substitute, obviously, but you get my drift. How difficult is that?"

"I am. I do. I mean, I will. Of course."

"So problem solved."

He hung his head. "I'm overthinking everything. Going crazy."

"Which is why I think you should take the semester off and get some counselling."

"I can't do that. No...."

"I'm sure anyone in your situation would benefit from counseling. It doesn't mean you're crazy. Everyone can benefit from talk—"

"Talking about how I feel?" He was angry. "I'm empty, that's all. I've had the shit knocked out of me. I need time to fill up again. With...I don't know; purpose, I guess. Something to do. A reason to go on. And that's in the classroom. Please don't send me off to a psychiatrist."

"Well, Bill. You see...it's also for the good of our students that I want you to go see a psychologist, a counselor, whatever you choose. It's also covered by your health insurance plan. Heck, you can even see my wife, if you like. Hannah's good. It'd be like a regular everyday conversation. No pressure, just talking."

Bill was nodding. "I suppose that would be all right."

"Great," said George. "You met her at graduation last spring."

"One other thing...."

"What's that?"

"If you have some time, I need help getting Barb's car home. It's still at the mall."

George seemed surprised. "Sure, I can help you with that."

"Today would be good. Then I won't need to rent a trailer."

"After lunch, then."

*   *   *

Bill stayed to have a go at the buffet table, then he drove the two of them down to the mall.

"She won't be alone," George said. Bill thought he was referring to Barb being in heaven, being there with Becky. "Yep. We have students from five countries this year. One from Nigeria, three from Asia, including your girl, and a Swedish fellow who'll help our basketball team."

"That's great," said Bill, almost a sneer. "Is there an international students' club?"

"Not yet." George laughed. "You can start one, if you like. Being the English teacher. Second language for all of them, right?"

"But you're not letting me teach."

"I just said to get counselling."

"So I can have my classes?"

"Maybe half schedule...give you time to ease into it. You should take that time. Extended leave is in our medical plan."

Bill scowled. "I'm not on I.R. I'm ready to play."

"I'd rather you not rush back from your injury. Don't want to make it any worse. You know, if you come back too soon—"

"You think I'll flip out, don't you?" Bill roared.

George's face tensed. "Would you?"

He was on edge, nearly ran a red light but slammed on the brakes.

"Possible. Anything is fucking possible, you know."

"You see?"

George stared out the side window for a few blocks.

"Bill, you've suffered an injury. As much as if you were right there yourself. You need help just like those that got shot." He turned to Bill as they slowed to a stop at another light. "No, I think you better sit this one out. It would be best for both you and the team."

Bill nodded until the light turned green. "And the fans, too."

"Yeah, maybe them, too." He gave a dry chuckle. "Talk to Hannah. Take your time. I want you back to full strength. We'll see you in January, ready to play."

"All right."

Bill turned into the mall, followed the lane lines over to Barb's Lexus, pulled alongside it.

As they approached the house, George following in the Lexus, Bill saw an unfamiliar car parked along the curb: a late model sportscar with dull orange finish, dented bumper, cracked rear windshield. It did not fit the neighborhood. As Bill negotiated the curve of the street, slowing to make the turn into his driveway, he realized the car's front end was blocking half of it. Stopped in the street, he glanced around to see if the driver might be out and able to move it but he saw nobody.

Instead of the driveway, he pulled along the opposite curb in front of his house. He stuck his arm out the window, waving for George to pull around the errant car into the driveway.

George locked up the Lexus and walked down the driveway to Bill's Escape, got in.

"What's with that orange car?" Bill grumbled. "Blocking us that way? Not from this neighborhood. Never seen it before."

"Must be a visitor," said George, flipping the sedan's keys to Bill.

He was about to shift into Drive and pull away from the curb when he saw a man come out from between his house and the neighbor's.

"What's this?" Bill snapped. George turned to look. "The orange car guy." The young man was getting into that car. "Just came out from between the houses."

"Could be casing the place," said George.

"You think?"

The man started up the orange car and slowly eased away from the curb. Bill's Escape was running, so the guy had to know there were people inside it, watching him. Pulling up beside the Escape, the man glanced at them, displaying an angry scowl as he passed, then sped up to exit the neighborhood, blowing past the stop sign at the end of the block.

"You get the license number?" asked Bill.

"Didn't have a tag."

"Strange." He pulled away from the curb a bit, then stopped. "Let me check back there."

Bill shut off the engine and climbed out, went to the gate on the side of the house, the opposite side the young man had come from. Stepping through the high grass, Bill recalled how he'd promised to get to it that Saturday they headed to the mall—then didn't mow. Now it was a jungle.

The thick grass bent low where he stepped. Same for the other guy. He saw the trail from the other side of the yard, coming around from where the man climbed over the wooden fence and gone to the patio. The trail ended at the stairs leading up to the deck. Bill stood at the bottom of the steps, examining the rear of the house. Windows intact. He went up the steps and checked the sliding glass door. Still locked, no damage. He bent to look inside the house, got a clear view of the living room and part of the kitchen. Enough items of value visible to entice a burglar. He cursed.

Returning around to the front, he waved at George, then unlocked the front door, picking up another bouquet of flowers on the stoop. Inside, he tugged the curtain at the sliding doors to block the view. He did the same with the kitchen window. He checked the locks. He went from room to room checking each window. Finally, he exited out the garage. Sitting in the driver's seat of the Escape again, he pushed the clicker to lower the garage door.

"Some punk looking for an easy score," Bill growled. "No harm done. But now I have something else to deal with. Watching for a punk thief."

"Well, he saw you. He knows you know him. So he'll go to some other neighborhood. Easier target."

"But I still have to do something. I have so much to do as it is. I mean paperwork. Probate shit. Insurance. And I need to go down to the police station to pick up some papers and whatever they have for me." He had to pause to catch his breath. "From the coroner, forensics, whatever they call it. Things they recovered from the scene."

"Bill...?" George reached over, pinched his friend's shoulder. "How about I drive us back?"

He nodded, tearing up. He unbuckled his seatbelt and climbed out as he wiped his face.

"I need to mow the yard," he said after he'd gotten in the other side and closed the door. "I promised."

A handful of teachers were hanging around the office when Bill and George returned. One called out to George, had questions for him. Another pointed out that Bill was with him. They got quiet. A couple of his colleagues went up to him and expressed their sympathy, wishing him well. He thanked them, his toughest job.

"Bill was just bringing in our new exchange student, a girl from China," George announced to them to save him from further scrutiny.

"Yes, her name is Wendy—her English name, that is—last name Wang. Wu Ting is her Chinese name. From Beijing. Her English is pretty good. Too good for my classes, it seems. So I'll be sitting out this term. There's still...you know...so much...."

"So much to do," George jumped in. "Dealing with the aftermath of that awful situation, you can understand. I think it's best he take some time to do that."

They agreed. More well wishes. A get-well-soon tone in their voices that made his stomach churn. It seemed, given enough time, the virus he had could be eradicated and he would be able to breathe freely again. Bill nodded thanks, shook hands with some of them, got a hug from Jennifer Claybourne, another English teacher. She was a widow, her husband killed in a car wreck five years before. A drunk driver crossed the center line. He gave her an extra look, wondering how she coped.

"Thank you all," said Bill, gazing past them down the corridor.

Wendy and a few boisterous girls approached them. He could hear their happiness before they arrived. The teachers were crowding into the conference room in the office suite but Bill, uninvited, remained outside to greet the girls. He knew them from his classes but now they were dressed in track suits, official school shirts and shorts.

"Hi, Mister Masters," said Kristy Henderson, the redhead.

"How're you doing, Mister Masters?" Gloria Suarez asked, putting her hand on his forearm like a nurse comforting a patient.

"Hanging in there," he replied, modulating his voice between melancholy and flippant. "So...looks like you've met my daughter. My Chinese daughter."

Wendy was smiling fully, like Bill had never seen her smile since her arrival. That pleased him.

"They showed me around school," said Wendy in a bubbly voice. "Every place here. Very big school. And I can join swimming team, if coach say yes."

"Swim team?" asked Bill with feigned shock. "I thought you were a tennis player."

"I can play both," she practically sang. "I can run very fast, too."

"She can," confirmed Kendra Willis, making speed waves with her hands, her brown ponytail likewise waving. "We were running on the track."

"In that dress and those sandals?" Bill made a disbelieving face.

"Yes—I tried." Wendy pouted.

"She ran without shoes," Gloria explained.

"Barefoot!" laughed Kendra.

Wendy stepped forward, pouting like a little girl who wanted to ask for something from her daddy. "If I got running clothes and shoes I can win, I think."

"She beat two of us dressed like that," Gloria admitted.

"Good to know...if I need to run away from you." Bill laughed and the girls felt awkward, their faces reflecting the inappropriateness of his humor. He was supposed to be in mourning.

"It's okay," said Wendy, recognizing the uncomfortable pause.

"Wendy taught us *Nihao*," Loni Freitz exclaimed, her blond curls bouncing. The girls all shouted *"Nihao"* in unison. "It means 'hello' in Chinese," Loni explained.

"I think we're gonna be best friends," said Olivia O'Donnell, the quiet one of the group. He sometimes heard her called 'Double-O'. She gave Wendy a big hug. "See ya, Double-U!"

The girls broke into a chorus of farewells, departing loudly out the front doors.

"I'm glad you made friends already," he said, watching the girls pile into a van driven by someone's mother.

"Oh, yes. They are very friendly to me."

"Great." He looked her over. For someone running the track in a nice dress, she appeared remarkably fresh. "Guess we need to get you some athletic clothes. Unless you brought some with you. If you're on any sports team, they'll provide a uniform for you."

"I need swimsuit," said Wendy brightly. "If I have swimsuit I can swim with girls tomorrow. I can meet coach."

"Meet *the* coach," he automatically corrected.

"Yes," she confirmed. "Missus Delmar will be here tomorrow."

He put away his exasperation. Not worth it. He only wanted to get out of the school as quickly as possible, and then drive somewhere, somewhere far away, and never return. Handling everyone's sympathy, even assuming it was genuine, was pure torture.

"Ready to go?" he asked her.

He walked with her out to the Escape. As he unlocked the door for her, he glanced back at the windows of the conference room and saw George standing there, perhaps needing a break from the meeting. He raised his hand to wave goodbye to Bill and Bill responded in kind. He would give Hannah a call tomorrow, set up something.

"So you got your schedule for the semester?" he asked Wendy as they drove home—close to the same time they would be going home during the regular school day with classes, he explained.

She pulled a folded paper from her tiny purse, opened it. "I have the History in the first period. In the second period is the Calculus. In the third period is the American Literature—"

"Now she uses articles," mumbled Bill.

"And in the fourth period is the Fine Arts. It's the Art History. I like to draw anime, you know. The fifth period is the Computer Science. The sixth period is the Advanced Composition. The seventh period is the Band."

"What? Band?"

"Yes. I play flute."

"Flute, too? You are a lady of many talents. You know, in the Fall the band marches during football games."

"They do?"

"Is that what you want?" He shook his head, amused.

"We don't march at games in China. We only play concert."

"Then you may want to rethink that. Especially if you want to be on the swim team, too."

She switched into contemplation mode, lost in thought until they arrived at the house. He recognized she was a quiet girl, much like Becky, which made her seem smart, always observing and noting everything around her, not speaking until ready to say something important. But with the other girls, she appeared lively and outgoing. Just like Becky.

"Take your time," said Bill. "Classes begin next week."

The orange car was not there, thankfully. He raised the garage door and drove in. With Wendy seeing the Lexus parked in the driveway, he had to give her an account of the operation to bring Barb's car home. He told the story without the rough parts and she was pleased he was successful.

Bill regarded her in the passenger seat.

"Can you drive? Did you get a license in China?"

"Oh, no." She shook her head vehemently. "I never take lesson. I ride bus and subway. Sometimes take taxi. Also ride bicycle. We must be eighteen for license."

"Just wondering. I thought you might be able to drive yourself to school and back."

"Me? Drive car?" Her chuckle was a tinny bell. "Oh no, too busy for me. Not here."

"Too difficult, you mean? Not really. Becky took the driver's ed class but she...she never took the driving test. Too much to do, she always said. She said she'd get to it...eventually."

That stopped him. He shut off the engine and lowered the door.

"Literally everything reminds me," he muttered. "Reminds me they're gone. That it's just me now. And I need to save myself."

The sounds of the garage settled in. The automatic light clicked off.

"Mister Masters?" came a soft voice.

Facing forward, he replied: "Yes?"

"Can we go inside house?"

"Yes, of course."

"Maybe you feel better in a light room."

"You think so?"

"I use article for you."

"Yes, you did." He cleared his throat of the emotional phlegm. "You did use *an* article."

"Thank you."

"No, thank you, Wendy." He coughed. "I'm glad you're here."

He opened the car door and she opened hers, and they went into the house, pausing in the kitchen.

"So much food we got yesterday and not started eating any of it yet." She grinned at him. "I can cook for you. You like Chinese food? You got wok? Please, you relax and I make the dinner for you."

He breathed deeply, feeling his anxiety wane. George was right. He did need help. He couldn't continue living with triggers everywhere reminding him of his tragedy, provoking his emotions.

"Thanks."

"Please wait some minutes. I will come back." She flittered away, down the hall to her room—Becky's room.

Bill smiled to himself, recognizing the calming effect her presence had on him. She must be an empath, he mused. She seemed to know just what to say to bring him out of his pain. But his pain was always there, ready to pounce on him if he let his mind go free.

He remembered an appointment for the next day.

"Oh, something else...," he called, then headed down the hallway to her room.

The door was open enough for him to catch her standing beside the bed, her back to him, wearing only bra and panties as she arranged the green dress on a hanger. He instantly spun around so his back was toward her, then reached behind himself for the doorknob, and pulled the door shut.

"Remember to close the door," he called to her and heard a reply but could not make out the words.

He replayed the vision: a glimpse of youthful beauty, of innocence. Her white skin, white underwear, dark hair streaming down her back.

"Listen, Wendy, I was going to tell you, uh...I have an appointment tomorrow. So I'm wondering what you want to do. You could stay here or.... Don't you have something going on at school? It's probably not good for you to go with me. What do you think?"

Instead of an answer, the door swung open. Wendy stood wrapped in a big white towel, her hair piled up on her head, held with a clip. He gazed down to her bunny slippers and up to her smiling face.

"I take shower, okay?" She grinned.

"Sure...okay."

"I run too much." She made a stinky face, wrinkling her nose, and laughed as she sauntered down the hallway to the bathroom and closed the door.

Bill stood in the hallway, staring at the door, feeling hungry.

6

DRESSED IN A T-SHIRT, too short to cover all of her flat belly, and a pair of loose, casual shorts, Wendy moved about the kitchen like a pro. She explained how her mother ran a small café back home, a hole-in-the-wall lunch counter popular with office workers. She helped out when she could. She learned to cut everything in clever designs and stir-fry using a wok. However, she made do with a skillet from the cabinet and the electric stove. Bill helped with cutting the steak into strips. The rice came in a pouch that he microwaved. Close enough, he decided.

"It taste good for me," she said with a smirk, flicking her chopsticks in the air, then snatching another morsel from the family-style plate.

"Yes, you could run a restaurant here," he confirmed.

"Maybe I hire you for cutting meat?" She smiled and he enjoyed that, the way she was settling in, sharing her humor.

Life was a string of ironies, he realized, perhaps remembering an old philosopher's words of wisdom.

"I'm sorry," he said, settling down on the couch after dinner, belly full. He pursed his lips. "And I'm sorry for saying I'm sorry so much. Listen, Wendy, I tried to find another family for you to stay with, but it seems nobody has any spare bed. There are still a couple families I can ask."

"I want to stay here," she said with no emotion in her voice. "I told my mama I want to stay." When he'd stared long enough, she batted her eyes. "This is Becky's home. We talk a lot so I feel I know it. I saw pictures of this home. It feel good here. Not busy. Not noisy. It's very nice and clean. I can study here."

He nodded, listening. "Well, if that's what you want. I mean, I can certainly keep calling around. Several families have daughters going to our school."

"Thank you." She flashed him a grin. "This is home."

"You probably overheard us talking outside the office. It seems I'm not going to be teaching this semester. I have to go to counselling. Get my head fixed." He tapped his temple.

"Your head hurt. I know it. I'm sorry, too." Wendy got up from her chair at the kitchen table where she was flipping through one of Barb's travel magazines, trips she never got to take. She stepped around the couch and came up behind him. She patted his head like he was a wounded kitten. "I want you to fix your head."

"You do? How kind." He didn't mean to sound sarcastic. "I do appreciate you feel that way."

Her arms dropped around his neck, formed a ring resting lightly on his shoulders.

"In a family everyone take care of everyone. Isn't it true?"

"Yes."

He tried to turn and gaze at her face. His eyes became wet and he stared across the room instead, seeing the wall of framed pictures, until she released her hug and returned to the other side of the L.

"I guess we are the family now. You and me." He breathed quicker. "Strange how things turn out sometimes. Never could've foreseen these circumstances. Six months ago, who would've known? You applied, got accepted. We said okay. Arrangements were made. That's the way it's supposed to be. Then all hell broke loose." His voice fell off, choked. "Who could've known?"

"Mister Masters, I'm—"

"It's Bill."

"Bill—I'm sorry for your loss." She took a breath. "I see you hurting so much." She sat diagonally across from him, the cluttered coffee table between them. He had one leg crossed over the other, bent at the knee, ready to plop it on the table, but hesitated. "I am hurt, too. I see you and remember my daddy. If he live now."

"Yes, I remember you mentioned him. He had an accident?"

She gave a nod, regarded him with a tilt of her head. "He fall off building. It happen when I'm seven years old. Mama cried for long time. I was too young, didn't understand. Only what I know is he doesn't come home at night."

"Oh, my goodness." He shook his head. "I'm sorry."

She wiped her cheek. "I think about him sometimes. Mama want me to forget him so I will not be sad."

"Is that how it's supposed to work?" He closed his eyes a moment. "How long until I forget my wife and daughter?"

She bit her lip, like she was afraid of what she would say next.

"I am seventeen last April and I don't forget him."

"I'm sure you never will. How long will I cry for my ladies?"

She got up, moved around to his side of the couch. He tried not to flinch as she leaned down and hugged him. It felt both good and a little strange. She smelled savory like the dinner she'd cooked.

"Don't be sad, Mister Masters," she spoke in his ear, then leaned away. "I know you feeling sad. I feel sad, too, for my father. And for Becky and Missus Masters, too. They are my friends but I never can meet them. But I want so much to meet them." A tear dropped. She caught the next one on her fingertip, sniffling. "I wish they can be here and I...I wish for you can be happy."

With her arms still encircling Bill's neck, she lowered herself onto his lap, laying her head against his shoulder. Her hair brushed against his throat and tickled his chin.

"Detective Logan," Bill asked at the front desk. He waited patiently while the female officer stepped away. Leaning against the counter in his casual school clothes, he studied the three fellows sitting on the chairs there, one in handcuffs. He thought of the guy driving the orange car.

"He'll see you now," said the officer, returning. "Follow me."

Bill knew the way through the desks and down the hallway. He had been there previously, too many times, cooperating fully, telling them everything he knew, even getting derided for his on-air remarks. They all knew him, some giving a wave as he passed by.

They greeted each other, shook hands, and Bill took a seat beside the detective's desk. On the desk were several clear plastic bags full of items he recognized as belonging to Becky and Barb.

"I see you have them ready," he quipped, pointing to the bags.

"They went over these before," said Detective Logan, a man Bill's age with an unevenly trimmed moustache. "Forensics is finished, so you can collect them." He waited as Bill stared silently at the bags. "Or we can dispose of the items. Your choice. Some people'd rather not be reminded. Others want them as keepsakes."

"Keepsakes?" He *tsk*ed, picking up the nearest bag. He saw Barb's wallet inside. "Can I open the bag?"

"Help yourself. It's yours."

He took his time fingering the bag, hesitant to break the seal.

"You know, I saw a guy casing our house. Had an orange car parked in front. I happened to come home early, saw him coming out from between my house and my neighbor's. He climbed over the fence. I checked the backyard. I haven't mown the grass so it was long and he made a trail through it, right up to the steps going to the deck. Nothing seemed damaged, not like he tried to break in. But I wondered...why my house?"

The detective shrugged. "Coincidence."

Bill pointed to the wallet in the bag. "Where's her car keys?"

Opening the bag, he retrieved the wallet, unsnapped its catch and opened it, saw the empty slots where credit cards would go. Barb's driver's license was missing, too. He showed the wallet to Logan.

"See? Someone took her cards and her driver's license." His chest felt tight. "With her address on it. I've heard of that. The thief gets a person's license and then goes to check out their home."

"That can happen." Logan studied Bill as he picked up the other bags, giving a quick look through each side. "In this case, the perp is dead, shot by S.W.A.T."

"Then who is the orange car guy? And why my house?"

"Do you want us to send a patrol by once in a while?"

"What's that going to do? He's not there all the time."

"Make you feel safe...?"

"I feel safe." He stopped, coming to the last bag. The clear plastic did not hide its contents. "What's this? A tissue? And what's that stain on it?"

Logan leaned over. "Dried blood, looks like."

"Blood on a tissue. But not a wound. Something else. Nose bleed? She used the tissue deliberately, but not for a gunshot." He held the bag up to his face. "Was this tested? Is it her blood?"

Logan picked up a folder from the desk, flipped open the cover, read down two pages. "Yes. Blood is...your daughter's."

"I wonder...before or after? She wouldn't use a tissue on a serious kind of wound, would she? She would know it would be useless."

"You're turning into quite the detective, Mister Masters."

"I'm an English teacher. I read fiction—literature. I try to write stories, too. I have to think like the protagonist thinks. I try, anyway. Plots. Always plots, motivation, scenarios. It's a curse sometimes."

Logan sat back in his chair. "We appreciate that."

Bill squared his eyes at the detective. "Is it possible there was a second man? Someone who got away?"

"We interviewed all the survivors. They confirm only one shooter."

"I don't mean another shooter. I mean...someone else...in the store. Maybe not related to the shooter, just another bad actor. Someone taking advantage of the situation."

"A customer?"

"Or staff. Who knows?"

"None of the people we interviewed said anything about that."

Bill leaned forward. "But it's possible, isn't it?"

"I'm not sure I know what you mean."

He lowered his voice, but it grew in intensity as he spoke: "I mean...a guy forces everybody into a corner, customers and staff. One of them offers to cooperate and gets rewarded, part of the money, let's say. And when the shooting goes bad, that person escapes. Out the back door maybe. Or maybe he just blends in with the crowd."

"There wasn't any crowd at that time. Only the S.W.A.T. team."

"Every store has a back door, right? All those mall stores have a back door, a long hallway, a fire exit. I worked at a mall when I was a teen. Spent a long time in the back hallway moving stock."

Logan sat up quickly, hands flat on the desk top. "I assure you, Mister Masters, we've checked every angle of this incident."

"Incident...." He chuckled. "Yes, incident. Then who has my wife's car keys and her license? Who has her credit cards? Not the shooter—not that bastard. He's dead twelve times over. Right? You didn't find them on him, did you?"

Logan glared at Bill. "No."

"The report said he didn't collect the hostages' valuables. So he wasn't interested in robbery. Then why are they missing? Anyone else report items missing?"

"I'm drawing a blank," said Logan, absently tapping his temple. "But I don't think so. Just your two."

Bill shook his head, glaring at the detective. His eyes slid to the pistol holstered on Logan's belt.

"Then who has them? Someone else there? Someone who had access to personal items? To what my ladies had. Someone knows where they live—resided. Orange car guy?"

Logan leaned on an elbow, regarding Bill. "Interesting theory. Have you checked the credit card companies? Banks? Any unexpected charges? That would be the thing to look for."

Bill's face reddened. "Well, no. I've been kinda busy. Funerals and all. Then a good bout of mourning. Followed by depression. And anger. You know the drill."

Logan tightened his lips a moment, rolling a pen over the desktop.

"What would you like us to do?" He turned away, called to a colleague who came over. "We can interview them again, I suppose."

He turned to the new guy and explained Bill's concern.

"Do that." Bill regarded the bloody tissue once more. "And this? I think she put this to some place that was bleeding prior to the final shot. Or shots. Nose bleed? Was she hit in the face? I think I want to read that report now."

The new guy, Sergeant Ramirez, leaned down, both hands on the desk, giving Bill a stern look. "You identified the bodies so...."

Bill nodded. "Yes, but I couldn't read the report. The coroner's report. I just assumed cause of death was gunshot. Like all the victims. Execution style. One every hour, like he said he would do. Then it went on only five hours, so he had to rush the last two."

Logan lowered his head in sympathy. "An unspeakable crime. We are all very sorry for your loss. The whole city is."

Bill looked at his hands, feeling tension there, like he could wrap them around a certain person's neck and break some vertebrae.

"I think there's another one out there."

The detective blinked. "We'll take a look at that possibility—"

"Someone who participated, but got away."

Bill stood quickly, defiantly. He leaned down and swept up the bags in his arms. When he turned to go, Logan pointed to other bags on the next desk.

"Don't forget those."

Bill spun around, surprised. The larger bags contained clothing, folded neatly like they were coming back from a dry cleaner's, ready to be put away in dresser drawers. He dropped into the chair, holding the smaller bags in his lap, an exhausted sigh escaping.

Logan twisted in his chair as Ramirez departed. "Barbara, could you make a copy of the forensics report on the two Masters females? Thanks." The detective regarded Bill, whose face was red, tears welling. "Different Barbara."

"I guess so," Bill muttered.

They waited in silence, occasionally meeting each other's stare.

When the woman in white blouse and dark blue slacks returned, she laid the sheaf of papers on the desk in front of Logan. Once she left, he slid them across the desk to Bill.

"You may not like what you read. But it's your right to know."

"I can handle it." He picked up the papers, stapled in the upper corner. He had handled plenty of student essays. This felt like twenty-five pages total, about one set of essays to read.

Fumbling with the bags and the papers, he pushed himself up from the chair and crashed through the aisle of desks, like a bull in a china shop, out to the lobby, out the door to his SUV. He fumbled with the keys, got the door open, and tossed everything into the driver's seat. He took several breaths, thinking of what else he needed to say to them. It wasn't finished.

He got his phone out, poked around on Google to find the number of a locksmith.

"Yeah, hi. I need the locks on my house changed. Like today, if you can come over. All of them."

*   *   *

The house seemed unusually quiet when he arrived. With his mind running a new scenario, he imagined walking into the house and finding a body on the floor, killed by an intruder. His heart raced. But there was no body. He took several deep breaths. He checked the front door and the sliding door in the kitchen. Everything looked in order.

After carrying in all the bags—two trips, deciding with the first bundle to put them in the master bedroom, out of sight for his guest; he would deal with them later—he went to Becky's room.

"Hello," Wendy sang from the bed. She rested on her belly, wearing a pink tanktop and white shorts, her bare feet kicking the air, knees bent. *The Scarlet Letter* was open between her hands.

"Still reading that?" he asked, leaning in. "What do you think?"

"It's very strange," she replied, making a disgusted face. "Everyone is hurting everyone."

"Probably where all our problems began," he said, staring across the room at Becky's bed.

It was made-up, the blanket and pillow neatly arranged, as perfect as a hotel room. Barb insisted on made beds in the morning. He was the slob in this household. He hadn't made the bed in the master bedroom since the morning they left for the mall. He didn't feel guilty about it, though. He wanted to keep the same sheet she had lain on. But he'd ruined it by now, with his rolling around, sweating, crying. It was only him now. Time to change the bedding.

"What problems do you mean?" asked the girl, breaking his trance.

"What?" He refocused. "American society. Our system of morals. Our concern for our fellow man. Infidelity. The letter, the mark of sin."

"But she got husband. And got boyfriend. Very lucky girl."

"Well, they didn't think in terms of boyfriend back then. Lover would be more apt."

"Lover...." She seemed to be checking her pronunciation. "So she finally meet somebody make her feel happy, not lonely."

"Lonely? I suppose that's true."

He felt like stepping further into the room. He wished to survey the items arranged on Becky's desk and shelf, the tokens of her life from childhood on up. She had deemed them important enough to keep them out where she could see them. Prominent among the collection was a portrait of her parents at a picnic in a park, Barb grinning like she hadn't wanted her picture taken and Bill mugging surprise. Out of the frame, but fixed in the center of his memory, was her big belly, containing a baby who would be named Becky. Not Rebecca with a nickname but Becky. Becky Jane. Jane after Barb's mother.

"Are you relax?" asked Wendy, watching him lean in the doorway.

"Actually, Wendy, I have a guy coming over soon to change the locks. All the locks on the house. For our safety."

He entered the room and went to Becky's bed. He was hesitant to sit there, to mar the perfect press. He pulled out the chair from the desk and positioned it against the bed, sat there.

"You need to know...."

"Know?" She rolled on her side to face him, sliding the book under the pillow to hold the page.

"I went to the police station today. To gather the things leftover from the investigation. You don't need to concern yourself with any of that. The thing is, my wife's car keys are missing. The keys to the car you saw out in the driveway. I used the spare set to drive it home. But there are house keys on that key ring, too. Whoever has them can get in here. So I—"

"Get in?" She was alarmed now, sat up on the side of the bed, legs draped off the edge. "Who? Bad man?"

"Yes, a bad man." He gazed at her: so innocent yet gets straight to the point. "Don't worry. It'll be fixed today. I'll give you a set of keys so you can come and go as you please. Just remember to lock the doors when you leave. We need to have a protocol."

She had a wry grin. "I never lock doors my home in China. Mama always there when I go and I come home. Maybe she lock doors if she go out but not me."

"It's a different world here. The more you have, the more people want it. People who don't work for a living. The more peace you have the more people want to take it from you." His voice was growing gruff. "This is the American dream, Wendy. Work hard, accumulate stuff, keep it locked up, hope some bastard doesn't try to steal it or break it."

"American dream?" She smiled awkwardly like she doubted him.

"A saying. A myth. What we like to believe is our fate, our destiny, just by being born here. So many people come here trying to get it.

Work hard and you'll be rewarded with comfort and prosperity. That's what we believe."

"Is it true?" Again she seemed to have doubts.

He shook his head, ready to go out and wait for the locksmith.

"Listen—Wendy—you can still move to another family, if you like. I won't feel offended if you do. This house seems to be targeted by a burglar. I would feel better if you were someplace else. Someplace safe. It's not over yet."

"What's not over?"

"The crime," he snapped. He looked away, unable to meet her eyes.

"Not...over...?"

"Not finished."

"It's not?"

"No. It's not finished. Someone out there may try to get in here. The keys, remember." He began shaking his head, rubbing his eyes. "I have a theory, but I don't like it. I told them at the police station but I'm not sure they take me seriously."

He looked up, found a spot on the wall beside her to stare at instead of at her concerned face. It hurt to make her afraid.

"First the locks. Maybe a security system, too. Outside lights. Then I've got to mow the damn yard. Then you go to school. But not me. I start talking to a psychologist. By then it should be Christmas, hah."

"Ah! I love Christmas!"

She described Christmas in China, a 100% commercial enterprise, more Santa than Jesus—just as he'd experienced while living in Japan years ago. They talked until the doorbell rang.

As the locksmith worked, Bill called a home security company to set up an appointment, then called the garage door company to come out and change the code. The house had to be secure so they would feel safe. He wasn't used to worrying. Now he had the girl to protect—the last one, like she was one final test for him. And he would not fail.

7

THE OFFICE HAD A NICE, HOMEY FEEL. A couple couches, lots of plants, the ambient illumination from a pair of windows and some track lighting, a coffee machine close at hand. Bill relaxed as the woman took her seat at the end of one couch, perpendicular to where he sat on the other couch, a configuration much like at his home. He crossed his legs. She crossed her ankles, grabbed a notepad from the table between them.

"I want to begin by assuring you that whatever is said here today, and any future meetings, is and will remain completely private, and that I will not share any of our talks with anyone. Especially George." She seemed serious yet gave him a tiny smile, more like an obligation. "Also, I already know why you're here—that terrible event—so perhaps we can get right to your issues. Or we can just chat for a while about anything you like. Whatever you wish. How does that sound, Bill?"

"That's fine," he responded, glancing at her, then down at his shoes. The Griff had married well, he mused, giving her a longer look. Dr. Wisniewski—Hannah—dressed in a somber black dress with pearls was a graduate student from Poland. Lord knows how they met or what first attracted her to the football player. What had attracted the Griff was obvious.

"How are you doing today?" she asked after a long silence.

"I'm here. Got some free time so I thought I might stop by and talk your ears off."

"I'm glad you have your sense of humor."

"Have to. These are trying times. Yeah, sense of humor. I guess it's a part of me, ever since childhood. Defense mechanism. Is that what you call it?" He chuckled to himself. "I know all that childhood stuff and how it impacts adult life. I've read a lot. I was writing a story once and needed to research that, came upon a lot of interesting material. So I know that, for example, as an only child who spent a lot of time among adults—that is to say, not with other kids—I learned two things about life and my place in it: first, that I was a darling little boy who adults thought was cute and clever. Second, if I could be funny, like tell a joke, play dumb, then I would be liked. I've known that for many years. Therefore, I tend to tell jokes. Especially in tough situations. I speak with a sarcastic tone. Especially in class. It keeps the students on the edges of their seats, you know."

"Yes, I understand the themes. But do you believe them? Have you tried being any other way?"

"Other way? No, it's been part of me since childhood. Besides being shy, I used humor to make friends, to ease tension, to escape from a bad situation. Like getting a bully to laugh so hard I could run away."

"You had a bully?"

"Not really. I grew up fast, so I was one of the bigger boys. Nobody bothered me. I stopped growing in my sophomore year."

Bill was happy to recount his childhood, year by year, musing at some incidents, shying away from others, until a pause allowed the doctor to ask him about the elephant:

"Do you feel any guilt for what happened?"

That stopped him. He studied his shoes once more. There was a scratch on the inside of his right shoe, something catching the leather and scoring it along the arch. Unsightly. He really should get a new pair before classes began. People notice how you take care of your shoes.

"I'm not a victim," he mumbled.

"I asked if you felt guilty."

"You mean survivor's guilt?" He leveled his eyes at her. "Sometimes I do feel I should've been there. Maybe take a bullet instead of them."

"And would you have?"

"Of course." He felt insulted. "What do you mean?"

"At that moment. Facing the gunman. Would you have pushed your wife and daughter aside or stood in front of them?"

The image flashed into his head: standing between the shooter and his ladies. He saw the black gun in the hand of the young thug, arm raised like he wielded a magic wand, like he was a wizard ready to remake the world in his own power structure with him at the apex, claiming through magic whatever he hadn't been able to attain through hard work. He saw himself twisting to see where his ladies stood, then one arm shoving Becky to the floor and spinning around to push Barb to the side. When he righted himself and faced the gunman again, the bullet would be on its way, unable to stop it or dodge it. He would feel it tear into his chest, shatter his sternum, dig into his heart, and a fountain of blood would erupt, filling the screen of a shocking crime movie. And he would collapse in a heap; Barb and Becky would rush to him. And the gunman would simply shoot them as they bent over his body, screaming, then silent—

"Bill?"

He opened his eyes, found them wet, wiped them with his fingers as though hiding the fact he had any tears.

"Are you all right?" she asked.

"Had a moment there."

"Have you had a lot of those flashbacks?"

"Not flashbacks. I wasn't there. More like scenarios." He shook his head, weary. "I guess that's why I write stories. My head grabs hold of some odd moment in time and won't let go, runs with it, creating all sorts of elaborate scenarios, like a causal chain that may or may not come true. It's a kind of curse."

A moment of repose, the air conditioning humming.

"Do you feel you've been cursed?" she asked.

"Cursed.... Is that the right word? Best word?" He thought for a while. "I don't know about curses. But it has been a rough three years, I suppose. Yeah.... I—I don't know what else to say. I love my wife. I *loved* her. I wanted us to stay together, and not just for Becky's sake. So I promised her everything a good husband should promise. And I've been that guy. But it wasn't me fooling around."

The good doctor sat up. "Your wife was...unfaithful?"

"That's a crude word."

He looked out the window: royal blue sky, fluffy white clouds, the sunshine's golden nothingness.

"She had a fling. She admitted it."

Note-taking.

"That's something unexpected," said Dr. Wisniewski.

"I was busy writing, trying to get published. I ignored her a lot. I went to a conference and she thought it was me having the fling."

"Did you?"

"No!" He caught himself, sighed. "No.... I was too tired for that kind of nonsense. The National Council of Teachers of English conference. I was presenting a paper on folk tales. I was nervous. Also, I was twenty pounds heavier then. Not interested in exerting myself, you know?"

"But she suspected you were?"

"I guess. But she was having hers then. Maybe because she thought I was. Who knows? Like a revenge affair. Right? People do that. He's doing it so I will too, just to make things even. Like that. Anyway, she left that company afterwards and started her own business."

"Did your daughter know?" The doctor's voice was perfectly flat.

Bill gazed at the wall behind the doctor, examining it inch by inch, looking for a crack he could exploit.

"I guess she suspected things were not all that copacetic between her parents, but as for the details—what exactly the cause of it was—I don't think so. People fall out of love with each other. That's probably what she thought. We acted courteous with each other, never shouted." He laughed. "We thought we were so clever, putting on an act, so she wouldn't think anything was wrong. But that was our curse. We never had acting lessons. We were so phony. Becky had to have noticed, even at, what, thirteen? fourteen?"

"Children can often be particularly acute."

"Yes, her. Acute. Very observant. But she never said anything. She played along, I guess. Busy with school. School and her friends there, that was her life. Not at home."

"Since then.... You said you made promises."

"I promised to be a model husband. To never give her any reason to worry. I dropped the twenty. We got romantic again. We fell in love once more, started having sex. Hah! I remember Becky complaining we were having too much fun. Noisy fun."

She made a note. "You were married how long?"

He had to stop and think. "Eighteen years. We got pregnant a little before the wedding."

"That's a good length."

"It would continue. If, you know, she survived. We were making plans for our golden anniversary, you know."

"There's the humor...."

"There goes the humor—" he flipped his hand toward the windows "—right out the window. Good riddance. I need to stop that. Nothing now deserves humor."

She sat back with a knowing sigh. "Even Shakespeare used humor in his tragedies."

"Shakespeare? You're throwing him at me? Hitting me where I live. Yes, after a violent scene he brings out the comic to tell some jokes. I hate that. I want to revel in the horror of the previous scene, and feel the visceral emotion of what I witnessed."

"And now? Do you want to revel in the horror?"

"The thing is, it's a play. My horror was real." He shook his head, pinching his forehead like he felt a pain. "I've been reliving it every night. I can't sleep and, when I do, I have dreams, nightmares, or I toss and turn and it's pure darkness. An abyss. Like something from Dante. No, I don't want to revel in the horror. Geez. Not that horror. Damn. What a question. No."

He squared his gaze at the doctor for a full minute.

"I wish it never happened. I want my family back. I'm not reveling in the horror."

He fingered the long leaf of the potted plant next to him, found it to be unconcerned with his plight.

"I apologize," said the doctor.

"Maybe you're right. I do want closure. Is that the right word? I wasn't there. I didn't see everything in vivid technicolor, you know. I can only imagine the scene from the facts they reported. I've been in that store before, so I have that info to reconstruct what happened in the theater of my mind. Like I'm watching from the cheap seats as the actors on stage go through the play. But there's no comic. Unless it's me, *pfft*. I can imagine what happened. I see it in my imagination. Very clearly. That's the curse coming back."

The doctor finished a note, regarded him with a stone face.

"Perhaps seeing it again, in your mind's eye," she spoke in a level, sterile tone, "through your imagination, is a way for you to understand what happened, how it happened. Hear me out. You put it all together so you can examine it, walk around it as though it were a statue. You're looking for an angle, something perhaps overlooked by the police, something that if you could see it, find it, might give you the ability to prevent it. You're trying to make sense of it, of course, but perhaps also you are trying to convert it into, not reality, but a story. A story you can then close the cover on. Because it is only a story, a piece of memory you can choose to put away and never read again. Then it won't be real. Then it won't hurt any longer."

Bill was nodding as she spoke, continued after she paused.

"I guess."

"And if it's no longer real—as only a story you read, and now it's finished—you can move on."

"Move on...."

"And then, moving on...what will you do next?"

"What do I do now?" He grimaced like he'd walked into a surprise party. "That's what I keep asking myself."

She leaned forward. "And...?"

"I probably should mow the lawn. I promised."

8

DETECTIVE LOGAN WAS RIGHT, he realized as he opened the first bill retrieved from the mailbox. New charges.

The charge for bedding at that store stood out. So they made their purchase, were ready to leave the store. But the cash register was at the rear of the store, as far from the entrance as possible. They'd almost gotten away before the gunman entered. Thirty seconds to walk out, then head home.

Raindrops spotted the page and he gazed up at the clouds. It was going to rain. The mowing would have to wait. He was both glad and angry. It would be harder to mow with each passing day. Everything would be harder with each passing day.

Taking the mail inside, he listened for Wendy in Becky's room, quietly reading. Probably take her longer to get through the chapters and understand everything, maybe have to look up words. He had reminded her he was available to help, to answer questions, to give definitions or explain concepts. He wasn't much good at the math, however.

The next bill floored him. Seven-thousand dollars. An auto parts store. Three stops at liquor stores. Gas stations. Online purchases. Membership to an adult website. Two sites. And lots of downloads. Definitely not Barb's charges. In fact, they were all made after the day of the shooting.

He almost crumpled up the bill, but he had to show this evidence to the detective. There was someone out there, someone who wasn't shot dead, who got away with his wife's cards and keys—

Something didn't seem right. Bill had a feeling of the world being off-balance. He returned to the front door, opened it and stared. His eyes fell upon the driveway. The empty driveway. Barb's silver Lexus no longer sat there. Gone.

"What the fuck?"

He should've pulled it into the garage, but that side was filled with lawn equipment and boxes of junk he was supposed to get rid of. Usually he parked outside and let her have the garage, so her car would be nice and warm in winter and the windshield not need scraping.

"Gone," he cried into the phone.

"What is?" asked Detective Logan.

"It's just like I told you. Somebody got away. He has my wife's car keys, drove it right off the driveway during the night. And there are charges on her card. I got the bill today. Everything is posted after that date. Porn sites? That's not my wife's charges."

The detective agreed it now seemed true. Logan advised him to come in and they would gather more information, re-open the case.

He had just hung up the phone when Wendy pranced out of Becky's room, dressed in a t-shirt with anime characters across the front, a pair of pink shorts, padding in her bunny slippers.

"Remember, I need to get swimsuit," she called to him. "I can pay for it with my money, okay?"

He stood at the end of the hallway, facing the living room, and quickly lowered his hand holding the cell phone.

"Wendy, there's more happening. My wife's car has been stolen. The keys.... I told you her keys were missing. That's how they probably got in. Just drove it away."

Her face went pale. "What?"

"We've been robbed." He set the phone down and waved the billing statement. "And here, too. Her credit cards."

He went around the kitchen, ranting, shaking his head.

"Wait," she called. "Please."

He halted, stuck between the refrigerator and the table, hand on the top of the chairback, unable to decide where to go.

She rushed to him, embraced him, pressing her cheek against his chest and holding him tightly, as tight as she could.

"Please, Bill. Be calm. It's okay. It's okay."

A spasm ran through him, closer to a bolt of lightning, and he felt her breath on his chest. Not right, he decided, and peeled her off of him. He held her wrists as he walked her backwards into the living room, dropping her gently on the couch. He released her wrists and sat down on the other wing of the couch.

"Wendy," he said, then took several long breaths. "You have to stop grabbing me. Like that." He gazed at her. She looked surprised. "Maybe you've watched too much American TV. I mean, while I appreciate your affection.... Is that the right word? It's.... I'll be all right. Yes, I'm hurt. I've been wounded and a good hug helps. But...it's not quite right the way this...this situation has turned out. I mean, you being here. My wife and daughter killed. Me being a man, alone, and so...so fucking torn apart. I...."

She started to get up but he waved her down.

"Becky...she pretty much stopped hugging me when she got to be a teenager. That's what happens, I guess. You don't show affection to your parents, especially not in front of peers. And Barb...well, she was cordial but, well, not exactly affectionate. I mean, we didn't kiss or hug most days. Long story. We had some difficulties...a few years ago—"

Wendy raised her hand like she was in class and wanted to answer a question.

"Yes?" Bill called on her.

"I know," she said with a pout.

"You know...? About what?"

She looked down, like she was ashamed to have that information. "She said. Becky told me. We exchange email long time. She say you have problems. Maybe you getting divorce. She told me you try to act like normal parents but she know truth."

"What truth?"

"Missus Masters."

"Yes? Go on. Missus Masters what?"

"She go out to see other man. Becky said it."

"Oh?" He chewed his lip. "Did she say any more? Like who it was?"

"She think he was man from her office. Co-worker. Name...I don't know. Becky didn't know."

"So what did Becky think?"

"She worry you getting divorce and she have to go live with you or with Missus Masters and not have happy life. She use crying emoji a lot."

Bill let his chin settle on his chest. It all made sense now. He made himself regard her, saw the girl gazing at him with puppy dog eyes, a little teary.

"We had some rough patches, sure. The time you're talking about, well, we just had some misunderstandings. But we fixed it. Becky had to have noticed how things changed. Did she say anything about that? How we were back together?"

She shook her head. "Only she tell about boyfriend."

"Barb's boyfriend?"

"No, her boyfriend. Becky's."

"Oh. You mean Bobby? I know him. Decent fellow."

Then Wendy, shaking her head, burst into tears and covered her face with her hands.

"What? What did I say?"

She was shaking her head as he moved to the spot beside her.

"Not you. Bobby," she mumbled.

"What happened? Did she tell you?" He glanced at the clock on the wall. "The dad is always the last to know."

"She say—said—he hurt her. After school." She pointed down the hallway. "They come here and playing in bedroom."

"Playing? What...? He assaulted her?"

"She say he want sex with her but she didn't want so he hit her."

Bill let out a huff. "I knew it. He stopped coming over. But she never said anything. Maybe she told her mother, I don't know. These boys.... Raging hormones. Yeah, I remember. I had raging hormones, too. But I was kinda pudgy back then, had pimples, so I didn't need to worry about.... But I never.... Why couldn't I protect her?"

He watched her sobbing, dared to put his hand on her shoulder to show sympathy. They needed to calm each other. So much trauma in the world. So much need for calming. He wanted to brush her hair, tell her everything was all right, as though she'd done something wrong. He wanted to believe it was true, that everything would be all right.

"Do you have a boyfriend? Back in China?"

He sat up straight, leaving a gap between them. He just wanted to change the subject.

She dropped her hands. A tear ran down her cheek.

"No.... Nobody."

"I'm sure in your culture it's not a thing. When I was in Japan—I told you about that time? Years ago—all the students were too busy studying to have any relationships. Oh, I suppose there were crushes. A few infatuations, maybe actual love. Unrequited love. A lot of that. So it's probably the same in China. Asian culture, right? Study hard. Then an arranged marriage designed for a good, stable economic future. And pretty babies."

She nodded, wiping tears from her eyes.

"I'm sorry." He forced a smile. "I didn't mean to offend."

He waited until her tears stopped rolling down her cheeks.

"Didn't mean to invade your privacy, either. Your relationships are none of my business."

She licked her lips, started to speak then stopped. Closing her eyes, she inhaled slowly, then let it out even slower.

"My father died. Falling off building. I told you. Sometimes I hear he got push off building. It's story. So Mama was alone. Sometimes Uncle visit us. He is elder brother of Father. He sleep with Mama."

Bill sucked in a breath. "Oh.... I get it." He gave her a longer look. Not such a perfect life, after all. He felt pity for her, not for losing her father but for how the uncle inserted himself into her life. "Yes, that would be...awkward...to talk about. You don't have to say anymore."

"Uncle was...."

"A bad man?" he finished for her.

She shook her head, deciding not to say more, then stood suddenly, like she was ready to march all the way home. With a swift wave of her hands, she indicated he also should stand.

"What's this?" he asked, getting up slowly.

She only came up to his shoulders, but she tilted her head up to gaze at him. He got the idea, lowering his chin so he could meet her eyes. When he looked into her eyes his body filled with energy, an odd, indistinct sensation he could not identify, something youthful and raw.

"Can I touch you now?" she asked softly.

"Touch me?" He wasn't sure what she meant. It could be construed as a romantic suggestion, or probably quite simple and innocent. Like a child would want to touch a parent, a show of affection.

"Can I hug you?" she spoke, holding her arms out.

"Ah, I see what you did there." He pursed his lips. "Sure."

She leaned against him, her arms closing behind his waist, her hands clasping in the small of his back as her head turned and rested against his chest. His arms encircled her shoulders. How narrow they were. How strong, too.

"Thank you," she murmured.

He remembered what it felt like to be held that way, whether it was Barb or Becky. Different hugs, but just as warm, just as appreciated.

Bill threw the billing statement down on Detective Logan's desk.

"See? There is somebody else," he grunted. "Look at the charges. All after the date of the shooting. Look what they're for. Porn sites? Online purchases? Barb hated shopping online. She always had to feel everything in a store. No, not the shooter—who is dead. Someone else has her cards, her driver's license—so he knows her address, and has her car keys so he can just drive her car right off our damn driveway in the middle of the night."

Logan nodded repeatedly, then stood awkwardly and called over a couple of his colleagues, Ramirez and Drake.

"Tell them what you told me," said Logan. "Your theory."

So Bill launched into a passionate description and led them on a walk down Logic Lane through the Cause and Effect garden, pointing out this flower or that bush, noting how the sunshine illuminated the leaves on that tree or how the bees seemed to like a certain plant.

"But it could just be coincidence," Ramirez declared. "Maybe her card was lost or stolen before."

"No, look," Bill growled, pointing to the line on the statement. "She used that card at the store. On that day. She finished her purchase. Right there. See? She was ready to leave." He glanced at Logan, hoping to see him understanding. "Thirty seconds and they would be alive."

Logan looked away, rubbing his head.

Bill glared at Ramirez. "Then someone else uses it. After. Got it? Dead men don't shop. So the question is—what the good detective here calls my 'theory'—who was able to take those things out of my wife's purse right in the middle of a hostage situation? And start using the cards, casing the house, and stealing a car after?"

"We need to talk to the survivors again," Detective Drake spoke up. "He's right. It's not the gunman. Has to be somebody else there, who walked out alive."

"All right," said Logan, scratching his chin. "Let's do this."

"My theory..." Bill cleared his throat. "...is that whoever has my wife's things may have known the shooter. Maybe they were partners. An inside guy. I don't know if it was planned that way or the guy was already there and saw a way to save himself—help the shooter, you know? I propose this person is the same as Orange Car Guy."

He had to explain to Ramirez and Drake about the orange car, the guy climbing over the fence to have a look in the windows. Probably the orange car had a few upgrades now by the look of the auto parts store's charges. Maybe a paint job, too, so it might not be orange any longer. Look for that.

"And I presume you've cancelled the cards?" asked Ramirez.

"I tried. But you know how customer service can be. I need to tell them a PIN or answer her security questions. Hell, how do I know what her lover's dog's middle name is? I did manage to file a disputed charges complaint, at least."

"You can give the car description to Barbara there," said Logan.

"I'll drop the insurance on it, too. Then the bastard'll get ticketed for having no insurance."

The detectives did not share his humor.

"I got all the locks changed on the house, too. And a security system installed. I have a teenage girl at home I need to protect."

The three detectives looked at each other, deciding who should speak first, what they all were thinking.

"Teenage girl?" asked Logan finally.

Bill grinned, shaking his head. "Oh, I know how it sounds. She's the exchange student from China who was already scheduled to come live with us for the year. She didn't know anything about the 'incident'. She just arrived. I forgot about her. My wife was supposed to pick her up at the airport. She's going to school—like a sister to Becky, my daughter. They would go to school together. That's all it is."

Ramirez and Drake stepped back to discuss an issue under their breath but Bill heard the word 'trafficking' among their verbiage. Bill knew from news reports that Oklahoma City, with its central location and confluence of highways, was one of the worst for trafficking.

"It's all legit, I assure you. I have paperwork at home. Exchange International is the organization. In fact, I tried to find another family —faculty who had daughters—where she could stay instead of with me. I'm in no condition to deal with her now. I can't be a good host family, not by myself. Besides, they made me take the semester off, said that's what extended sick leave is for: getting help dealing with your feelings after a traumatic event."

He was fighting through every word, holding back a tsunami of emotion filling his head.

"I'm doing the best I can. And now all this mess with stolen cards. Something else I have to deal with. I don't need this shit."

"We understand, Mister Masters," said Logan. He sat back in his chair. "Look, we're gonna talk to some people, see how their answers match up with other people's answers, and we'll get back with you. Okay?"

"Okay," said Bill, pinching his eyes and sniffling back some tears. "It's like God's given me another chance to not fuck up. I have another girl to save from harm. And I will."

9

BILL DROVE SLOWLY HOME, not paying attention to the traffic, worrying about Wendy. With her safely in school, he was free to play detective.

He worked the phone as he drove, digging for information, drawing out as much as he could, playing the part, whatever he needed to be. A lawyer seeking info. Another customer service rep. If he could invent characters for a story, he certainly could act like one during a phone call. Online purchases? Mostly clothing and electronics. It had to have been delivered somewhere. But the package was returned, he lied, so need to confirm correct address. No, not to the card holder's address, another address. Must've been a gift. Oh, looks like we missed the apartment number. That's the problem. Thanks. He wrote it down: an apartment in one of the many complexes around the mall.

Checking the time, he turned the Escape around and headed down the highway to the mall. He hated crowds, hated traffic more. Both merged in the neighborhood of the mall. You could take ten minutes going between lights that were only a block apart. Then another set of lights a block away. It was ridiculous, he complained to anyone who would listen. Best time to go to the mall was about 3 a.m. But he was not going to the mall, might never go to the mall again. Instead, he was interested in the apartments.

When he first arrived in Oklahoma, he'd arranged for an apartment over the internet, just a cheap base while searching for a house. When he pulled up in front of the office, he saw the complex actually looked rather shabby and he balked. Looking down the street he saw a nicer place and went there, signed a lease, moved in. He could see the mall from there, across the highway, and he recalled thinking it would be convenient.

Now he was turning into the Quail Meadows complex like he still lived there, like he was a bachelor and not just getting everything set up for Barb and Becky to join him. The place looked the same: red brick and beige stucco, with cars and trucks of various degrees of dents and hanging bumpers—as it was before. He slowed in front of his old place, gave it a stare, not believing it had been so long.

Eventually he found a nice house and Barb joined him with little Becky. It was the American dream at last but without the white picket fence. He had looked for a house with a backyard, envisioning many hours playing there with Becky, wanting to be the fun dad. However, Becky preferred her room. Or the living room and its TV. Electronic games were more interesting to her than kicking a soccer ball into a net in the backyard. So the yard's purpose devolved into a square of land that needed to be mowed once in a while, and occasionally seeded, fertilized, groomed. All his free time seemed to go into caring for the yard. Apartment living had been a lot easier.

He drove on, circling around the buildings until he came to the one he was looking for. He expected to see an orange car parked there but there wasn't any. Barb's Lexus wasn't there, either. He expelled a rough sigh. Perhaps he hoped for a confrontation. He didn't know how car theft worked. In the movies they would take the car to a 'chop shop' and divide it up for parts, or else someone drove it to Mexico.

He studied the address on the wall.

"Nope. No confrontation. Not without back-up," he muttered, "not without protection." He flexed his hand, imagining how a gun would feel in it. He remembered the pistol at home.

After arriving at school to pick up Wendy, Bill had to wait through an extended session of good-byes between her and her new circle of gal pals. He was glad she made friends. She was sweet. As she climbed into the Escape, some of the girls waved to Bill and he waved back.

They rolled down the long drive out to the street.

Wendy reminded him of her need for a swimsuit. Bill agreed. He promised her that, so he would take care of it. He would take care of everything. She was delighted, sitting in the seat beside him, like a princess in her royal carriage. She began recounting her day as they headed to the mall.

"The mall." He stared out the window of the SUV as they sat in the mall's parking lot, intending to get Wendy a swimsuit. "I'm not sure what store has swimsuits. But it's the end of summer now so they've probably put away their summer inventory."

Even if there were a hundred swimsuit stores inside, he could not enter the mall. Not yet. Maybe never.

He looked in the rear view mirror, saw the line of stores along the main street, off the mall property. There was a sporting goods store.

"How about Dell's?"

She screwed up her face. "Dell's?"

"It's that sporting goods store. Over there. They'll probably have swimsuits. It's a year-round store."

He drove them off the mall property and down the side street to the intersection, crossed into the strip mall's collection of shops. A haircut place, a phone place, a taco shop, a nail salon, a pet food place. He ran his fingers through his hair. Could use a haircut. If not the lawn then maybe him. And the phones.

"How about we go in that phone store first?"

He pulled the Escape up to the storefront. He felt more comfortable not being so deep within a building that he couldn't get out easily. Not like a mall with a ten-minute walk from the entrance to the store you actually wanted to shop in. Wendy jumped out the other side, nearly tripping when she underestimated the distance.

"Careful," he called to her.

"I'm careful girl."

She bounded around the SUV, her sneakers still incredibly white and her bare legs long and pale. The top she wore, which had anime characters on it, made her look younger. Putting her hair in pigtails didn't help alleviate that impression. But the shorts were still short, because comfort trumped modesty in the late summer heat and humidity. She followed him inside.

"Cute shirt," a saleswoman chirped, then offered to help them.

Bill explained what he hoped to do: cancel the phones of Barb and Becky, which had been 'lost'—or stolen, who knows? Again with the secret questions! He explained the situation, divulging the notoriety of the users, victims of the mall shooting. The saleswoman, Georgia, gave a genuine expression of sympathy. She excused herself, saying she would call another office, a higher-up, to see what to do.

As she talked, Bill wandered around the store.

"You know, Wendy, I really hate for you to keep calling China every time you want to call me. The roaming charges must be a lot." He came up behind her. She had only called him twice so far, to be picked up from school. But the call had to go from her phone all the way back to China, then was rerouted back to the US to arrive at his phone. "We can get you a phone to use here. You can still call your mother on your Chinese phone."

"It's good idea," she replied with a happy face.

Cancelling two lines would save on the bill. Adding one back would still be a savings. Besides—he scolded himself for thinking in terms of money—it was the right thing to do.

"I'm sorry," said Georgia, finding him among other customers. "It doesn't seem possible to cancel those phones. Not without the users' okay. Now, I understand the special circumstances, but corporate doesn't get it. Now, you have a family plan. And you're the principal. Hmm, let me see what I can do. Might be a little...mmm, off-label, if ya know what I mean."

She led him back to the counter and fiddled on the computer there for a while. Meanwhile, Wendy came to him with a pink phone she thought would be perfect. He approved.

"Great," Georgia mumbled. "Oh.... Yeah, okay...."

"Not working?" he asked.

"Just about...there." She smiled. "Got it. I have just cancelled those phones on your account. I overrode the PIN firewall. These systems they have, always making you go through hoops."

"Yes, systems. They suck."

Georgia laughed as Bill put the pink phone on the counter.

"If you wouldn't mind, please add this one for my other daughter."

Wendy stood nearby and when she heard him say 'daughter' she swept up to him and took his arm in hers. "Thanks, Daddy."

Inside the sporting goods store, every sport was represented. Wendy stood in awe. So did Bill. He had only played football one year in high school. He'd sat on the bench while the coaches' favorites got time on the field. Tried baseball one semester in college, but bombed out.

"Plenty of stuff here," he moaned, standing beside Wendy at the entrance. "It's been a while for me. Playing sports. You said you play tennis. Do you need anything? I guess the school has rackets."

"Swimsuit," she responded, scanning the store.

"A swimsuit to play tennis.... Could be interesting."

She laughed, pointed to the clothing section.

As they strolled down the aisle, Bill couldn't help but notice the rifles on the far wall. The hunting section. He had never been hunting although his father told stories of getting some deer when Bill was just a toddler. A few years in the National Guard while he was in college gave him his only shooting experience. But he found he was pretty good at the targets, better than a lot of the good ol' boys who played with their guns every day. He had a steady hand and a sharp eye, the sergeant told him.

They reached the clothing section. No swimsuits. A salesman came by, asked if he could help. The swimsuits were over along the other wall, with the pool gear. That made sense.

"Hey, why don't you go on over and see what they have," Bill told Wendy. "Try on anything you like. The fitting rooms are there in the center of the store. Remember to keep your underwear on when you try on a suit. I'll check back with you in a few minutes." He pointed to the wall of rifles. "I want to check something over there."

"Okay," she sang out cheerfully, practically skipping away. "See you later!"

Bill walked with determination over to the gun counter, breathing deeply so he wouldn't be nervous and trigger an emergency response, like there was a crazy person in the house. He arrived at the counter and stood looking down at the handguns in the glass case. A burly salesman came out of a doorway behind the counter, asked if he could help.

Bill looked up from the handguns. "I'm interested in getting some ammunition. It's for a...a Glock pistol."

"Okay, what model?"

"It's.... Let me think. It was my father's. I inherited it. Got a clip of bullets...nine millimeter, I think. I wonder if they're still good, though. It's been eight years I've had it. I don't know how long before I got it that they've been in the clip."

"That's magazine."

"Right. Magazine."

"With a Glock you got a seventeen-bullet magazine."

"Seventeen, huh?"

"They should be good to fire."

"Great. Wonderful. So, umm, how about some more, just in case?" He felt his face flush. "I mean, I have I think five or six remaining. Maybe another box?" He leaned over the counter, lowered his voice. "I've got burglar trouble. Need home protection, you know?"

"Certainly, sir." The man turned to get a set of keys. When he opened the case, he retrieved a handgun, laid it on the counter. It looked similar to his pistol but smaller. "This is our most popular weapon for home security. The ladies like this. Light-weight, not much recoil."

Bill straightened up. "I have a gun. I just need some ammo."

The man seemed disappointed. "Thought you wanted a gun. My bad." He tapped on his ear. Maybe too much time at the gun range, Bill guessed. "You have a permit?"

Bill didn't seem to understand. "A permit to buy bullets?"

"To carry. You need a permit to carry and to fire it. Even if you inherit it. That's the law in Oklahoma."

"Oh." He took a step back from the counter. "I see."

"You can possess it, carry it on your private property, no problem. But firing it, assuming off your property, like at a gun range, you have to transport it lawfully. As for carrying it, concealed or not, you'll need to get a permit. You can apply here."

"Yes, of course. Can't have the wild West going on."

"You want to apply for a carry permit?"

"No, I don't think I'll need to be carrying it off my property. Or using it. But maybe at a range?"

"You can't transport it loaded."

"I know. Gun and clip—magazine—have to be separated."

"You need to take and pass a gun safety course, too, for any permit. We can sign you up for one. Here's a pamphlet."

"That might be good. Been a while since my Army training."

"And, naturally, a background check."

"Background check. Certainly. I'm sure I'll pass that."

The man stared across the glass case at Bill. "Not a convicted felon? Ever been in a mental institution?"

"No and no." But Bill wondered if his current mental state might disqualify him. A man upset over the deaths of his wife and daughter wouldn't be in a stable frame of mind. Other people would think that. And he was seeing a psychologist, after all.

"Gimme your info and I'll run it through the system."

Bill balked, pursing his lips. "No hurry, I guess. Actually, I'm here with my daughter. School sports, you know. Just thought I'd come over and see what's what."

"Come on back anytime, sir." The man put away the handgun. "And we'll get ya fixed right up."

He thanked the man and stepped away, slowly, no sudden moves, and only when he was a good distance from the glass case did he spin around and leave his back side vulnerable before hurrying away. He crossed the store, over to the pool section and racks of swimsuits.

Not seeing Wendy there, he went to the fitting rooms and called out her name.

"I'm here," a girl's voice called back.

He smiled, remembering that first phone call, when she was down at the airport, like he was supposed to know what that meant.

Taking a seat on the bench there, his thoughts returned to his gun. He always thought of it as his father's. Had to check it carefully once they returned home. Had to be sure he was ready to use it—

"How do you think?"

He looked up and saw his young guest posed before him in a blue one-piece suit, cut low in front and high on the hips. She had a good figure. Bigger in the chest than he had thought.

"Is that the style you have to have?" he asked, trying not to stare too hard. "Can you swim in that? Or is it just for sunbathing and, I don't know, fashion shoots?" He caught himself, intending only humor, then bit his tongue. "I mean—"

"It's for daily practice." She grinned like she knew she had excited him, turning around to show off the suit, posing deliberately. "We get school style for tournaments."

"I think it's wonderful." He nodded approval.

The way she stood there, barefoot on the carpet, hair tied up with a clip, she looked quite lovely. She could be a swimsuit model. Except she really had no butt. Upon further scrutiny, he decided she was too thin, had no muscles. He wasn't sure how much of an asset to the swim team she would be.

"Okay, I will buy it," she sang, happily.

"That's all right. Let me pay for it. A welcome gift."

"But I have brought money."

"Like I said, it's a gift."

She ran up to him, planted a kiss on his cheek, then disappeared into the fitting room.

Bill slowed the Escape as they approached the house, expecting to see something else that might not be quite right. That was his life now, looking for evidence, clues, taking on another task. But the driveway was empty and he pulled in as usual, rising the garage door and pulling in, shutting off the engine, lowering the garage door—as protocol dictated. He was getting back to business.

In the car they had been discussing the school year and the way things were done at Vista High School. Sitting at the kitchen table as Wendy cooked the dinner, he continued reciting the customs and procedures. Then he mentioned the memorial service for Becky that the school would be having on Friday.

"You know," he said, standing suddenly. "Umm.... I'll be right back. I just want to check something."

Slipping into the master bedroom, he closed the door, considered for a moment locking it. He went to the chest, slid open the top drawer, felt inside for the pistol and retrieved it. The pistol had *Glock 17* chiseled on the barrel. The black finish shone like polished stone, cold to his touch. It was heavier than he expected.

Remembering his National Guard training, he turned to face the far wall and pointed the pistol downward—the bed's mattress would catch an errant shot, he guessed—and checked that the pistol was not loaded. The magazine was out of it, too, stored in the bottom drawer. Perfectly safe now.

He took a stance, more from movies than training, pretending to fire at the wall. Holding up his arm, he looked down the sight line, aimed at a picture hanging on the wall—

Blinking furiously, he lowered his hands, brought the pistol to his side, realized he was breathing hard. His shot would've been off. Had to control his breathing, he knew. But the picture he aimed at undid him: Becky, a grinning toddler, the first two teeth shining for the photographer in her first studio portrait, wearing a red jumper, her dark hair cut short, a cute bob—"She looks like a boy," he complained when Barb brought her home from the salon, claiming she was ready for her portrait.

No, he hadn't meant to aim at her, not at her picture on the wall, not at anything, really. He felt the pistol weighing in his hand and brought it up to his waist, gazing down at it. He began to understand the feeling some people might get when they had a weapon in their possession: the power of absolute decision. *Do this or I will use my weapon to harm you. Do it! Now!* The steel could turn any weak-willed lame-ass into a crazed monster believing he was God.

"Mister Masters?" called Wendy from outside. "Now is dinner."

"All right," he called back. "Be right there."

Barb probably knew he had the pistol but never would've thought of it, out of her consciousness. Becky likely never knew he had it. His father had a pair of hunting rifles, too, but he was not in a mood for hunting when he sold them to his cousin who loved to bring home a deer every fall.

And yet, if someone came to the house....

If someone tried to break in—or *did* break in, home invasion style—would he—could he—raise that pistol and aim it at a human—yes, a bad human, a violent, dangerous person—and squeeze the trigger?

10

"YOU MAY NOT LIKE WHAT YOU READ," Detective Logan had told Bill, sliding the freshly copied forensics report across the desk. But Bill had insisted on being able to see it for himself, to know the details of his wife's and daughter's deaths. It would read like a cold detective novel, he imagined, with lots of vivid, evocative adjectives and adverbs, putting him there at the scene of the crime.

It wasn't a narrative, he discovered, not like a story, but short statements of clinical fact or professional opinion, presented in rough chronological order with explanatory notes, prepared not for pleasure reading but for legal use. To give a set of details to authorities of one kind or another. To make things clear, unequivocally clear. He wasn't supposed to enjoy it.

"No...."

Bill looked up from the pages in his lap, his eyes falling on the bed beside where he sat.

"No...." His voice was a scrape through the chilly air of the room.

It was late and he readied himself for bed after thanking Wendy for another great dinner, more Chinese food or as close as she could make with ingredients available in the kitchen. He was conflicted, wanting to get on with his tasks but at the same time feeling in a better mood, feeling more relaxed after securing the house. He had the pistol and he believed he knew how to use it. But trying to sleep was impossible, as busy as his mind was, thinking through every scenario, preparing a response to each situation.

So he had gotten up, turned on the light, and finally decided to read the report that had been tossed on the nightstand on a busy afternoon. He intended to get to it when he wasn't distracted. But that never came. He sat up, rubbing his forehead, squinting against the light, and grabbed the papers, almost at random, tearing the top two pages from the staple.

"How much worse can it get?" he muttered, returning his burning eyes to the page.

He thought of the tissue with the blood soaked through it, still in the plastic bag, in a pile of bags on the chair at the side of the room, the chair where he usually tossed his half-worn clothes. He had believed the tissue was for a nosebleed, something small. Definitely not for a gunshot wound. No, apparently it was for...

"...rape."

Someone during the hostage situation had forced his daughter down behind the cashier stand and assaulted her. There was blood. Afterwards she, or someone, had put a tissue to her wound. Witness corroboration. But they couldn't do anything, not with the gunman pointing his gun at them. While someone. Someone else. Pushed her down. While a second person. A second person took advantage of the situation.

Barb cursed at the assailant, surviving hostages confirmed. That was when she was shot. Front of her shoulder as she faced the gunman, then, as she spun around from the shot, a second one entered the side of her head, just below her ear, shattering her jaw. She dropped immediately.

Tears began to wet the page and he carefully dabbed the paper with his pillow, not wanting to smudge the ink—

"Oh, God!" he erupted. "Oh, God. No!"

He sobbed as he rocked on the edge of the bed, feet stamping the carpet, his t-shirt wet. If only he could've been there. If only he'd gone with them on that simple errand to get the damn bedding. If only he'd carried that pistol with him. If only they were not hosting an exchange student—then there would be no need to get any bedding, no need to go to the mall that day. And he would be reading about someone else's family and thinking he wasn't involved and, while tragic for them, his life was safe and his family secure—

A gentle knocking interrupted his anguish. He knew it would be that girl from across the hall, from across the ocean.

The door opened a few inches. Wendy peeked in, her expression full of concern.

"You okay?" she asked timidly.

"No, I'm not." He stared down at his feet. "Why does everyone keep asking me that? Isn't it obvious I'm not? Even if I act normal I'm not normal. I'm special. I was selected to be a survivor, and have to deal with all this shit. Have to live with it forever."

His rant overwhelmed her and a tear rolled down her face.

"I'm sorry," she said, her voice choked. "I heard shout, so...I worry for you."

"Yes, worry about me. Worry about the whole world. The crazy, fucking world." He turned and glared at her. "Please go back to your room—to Becky's room."

"Back to room...?"

"Yes," he growled. "Get out. Leave me alone."

"But Mister Masters—"

"Go away!"

She backed out of the doorway but left the door open.

"Sorry, Bill."

He sprang from the bed and with a wide swing of his arm slammed the door shut with a loud bang.

When the echo had faded he could hear sobbing outside the room, in the hallway. He wished he hadn't slammed the door. But rage had overtaken him, made him act irrationally. Made him focus on his hate. And nothing was more satisfying in that moment than feeding his hatred—

He had done nothing wrong, a perfect citizen with a perfect family. It was the thug who was wrong. And there was no excuse, no good reason for acting as he did. No bad childhood, abuse, alcoholism, drugs, bullying, paranoia, nothing that would serve as an adequate excuse for taking hostages in a store and shooting them. And letting someone, a partner or co-conspirator, an accomplice, hurt his daughter that way. Did you need money? Need some bedding? Just take it. Go ahead with your theft. But no need to kill anyone. No need to assert your gun-infused authority over innocent people.

He dropped off the bed, hit the floor with his knees. He scraped together the pages of the report, shuffled them, and smacked them on the nightstand to make them even, laid them flat.

"Everything began with her," he mumbled, then glanced at the closed door. The sobbing had stopped. Maybe she had gone into her room and closed the door. Maybe she had stopped crying—from his violent actions which frightened her. Or maybe he just couldn't hear her anymore. His blood was gushing so loudly his ears were numb. Maybe she was calling her mother even now, begging to come home.

We all want to go home, thought Bill, staring at the page, feeling a primeval punch to his gut.

Kneeling, upright from knees, unclothed below waist, w/ vaginal hemorrhaging visible on thigh, ponytail swept to front. Barrel to back of head, just above first cervical vertebrae (transversalis cervicis). One shot. Exit upper jaw/nasal cavity, removing front teeth & nose cartilage. Fell forward. Jacket draped over head & shoulders by other hostage. Found prone beside #2 (mother).

Awakening in a dark cloud, Bill was unable to bring the details of the night into his consciousness. He hadn't been drinking, no pills to sleep, just rage. He recalled the rage and he recalled vaguely the cause of the rage. That Chinese girl. His heart thumped hard in his chest.

"Oh, shit," he muttered, rolling off the bed, standing and swaying beside the bed. His head hurt but it wasn't a hangover. His chest was tight like he'd run far and his breaths were labored. He sat back on the bed, forcing himself to breath deeply.

As images returned to him, he realized how angry he had been, which caused him to act badly. It wasn't her fault. His head knew that, but his gut still blamed that Chinese girl for entering their lives, for causing their lives to be cut short.

He opened the bedroom door, saw the door to Becky's room closed. He tapped on it. "Wendy?"

No answer. He glanced back into his bedroom and noted the time. He had slept late, like he had gotten used to doing during his required period of mourning, the three days of numbness.

"Wendy, are you here?" he called out in the direction of the kitchen. No response.

"Well, it's late," he said to himself.

But where was she? Maybe she got the idea she had to leave. He told her to leave him alone, right? Maybe she was on a plane back to Beijing at that moment. He thought of that: the cabin of the plane, her leaning against the window, tears rolling down her face—her pretty, innocent face. Her experience living in America ruined.

She wasn't supposed to be here. An artificial situation, an anomaly, a quirk of fate. He had punched the wall. His hands hurt; he wanted to feel pain. It felt good. He deserved it. No, she wasn't supposed to be here. She shouldn't have come. If she'd stayed in China, his ladies would still be alive. Damn her. Damn that Chinese girl for forcing this fate on him and his family.

He should've tried further to find another family for her. He had the right idea. He would try again. She had to get out of his house. Now there was no friendliness within him, no polite urge to do the right thing for an innocent girl. She was not innocent, not now. Not to him. Better if she did go home, like her mother wanted her to. America was a violent, dangerous place. Even in a peaceful suburb.

In the kitchen was a note, left on the table by the chair where he usually sat. A farewell address, he presumed, picking it up. Just a page torn from one of her cute notebooks, a pink kitten smiling from the corner. The writing was pink, too.

> *You are sleeping. I call my frend Jackie & she take to school.*
> *Swimming today. See you later!!!*

And she had drawn a heart where the signature would go if this were a formal letter of resignation.

He sat at the table with a long sigh, holding the paper and studying her handwriting. So neat. One misspelled word. A missing object— 'take *me* to school'. The important thing, he noted, was that she left a note for him. And the note didn't say 'good-bye'.

His gut felt funny: empty, of course, needing to eat, but also like butterflies that fluttered when preparing to go on stage in front of an audience and you're unsure of your lines, hardly confident in being able to pull off the role—the role of host parent. Especially when you were beaten up on your way to the theater, hit about the head and body, yet still expected to perform. Your fellow cast members expect the show to go on, no matter what might've happened outside the theater, there in the real world. Indeed, a world so different than the stage, than the simple passage from home to school and school to home, with everything in its place and the sun shining and the birds singing and the bees buzzing—maybe not so many bees, he decided.

Seeing the collection of pictures on the wall in the living room— Becky at different ages, smiling in all of them—he began to cry, hunched over the kitchen table, crumbling the note in his fist, slamming his fist against the table.

11

DR. WISNIEWSKI LOOKED OVER the top of her black-rimmed glasses, Bic pen poised in one hand, wire-ringed notepad balanced on her knees, pressed together below the hem of her black skirt. She gave Bill a stern look, a rare display of emotion, then glanced at the clock on the wall behind him, positioned so the patient couldn't see it.

"I did say you do not need to talk if you don't want to," she said to break the silence.

A pair of nods.

"I only come here as something to do," he responded a minute later. "It gets me out of the house."

"And you feel you need to get out of the house?"

"Yes."

A few minutes.

"The house is too full of memories."

"Tell me about them," she suggested, moving the pad to make a note.

Bill let out a long, loud sigh, like he'd been holding it in all session. It seemed to be getting harder. At first she was easy to talk to. He would simply share his thoughts and would feel better at the end. But each time he had less to say. Each time it was more difficult to say anything. The longer he remained alive, the sole survivor, the less he wanted to talk about it.

He told her how he went through the dresser drawers and gathered up Barb's clothing, every last piece, and packed them into plastic boxes with lids, taped the lids, moved them into the garage with the other boxes of junk he was supposed to get rid of. He had promised Barb. He had gone through the closet and done the same with her clothing. He told the doctor about that. Maybe someday he would feel comfortable giving away her clothing to a charity.

The same for Becky. But with the Chinese student staying there he didn't want to disturb the room.

He'd gone around the house removing anything that smacked of memories. The photographs on the wall were the most devastating. They were all pleasant memories, special times when the people in the pictures displayed their happiness. To see Barb smiling hurt him more than if she wore a more perturbed expression, which she often had off-camera. And seeing Becky's childhood photos reminded him of the potential she once had, a bright light that would shine over the world someday. He allowed only one framed picture to remain: the three of them at graduation, when Barb had gotten her MBA and stood in her cap and gown beside him while he held Becky, a fussy toddler grabbing at her cap's tassel.

"And...?" the doctor prompted.

He looked away, avoiding her.

"Have you done any more packing?" she asked.

Still regarding the windows, he took a breath. "This is, what, our fifth session? I feel less like it's helpful. I guess you're frustrated by my lack of talking. The talking cure doesn't work for the silent type."

He tried to laugh. She made a note.

"There's nothing to laugh about. All the joy has gone from my world. There's nothing left. Nothing but memories which haunt me. It's too hard to start over. How am I supposed to do that? I don't want to 'start over'; that just closes the door on them. I want to remember them but I don't want to hurt so much every time I remember them. If that spot in my brain that links anything about them to the way they left me, to that day, I wish it could be cut out. Or zapped. So it doesn't hurt. The closest thing I can think of that does that is a cheap bullet."

He took a breath. Another.

"That's what I've been thinking. If I had one cheap bullet I could've stopped it and we wouldn't be talking now."

She scribbled on the pad, then looked up.

"Yes, the memorial for Becky went well. I told you about that. It was well-planned. Touching. Truly touching. The entire school cried. It was good so many liked her, that she was respected by everyone. It was moving. I was pushed to say a few words but, you know me, I didn't get very far before I lost it. Too choked up to continue and your husband rescued me. At least everyone could see what a wreck I was, and that was the reason I was out for the semester. The other kids who spoke...I really appreciated what they said. Becky was popular. They made a permanent memorial next to the trophy case."

A moment's pause.

"And Wendy?" asked the doctor.

"I told you. Even when most didn't know who she was, she spoke. Said some good comments about Becky. She was ready. I know, she comes off as shy but she does assert herself sometimes."

More breaths, labored, noisy.

"Of course she never met Becky, but the two of them had a lot of correspondence. They were good friends. Now.... It's strange because at home we hardly speak. Not after my blow up. She's afraid of me. I get it. Besides, she has her school friends to take care of her. She comes home late—well, nine or so. I presume she gets dinner with one of her friends then studies or whatever teens do. She's gone when I get up in the morning—as I sleep late."

"Are you deliberately trying to avoid her?"

"Doctor, we have discussed that already." He laid his head back. "I think that was our third session. I said I hated her for starting this whole scenario, causing it to unfold. Yeah, I know she's not directly involved but she had a hand in it. And she...survives. Like me."

He glanced around the office, looking for an escape route.

"She was strangely affectionate when she first arrived. I was kind of alarmed, then dismayed. I didn't think Chinese were so touchy-feely. Then, well, I thought it was a teen thing, or maybe her trying to be more Western, you know."

"Did you like it?" She'd asked the question several times previously, and he had answered the same way.

"As a family man, it felt odd. As a man, it felt good. As a man who lost his family, it made me fear. I told her the rules of the house."

More writing.

"And I finally got the damn yard mowed. It was quite a jungle. Took the whole weekend. All day, both days. Pushing the mower through the wall of grass, a foot high in most places. But I got it done. Finally. I promised Barb I'd do it while they were at the mall, but I delayed. Yeah, I got so sweaty I had to pull off my shirt. It felt good to be exercising like that. Half naked with the sun on me, breeze blowing against my skin. And then she comes out to watch, sits on the deck like some princess watching the serfs labor."

"How did that make you feel?"

"I didn't care what she did. Every glimpse of her reminds me why she was here. Why they're not. I tried—really tried—to get her placed with another family but I couldn't find one. And she wanted to stay, wanted to be in Becky's room. Said it was cute. The anime theme, you know."

"I see." More scribbling.

"So I'm busting my balls there—excuse me, my *back*—fighting with the mower, and she comes out into the yard, walks right up behind me so when I back up there she is and I bump into her. And she's got on one of her skimpy tanktops, you know, spaghetti straps barely holding up her...uh, breasts. And her short shorts—thank God for this lingering summer heat."

"And how did that make you feel?"

"I'm a man." He shook his head. "I felt what any man would feel."

"I remember you said she brought you a drink."

"Yes, she came out to give me a glass of lemonade. Or, at least, lemon flavored water—ice water with a couple slices of lemon in it. To refresh me, she said. Yeah, even though we didn't speak to each other, she made that drink for me."

"How did that make you feel?"

"Grateful, I guess. I needed to...what's the trendy word? Hydrate? I was sweating like a dog. Quite yucky. So as I'm stopped, drinking, she pulls out a towel and wipes me down. Like I'm a race horse. More like an ox in the field."

"Then she resumed watching you 'labor'. Is that correct?"

"Yes."

He fell silent, remembering every detail of that afternoon, playing it back in his mind, feeling the rough towel against his back, the cool liquid down his throat, the jiggle of her breasts in the tanktop. After she took the glass away he remained self-conscious, aware of her watching him, his body running with sweat once more.

"Enough talk for this session? Did I make up for my silence?"

She looked up from her writing, flashed a polite smile and adjusted her glasses.

"Whatever you say is helpful. Silences say something, as well."

"That's poetic. Maybe turn it into a haiku."

She tilted her head. "Are you writing again?"

"Writing? You mean like haiku?"

"Anything. Isn't writing a source of pleasure for you?"

He scratched his nose, kept his hand half-covering his mouth. "Used to be. But now I feel...well, if I get into a fictional scenario, it's like I'm cheating on them. Like I'm closing the book on them."

"Any poetry? Have you expressed your thoughts and feelings?"

"Thoughts and feelings...." He raised his arm, finger pointing to the clock he knew was above him on the wall.

"Yes," she said, flipping a few pages over, closing her notepad. "We can discuss that next time."

Bill nodded, stood and stretched. "Deal."

As he rode the elevator down, thoughts came to him of the day he went to the indoor range and actually fired his pistol, the Glock. The quartermaster helped him understand how to maintain the weapon and load it, and an instructor taught him a proper firing position. He bought additional ammo at the range, used all of it. After two hours of practice he could hit the bull's eye consistently. Other shots struck head and shoulders. Any of them would halt home intruders, said his instructor. He wondered if he should've divulged that to the doctor. Probably not.

He paused outside the medical office building and sucked in air. There was a hint of autumn coolness that comforted him. Besides the enjoyment of autumn, it meant that time was moving on. The ever-oppressive summer could not last forever. Life went on, even in the season of dying. He remembered the days in his childhood when the autumn held so much promise, so many opportunities.

Four weeks into the semester, he considered as he drove home. Her schedule was set, her routine established. She got herself up in the morning while he stayed in bed. He would see the remnants of a breakfast produced from the groceries he bought during the day when she was at school. Sometimes there would be a note—most mornings, he corrected himself, thinking how he would phrase such revelations to the doctor. The notes would inform him of her schedule, something happening at school or after school.

Often she would go home with a friend, have dinner with the family. Everyone was happy to get to know the girl from Beijing—from 'a small town near Beijing' that had a million people, she explained. Several families wanted to have her as their guest. She had been enlisted to teach Chinese to one family's eight-year-old girl who was adopted from China as a baby. Some students in the high school also wanted to learn Chinese so she tutored them. By all accounts, Wendy— Wu Ting whenever she taught Chinese—was popular and well-liked. It made life easier knowing that others could take care of her, pick up some of his duties, and, moreover, that her visit to America was not completely ruined by his circumstance.

She usually came home late, dropped off by one of her friends, which he thought was permissible. He would be in his room, door closed, as he listened to her entering through the front door with her key, making her way to the kitchen for a drink or a snack, then to the bedroom that was formerly Becky's. He checked in the room during the day, found nothing amiss or out of place. She kept Becky's side of the room immaculate—like a shrine. He would step out for a drink and snack after she returned. Seeing the light on, he presumed she was studying, likely reading, or on WeChat. Sometimes speaking Chinese, probably on the phone. The light would go off at midnight.

Other mornings the note would be just a heart or a smiley face or her attempt to draw one of her favorite anime characters. No words, only the drawing. But she was communicating with him. She seemed to understand by then how she was a trigger for him, how her mere presence caused him grief because of the way she reminded him that his wife and daughter were no longer there. She respected his wish to avoid her. Anyway, she was busy now. No need for him to interfere with her experience living in America.

Sometimes, on those days when she got home in the afternoon, she would knock on his bedroom door, gently, as though she still feared his angry response.

"I made dinner."

Her voice sounded grateful for the food he had bought which she could put together as she liked. When he left a rare note, he offered to get whatever she wanted, just make a list. And she did.

When he came out to eat the dinner she made, she had finished hers and retreated to her bedroom. *Her* room, he thought. It really was Wendy's room now. When she was out, he looked in and saw how she decorated her side of the room, posters and drawings taped on the walls, a new stuffed kitten on the bed—a gift?

Occasionally they met in the hallway, he going one direction and she the opposite. A polite nod maintained the protocol.

He passed her room one Sunday morning, after she had showered, and caught her sitting on the bed still wrapped in the towel, with her feet up, painting her toenails one by one. Hot pink. She glanced up, grinning like she knew exactly how he must be taking in the sight of her, toes wiggling before him, yet continued her careful painting as he stepped away.

Should I tell Dr. W about that?

He pulled into the garage, shut off the engine, lowered the door.

That was the same day, he realized as he entered the kitchen. She had stayed up late, on a school night, to finish reading for class. It must have been about midnight but she kept going to finish the assignment, so maybe 12:30.

He heard a scream and the door to his bedroom flew open and in she rushed, saying there was somebody outside who had peeked in the window. She was shaking as he jumped up from the bed and went to her room. He didn't want to look out the window for fear whoever was there might be waiting for him to look and fire a shot.

Instead, he returned to his bedroom and got the pistol from the top drawer and the magazine from the bottom drawer, snapped them together.

"What's that?" she gasped.

Not answering, he rushed to the front door. "Lock this after me."

Running barefoot in shorts and t-shirt, he entered the backyard through the side gate, saw somebody climbing over the fence on the opposite side of the house.

"Hey!" he shouted, holding the pistol up but not aiming. "Stop!"

The wiry young man was too quick and sprang over the fence.

Bill raced back through the gate, around to the front of the house, feet padding on the driveway—just as the tail lights of a car roared away down the street. In the darkness he couldn't determine if the car was orange.

He sat on the front stoop, breathing hard from the exertion, heart racing from the confrontation. Catching his breath, he returned to the backyard, dark but for the security lights which snapped on when he waved his arms. The window of Wendy's room was high enough. The only way to look in was to be on the deck and lean way out over the railing. Or stand on a ladder under the window.

Weighing the pistol in his hand, he wondered if he should have fired a warning shot, make the punk stop, then call the cops and be done with him.

"Is he gone?" asked Wendy when he entered. He had to knock their secret code on the door and wait for her to identify him through the peep hole. "Are you okay?"

"Yes and yes," Bill said with a grunt. He was soaked with cold sweat but she latched on to him anyway, held him tight, wouldn't let go.

Maybe he should tell the doctor about that episode. It seemed important, a demonstration of his parental concern, his determination to be a good citizen and rid the world, or the neighborhood, at least, of bad actors. His silent sessions likely made her think he was slipping, losing his grip on reality, sliding into the abyss like a jungle explorer disappearing into quicksand.

Or maybe he shouldn't.

Wendy remained afraid, nervous that night. She had hesitated returning to her room. Even pulling the shade down did not alleviate her fear. So he gave in and let her sleep in the bed with him. Although he felt her bump against him a few times during the night, when he awoke in the morning she was already up and off to school.

12

THIS TIME HE WAS ESCORTED to a conference room where a grim Detective Logan and a somber Detective Ramirez sat, papers spread across their end of the long table. As Bill entered, Logan got up and stretched out to shake hands, returned to his seat, inviting Bill to take a seat. He pulled out a chair where he stood, four seats up from Logan's at the head of the table.

"You call me in, you must have something," said Bill with awkward jocularity. "Well, I have something for you guys, too."

He launched into the telling of his midnight encounter with the peeping Tom, the presumed burglar, possibly Orange Car Guy, as the detectives listened patiently. They got the report from the police officer who had stopped by the house the next day, a regular patrol past the house, as they'd promised. Bill flagged him down and reported the trespassing. Yes, it could be related.

"Turns out you were right," said Logan, steepling his fingers over the report pages on the table.

Ramirez took a page of the report. "We interviewed the survivors again. Two saw what you've alleged. One confirmed—" He read from the paper. "—'the girl was dragged behind the cashier stand and we just heard her crying then a scream like she was in pain and we figured she was being assaulted, but couldn't see nothing.'"

He glanced at Bill, who remained silent, frozen.

"Another reported that she, the witness, quote 'never noticed the fellow until the girl screamed behind the cashier and the mother was on her knees begging for them to leave her daughter alone' unquote."

Again Ramirez checked on Bill: granite.

"Descriptions of the assault suspect would indicate he was just another customer in the store. He was there prior to the gunman entering. Could've been planned that way. Two witnesses said it was possible, said the suspect seemed out of place, pacing around the store, uninterested in choosing merchandise. 'Young men don't usually go into bedding stores alone like that,' one said. The suspect reportedly looked around eighteen. Another said 'a little older than the girl'. Thin, 'casually dressed but in a neat way', and 'only became loud when he took the girl away.'"

Finally Bill hung his head, unable to speak. He had started to make peace within himself about what happened. But there were so many triggers out there to remind him, and then he would feel that lightning bolt zap through him. He felt it again and leaned forward against the table. The tear ducts which had eventually dried up broke open.

"Sorry," said Bill, wiping his eyes.

"We checked store surveillance cameras early in the investigation. They seemed to have been turned off just before the gunman entered. Likely could only have been done by an employee. Perhaps working with the gunman. It was planned, coordinated. Not random."

"Sorry to tell you," said Logan, hand slowly tapping the table. "It was a good tip, a viable theory. Thanks. And you were, unfortunately, correct."

"Now to find the punk," Bill muttered. He looked up, eyes wet.

Logan gave a nod, shuffled some of the papers. "Actually, we have someone. Fits the description you gave. Driving your car, the Lexus. Vehicle was found in a ditch out I-40, one-car accident, veered off the highway couple nights ago, hit a road sign. Driver evidently walked a ways down the highway and was picked up by OHP."

"It's still on-going," Ramirez spoke after a moment, "but we want you to look at some photos, identify anyone you recognize, and maybe answer a few more questions. We think we have the narrative now."

"If you want to hear your theory put to a narrative," said Logan.

"Who doesn't like a good story?" Bill tried to grin, failed.

"It's not a good story," said Logan.

"We think this is what happened," said Ramirez, modulating his voice. "Your wife and daughter enter the store, find what they want to purchase, go to check out at the cash register at the rear. Already in the store are four employees, one in the back room—we believe he shut off the video feed—the assistant manager, hired two months earlier. The other three were out in the store. Names don't matter at this point."

"Assistant manager was working with the gunman, we believe," said Logan.

"At the same time, there's another customer—the young man that some witnesses confirm assaulted your d—"

"Raped."

"—your daughter. We believe he knew her. Could've followed her into the store seeking to either stalk her or perhaps speak to her. But he stays away until the gunman declares. None of the witnesses—the survivors—remembers the young man prior to when he grabbed the girl and—"

"My daughter."

"Yes." Ramirez met Logan's eyes, and Logan nodded. "So when the gunman declares his authority, and pulls out the AR-15 from his coat, the accomplice—"

"And who the fuck," Bill burst, "wears a goddamn trenchcoat in the fucking heat of an Oklahoma summer? No security guards at the mall entrance? No metal-detectors? They have 'em at some schools, you know."

The detectives nodded in agreement.

"It was not intended to be a robbery," Ramirez continued, "but a deliberate hostage situation. The gunman left a manifesto on his phone, a rant about how the world mistreated him all his miserable life, the usual complaints, nothing political, nothing religious."

"Just a piece of shit who wanted to go down in a blaze of glory, with an entourage," Bill grumbled.

"Assistant manager participated, as I said. When it started, he stayed in the back room, only came out later, after it ended. He claimed he was scared and hid there."

"He's in custody as we speak," said Logan.

"And the rapist?" asked Bill.

"That young man stood among the hostages. At first. He was beside your daughter, one witness confirmed."

"You know the news report, Mister Masters. The gunman, Fredrick David Singleton, who was killed at the scene, ordered the hostages to kneel on the floor, backs to him. As they did, the young man pulled your daughter behind the cashier stand. Evidently, the gunman didn't notice or didn't care. Your wife reportedly shouted for him to leave her alone. At which time the gunman shot her. Shouted for her to 'shut up'—witness reports. None of the other hostages moved to help."

"Lot of coincidences coming together," Logan said with a sigh.

Bill stared at the detective. "The young man?"

Logan shuffled the papers, held up one to read. "He is Robert James Kendall."

"Bobby...."

"You know him?" asked Logan.

"Ex-boyfriend." His chin dropped to his chest. "Haven't seen him for months. I understand he tried to...you know...assault her...at our house last spring, but she rejected him."

"Got it." Logan regarded Ramirez.

Bill pinched his eyes, looked up. His voice wavered: "Not a very good story. Several plot holes. Not very good character development, either. Needs work."

"Again, we're sorry. It was a horrible incident."

"Incident.... Pfft!" Bill slapped the table. "One random store. Why that store? Why that day? At that hour?"

"Singleton and the store manager—assistant manager—already knew each other, planned it together, had the same mindset—"

"To make a statement." He wanted to roar but he let his anger go into his fingers as he gripped the table, ready to break off the edge trim. "To be sure the world paid attention to them. Is that all?"

Ramirez shook his head. "Isn't that enough?"

"And Bobby sees her in the mall, follows her into the store, waits until someone totally at random halts everything, and right then he sees his opportunity. And there's no connection between Bobby and the gunman-slash-assistant manager team?"

"Apparently not." Logan set down the paper. "Coincidence."

Bill rubbed his forehead, eyes closed. "We call that 'serendipity' in the English department."

"Are you ready to look at some pictures?" asked Ramirez.

He let out a groan. "I guess so."

The detectives led him out of the conference room and into another room with a computer set up. The technician there pulled up a set of pictures, selected one, enlarged it to fill the screen.

"Do you know him?" asked Logan.

Bill stared.

"Well?" asked Logan after a minute.

He exhaled slowly like he was finishing a cigarette.

"That's Bobby Kendall."

Despite the badly beaten face, Bill could recognize the boy who once seemed nice, a good student—perhaps too good, like he was putting on an act just to get on the good side of a girl's dad. That kind of bad boy. But after poorly written papers and lowering grades, he'd switched to Mrs. Claybourne's class. He was glad at the time the boy moved. Then he showed up at the house to see Becky. He tried to give the boy the benefit of the doubt.

"He was in a class with me," said Bill, suspicion in his voice. "Why does he look like he was beaten up?"

"He had a scuffle with a couple other boys," said Ramirez. "Three months ago. We brought all of them in. Assault and battery. Kendall was the victim in that case. Football player versus computer nerd. No contest. Something about who had rights to a girl."

Bill closed his eyes, facing the screen. "You mean my daughter?"

"Apparently," said Logan.

"So he stalks her and gets a chance to rape her...."

Logan, standing behind Bill, cleared his throat. "And he died in the shooting."

Bill felt his eyes getting wet again, his throat tighten. He had to hold it together. Mourning was over.

"Then who is casing my house? Looking in my windows?"

"Don't know," said Ramirez with a theatrical shrug.

Logan gave another nod to the technician, who made the picture disappear off the screen and brought up another.

"Know this one?" asked Logan.

Bill regarded the mugshot. "This is supposed to be...?"

"Do you know him or not?" asked Ramirez.

"No." He continued to regard the ugly face: scraggly beard covering a long scar down the side of his cheek, a bit cross-eyed, a previously broken nose by the look of it. "Never saw him before."

Ramirez nodded. "The assistant manager that day."

"Howard Thomas Payne," Logan announced, reading the paper.

"Had an embezzlement complaint by a different employer a while back," Ramirez explained, "thrown out when the company settled out of court. Got this job at the mall. Happened to know a crazy person."

"Singleton?" asked Bill. "That's who you mean?"

"Apparently," said Logan. "Last employed...." He searched through the folder of loose papers. "One of the stores in the mall. A different store...." He kept shuffling, reading.

"Fired, of course," Ramirez added.

Bill sat back, stretched. "That's all right. Doesn't matter. It's over. Singleton's dead. Shot by the S.W.A.T. guys. Lots of bullets. Good. I feel sorry for his mother, though."

Logan was nodding, his face frozen.

"Payne is in custody now."

"Good to know."

"Well, you shouldn't have to worry any more."

Bill stood up, shook out his shoulders like he had sat through a three-hour movie. "That's good."

"Okay, then," Ramirez spoke. "That's all we need for now. We'll be in touch. May need you to testify, so stay in town."

"Oh, one more thing," Logan perked up as Bill was reaching for the door. "We turned in your credit card fraud case to OSBI. They nailed the guy. A whole ring of thieves, turns out. Buying and selling people's data. You did good."

Honk, honk, honk. Bill looked up at the rear view mirror, saw the guy in the truck behind him waving his hand, finger raised. He glanced up as green turned to yellow, then rushed through the intersection, leaving truck dude behind.

At the next light, truck dude pulled up loudly beside Bill, the engine deliberately roaring, and leaned out the window shouting at him.

"You fucked up two lights! What's your problem?"

Do not engage. Bill kept his eyes forward, watching the lights, hands on the steering wheel. What was his problem? A fair question. He considered rolling down the window and shouting back that his wife and daughter were murdered. That was his problem.

He recalled seeing a poster at school, how we can never know what another person is dealing with so always be kind. When the light turned green, he waited, let truck dude go ahead, and without surprise the truck charged past and swerved into his lane, continued speeding down the boulevard.

A police car sitting under the shade of some trees by the Home Depot pulled out and chased after the truck, lights flashing.

Bill rolled on, not slowing to gloat or wave or flip a finger. Just keep going, keep on truckin' as he glanced at the officer getting out of the patrol car to go up and write a ticket.

Keep going. That's the standard mantra, isn't it? What else can a person do? Can't go backwards. Can't truly stand still. Except for death. Death kinda freezes everything, locks everything at that one point in time. And saddles the mind with a lot of baggage that never makes it home.

He turned into his driveway, clicked to raise the garage door, and slowly pulled inside, lowered the door. The engine was running and when the exhaust began to choke him, he shut it off. He coughed, at first lightly, then with desperation. He grabbed the clicker to open the garage door as he fell over onto the passenger seat, heaving.

Tumbling out of the SUV, he tripped out of the garage, sucking air, dropping to the pavement. He sat leaning against the brick column between the two garage doors, catching his breath.

Staring across the street at his neighbor's house, he noted their well-groomed lawn; they always had a seasonal display. They'd put up the autumn one already, pumpkins and corn husks, all orange and yellow. Soon they would set up the Halloween display, skeletons and ghosts usually. The Masters family never did anything like that. Their house was strictly functional, not a public work of art.

A late model gold car sidled up to the curb in front of his house. Out came a man in a suit. With a priest collar.

"Bill Masters," called the man, daring to walk up the driveway.

It was Father Michael from Barb's church. Or Reverend Michaels.

He was never clear which.

"Thought I'd stop by and see how you're doing," said the clean-shaven man with thinning hair combed to the side. His teeth were very white. "Funny I should meet you sitting out here."

"I just returned home," Bill said with less breath than he wished. He drew in some air. "I was at the police station looking at pictures."

"Pictures? At the police station?"

"That's what I said."

"But didn't they...shoot the man?"

"That man, yes. But not enough. There's someone else."

"There is?"

"Father—Reverend—whatever you are, no offense—I just want to be alone. I don't need any preaching. No prayers. It's done now. Let it all rest in peace. Let them rest in peace."

The man of God bowed his head, pinching his lips. "I understand."

"Good."

"Seeking the Lord's help through quiet contemplation is often as good as hearing some words spoken."

"Yeah, quiet contemplation rocks," Bill grumbled. He'd done that for three days, mostly in bed, then crawled out of his cave when it was time to pick up a girl from the airport. He didn't feel he had gotten enough of that quiet contemplation.

Michaels gazed upward as if searching for God in the clouds.

"You know, I remember something Barbara said to me the last Sunday before the, uh, incident. She came up to me after the service, as everybody was filing out, and you know what she said to me? She said to me 'Father, thank you for a lovely sermon'—"

"Yeah, she was always saying 'lovely'."

"Wait, that's not all, Bill. That sermon was on forgiveness. She told me there at the door that she was inspired to forgive someone. I asked her who and you know what she said? She said you. That's right. She had a tear in her eye, in fact. That really touched me. I could see she was serious. Now, I don't know the whole story but she did speak with me another time about some difficulties you and her were having in your marriage. And you know what she said? She said—"

"Stop." Bill glared at the reverend. "Just stop it." He dug his shoe against the pavement. "That's none of your business. It wasn't then and it isn't now. I'm fine. Just need to work through the five damn stages of gut-wrenching grief." He looked away. "I have a psychologist."

"Oh, that's good." The reverend tried to laugh. "About the same, but without God."

"It's working so far."

"Glad to hear, glad to hear." The reverend sought another spot to fish. "Missus Garver, who you may know, she delivered a casserole one Sunday past, I do believe. She said you evidently have a guest. She was quite surprised." He chuckled. "A gossipy woman like her is one to talk. Am I right? But you know what she said? She said you looked happy. I mean, having that girl stay over."

Bill glared sideways at the reverend. "She's the exchange student who was already scheduled to come here. That old woman can mind her own business."

"That's fine with me. But I couldn't help overhearing her talking to the other ladies of the Outreach Committee. You know what she said? She said they didn't need to be delivering any more care packages to you, that you had dessert already." He forced a laugh. "Imagine that. They do love to gossip."

"Reverend, this is not the time."

Bill saw the grass was getting tall again. Recent rains had helped. Better not let it get too long this time. And in the middle of a clump of grass he had skirted last time because it was too close to the tree trunk, was a rabbit. A bunny. Cottontail, long brown ears flicking, munching away. There! The meaning of life. Eat your veggies and shut up. Yep, there's nothing in the world for us but grass and sky, no pleasures but reproduction and eating. He stared a moment.

"Thanks for coming by, Reverend."

They said their farewells.

Bill watched him drive off.

How do you deal with such horrible events?

He looked again at the rabbit. Sensing a stare, the rabbit bounded off across the driveway and out of sight.

There was nothing more he could do for Barb and Becky. All that remained were memories. Tokens. Various objects forever infused with their auras, to hear a TV guru describe it. He'd watched a lot of strange programs on late-night TV when he couldn't sleep. His ladies would always be in his heart, to use the Romantic vernacular, and in his mind, to use the concepts from psychology.

So what's left to do?

Him. Himself. He was the one hurting now. He had physical pain the same as if he also was shot. Every thought of them made his gut ache and his head rage. He had to save himself. He had to rid himself of the pain. He knew ways to do that, at least temporary ways. Get stinking drunk, stay unconscious. Or run through a long checklist of indulgences, a bucket list of hedonistic pleasures.

Or a more permanent solution—

As he rose, legs unfolding, sliding his back up the column, another car arrived, turning into the driveway. He could see by the gaggle of girls laughing out the windows they were dropping off Wendy, giving her a ride home after school.

Out she stepped, wearing a bright red Chinese-style dress covered with embroidery. She wore little black slippers and had her hair put up with clips and ribbons. She looked like a Chinese princess.

"Well, look at you," he said automatically, grinning, forgetting that he'd resigned himself to speak as little as possible to her lest he say anything in anger. "What, is this Chinese day?"

"We have International Day today," she explained, then turned to take some bags from another girl before they drove away.

"So you represented China. How'd it go?"

She told him about the assembly, when each of the foreign students talked about their countries, customs and history, showed traditional costumes, played traditional music. He remembered her busy in the kitchen, cooking several dishes. He thought she was working ahead making lunches so she could spend time studying. No, they were for International Day. Of course, everyone knew Chinese food—but not real Chinese food, she explained. One of her friends had driven her to an Asian grocery where she bought the food products not available at Bill's grocery. She paid for it with money drawn from her suitcase.

"I hope you'll make some for me—for us."

They went inside and she unpacked her bags. A few Tupperware from the kitchen. She apologized for using them without asking for permission and he waved off her apology. He had been sleeping.

"Please excuse me," she said, batting her eyelids with their long lashes, "I go change clothes then I wash boxes."

"It's okay," he said with a nod. "I'll wash them."

She smiled back at him as she left the kitchen, something not quite confident, a bit on edge, perhaps wondering why he was being nice all of a sudden, maybe because of some evil plan he had concocted.

But he was sincere. He took the Tupperware apart and washed every piece, set them to dry on the rack on the counter. He was finished when she returned, wearing casual lavender slacks and a long-sleeved gray pullover with a yellow character front and center, something like a squirrel but more Cubist art. He thought it must be a Pokémon.

"I guess you had a good day?" he asked, sitting at the table.

"It was great. A lot of fun." She was clearly delighted, holding up her phone. "Here are pictures." Shot after shot of her friends, of her and her friends, of only her in the red Chinese dress. "We were told to bring things from our countries to share at special day like today."

"That's wonderful. I didn't even know there was any event going on today. I'm so out of the loop now. I should've attended."

"But you are off leave. So you stay home."

"I'm *on* leave," he corrected. "I'm *off* work, or off-duty. I'm excused from work. Because I've been wounded." He tapped his head. "And I don't simply stay home. For example, today I had to go back to the police station to answer some questions." He lost the smile he'd been wearing since she arrived home. "Lovely pictures. Good memories for you. Can you send the ones of you in that dress to me?"

"Sure I can."

Then, as he clicked onward thinking the pictures would continue, they became pictures of Becky. Obviously she'd sent them to Wendy. Bill had never seen them. Lots of school poses. Some out shopping. Their trip to the Chickasaw Cultural Center last spring, and in the Arbuckle Mountains, posing with such a great smile. The braces had worked, her teeth straight now.

"Oh, those are Becky," said Wendy. "Sorry."

"No, don't be sorry. I'm glad to see them. To see her—Becky. Could you send them to my phone, please? I'd like to save them, put them on my computer."

"Yes, I can do it."

"Thanks."

The next picture was strange. It had to have been taken inside the mall. Some event going on. For kids, it seemed, but Becky had posed beside a clown there. Not a typical circus-type clown but something decidedly post-modern. More like a ghoul.

He shivered. Seeing the date of the photo he realized the picture was taken moments before they entered that store.

Handing the phone back to Wendy—"Thanks."—he retreated to his room, closing the door.

13

THE WARM AMBIANCE OF THE OFFICE was no longer comforting. It felt sterile, even with the potted plants always green, taunting him with their life-boasting fullness. But the sooner he said everything, the sooner he could leave.

"I couldn't stay there," Bill explained. "I was ready to explode. Seeing the pictures Becky sent to her. And then...the picture of Becky at the mall that day, posing with a clown...right before they went into that store. A 'fun' pic. Social media is so demanding. So cruel."

"How did that make you feel?"

He could anticipate her questions. She had four different questions, it seemed, and they cost a lot. Fortunately, his mental health care was covered by employer insurance. They had anticipated every need in his life, it seemed, and he smiled to himself.

"It was amusing?" asked Dr. Wisniewski.

"No, I was thinking of something else." He regarded the doctor. "I was thinking about the day I checked the box that got me the coverage for help like this. I never thought I'd need it but, being a teacher in a high school, they must have expected I'd get frazzled someday."

"It can be a stressful occupation, I'm told."

"Well, that's not why I got into it. Not for the stress. No, not for the excitement of the everyday drama. No, I like to write and I'm good at it. So I thought. I want to share my love of writing. And maybe get some time to do my own writing. It was working.... Until now."

"Have you been writing?"

He chuckled to himself, looking out the windows. "You mean the haiku? No. Nothing. There is no spark left in me."

"You said before you wrote fantasy stories?"

He didn't know whether to smile like he knew some secret or like he thought she was being silly.

"Fantasy. Like Tolkien. Or like Zelazny and Moorcock. Knights and princesses, dragons, elves and trolls. Like that, yes. Don't judge me. 'Fantasy' can mean a lot of things. What I write is not the erotic kind of fantasy stories. I'm not a pervert. In fact, all my stories are rather mild, nothing sexy, more the romantic kind. They all have happy endings. Not enough conflict. Which is probably why they never sold."

"But you haven't written anything recently?"

"Nothing for a couple years."

She started to ask another question but cut herself off, slowly twirling her pen between her fingers. Then made a note.

"I'm too consumed with the list," he spoke after a moment. "The checklist. All of the things I have to do. *Have* to do. Forced to do. Paperwork mostly. Collecting Barb's insurance. Becky had a small policy, too. For final expenses, really. But now it's tracking down the unauthorized charges on credit cards, cancelling phones, finding her stolen car, getting a security system for the house, and protecting my guest, my substitute daughter, hah, my...my substitute wife."

He wasn't sure if he should've said that last bit, but it was out now. Hannah knew he had a guest but hadn't included Wendy in her line of questioning. Thankfully.

"She goes on her own schedule, like Barb did. She gets breakfast, goes off on a life of her own, comes home whenever she wants, like a grown woman. Her only limitation is she can't drive herself anywhere. No license. So she gets rides with her friends."

"And you said she slept with you...?"

"Not—not like that. The night the creep was looking in her window. She was too afraid to go back in there so I let her sleep...yes, in the same bed as me. But, honestly, I was too tired to do anything but sleep. I'm not a creep. I would never do anything improper. Or illegal. Or immoral. I have standards. She's my guest. My substitute daughter. Daughter. My role is to protect her."

"And yet you frightened her...you said."

"Being a protective parent." He clenched his fists. "I sent her out so I wouldn't hurt her. Yeah, at that moment...I hated her. I wanted her to go home, out of my life. If I didn't have that last tiny glob of a soul in me, I might've punched her in anger. But I didn't. I held back. I'm still a sane, rational human being."

"That's a good accounting, Bill."

He thought of the nights in the backyard, dark but for a distant streetlamp cutting into a corner of the yard. He sat in a lawn chair in canvas pants and dark t-shirt, boots ready for running, holding the pistol. Balanced in his hands, over his lap, the magazine inserted, locked and loaded as they say. He felt like a soldier on patrol. He had done that in his National Guard days: stand guard, signal if you encounter the enemy. That was easy. Now the gun had real bullets and there was a real enemy. He wouldn't be stupid or weak this time. He had someone to protect. So many nights watching the lighted window of Becky's room—Wendy's room—until the light went out. He would remain a while longer, just in case, then pack it in and go inside. He started leaving his bedroom door open, in case she needed to get out of Becky's room.

"I feel like I'm splitting in two. Part of me continues to mourn and wants to die to end the pain. And part of me has moved on, it seems, and acts normal, even friendly, to the outside world. But these two sides pull further apart with each day. That worries me. What is that, schizophrenia?"

"It could become schizophrenia if you continue to pull apart. Let's talk about the first part. Where you want to, as you stated, die to end the pain."

He had to smile at her serious tone. "That's just a metaphor. People say things like that all the time. 'It's to die for!' 'I'd kill for that.' But I do want the pain to go away. Can you prescribe something?"

"I don't prescribe medications." She flashed a smile, a requirement, he supposed, when talking about drugs. She regarded him. "But do you think that way? When you're alone?"

He leveled his eyes at her, turning serious. "Yes, I have. But I won't do anything. Not like that. I mean, now that I have something to do, someone to protect. I have to stick around to fulfill my obligation to

Barb and Becky, to take care of the girl they brought here. I don't want her to think bad things about us. About America, either."

"Then it's good she came."

"Yes." He shook his head, rubbed his forehead. "I don't know. Yes, it's good she's here. But being here also reminds me that Barb and Becky aren't."

She regarded him over the top of her glasses.

"These new pictures—"

"—remind me what I missed, what I will be missing. How does anyone move on from something like this? I know there are supposed to be five stages of grief, but I must've gone through seven or eight of them by now. When will it stop? When will it?"

She pushed her glasses up on her nose. "Sometimes it doesn't."

The trees were in full autumn splendor as they pulled up alongside the curb, staring out at the gentle slope of the cemetery. Bill wore a dark suit and tie, not what he'd worn to the funeral. Wendy wore a serious dress also in dark blue but with thin white vertical stripes, the closest to a funeral costume she had brought. Her heels raised her three inches and made it difficult to walk across the grass.

"Here," he called in a low voice, pausing before the small signs poked into the ground. The two headstones had not yet been put in place, though they should have been. He'd need to make a call to check on them. Something else to do. He ordered a joint stone for him and Barb. He would join her soon enough. And Becky would have her own beside her mother. "'Beloved Wife and Mother'," he read on the sign, noting the years. Such a small period of time in the greater scheme of the universe, he thought. "'Beloved Daughter.'" Yes, very beloved.

Two people meet at random, make a third. Bill pulled his hands out of his coat pockets. *Like it was meant to be. And they do things to make themselves happy. And time continues counting. Then they are gone. All of them. And time continues counting.*

Wendy approached the site but stayed behind him, holding the flowers she purchased, a separate transaction from Bill's. She said she wanted to buy her own flowers. She missed them, too. She had tears in her eyes as she said it. He had intended to go alone but when he told her where he was going on this cool Saturday morning, she insisted on accompanying him, to pay her respects. After a moment to reconcile his feelings, he agreed.

Sensing her presence behind him, he turned and waved her up. She stepped lightly until she stood beside him, gazing down at the plots, hard to distinguish from an ordinary lawn.

"And that's how we do it in America. We bury the dead. In a park. Or a pretty place that's like a park. To help them rest in peace. That's what the R.I.P. means. 'Rest In Peace.'"

He breathed for a while, his heart beating stronger, knowing stress was building inside him. Only a short time before it would overwhelm him. But he couldn't rush this.

"And we hope they do rest in peace. Some people die peacefully, just go to sleep and never awaken. Like old people. Others die without peace. Those are the ones we wish to rest in peace the most. I don't know if you believe in ghosts, but we believe the ones who die violently are the ones who come back to haunt us." He turned to her. "It's just some American history. Nothing to be afraid of, okay?"

She gave a nod and reached for his hand, took it in hers.

At an unspoken cue, they both leaned down and placed their flowers on the grass before the signs, Bill's bouquet on Barb's plot and Wendy's on Becky's.

They stood straight again, still with hands clasped.

"I remember that day was so hot," said Bill, glancing wistfully around the cemetery, the trees casting shade here and there over the leaf-strewn lawn. "I was sweating so much wearing a suit. I could barely breathe. And everybody was so miserable. I just wanted to get out of here. I know it was supposed to be a solemn occasion, but we knew what it's about. We knew our lines. Strangely, I didn't cry that day. Maybe it was because of being in front of everyone. I said the words, dropped handfuls of dirt, stayed quiet otherwise. They shook my hand, hugged me, told me how sorry they were, to call if I needed anything. And I said—stupidly said—I just needed time. I guess time to get over it, for it all to fade away. Fade away. Like it never happened."

He felt the other hand squeeze his hand and then she was against him, holding him tight, her head digging into his chest. He heard sobbing and felt his shirt getting wet from her tears. He raised his arms around her.

"My parents were already gone, but an aunt came, and my cousins, two of the four, anyway. Barb's family came. Her parents, her older brother and younger sister. And their spouses and kids. And a few kids from school, too. I didn't really pay attention to them so I'm not sure who. I just figured they were from the school. And people from her church, too. I didn't know most of them. I seldom went to the church with her."

"I'm sorry, I'm sorry," the girl mumbled against his shirt.

He hugged her tighter, then loosened his grip.

"I know. Yes, I know. Nothing happens like it's supposed to. Far too many variables. Too many anomalies floating around out there, just waiting to get caught in our plans, to screw things up. And the rest of us...we're left to fix things, to clean up, to make it all right again, and then...then we have to keep going, like nothing bad happened. Like all the people who never experienced such a horrible event. The people who never had to work through a checklist. Or bull their way through stages of grief. The people who don't know what happened, and live their lives in harmony and bliss. I want to be one of those people. The ignorant ones. Yes, I loved my wife and my daughter and I will never forget them, but I want it not to hurt whenever I think of them. I don't want to feel a trigger being pulled whenever I see a photo or remember a moment with them. I don't want to hurt anymore."

She squeezed him once more, then gently pushed herself out of the hug but remained against him, shoulder to shoulder, her hand on his arm, clenching his elbow.

"Please rest in peace, Missus Masters," she spoke, a catch in her voice. "Please rest in peace, Becky. Thank you so much for everything to arrange me coming here. I wish I can meet you. I always remember you. I love you."

Her words moved him to embrace her again and kiss her head.

"Thank you, Wendy. Thank you for being here. It's like you are my last tie to them. Holding you is like holding Barb, like hugging Becky."

It wasn't a particularly good day for it, but Wendy insisted. Her friends agreed to help, so when Bill returned home from errands, they were ready and threw confetti at him and shouted "Happy Birthday!"

Dressed in old jeans and a worn sweatshirt, Bill wasn't expecting a party. Having students he had in class in his house was a bit alarming. But he played along, pretended to be happy. He accepted the well-wishes from Abby, Kitty, Kristy, Kendra, Gloria, Loni, C.J., Nancy, and Debbie, as well as boys named Marcus and Jimmy. Bill ate his cake carefully, despite his hunger, and listened patiently as they sang the special song, laughing at their odd rendition.

The girls each gave him a hug as they left, the boys handshakes. Wendy smiled as he closed the door and turned to her. She practically jumped on him, giving him a big hug, and just as quickly let go and dropped to her feet.

"You arranged all this?" he asked, breathing hard.

"Oh, yes. Are you happy?"

"Surprised, yes. Happy...well, I guess." He made a strange face: embarrassment or delight, a mix of both.

"I saw it's your birthday, so I wanted to make party for you. It's marked on calendar."

"It is?"

She led him down the hallway to the door of the third bedroom, a door which hadn't been opened since she arrived. Tacked on the door was a paper calendar. It showed August still, but Wendy lifted the pages. On the October page, one day was circled in red ink. He saw it was Barb's handwriting: "Bill is 43" with a heart. He had to smile, seeing those words, her heart. He flipped up the page, saw the writing on the following month: "I am 42" with a frowning face instead of a heart. Another page up and he saw: "Becky is 18" with a heart.

He released the pages and they fell into place against the door.

"What's this room?" asked Wendy.

Bill stepped back. "This is Barb's office. Yes, it's a bedroom...but she made it her home office. We don't go in there. It's a rule. And we can't disturb her while she's in there working. Another rule. Actually, sometimes she let me use it to grade papers, so I wouldn't be bothered by Becky and her friends making noise in the living room. I have a tiny desk on the side. Her desk is the big one in the middle. Sometimes I write my stories there. But not for a long time."

"You write story?" She gazed up at him like he was famous.

"A few, yes. Nothing serious. Fantasy stories."

"I can read?"

"Hah. If you want to. But school work comes first, right?"

Big grin. "Yes, then I read your stories!"

"Well, don't get your hopes up. It's not quite *The Scarlet Letter*. Did you finish that?"

"Oh, yes. Sad story. But got A on report I wrote."

"That's good. Missus Claybourne is tough."

"'Do anything, save to lie down and die!'" she declared, one hand on her chest, the other in the air, like a practiced actress.

"What's that?" he asked.

"It's from *Red Letter*."

"Oh." He studied her: eyes gleaming, face cherubic. His birthday seemed to mean more to her than him. "I don't remember that quote. Perhaps I should."

She flashed a smile, happy she managed to teach him something. "Missus Claybourne says it's better to do something, even if it becomes wrong instead of do nothing."

He had to nod his head at that. "I get it."

Later, Bill decided the cake and ice cream were too much and he didn't need a full dinner. He made a sandwich instead. He wondered if Wendy wanted one, too, but she was still in her room. Her room, he thought. A warm glow formed in his chest then transformed into a stone in his gut. She must be studying, forgetting the hour.

As he approached the closed door, he heard talking inside.

Chinese words, pressing his ear to the door. Must be talking with her mother. He listened, merely curious how she sounded speaking Chinese. When he heard no more, he tapped on the door.

Wendy opened the door immediately, like she was ready to walk out anyway.

"You called your mother?" he asked with hesitation.

"No."

She seem sad or upset at something as they went to the kitchen. She pushed past him and he followed. Her first stop was the fridge where she retrieved her bottle of tea and took a long drink from it.

"I made a sandwich for you. We had dessert earlier, didn't we?" He gave a chuckle, pointing to the last two pieces of cake in the pan.

"Thank you, Mister Masters," she said, and her voice was definitely not her usual cheerful persona.

"Bill, remember?"

She sat at the table, pouting. She stared at the sandwich on the plate for a minute then picked up one half, took a bite, chewed.

"Are you all right?" he asked.

She shook her head, chewing. Wiping her eye, she took a second bite, chewed.

"Sandwich okay?"

She gave a nod. When she swallowed and cleared her throat, she spoke: "Uncle call me. He want me go back—come back home. He say Mama is sick."

"Oh. That's important. So are you going?" He tried not to sound hopeful, like he was finally getting rid of her. He liked having her in his life now. Having someone in the house. Someone to worry about. "I mean, what does he want you to do?"

"Mama is not sick. She told me. Uncle...want me come home."

"He wants you to come home?" he said both to ask and correct.

She set the sandwich down on the plate, wiped her eyes. But tears ran too fast. Sliding off the chair, she stood before Bill, wanting a hug. It was becoming a thing. He obliged. He brushed her hair with his fingers, like he'd done with Becky when she was young and needed comforting.

"So he's not telling the truth? Saying that only to get you to return, huh?" He waited for a response, none. "Not the good kind of uncle then."

He felt her shake her head against his chest. "No, he is bad uncle."

"Oh." He had only thought to make a joke to help calm her, not uncover the truth. "You said he...visits your mother...?"

"I said." She looked up at him. "Not my mama. He visit me."

"What?" He held her away, his hands clasping her forearms, trying to meet her eyes. "He visits you? What do you mean? Does he hurt you? Abuse you? What?" He became angry, as though whatever this unknown uncle did to his new daughter was as bad as what the rejected nerd from the high school had done to his daughter in that store. "Did he do anything to hurt you?"

She tore away from him, her face wet, and ran down the hallway to her room, slamming the door with less than full force. He followed. Hearing her sobbing inside, he decided not to bother her. She clearly wanted to be alone. He knew the feeling, but she was way over here in a strange land, among strangers, and he, as flawed as he was, was her only champion.

He waited outside the door, leaning against the wall, expecting to hear another phone call, or to accept her when she came out of the room. He recalled the times Becky came to him when she was upset and a good hug would lift her spirits, give her confidence. But nothing happened. The sobbing lessened, faded away. He thought of knocking on the door to check on her.

All he could think of was that, like many broken homes, the uncle had molested the girl, the daughter of the woman he supposedly was visiting. It never occurred to him that a perfect exchange student could have problems back home. And flying to the other side of the world might be the only way to escape. These students were supposed to be the cream of the crop, the best representatives of their countries, the bright ones who would promote international cooperation.

Returning to the kitchen, Bill began cleaning up, thinking more about his guest. He realized she had become more than a guest. She was part of his household, a member of his family. He thought of her through the days and welcomed her arrival home each afternoon or evening. He missed her when she was gone and enjoyed her presence permeating the house when she was at home.

Otherwise he was alone, a miserable figure lost in bad dreams, ready to end the pain. But she was restoring him. Who knew? If she hadn't called that night, he might not be alive today. They would find his body, carry it out, and someone else somewhere would be deciding what to do about the house and everything inside. Because he would be free from pain, and on his way to a reunion with his ladies.

14

AN ORDINARY DAY, sun hiding behind clouds, a breeze blowing from the southwest, leaves fluttering from the trees in the backyard as Bill set the mower to rest in the far corner of the yard, where they had buried Becky's cat long ago, hit by a neighbor's car. He went to the garage for more gas. He made sure to close the garage door after retrieving the gas can, noting reports of thieves taking what they wanted from open garages. He filled the mower. As he knelt in the grass to screw on the cap of the canister, he noticed someone in the yard.

As if on cue, a young man had entered the yard by climbing over the fence, especially odd with the gate available on the side closest to where Bill knelt. He remained quiet and watched.

Had to be a burglar, casing the house in broad daylight, the way they did these days, hitting while the family was away at work.

The figure wore a hoodie, torn jeans, and work boots, dressed for cool weather and perhaps to help hide his identity. He stood behind the house, staring at each window, then moved to the stairs up to the deck. Stepping lightly, he got to the top and again paused to survey the situation. Satisfied, he went to the sliding doors, tested them. Locked.

Bill didn't have the pistol with him but he had his cell phone—in his back pocket, in case he had to call for emergency help, like if he backed the mower over his foot.

He stood up beside the mower, felt his legs strain from the squat.

"May I help you?" he called out and watched the young man startle, twist around and start down the stairs two at a time, in a panic, rushing to the fence.

"You know, there's a gate on this side," Bill shouted.

But the young man was scrambling to get up the fence as Bill jogged over, grabbed an ankle and pulled him roughly down to the grass. The stranger was small boned, easy for Bill to hold him down, face in the grass, his knee in the small of the young man's back, even with legs kicking.

"Calm down," Bill grunted.

"Lemme go!" growled the young man. But the voice was not what Bill expected.

He yanked back the hood and found a girl, short brown hair, face a mask of shock and defiance.

"What the hell are you doing here?" he demanded.

"Nothing!"

"You're looking for a way to get in my house? That's not nothing."

She wriggled harder and he let her up, but as she got to her feet, he pushed her against the fence along the side of the yard.

"How long've you been casing my house? How long? Huh?"

His fist on her chest held her pinned to the fence. She looked like a boy, a skinny tomboy. He reached back and pulled his phone from his back pocket, held it up. Fumbling with the phone, he managed to snap a photo even while she tried to look away.

"All right, I'm going to let you go, but you better not come back here. Got it? Or I'll call the police. I have your picture now. Even if you don't break in you're still trespassing and that can get you arrested. Understand? I'll show your picture to the police if you ever return."

She nodded frantically. He stepped back and took his fist off her. She was quick, breaking into a run around the house, to the gate side. Bill followed, watching her escape. She ran down the street, settled into an innocent jog, and disappeared around the curve of the street.

He finished mowing the yard and pushed the mower around to the driveway, let it cool off. He thought about the visitor. Wondering if this one was the same as the nighttime peeping Tom or just a regular thief. But, again, why his house? Why was his house being targeted? Was it because Barb's keys were missing? He had changed the locks and the garage door code so whoever might have those keys and door remote wouldn't be able to get in and, he expected, would give up.

More charges hit the cards that were missing, even after he'd called to cancel the cards. He kept getting the run around. It was almost as though they believed Barb actually had run away, maybe with a new lover, and was using her cards, so he wasn't allowed to cancel them on her. Well, he wasn't going to pay for them, he retorted. Let them go unpaid. Let them send her account to a collection agency. He knew he was right. Let them ruin her credit, as though she cared anymore.

It would never end.

Stopping where he stood in the driveway, he let the breeze wash over his face. He wiped his face off on the sleeve of his sweatshirt. Clouds drifted by overhead, the sun casting a beam here, there, the trees of the neighborhood gold and red. The neighbors across the street had put away their Halloween display, started on Thanksgiving.

"Thanksgiving," Bill muttered and Dr. Wisniewski made a note. "What do I have to be thankful for?" He gazed out the windows at the gray day. "I'm alive. Even so…. Yes, I suppose that's something. But it's not a full aliveness. It's…I don't know…like being only half alive. Like being a kind of zombie. I just walk through each day, sometimes with an errand to do but mostly absent-minded, with nothing to engage me. Like a zombie. But instead of searching for brains, hah, I'm searching for something to stimulate my brain, some *thing* that will engage my attention. Know what I mean?"

"Yes, I understand. Go on."

"Time just keeps going on, like a river, and I'm like a piece of wood, a branch cleaved off an old tree somewhere on a hillside, now floating along, being carried away, down to the churning ocean, turning into a ragged piece of driftwood mile by mile. No will to act, no agency, no motivation."

"That's poetic," said the doctor, holding her pen to her cheek.

"Is it?"

"Could be a poem."

"I suppose. Mourning is such a great time for poetry, huh? Just keep going, they say. Doing what?" He flashed a grin. "Your husband called me, to check on me. You have a job, a profession, don't you? Do that, he said. Lots of people get by focusing on their jobs. I'll be trying that in a couple months. Right now, I don't see how getting up and going to school again, doing my classes, will be enough to keep me going, to give my life purpose. My life was rolled up in the family I had. I had responsibilities—didn't always follow them, sure, but I had them. I did my best. To love and protect. To cheer for them. To care for them. To...I don't know...."

"And your house guest?"

He blanched. "What about her?"

"Does she fulfill any of those roles for you?"

He rubbed his chin, counting the whiskers he had let grow out.

"She fills the house. I always know when she's home. That's true. Like a stray puppy you adopt. You want to protect her, care for her, without any thought of what you get out of it. I know what you're asking. Yes, I feel something like love for her. Meaning I don't want any harm to come to her. I learned about her uncle. Back in China. She loses all her cheerfulness when he becomes the topic of conversation. But here she's safe from him."

"Do you feel you're a protector? Her protector?"

"Yes, of course. But not much I have to do. She's far away from him. I fear for her when she returns, though. Seems he didn't like her coming all the way over here. Out of his control."

A scenario flashed through his head, like a fictional role-playing game, where the angry uncle arrives in Oklahoma, a gang boss with henchmen, coming to his house demanding she leave with him and he being too weak to stop it. Then she would turn and grin at him like she was finally revealing how the joke was on him all along and she prefers going with the uncle than staying with him, the stupid English teacher and widower. He cringed.

"Something?" asked the doctor.

"No." He shifted in the chair, switched the position of his crossed legs and faked a yawn. "I keep going back to the...to what happened to my daughter."

"The assault."

"Yes, let's call it that." He stoked his fire. "So the nerdy boyfriend tries to get fresh with her, she rejects him—as she should at her age.

Maybe he vows revenge at that point. But then a football player who happens to like her, too, decides to make it clear she doesn't want the nerd. Whether she asks him to do it or he decides on his own doesn't matter. The football player beats up the nerd, enough for police to get involved, to get a mugshot of the kid all beat up. He doesn't graduate because he doesn't finish the semester. All his troubles stem from her rejection, he believes. So he either follows her into the mall or he just happens to see her there and decides to follow her."

"And...? Your point?"

He regarded the doctor, poised to write another note.

"I think he wanted to get back at her and the football player both. By...by claiming her. By marking her, as it were. Crude, I know. But why else take that risk? He had to. But why the hell did the gunman let him go ahead while everyone else was kneeling, hands behind their heads? That was in the report."

"Again, I'm sorry. It was an awful thing to happen." She flipped back a page in her notes. "And yet you seem to be processing it better. Making sense of it."

"I guess." He shook his head and uncrossed his legs, sat up. "I'm still waiting to go to court to testify. When they call me." He took a long breath. "Twenty-four hostages. Eleven wounded. Seven killed. Barb was the first, the one he made an example of for the others. And she was only trying to stop the assault. The S.W.A.T. team kills the shooter. One hostage was also hit, an old man who died later. The assistant manager, hiding in the back room through the whole thing, turned off the store video feed. Somehow he gets Barb's keys. Then steals her car right off our driveway one night, wrecks it. He's in custody. And the kid who raped my daughter? Dead. One of the victims, thankfully. Not execution-style like the others but hit by the shooter as he tried to escape during the S.W.A.T. entry. They compared bullets."

"It seems you've learned a lot." She studied him, twirling her pen. "You're still obsessing over the details."

"The details remain. They haunt me. I guess that's clear."

"Will you come to a point where the details no longer interest you?"

He decided to check on the rubber tree beside his chair. "It's possible, but likely? Who can say? If I'm making sense of it, as you say, then I have to understand every aspect of what happened. Even if it means having nightmares sometimes." The tree was doing fine.

"Nightmares?"

"A few." He sat back.

"Tell me about those. About a recent one."

He tried to laugh, feigning embarrassment. "One?"

"If you can. What typically occurs in the dreams?"

"Mostly I'm there, right in the store, seeing it all unfold, moment by moment. Sometimes I'm in the corner watching, shouting warnings to people who can't hear me. Or I'm one of the hostages and I get shot. Or I'm on the S.W.A.T. team, armored-up and ready to take down the fucking shooter. Or I'm stuck in the crowd outside the mall, trying to get in, to save them, but the police hold me back. 'I have to get in there,' I shout. 'Let me in!'"

"Do you awaken from these?"

"Usually."

"Do you awaken with a verbal utterance?"

"You mean screaming?"

She nodded, putting her pen to the notepad, ready to write.

"Sometimes. In fact, one time—this was back in October—I had a nightmare. I think I was one of the hostages, seeing my daughter pulled away, shouting for him to stop—that kind of dream, intense—and my shouting in the dream became my shouting for real, in the bedroom. I guess I was loud because Wendy came rushing in, quite alarmed. She had to shake my shoulder to wake me up, and...."

"And?"

"Well, she stayed with me until I calmed down. She asked if I wanted her to sleep with me. Meaning sleep, just sleep. She said she often slept with her mother, for her own peace and for her mother's, too. I was too exhausted from the nightmare to argue. I rolled onto my side, facing away from her, and she did the same, facing away from me. But through the night I kept feeling her butt against the small of my back. Or her arm over me, kind of holding me. I didn't sleep well, but at least not falling into a deep sleep I didn't have a nightmare."

"How often now does she sleep in your bed?"

He laughed. "You're trying to make a bigger thing than it is."

The doctor sat up, leaning forward, notepad rocking on her knees.

"Do you have nightmares as a way to draw her to you?"

"No!" He looked away. "Definitely not. How do I have nightmares on purpose? That's ludicrous."

"Do you enjoy having her there with you?"

He let out a long sigh. "There's nothing down that rabbit hole, doc."

She nodded, made a note, sat back in her seat, studied him.

"Would it be possible for you to bring her to a session?"

"Wendy? To my crazy-talk session?" He chuckled, a hollow sound. "I don't think she would be amused."

"I'd like to get a sense of her. Nothing psychological, I assure you. I'd simply like to meet her."

"All right. I'll see. Maybe—" A thought interrupted him. "You know, she dressed up as a witch for Halloween?" He chuckled. "Yep, Wendy the witch. It fits. She said her friend suggested it. She didn't know any Wendy the witch. But wearing those striped stockings, all the way up her legs—like the witch in *The Wizard of Oz*, you know? And a fake nose and green face paint. The ragged dress and scraggly hair. The big hat and the broom. She looked very authentic. Actually scary. And a little sexy, too. She got lots of treats that night, I'm sure. In fact, she shared some with me."

The doctor was scribbling fast.

"Please. Is that necessary? Treats just means candy."

15

FRESH FROM A SHOWER, Bill paused at the junction of his bedroom door and her bedroom door, both open wide. She was still at school, so he had the opportunity. Curious how much work it would be, he decided to take a quick look.

Wearing a towel around his hips, he stepped into the room, lightly, as though not wanting to make a sound.

He studied the bed, immaculate as always, the same bedding as back in August when Becky had made-up the bed before going to the mall. Next to it was her dresser, the mirror stuffed with pictures and artwork, decals and souvenirs that could be stuck into the frame. He noticed one picture of Wendy.

She wore jeans and a beige jacket, the background dark, her face illuminated by camera flash. It seemed to be a festival of some kind. Lots of people behind her, a hint of fireworks. A hand was on her shoulder, coming from an arm behind her, the arm of a boy standing with her—no, a man. Not a high school boy but a man. Her uncle? She looked about the same age as now, so the photo couldn't be too old. He wondered. The man was Chinese, had a ruddy face, or was colored by the night's artificial lighting, a thin scrape of beard around his chin and cheeks, wearing a knit pullover with an Izod logo. By all indications, they both were having a good time. Her smile didn't seemed forced.

And she had sent the picture to Becky, part of their correspondence over the past two years. He reached for the picture, paused. He was only curious if there was a date on the back, but he worried he wouldn't be able to put it back again without its removal being noticed.

He got so consumed surveying the images Becky had collected on her mirror that he forgot that his reason for coming into the room was to remove Becky's clothing from the dresser drawers and the closet so Wendy wouldn't need to keep living out of a suitcase. He had intended to do that at the beginning but there were memories getting in the way. And his guest hadn't worried about it. She was such a polite, easygoing guest, he thought.

"Hello," a voice spoke behind him and he knew he was caught.

"Hi," he said, grabbing his towel to be sure it was secure. He turned around to face her. "I was just looking at all the things on her mirror. Sorry to be in your room."

Wendy entered and set her school bag on her bed. "I don't mind. This is Becky's room. Please look as you like." She waved her hand around.

"I think I'm ready to clear out her things. That will give you more space. You can use the dresser and the closet. I'm sorry I didn't do it right away, but...you know...memories...."

"I know." She smiled like she understood. Then sniffled. "I miss her. She always tell funny jokes. And we both like anime. And she's so pretty. And she run very fast. We planned to have a race."

"That's wonderful. Thanks for telling me." He grinned sheepishly. "Let me get dressed and I'll come back to take her things out."

"It's no hurry. It's not bothering me."

He padded into the master bedroom, closing the door behind him. He knew the door didn't catch when he swung it shut but he intended to be quick and she was over in her room, so he had no concern as he pulled open a drawer of the chest and grabbed a pair of shorts. He shook them out, then tossed his towel onto the bed.

The knock on the door startled him.

"Just a minute," he called, but she must have thought he said 'Come on in' because she did.

"Bill...?" And there she was, standing in the bedroom seeing him butt naked in his 'dad bod', holding a pair of shorts in his hands.

"Excuse me," he said, his backside toward her. "I need a minute."

"I see Uncle many times," she said with a giggle. "I turn my head."

He bent over to step into the shorts, then slid them up. With a sigh of relief, he turned to face her.

"Sorry about that," he said, standing boldly in front of her.

She seemed to study him, from his knees to his face. "I only want to ask...what is for the dinner?"

"I have no idea," he replied, realizing his voice was strained.

He reached for the clothes he had strewn across the bed when he got home and undressed, the blazer and white shirt, a necktie and the slacks, socks dropped on the floor. She watched him sort the clothing, distribute it about the room, some to a laundry basket, some to hooks on a closet door, all while wearing only his shorts.

"I had a meeting today," he said to answer the obvious question. "About Barb's business. Sold it to her partner. Barb's half of it, I mean. Now it's all hers—Barb's business partner, Lexi. Had to sign a bunch of papers today, so I thought I might as well dress up a little."

She smiled, nodding. "It's good day for you."

"I don't know about good, but it had to be done. No point keeping any ties to it. I can't help there. Not my field. So it's best this way. Let Lexi continue it, keeping the same name: Masters and Johnson Marketing. Well, Barb thought it was cute."

The clothes put away, he flopped down onto the bed with a loud huff, comfortable wearing only the shorts. He never bothered to make a fuss in front of Becky. He was dad, no big deal. Stretching out like he was planning to nap, he bent his arms up, slid his hands under his head, let his bare torso rise with each breath.

"What would you like?" he asked, staring up at the ceiling.

Her giggle was cute, disarming. He dared to grin as she sat on the edge of the bed by his knees. She leaned back on an elbow as she gave him suggestions. He pooh-poohed each choice; they'd had it already, several times, in fact. Noticing her gazing at his body, he tried not to feel any embarrassment, fighting self-consciousness.

"Well, what did you have for lunch at school today?" he asked.

She answered in a sad voice, apparently not satisfied with today's offerings. But her answer reminded her of certain episodes at school. Launching into a lively story of her girlfriends, she talked about their problems, each in turn. Who broke up with who, who was dating who, who kissed who, and who cheated on a test, who got caught smoking, who got kicked off the swim team. Typical high school drama. He chuckled. As she talked, she waved her hand like she was conducting the story.

When she paused to switch to a new story, her hand fell casually upon his chest. She grinned, like she was sorry her hand landed there. The swath of dark hair filling the center of his chest formed a triangle.

He got quiet, her fingers poking around as she talked. Was she playing innocent daughter, being silly as she teased Dad, he wondered, or was she trying to tempt him? He felt his body tense as she talked about some of the boys at school.

"And have you found someone to be your boyfriend?" he asked in a cheerful tone, lifting his hands from under his head and bringing them down along his sides. He thought the motion would shoo her away from playing games, but her hand returned to his chest. Heel flat, she strummed her fingers against his chest.

"No, no boyfriend," she said, feigned sadness in her voice. "Some send message to me. Very strange. And sometimes they speak to me with strange accent. But I don't sound that way. I think they try to tease me." Then she brightened. "Anyway, too much study to do." She laughed, then listed all the work she had, the readings and the papers she had to write. No time for relationships.

"It's good to have friends," he said. "But they should be the right kind of friends."

No time for any boyfriend drama like her American gal pals. Just as he would wish of Becky. Of course, his attitude had been different when he was a teen boy, seeking a relationship each month and usually failing. That boy Becky had liked, who came to the house to see her, turned out to be a problem. If only he had known how dark that boy, Bobby, could be—

"Are you coming?" he heard her ask, as her fingers walked south to tickle his belly, following the line of hair down to the top of his shorts as though she had never seen such a thing before.

"What?" he said, alarmed.

"To the kitchen."

He had been lost in his thoughts, hadn't heard her. He was focused on her seductive hand, her curious fingers. The way she modulated her voice, sliding seamlessly from a light, girly tone that made him think she was only ten to a womanly timbre that sent a rush of electricity through him.

"Yes, to the kitchen," he stammered. "For dinner."

She sprang up from the bed.

"See you there!"

As she skipped out of the room, he realized that, for the first time since the incident at the mall, his lower region had come alive. It had firmed, had felt excitement. Immediately he felt guilty. He didn't know whether to be horrified or to be elated.

He pulled on a pair of sweatpants, wondering what had happened, then added socks, put his feet in slippers. The house was cool, the days of air conditioning long gone, although in the peak of the afternoon, the house warmed too much. He hated to open windows because of the security system, so he toughed it out by wearing as little as possible during the days when he was home alone. But as Wendy returned in the afternoon, he had to quickly dress. Slipping on a t-shirt, he went to the kitchen.

She was hard at work when he arrived, pulled out a chair.

"Maybe we can go out for dinner sometime," he said, sitting.

Chinese food again. He liked what she cooked but he was starting to get tired of another stir-fry. Changing vegetables or meat or sauce gave some variety, but they had gone through the rotation a few times.

"Thank you for cooking again, Wendy." He smiled at her as she cut the veggies.

"You're welcome, Bill," she responded, focused on her work.

"You're very good at this. I think I've gained back all the weight I lost before you arrived. Or it's simply that I tend to gain weight in the fall anyway."

"Me, too." She patted her belly, but he didn't see any paunch there, as flat as ever, her t-shirt hanging loose over her lounging shorts. He gazed at her bare legs as she stood at the counter working the knife. One foot had come out of the bunny slipper and folded against the other foot, toes clenching her other ankle. "I must fit in swimming suit on Saturday."

"On Saturday? What's happening?" he asked, taking a seat.

"Swimming tournament."

"Oh, great. I should come watch you."

"That is good. I hope we win. Then it's better for you to see."

"It's always better to watch a win."

He thought of football, the games he usually watched all weekend, college on Saturday, pro on Sunday. He gave up Monday night games unless his team was playing, a compromise with Barb who had her shows to watch. The thought froze him. The season was more than half over and he hadn't felt he was missing it. He had a lot to distract him, of course, to take his attention away from how his team was doing. But something had changed.

He had stopped watching anything on TV. Sure he would turn it on during the days, just to have some company from the inane voices of the infomercials or soap operas or game shows, but he wasn't watching them. Late-night programming wasn't any different: he would stare at the screen and not see anything. But that didn't bother him. Missing football games was easy when he was so pre-occupied with his misery, the tragedy of his family.

Now he felt different. Was it the cool air of autumn? The colors of the trees? The fact that he had a new family? Was it simply that it had been long enough for him to mourn their passing?

He sat back in the chair, listening to the sizzling of the food in the pan, the *slap* of the spatula. It didn't matter how long it had been, not in days or weeks. There wasn't any official length of time required. Dr. Wisniewski told him he would know when a stage was ending and the next beginning. Or when all of the stages had run their course. It would be when his heart felt it was right.

But not because he'd gotten triggered by this girl coming into the bedroom like she had. That couldn't be the reason he felt different. That couldn't be the signal to end his mourning. Suddenly, he felt like going for a jog, just run up the street, make a turn, go down the avenue and circle back, about a mile, then do another lap, like he used to do, feeling his legs burn, chest heave, wind in his face—

Wendy was serving dinner, telling him about something he did not hear. He pretended he was listening, nodding and smiling.

"Sounds good," he mumbled when he heard a pause.

The food looked delicious, steam rising, smelling savory. And the bell on the microwave signaled the pouch of rice was ready.

"So I can?" she asked, flexing her chopsticks.

"Can what?" He blushed.

"I can stay with Casey after tournament."

"Oh, you mean sleep over there? With her?"

"Yes, girl night." She plopped a morsel into her mouth, chopsticks waving in the air. "It's when girls have home party and they do crazy games and tell stories and sleep on floor like camping."

"Yes, I know. Becky had a few of those. About every year, it seemed. Age seven, nine, ten, eleven, all the way up to sixteen. I recall thirteen being a peak year for sleepovers. But not recently. Like she outgrew them."

Her face was so cheery, her eyes hopeful, he had to smile.

"I can go?"

"Sure. Go ahead. I think that's an excellent idea. Very American."

"Thank you. I will call you when it's time to pick up me."

"Time to pick *me* up," he corrected, grinning.

"No, Bill. You pick up *me*."

Only a few students and a couple of the teachers recognized Bill and gave a greeting as he slipped into the aquatic center and found a seat half-way up the bleachers. The warmth and humidity of the place along with the scent of chlorine set him on edge, taking him back to that summer when he was eight and almost drowned. He was supposed to be learning to swim, but that day he was learning how to sink like a stone straight to the bottom of the pool and contemplate his future sitting in a lotus position over the drain grill.

He shook off the feeling, but a shiver lingered. He was surprised he wasn't past it by now. Some events were so visceral they always stayed with a person, he surmised.

He turned his attention to the rest of the audience, lightly attended, as he expected. Swimming couldn't compete with football. A game was scheduled for the afternoon and preparations were already underway at the stadium. The girls and boys of swimming had a couple hours to get their tournament in. He gazed across the bleachers to see if there was anyone else he knew. Not so he could wave at them or shout a greeting but so he could avoid them, keep his head down.

Waiting on the bleachers, he checked his phone. Five more calls he missed by turning off the ringer. Three left voicemails but he couldn't hear them in the echo of the aquatic center. Nine text messages, half spam, half follow ups to previous messages, including one concerning his experience with mall security. Was that a goddamn survey? He cursed. No, their security was not adequate! He deleted it. He scrolled down, seeing how many voicemails he still had. Dozens. He found one that was from Becky's phone and he froze. The phone company would have their robo-voice tell him to re-save any messages he wanted to keep or they would be automatically deleted. He continued to save Becky's: "Dad, where are you? Need a pickup." From school, he knew, and he did pick her up, and not too late.

With the temperature as uncomfortable as it was, Bill slipped off his jacket. He folded it on the seat beside him. Leaning forward, elbows on knees, he looked for Wendy.

The girls came out in a line in identical swimsuits, the blue and orange school colors. The boys followed, swim trunks in blue with an orange stripe. He stared, trying to find Wendy as they moved to their seats and huddled together for a pep talk. The announcer began to welcome everyone to the event and give instructions and information, which Bill ignored. He couldn't tell which girl was Wendy as they all had caps on their heads. He was too far away to distinguish faces, but he settled on one girl being Wendy only to realize he was wrong after the first race and the announcer named her.

Finally it was her turn, and Bill watched intently as the girls dove into the water and slapped their arms across the length of the pool, flipped over, and charged back across like a swarm of piranhas going for dinner. He was amazed at the energy they put forth, but Wendy only made fourth place of the eight positions. Well, it's just her first tournament, he thought, so that's still good. Later she got third place in breaststroke. She had the second leg in the team relay, which they got first place in. The Vista High team won the tournament over the other two schools, so they were happy about that. Bill applauded loudly when the girls bowed to the crowd.

After the tournament was finished, the girls getting their trophies and posing for pictures, Bill noticed someone who seemed out of place. A thin figure wearing a hoodie, which he found odd in the warmth of the aquatic center, standing down at the edge of the pool, near the girls team. Panic swept through him as he imagined a violent scene about to unfold. He stood, started down the steps, ready to stop whatever that figure who looked out of place was about to do. A jealous rivalry? An offensive utterance? Anything could set off kids these days. One quick act could ruin someone's life forever.

He got to the bottom of the bleachers, about a dozen steps from the figure in hoodie and jeans. Then he recognized the boots. It was the girl from his backyard. Same hoodie. Something was in the pocket of the hoodie. Was she on the verge of pulling out a gun? He could tackle her, but where she stood, so close to the edge of the pool, they would both likely tumble into the water.

But he had to do something. Or would everyone think he was crazy for tackling her that way? for falling into the pool?

Or preventing another shooting?

He took a step. So did the girl—toward the circle of swimmers. Her hands were in the pockets of the hoodie, hiding something. He tensed, ready to lunge at her—

Out came a hand, holding something—something flat—

His heart was about to burst—then shifted roughly into low gear as he identified the object as a small notebook. The gold rings on the spine caught the lights from above and looked like a metal barrel.

The girl simply wanted an autograph, it seemed. Of a minor figure in an amateur sport. Odd, thought Bill. Wendy took the notebook and pen and wrote on the page, handed back the notebook to the girl, who lingered to chat. Hoodie girl's body language indicated to him she was shy, maybe had a crush on Wendy. But Wendy was kind; at the end they hugged. Then hoodie girl vanished into the exiting crowd.

Bill took deep breaths, realizing how close he had come to making a fool of himself. Or preventing another tragedy. The line was so thin these days. He had to be cautious. Everyone knew he was on edge. He might blow up at some random trigger, a powderkeg of emotion. That was the reason he was on leave, everyone knew.

So, all right, that made a little more sense to him. A girl crush. She stakes out her house, tries to look in her windows, too shy to meet her directly. But she had checked the sliding doors as though she hoped to go inside. Creepy, thought Bill. Maybe she planned to go inside and take something that belonged to Wendy, like a keepsake, a memento of a relationship they never had. Teens could be that kind of crazy. He pulled out his phone and dialed up the picture he took of her. Even with her head turned in the photo, he could see it was the same person.

He waited by the locker room entrance for Wendy, what he felt was his duty as a parent, no matter how awkward it might feel to be seen there. Just another middle-aged pervert hoping to get a glimpse into the girls' locker room! He fit the profile.

Eventually she came out with other girls, dressed to go home. Or, in her case, to their after-tournament party, a girls' night out, whatever that might entail.

"Daddy," she cried out in front of the girls, some of them laughing at her effusiveness. Wendy swung her arms around his neck and gave his cheek a peck. "We won!"

"I know. Congratulations," he sang as she dropped from her hug and rejoined the girls. "You did well. Even better next time, I'm sure."

"Lots of practice," she said with a nod.

"So you're off to the party now?"

The girls spoke up for Wendy, confirming their plans. It sounded wild but with so many of them, he thought she would be safe. They would watch out for each other.

"Okay, call when you want me to pick you up," he told her.

"We can drop her off tomorrow," said Casey Turner, the team captain and, it seemed, Wendy's main friend in the group. Her long blond hair still looked wet and slick.

"That's fine," said Bill, accepting the bag of wet swimsuit and towel Wendy handed to him.

"Please take home," she said. "It need to be washed and then hang up for drying."

"Okay. I will," he called as she headed out. "See you tomorrow."

Dropping the wet bag on the passenger side floor, Bill sat in the Escape a while as he watched other parents leaving the parking lot and others arriving for the football game. The sensation of her arms around his neck stayed with him and he enjoyed it, not wanting it to fade. The kiss on the cheek—in front of the other girls. He had to grin.

The crowd of cars was getting serious, so he started out of the parking lot before he could get blocked in. Joining the exit line, he inched along, out to the street, and just as he got to the street, he saw, there to the side, parked on the grass with other cars taking the cheap seats, was a dull orange sportscar like the one he had seen in front of his house.

He hit the brakes, stared at the car. It still did not have any license tag. It had been more than two months. How did this car not get a ticket? Even if it was a new purchase, the buyer's tag would only cover it for two months. He felt like calling it in right then, let Detective Logan know. Was this a student's car? Or the parent's?

Snatching his phone from the center console, he snapped a picture of the car, as the truck behind him honked for him to move on.

Yes, I'm moving on, he sneered at the face in the rearview mirror.

16

HOWEVER, THE MEMORY RETURNED as he sat in the Escape in the dark garage, engine off, door closed. He remembered sitting at the bottom of the pool looking up, seeing other swimmers' legs kicking above him, the entire underwater world so blue and sparkling, like a universe he could float through—which he did literally float through, only it was downward.

One of the instructors jumped in and pulled him up. He thought nothing of the episode after the first few minutes of chest compressions and spitting up water and hating the taste of chlorine. If he had died that day, none of the present agony would have occurred. If he had drowned that day, his parents would be numb, forever wondering why they had signed him up for swimming lessons at the YMCA or why, on that day, he had chosen to jump off the diving board and land like a rock on his belly, which may have knocked the wind out of him as he sank. And then, if he had died that day, years later there would be someone else meeting Barbara in the library, someone else to be Becky's father, someone else to pick up a Chinese girl at the airport.

Bill stood in the living room, listening to the silence, feeling the emptiness of the house. The people who were gone....

"I don't need a house," he muttered.

With a sigh, he looked around at everything he had, everything that he and Barb had collected in the ten years they had resided there. The furniture, the decorations, the curtains, the vase with its wilted flowers, the jacket hanging over the chair, the reading lamp with its three tentacles, the wall of photos. He didn't need all that. And what did it cost to maintain this castle? With Barb gone, the family income was cut in half. Although he was still getting paid, it was not enough. He realized the date had just passed for yet another mortgage payment. Another thing he had to do.

He wasn't a deadbeat. He had a plan. Eventually, he would get a check from the insurance company that had assured them long ago that if Barb died he and Becky would be fine. And his policy? Minimal. He had never considered himself the breadwinner. Barb made more than he did as a mid-career public school teacher. He raised the death benefit twice already so it was respectable, enough to cover Barb and Becky for a few years. Until she remarried, he considered at the time. When the check came, he would pay off the mortgage, be done with it.

Be done with it....

He walked the hallway, thinking of how many times he had walked the hallway, either on his way to his bedroom or to Becky's room. On this afternoon, with the house empty, he went straight to the bathroom at the end of the hallway, the one for Becky's use and now Wendy's.

He found Wendy had strung up a line over the bath tub and hung her underwear on it to dry, colorful clips holding each one in place, presumably after washing them in the sink or the tub. No wonder she seemed to spend a long time in there. He thought it had to do with her period. There were never any undies in the laundry basket. She only gave him outer clothes and told him her mother warned her against using these Western washing machines and, worse, the dryers. Her mother warned her of mixing her clothes with other people's clothing, but she had laughed at that 'old wives tale' as she handed him her shirts, pants, and skirts. He was no scientist when it came to doing laundry, but with hers added, he tried to sort them like Barb did.

He fingered the first panties hanging on the line; it was dry now. Next to it was a pink bra. Next to that a pink panties, and so on, across to the shower spigot. Delicate items, some with lacey trim, pretty pastel colors. One with an adults-only lace crotch. Another with only strings at the hips. And a thong—only a strap for the rear side. He stared at them, surprised a teen girl would wear them.

On the towel rack was a thin towel with Chinese characters on it which she must have brought. On the toilet seat was another towel, folded over, protecting her from the cold ceramic whenever she would sit on the lid. The room was immaculate. They had wondered if Becky had obsessive-compulsive disorder; she was too neat, too concerned about things being in their proper place, which didn't seem right for a teenager. Precision was a good thing, Barb cautioned. Maybe Wendy was simply being a good guest by not making a mess or by following the customs of the house.

Bill opened the wet bag and pulled out Wendy's swimsuit, moisture running down his hands. He held the suit over the bath tub and let it drain. He remembered his promise to wash it, to get the chlorine out of it. He ran the water, held the suit under the stream until he no longer smelled the chlorine. Then he searched for a hanger and hung up the suit on the shower spigot. The towel he tossed in the laundry basket.

The same in the bedroom: neat and clean. Becky's bed remained perfect and untouched. Just as she left it that morning. But it was time, Bill decided, standing in the doorway. Time to pack her things. Finally. Some other girl could make use of them, perhaps, and be happy, and that would make him happy.

He noted Wendy's laptop was on, apparently charging. But the battery was full now so he thought to turn it off for her. He tapped the touchpad and the screen reverted to her last program. She had been writing a paper for school, a report on *The Great Gatsby*.

"That'll sure teach her about the American dream."

He read through it to where she had left off. It was standard with only a few errors of grammar or spelling, which he felt compelled to correct. He felt proud, though. She had some insights which even an American student would be hard-pressed to come up with. Comparison to a collectivist society was good. He wanted to save the file but all the commands on her computer were Chinese characters. When he figured it out, he went to close the program but hesitated. Would she know he had fiddled with her computer? But she left while it was charging. He could say he turned it off to save the battery.

Curiosity tugged at him. He wanted to look further at what she may have on her laptop. Her life in China? Her family? He wouldn't be able to read anything in Chinese, of course. But pictures translated easily. So did video. He sighed, wanting to know more.

But he closed the laptop and got up from kneeling against her bed. She used the laptop on her bed. He'd seen her laying on her belly on the bed, working on the laptop, the same as when she was reading. It looked comfortable. Maybe the little kid's desk in the room was too small, or she thought it was Becky's and shouldn't be disturbed. He should let her into the third bedroom, Barb's office, and use the full-size desk there.

If he sold the house and moved into an apartment, he considered then stopped. If he were to start a new life....

"As though nothing happened before," he finished.

The whole reason for getting a house was to be a family, a proper American household, a member of society. They had chosen a house with a backyard so their child could play there. Safe and supervised. He envisioned hours tossing a ball back and forth, or kicking a ball, or chasing her in a game of tag, or pushing the swing, or catching her as she came down the slide. Yes, a house with rooms for each of them. On a nice street with trees. Two-car garage, a wide driveway for learning to ride a bike. A large living room where they would live. He frowned. He didn't need any of that now. He thought of his college days, the studio apartment he lived in, a one room place that had all his stuff, kitchen at one end, bedroom at the other end.

With a big breath, he took a determined stance in front of Becky's white, ornate Young Miss dresser, as if he were about to lift a great weight. He opened the first drawer on the upper right, found what he expected: underwear. The drawer in the middle, also had intimates. He removed everything, laid them out on Becky's bed. Pajamas, t-shirts, underwear, loungewear, sports clothes, some clothing she must be keeping for memories because they were clearly too small for her now. He maintained their folds as he set them in rows across the bed. Then he closed each drawer slowly, solemnly.

The closet was neat, too. There were plenty of old clothes hanging there. On the floor were boxes of toys, shoes, books. He moved the boxes out first, carried them to the hallway. Then he went after the dresses, skirts, shirts, and slacks that hung in the closet, laying them neatly on the bed, on top of the items from the dresser. It was quite a collection. But girls need a lot of clothes, he thought, ready to affect whatever mood they wanted for themselves. He could appreciate that.

Barb's clothing cache was three times the size of his. He didn't think of his ladies having so many clothes in a negative way; he was amused. Going through the clothing filled him with memories: purchasing them, seeing Becky wearing them, washing them. He let the fabric settle against his hands, his fingers recalling the feel of holding his daughter as a baby, a toddler, a little girl, an adolescent, and as a teenager who didn't want to be hugged by Dad.

Just as he was feeling surprised he hadn't yet become emotional dealing with this collection of memories, the tears burst forth.

He dropped to the floor in the middle of the room, overwhelmed, sitting with legs crossed, bent over choking. It went on for a minute. He caught his breath. How often would he continue to be triggered by random things? For the rest of his life—an odd expression itself—any random moment something might occur. Something could flash before his eyes or he might overhear something and there he'd be: frozen, numb, unable to act or think or speak, and his body would return him to that abyss of sorrow so he could resume his drowning. It would never end, he knew, and continued crying.

Then he stopped.

"Be a man," he spoke and the words hovered in the air, turning frosty in the coolness of the room. He stopped folding Becky's clothes. "Time to man up." He stood, breathing deeply. "Time to get a grip."

Sure, anyone suffering the same kind of shock would be expected to cry, even the burliest men. But it had been weeks since the incident at the mall. It was pathetic now, the sign of an unstable, weak man. That wasn't him, not who he wanted to be. He couldn't allow himself to be hijacked by every stray sound or image. He wouldn't let every random thought trigger his tear ducts to launch a fresh stream or his heart race or his mind be flooded with memories. It wasn't that he no longer mourned, nor that he was ready to forget them, but it seemed the stage of grief where he finally accepted what happened and moved on was starting to fall upon him.

The first step of that stage was to become a different person.

He went to the master bedroom, to the chest of drawers, opened the top drawer and retrieved the pistol, closed the drawer and stared at the gun in his hand. He got the magazine from the bottom drawer, filled with the maximum number of bullets. What he needed to do, he considered, was return to the firing range and practice more. What he did before was good for a start, so he wasn't completely inept. He needed to become proficient, however. Who knew when their burglar would return? What about Orange Car Guy? Could even be a home invasion, which were becoming popular among the wretched and vile of the city who believed a locked door was rude. A locked door was not sufficient deterrent to taking what didn't belong to them and messing up the people inside who refused to give up their property. That was what a gun like this Glock was for, he decided, letting his hand slide into position around it.

You shall not pass!

He aimed at the far wall beside the master bathroom doorway, aligned the sights, and pulled the trigger, heard the safety click as expected. Good.

As Bill drove to the indoor range as before, he thought of the people in his life who had died. Not too many. Not like in some families where funerals seemed to be a monthly occurrence. The criminal class. Or those cursed with various diseases. Not his family. He had lost both sets of grandparents. One grandfather, Frank, had died when Bill was a little boy. The sights and sounds of the funeral seemed otherworldly, scary, and the body reclined in the open casket startled him. He had called to his grandfather, expecting him to awaken, but his mother corrected him, kept him close and calmed him during the service. His wife, Grandma Rose, passed several years later, and he was older then and knew it was coming, seeing her deteriorate year by year. He felt sorrow then and cried openly, not yet too mature for such a display.

His father's parents had passed away at about the same time. Grandpa Albert had smoked pipes and cigars all his life, been a wild sort, full of the rough country life, and nobody was surprised when he fell one day with a heart attack. Relatives on that side of the family had been cheerful at the funeral, compared to his mother's side of the family. They had a big dinner and told jokes, some of them about his grandfather. As a teenage boy, he both laughed and felt awkward. Running around with his cousins helped alleviate the sadness.

His grandmother, Helen, a nurse during World War II, was revered for her quiet demeanor and unbreakable determination. She collapsed in her home and was found by one of the grandchildren coming for a visit. Taken to a hospital, a tumor was safely removed from her brain and she was expected to make a full recovery. But it seemed that being in a hospital bed with relatives sitting around to keep her company was too much and a few days later she died. His family believed she had willed herself to die, unable to have other people take care of her when she had been everyone else's caregiver all of her life.

And there was Uncle Ray who had gotten a brain infection from an infected tooth—so his cousins insisted. And Aunt Fran who had been a life-long smoker, got emphysema, tied to an oxygen machine and later died in her sleep. His mother's brother, Benjamin, had died of a heart attack, but he was obese. They were all in their seventies—like all of his grandparents except Helen who was 81. They had hard lives: Great Depression, World War, and the ornery kids that tested them every day. But they'd lived long, full lives, and died of natural causes. Even his own parents had gone in natural ways a few years past. The people in his family were living longer, he considered.

He laughed, pulling into the parking lot of the gun range.

But his earliest encounter with Mister Death, which he'd almost forgotten, was Miss Riddle, his second grade teacher, who had such beautiful auburn hair and put her hand on his little shoulder whenever she visited his desk, who he planned to marry someday. Then one day she announced to the class that she was getting married—but not to Billy Masters. No, she would become Mrs. Ross, she explained to her pupils. Everyone was happy for her except him. She would be taking a vacation, something called a 'honeymoon'. The class had endured the cranky old substitute teacher, Mrs. Dawson, for only three days when news came that Miss Riddle, now Mrs. Ross, and her new husband Tim, had been killed in a car accident while going to their honeymoon destination.

17

SUNDAY MORNING, golden sunshine streaming through the kitchen windows, but the house was too cool for Bill as he got out of bed. He threw on his bathrobe, a heavy flannel thing he only wore during the colder months, a green and blue plaid that reminded him of forested climes he would rather live in more than Oklahoma.

He made coffee and stood by the sliding glass doors in the kitchen as he drank it, staring out at the backyard. It needed mowing again, possibly the last one of the year. He stared at the swingset, recalled times he had pushed his daughter back and forth, enjoyed her giggling as she pretended she was flying. He saw the neighbors were out on their deck, hidden well enough by the trees between their yards and the high fence. Life in America.

Setting the empty coffee mug in the sink, he realized how empty he felt. That Chinese girl had briefly filled his shattered life, kept him going, made him believe he still had a family, helped soften the pain. And now she was gone. And she would be gone forever when her year in America was up. Then where would he be? What stage of grief? He wondered what she was doing with her friends, what naughty games they might be playing—spin the bottle? truth or dare? or whatever girls did at those kind of sleepovers these days.

Most of all, he didn't know what to do.

Is this what a Sunday would be like if she weren't living here?

He glanced at the clock on the living room wall, guessing what time she might be returning. It could be as early as noon. He doubted the girls went to church. Probably they would push the sleepover through the afternoon. It would likely end prior to dinner time so the poor host family wouldn't need to feed the girls again. He checked the clock: a minute had passed. He should get himself ready so he could go out and greet her, wave thanks to the girls who dropped her off.

Freshly shaved and showered, Bill traipsed into the bedroom and dressed in lounging pants and a pullover sweater. Feet pushed into cushy slippers, he went to the third bedroom, Barb's office, what he would start calling the den.

Opening the door, he surveyed the room. Dominated by the large two-pedestal wooden desk in the center, computer monitor set to one side, the CPU under the desk; large, high-backed chair with headrest; oak shelves along one wall filled with books and binders, folders lain flat, decorative figurines and a few framed photographs; a window with closed violet curtains; and his little press-board desk on the side—more often used as a side table when she had papers to lay out. Two tall metal file cabinets against the corner by the closet. He knew the closet had boxes stacked up, office papers mostly, promotional documents.

So much to deal with.

"But it has to go," he muttered, not knowing where to start.

The easiest thing was to take the boxes out of the closet and stack them in the living room, ready to give to Lexi. He had already let her take a couple boxes that she needed. Lexi was the creative one, the artist, while Barb was the business person. They made a good team. She would be happy to have all the boxes, and he would be happy to make the room his.

The day they first looked at the house, Barb had claimed the corner bedroom as her office. He wanted a den where he could write his stories, hoping to become a great American novelist. But the new job, parenthood, and household chores had taken away that dream. He managed only short stories once in a while, whenever an idea struck him. Usually he would type them out in one sitting, short as they were. But he conceded the room to Barb.

It wouldn't be hers any longer. It was a simple fact, nothing more, he told himself. It wasn't that he was glad to claim it back.

He worked through the morning, clearing out the boxes. He got hot and stripped off the sweater and worked in a t-shirt, got that wet, too. But finally the boxes, a dozen or more, were stacked by the front door, ready to be loaded into his Escape or Lexi's Mercedes. The closet was empty and he closed its door.

He wanted to stop for a snack, maybe call it lunch, but he feared not being able to make himself return to the task. Checking the clock again, he calculated how much time he might have before she returned. He wanted time to clean himself up, not wanting her to see him so messy. She might hug him again.

Deciding to use his time better to make a plan rather than continue hard labor, he opened each drawer of the big desk and checked what was inside. He pulled out the contents of each drawer, set them on top of the desk. He would find boxes for them. He tested the computer; still worked, but it was dedicated to her business software and he had no clue how to get to anything he would use. The unit seemed good so he would keep it; he could use it for writing instead of the rusty ol' laptop he pulled out of his school bag whenever he needed to record grades or write a poem.

He sat down in the big desk chair. The cushion she put on the seat had an embroidered scene: autumn leaves and bunnies, a grinning cat among the branches. He held up the cushion, worn thin from many hours of sitting, and held it to his chest like it was Barb herself. A tear settled in the corner of one eye; he scolded himself for allowing that. Everything he touched had memories and each one poked at his emotions, which signaled his tear ducts to let one fly.

His mother would cry at the drop of a hat, he recalled, and he seemed to have inherited that fun feature. He explained to Wendy what 'drop of a hat' meant after she questioned why anyone would cry if a hat fell off. People like their hats, he had joked.

Of course he would save the cushion, put it with other special items he would keep forever.

He worked until he noticed the light had changed outside. A couple hours had passed and he'd made progress. He found the keys to the file cabinets, emptied their contents into neat piles beside them, leaning against the wall. The room was a mess now, but that was the first step—as he often told his students while they were doing research for their papers: you gather as much as you can, making a big mess, then you put things away neatly until the mess is reduced to a concise, well-organized paper.

With a loud exhale he plopped into Barb's chair to rest, realizing he missed the daily grind. The rhythms of the school day, the school week. Although reading student papers was often unpleasant, he relished finding the gem in the fodder. That was enough to let him know he was doing some good in the world. Soon, he thought with a sigh, soon. Five weeks until winter break. Then January and his return to school, full of good cheer, ready to teach.

What would that be like? Everyone would know why he'd been out for a semester. Would they greet him as usual, treat him normally? Or would a cloud of horror linger about him wherever he went? People afraid they would say the wrong thing, maybe set him off. He was not the crazy person. He was as much a victim as his ladies. None of it was his fault—except as he envisioned his efforts to protect them, but did not protect them in the end.

He was ready now. He had his father's gun, and he had practiced. When he returned home from the gun range the previous evening, it was already dark and he drove carefully, under the speed limit. He wasn't eager to be stopped for any reason and discovered carrying a firearm. He knew he was supposed to transport the ammo in the back of his vehicle, away from the unloaded gun itself, but with an SUV there wasn't any trunk and he didn't want a magazine full of bullets to be bouncing around back there. The handgun he set on the passenger seat in the leather case he purchased. He tossed a small towel over the case. The magazine he put in the glove box. He was technically illegal but he felt he was in compliance. He arrived home without incident.

Then he left the garage, closing the door, and went around the back of the house, in the dark, using a flashlight from the Escape to check each window and door. Probably someone would see a man with a flashlight checking out the house next door and call the police. Got a snooper. But nothing happened. His neighbors didn't look out for each other. None of his neighbors likely knew he was the one in the news, the guy who lost family members at the mall. They would only notice Barb and Becky no longer appeared in the yard or the windows, but a Chinese girl now did. Maybe they got divorced and the mom and daughter left and the girlfriend moved in. That's what the neighbors would think. They never talked except if they happened to cross each other's path and then only about the weather or some change to the garbage pick up schedule.

He cleaned himself up, figuring he had done enough for one day. He felt tired from his labor, satisfied at his effort. It was getting dark, the autumn evening coming early. She would be home soon. He wore street clothes, like he was going out on errands. He ran his fingers over his cheeks, testing for smoothness. Then he waited by the front door, gazing out the glass outer door for car headlights approaching.

Two false alarms.

Then a set of lights slowing...turning into his driveway.

He rushed out, then halted himself, wondering how it looked if he acted too eager, like a love-sick school boy. Stepping onto the driveway, he went around to the driver's door as Wendy climbed out the rear door, saying thanks and goodbyes to her friends.

"Thanks for bringing her home," he said to Casey, the driver. "Saved me a trip." He looked into the car. "So...you girls had fun? Busy with your book club? Discussing the merits of *Sense and Sensibility*, I'll bet. Or was it *Pride and Prejudice*?"

They all laughed like they were fresh from a party and half-drunk.

"Yeah! Sure did! Loads of fun!" they cried out. They pooh-poohed Jane Austen's novels.

"Well, I'm glad you're back safely now," he said, reciting a line his mother used to tell him when he arrived better late than never.

He straightened up from the driver's side window. Wendy was right there to greet him. She jumped up on him, throwing her arms around him in a big, flashy hug.

"I'm home, Daddy!" she sang, loud enough for the neighbors to hear. And planted a big kiss on his smooth cheek, exactly as he had expected—hoped. The girls giggled at the scene and he waved them off like it was no big deal.

"Night, Mister Masters," Casey called, backing down the driveway.

The other girls in the car were laughing, calling "Daddy, Daddy" to tease him. He worried what they would say at school. What did they think his relationship was? What had Wendy told them?

He watched the car depart around the curve of the street as Wendy went inside with her bag.

Realizing he stood alone in the driveway, he turned to go inside, as well, but paused and gazed up at the bright stars that seemed so cool, like diamonds, twinkling as if they were signaling to him. But what? That all was well? That everything would be all right? That the universe ticked on whether he was happy or not, whether he felt like pushing onward with his life or was ready to give up? He studied the patterns, recognized several constellations, recalling the telescope he'd gotten for Becky and the few nights they had used it before she got bored and they put it away in the garage. It was probably still there, like other memories catalogued and put into storage.

"Daddy," called Wendy as she leaned out the front door, "are you coming in?"

Bill entered and closed the door behind him, took care to lock it, all three locks, and set the security system for the night.

Wendy was smiling so big that he wondered if he had a bat or something sitting on his head. She was overjoyed by her weekend. No doubt she had fun hanging out with American girls, especially outside of school where the rules were lax. He worried what things she might have learned.

"So...seems like you all had a lot of fun."

"Oh, yes!" She couldn't calm down. She started telling him some of the fun she had, using her best freshly-practiced English to describe the odd things American girls do, some of it borderline naughty by his standards.

"Listen, Wendy," he spoke when she paused. "I need to explain a few things to you." He took a breath and she immediately had the look of having done something wrong. "No, you're not in trouble. I just wanted to explain.... Yes, the male parent is called father, or dad, or daddy. That's correct, and you probably learned that when you were younger, so 'Daddy' would be what was used in your textbook. Am I right? That's how it was when I taught English in Japan. So in America, we like to use a lot of slang."

"Slang?" she asked, cautiously.

"Yes, you know...words that have other meanings than the standard definition. Often they're used in a bad way, a not-nice way."

"How?" She was pouting. "Not nice...?"

"It's okay. I just want you to know how else 'Daddy' can be used in

America. See, when a girl finds an older man to support her, like pay her rent or buy her gifts in exchange for her, mm, giving her attention to him and...well, other ways to be nice to him...she will often call him 'Daddy' as though he is her biological father. Even when he isn't. It's kind of like a role-playing game. She plays his daughter and he plays her father, or 'Daddy'. We kind of laugh at that role-playing. That's what I wanted to tell you. It's not a big deal."

"I'm not role-playing be your daughter, I am your daughter," she stammered. "You the host family. You are daddy of host family, so you are my daddy. It's not right?"

He held up his hands as if to stop her from getting emotional.

"I'm sorry. I didn't mean to accuse you of anything. I mean...."

"I call you 'Daddy' because you are daddy." Her face tightened. "I like calling you 'Daddy'. It make me feel I'm in family. I don't have daddy in my home in China."

"I know. I get that. I'm sorry. Didn't mean to upset you." He took a breath. "But even so, you're seventeen, so calling me 'Daddy' is still a bit inappropriate. 'Daddy' is for little girls. That's why the role-playing kind of 'Daddy' is meant to be cute. And it is cute. That's why your friends laugh when you say it."

He dropped his hands beside his hips, ready to surrender. He had said too much, and it didn't need to be said, he realized. A twisted grin appeared despite his effort to keep a straight face.

"I do like it. I admit. I like having you here. I told you. And I like you jumping on me and hugging me and giving me a kiss. It makes me feel...like I have a family still, like I'm going to be okay. Like I feel loved."

She wiped her eyes, like she had tears, but Bill couldn't see any. Maybe she was acting, playing the upset 'baby girl' to his authoritarian 'daddy'. He would need to buy her a new fur coat to make things right.

"But I do love you, Daddy."

Her eyes were set at an awkward tilt where the light of the living room lamps gave her both a glow of innocence and a glint of sensuality.

"You do?" he asked hesitantly.

Her lips pursed. "You are my daddy." He understood then exactly what she meant and had a sigh of relief. "Of course I love you."

"Yes...of course." He breathed deep, calming himself. He shouldn't think such things, taking her innocent words and interpreting them in a way that favored his fantasies.

"Do you love me?" she asked.

"Of course, I do," he stammered.

"Will you please say?"

His throat was dry, but he pushed the words out: "I love you."

That made her smile, like she had won a bet.

He asked about her dinner. She had eaten with the girls at a fast food place on the way to the house: cheeseburger and tater tots, and a cherry limeade. She said she loved all of it. Loved it.

She loved him, too, like how the word was used for everything in the English language. Love was the superlative of like. Who doesn't *love* Chocolate Almond Fudge ice cream? Who could still *love* an older broken man like him? What man wouldn't *love* being with a sexy girl like her?

Eventually she retreated to her room with her bag, unpacked it. She saw everything stacked up on Becky's bed and called to him.

"Oh, I spent the weekend doing some packing." He leaned against the doorway. "I decided it's time. I did hold back some things, you know, for memory. The rest I'll donate. Maybe some other girl can make use of them and then I'll feel glad those girls are happy to wear her clothes."

A light bulb went on. He glanced at Wendy.

"You know, you and Becky are about the same size. Maybe some of her clothes would fit you. If you want them. If it doesn't feel awkward to wear them. They're clean, and unworn since they came out of the laundry. Anything that had some memory associated with them, I've already put away."

Wendy studied the items on the bed. The dresses and skirts and pants lay over the underwear. She lifted a couple of the outer clothes as if testing them for any ties to their former wearer.

"Well, you can decide," said Bill. "If you don't want anything, that's fine, too. Thought you might as well get first crack. You can set aside anything you want and I'll take the rest out tomorrow."

She held up one of the dresses, an off-white mid-length dress with pink ruffles along the seams, short V-neck in front, slits on the sides, feminine, fitting somewhere between school and church.

"That's nice," he said.

She looked up at him, holding the dress in front of herself.

"It's pretty dress."

"It's yours if you want it."

She fought to hold a smile but broke into a sad persona. Laying down the dress on her bed, she went to him and stretched up to hug him. She planted a kiss on his cheek.

"Thank you, Daddy."

He felt a tingle crash through him, which grew into a storm, a bull in a Chinese china shop.

"You're welcome...baby girl."

18

HE KISSED HER CHEEK—a big, loud smack—and set her down, bunny slippered feet flat on the floor. In the moment she had hung around his neck, he felt her weight. His neck became strained.

"I'm not baby girl," she said, pouting. "I'm full-size girl."

"Yes, you are," Bill confirmed, holding his hand out to the top of her head. "An ideal size."

"I'm perfect size," she insisted. "I'm tall as Mama."

He gazed at the girl: a cherubic face with the sexy body of a lingerie model. Like the *manga* he saw so much when he lived in Japan. The cartoon drawings tended to feature an overly cute face with an overly sexualized figure—how the teenage boys who bought the comics liked their heroines to be, he guessed.

She twirled around like a ballerina, consciously flirtatious, batting her eyes, teasing him.

"Don't you have some homework to do?" he said, taking back the role of parent. "Tomorrow is coming soon."

"I finished before swimming tournament." She giggled like she had played a joke on him.

"Then maybe call your mother," he suggested, wanting—needing— to extricate himself from the situation. He turned abruptly away from her, took a step into the hallway. "Anyway, I need to go to...to the bathroom. Excuse me."

He slipped into the master bedroom and on into the bathroom, closed the door, and leaned against the sink counter, hands on the edge. He was afraid to look but he definitely felt it. Arousal. He dared not be caught reacting to her that way. She was his guest.

Then he smiled at the mirror, a knowing display of regret he used on rare occasions. If another writer had seen him, he would know what he felt. The all too common trope of the lonely English teacher being tempted by the bodacious female student. The student would know she could flirt and tease without limit while the poor male teacher could do nothing but take it, trying to hide his excitement from the world. He'd experienced that before in school. Deliberate behavior like that was inappropriate and, in a way, rude, often cruel, even as he sometimes enjoyed it. He understood these teenage girls were merely trying out their sexuality, seeing how far they could go while using a safe target.

No wonder it was a trope, a common theme in literature replayed over and over in novels and stories, poems and plays. Some readers, he knew, vehemently decried such stories as being nothing more than a male writer's fantasy. But fantasies don't start out of thin air, he would argue. At some time in history it must have happened, and the man it happened to decided to write about it. For what purpose? Possibly to entertain himself or others? To make a point? A chastisement for young ladies? A cautionary tale for men? The same awkward situation occurring often enough to become a trope is what gives them their meaning, their power to cajole and wound and warn us of the state of Western sexuality in the late post-modern era—

He had to wipe his brow as he thought through a lecture he never intended to give, speaking to a hall of imaginary students, half of them female, all dressed in sexy outfits, smiling their temptress smiles, flipping their lovely hair seductively, pouting like they might benefit from a good spanking, blowing a kiss or two, crossing and uncrossing their legs, letting a shoe slip off their foot while winking in his direction, as he stood with strained heroism, fighting against nature and his training to maintain a professional demeanor.

"Who else writes these kind of stories?" he quizzed the man in the mirror. "Who else writes stories period? The English majors, the ones who love to write. Some of whom become English teachers. Who else? And there's the lived experience ripe for fictionalization." Indeed, their first effort at penning the great American novel was generally a veiled autobiography. He had started one years ago.

Nothing inappropriate, not really, he thought.

"I tried," he swore to himself. "I tried to get her another family."

But not all those English teacher vs. flirtatious student stories need bring about an uncomfortable conclusion in some May/December romance. That's fine for fiction, but not for reality. Nabokov tried that in *Lolita*, a famous example, but the novel made him uncomfortable even as he admired the elevated prose of the protagonist's narration, blithely explaining his righteous perversion in hopes of acceptance by the reader.

"Not me," Bill whispered, standing straight, feeling his body relax.

A knock on the door startled him, made him unconsciously turn away as he swung the door open.

"Thank you hanging up my swimsuit," she said with a slight bow of her head. "Did you wash?"

"No, but I rinsed it thoroughly, until all the chlorine was out of it. My mother always said don't put it in the washing machine too often or it'll ruin the fabric."

She grinned like she'd heard that warning before. "Okay, Bill."

He turned to face her fully. "Listen, I'm sorry to give you the speech before. I was...."

"It's okay. I learn something new."

"I'm sorry."

A thought came to him as he escorted her from the bathroom, paused in the bedroom, then waved her to continue on to her room.

"I wonder if you could help me with something," he said once they were back in her room.

Her laptop was open on her bed and he pointed to it.

"I need your help with the social media stuff."

He explained how he hadn't been online since the incident, hadn't let everyone know what happened. He phoned friends and relatives. However, he knew Becky had friends online who weren't at her school, people who may not know why she was no longer responding to their messages or posting anything.

"We only use WeChat," said Wendy. "And email. I don't know Snapchat or Twitter. I know Facebook but it's block in China. Except if you have VPN app."

"VPN, huh?" He was amazed how much he didn't know. "Well, we had her give her passwords to her mother—yes, to check on her, to make sure she was safe. I have those passwords. They're written down and I got the paper from Barb's desk."

She seemed puzzled. "What can I do?"

"I thought you could post a message, to let everyone know. And then, maybe after another month, to close the account." He sighed. "I guess I could do that, too. I thought you were on those other sites, so you could simply post a message telling her friends."

"No, only WeChat."

"I see." He scratched his cheek.

"I don't think she have other friends on WeChat. Only me."

He looked at her laptop. She had a school paper on the screen. He gazed from the laptop to the wall. On the other side of the wall was Barb's office. Wendy had been able to connect using the Wi-Fi from that room, which was always on. He hadn't thought of that, of making the signal available to a guest. The signal dubbed "BandB" continued to provide service.

"Don't worry. I'll take care of it. Go on and work on your paper."

"Paper is finished," she announced proudly. "Can I play video game now?" She pointed to the machine on the shelf of the TV stand, the controls hanging off the edge.

"Sure, go ahead."

He retreated to Barb's office and booted the computer under the desk. The icon for the browser was easy to find among the dozen on the screen. He typed in the first site he thought of and went to Becky's page. Not registered on that site, he used her password, checking the spelling from the Post-It note stuck in the top drawer, and logged in.

> Sorry to give you this news but Becky is no longer available on this site. Unfortunately, she has passed away.

He typed 'died' then backspaced and typed 'passed away', a softer phrasing he thought would be better for a short, impersonal note. Then he added a thank you for their friendship to her and typed his name as a signature—his real name: *Becky's Dad*.

He repeated the task on different sites, slipping further down into the abyss with each posting. Becky had accumulated a lot of messages, people wanting to know where she was or why she hadn't responded, all the events she missed, notes for class, and birthday greetings the sites told her to offer. And the little memories videos the sites made automatically, which Bill found painful to watch.

He heard some of the sounds from the video game Wendy was playing in the next room, and thought of Becky's playtimes there. He felt the dual realities pulling him in opposite directions again as he worked, listening to the next room. But it had to be done.

Eventually, he heard no more video games. Sensing Wendy had gone to sleep, seeing the light in her room out, he realized he had nowhere to go in the morning. It was routine now. She would get herself up and ready, and one of her friends would pick her up and drive her to school. He would awaken later and roam the world in a death shroud.

He wanted to do the same for Barb's online accounts but he had no passwords. He had his own, however, so he went to those sites and posted similar messages about his wife, about her no longer being able to respond to messages and posts. He made a note of the date. He would let both of them go to the end of the year, through Christmas and New Year's greetings anyone wanted to post. That would be long enough. If things went as he noticed previously on those sites, friends would post condolences for a while and fall silent. He could shut the pages down then. And turn out the lights.

Bill was surprised he awoke much earlier than usual. He yawned as he listened to the noise in the kitchen, Wendy making breakfast. He went to the bathroom and splashed water on his face, combed his hair with his fingers, put on his robe and shuffled out to the kitchen.

She was rushing to clean the dishes.

"I'll take care of those," he said gruffly, needing to drink something.

"Must hurry. Casey coming soon." She dashed to her room.

She was already dressed for the day, American-style blue jeans with a pullover sweater, her long hair in a ponytail. He smiled at the sight of her, always looking pretty.

Making a pot of coffee for himself, he had a full mug ready, holding it gingerly in his hands, when Wendy returned to the living room. A car was pulling into the driveway, giving a honk.

Wendy hurried to the front door, her school bag on her shoulder.

"Bye, Daddy," she sang, stepping out the door.

"Bye, Precious," he called to her.

She stopped on the stoop, looked back. "Why you call me that?"

"Because you're precious." He chuckled. He hadn't planned to call her that. It had simply come out. "Besides, if you're going to call me Daddy, I'm going to call you Precious."

Another honk from the car. She looked worried.

"Okay, Daddy. It's deal."

He watched her climb in and the car back out of the driveway. He felt like a parent again, seeing his kid off to school. As though nothing had happened to change that situation.

What the fuck am I doing?

He made a list in his head of things to do, things which would keep his mind in check, stupid and useless things. He got out the vacuum and swept it through the house, every room, under every piece of furniture. The effort left him sweating, all the bending and stooping, pulling the furniture or other obstacles out of the way and pushing them back again. He found some coins in the couch cushions and a pair of Becky's socks wadded up under the couch. Also, Barb's favorite *Mont Blanc* pen which she never could find.

During his task, he thought what else he could do to fill the day before Wendy returned. He decided to go to the indoor shooting range. He needed more practice. His draw was still slow and off-target.

"There ya go," said Chuck, one of the instructors, standing behind him in the shooting lane. "I think ya got it."

Bill followed protocol in handling the weapon, checking that it was unloaded, then setting it down on the shelf and stepping back.

"Excellent. Excellent."

"Feels good," said Bill, turning to Chuck, raising his voice to be heard with the ear protection on. "Feels natural now."

"Ya made some progress."

"And my shot pattern is tighter, too."

"Ya ready for the show."

Bill laughed. "What show?"

"The Wild West show!"

He grinned, feeling like someone else, not the guy learning how to protect his family. He could be a cowboy, sure. He reminded Chuck of his National Guard service years before. But that was with an M-16, a rifle not a pistol. Chuck had set him straight, fixing his stance and his two-handed grip.

On the way out of the range, he stopped to buy extra ammo.

"Gun's no use without ammo," Chuck always said.

As Bill drove home, he thought of stopping off for a few items at the Walmart but he worried how to leave his gun in the Escape. Out of sight, of course. But what if his vehicle was broken into? He couldn't take the gun into the store. He didn't have a carry permit, concealed or open. He thought of taking it in its leather case, tuck it under his arm, which may not be noticeable to anyone, shaped as it was like a big teardrop with a long zipper. He decided he could wait.

Pulling into his driveway, he thought of taking a nap before Wendy returned home. He tried to remember anything she might have said about today, whether she would be home for dinner or be home late. With the flustering over the weekend and the previous evening, he had missed it—if she had told him.

He raised the garage door and pulled in, shut off the engine and climbed out—quickly, this time.

He opened the door to the kitchen and stepped inside.

Standing at the edge of the tile, one foot on the living room carpet, was a young man in jeans and hoodie staring back at him. Behind that man was another young man, farther away, in the living room, near the entrance of the hallway. He carried something. It looked like Wendy's laptop. The closer man, empty-handed, frozen where he stood. They both seemed surprised.

19

BILL TOOK NO TIME to figure it out but grabbed the case from under his arm, fumbled to unzip it and retrieve the weapon. At the same time, the two young men bolted for the front door, fiddling with the lock. He pointed the Glock at the nearest man—but the magazine was still in the glove box in the Escape—

He dashed into the garage, opened the door to the SUV, dove across the seats to the glove box, got the magazine, inserting it as he scooted out of the vehicle and re-entered the kitchen, pistol ready—wary that the young men also might have a weapon. He took a stance, held the pistol in both hands as he stepped through the kitchen and around the corner to the front door.

They had managed to open it, security system be damned, and were out on the stoop by the time Bill got to the door. But they had dropped the laptop at the door. He pushed it out of the way with his foot.

"Stop!" he shouted, coming out the front door, but the two men were running across the yard to the street. A car roared up to meet them, a dull orange sportscar, and the two men tumbled in as Bill aimed at the rear quarter panel of the car. A bullet there would likely explode the gas tank, he realized, and held back. A shot into the air to warn them? No, it would fall somewhere and maybe hit a neighbor or a neighbor's pet or child or break a window.

"Hey!" he shouted, chasing them down the street a couple houses.

But they were gone.

He leaned against a parked car, breathing hard. He examined the pistol and found he had not chambered a round, and knew he could have done nothing to halt them.

Trudging back to his house, Bill cursed the security system and the company. All the trouble he had to go through each time he went in or out of the house, all the promises, all the hype. And why him? Aren't the other houses just as inviting?

He whipped out his phone—tried to, but he didn't find it in his back pocket where he usually carried it.

Returning to his house, he went through the kitchen and out into the garage, got in the Escape and saw his phone sitting in the center console. *This is why I sit here after I arrive.* Grabbing the phone, he exited the vehicle and returned angrily to the kitchen.

The ghosts of the two men remained before him, standing where they had been when he first walked in. If he had been a few minutes later, they would be gone.

He hurried to Wendy's room. Her pink suitcase was still there but up on her bed, like they had tried to open it. What did they expect to find in a girl's pink suitcase? Clothes? Of course, he knew she kept her year's worth of cash locked inside. Who would guess that from looking at the suitcase? And they tried to take her laptop, too. He retrieved the laptop from the front door and examined it. A scuff on the corner. He wondered how hard it had been jarred? Maybe it needed to be checked, possibly repaired.

In the master bedroom, the drawers of the dresser were half open, as though they had looked for jewelry or other valuables. But he had emptied them already. He went to Barb's office and everything looked the same, the computer in its usual spot under the desk. Maybe they hadn't gotten that far.

So these two knew where to go, had a plan for what to take....

"About six-feet, slim, maybe a hundred-seventy pounds, white with dark hair, what I could see falling out of his hood, a square face, no facial hair," he told Detective Logan. "Never saw him before. And the other guy, behind him, he was shorter, chunky. I'm extrapolating, of course, considering he was further away and would look shorter from my vantage point. So I'd say maybe five-foot-six, possibly Hispanic but with light skin, some acne disfiguring."

"You're watching an awful lot of cop shows," said Logan, writing.

"The closest guy had an OSU hoodie, black with the orange Cowboy face. The other one, the Hispanic guy, wore an OU hoodie, red with the white 'OU' on the front. Both wore blue jeans."

Logan laughed, but knew it was a serious situation. He wrote down all the details.

"And the orange car," Bill added. "It's all tied together."

"The Orange Car Guy."

"Exactly." Bill was beside himself. What if Wendy had been home? He didn't want to be the hero who failed twice. But he also didn't want to go to prison for shooting someone.

"So OCG sent his two buds to do the dirty work, huh?"

"It's all connected to the mall," Bill spoke up, breaking out of his trance. "As bad as that event was, it just keeps going. I want it to stop. I'm trying to move the fuck on. And every day there's more shit that slaps me back to that...to that *incident*, as you guys like to call it."

"This orange car now...."

"I saw it at the school, too. Parked for a football game. But it still had no tag. Don't you guys ticket cars with no license tag?"

"The orange car guy...is a student?"

"I don't know. Who goes to high school football games? Sometimes it can be former students. I know in the past we've had former students return just to cause trouble. One reason we have police at the games."

"Student, parent, another family member, or a faculty member, a staff member. Someone from the community looking for something."

"A drug deal," Bill offered.

"Possible. A crowd of people. Easy to swap something."

"But let's get back to the connection." He glanced behind himself as a pair of haggard young men were marched past. Not his guys. "My wife's wallet, her credit cards, driver's license, her car and house keys, all were taken at the mall. By someone who survived. That's a short list, isn't it? They know where she lives, and have a way to get in, and also to steal her car, a way to rack up charges. But they didn't. They handed over or sold the cards to some other person who started using them. And you know it was the assistant manager who stole her car right off my damn driveway. Then totaled it. But you have him in jail now. I got the insurance check for that, by the way."

"Okay, that's good," said Logan, sitting back with a sigh. "And you did report Orange Car Guy early in the investigation. He came by, you said, looking over your house, like he planned to break in."

"Instead he gets his buddies to do it and he serves as the getaway driver."

"Yes, something going on," said Logan, nodding pensively.

Bill leaned forward, elbows on his knees. "I sure don't know how they could get in, with the security system activated. Unless...*damn*. I went out this morning, in the backyard, you know, to have a look. I was seeing how much the leaves had piled up from my neighbor's trees. They're on his side of the fence but they drop all their leaves in my yard and I have to rake them up. Every damn fall."

"You could just leave them. I hear it's good for the lawn."

"So I turned off the system to go out the back door. You know, so it wouldn't sound an alarm when I came back in. I guess I didn't reset it. I was in too big a hurry to get to the range, I guess. They must've come in through the kitchen, through the sliding glass doors. Nobody would see them that side of the house. Those doors are easy to jimmy, right?"

"To the range? You mean a shooting range?"

Bill froze. "Yes, I went. Over to Hot Shot Shooting Sports in Yukon. It's an indoor range."

"I know it."

He gazed across the desk at the detective. "That's legal, isn't it?"

"Sure." He glared back at Bill. "You have a firearm?"

"I do."

"Did you discharge it today? I mean, at your residence?"

"I did not." He sat up stiffly, pulled in a shallow breath, held it a moment. "I wanted to, but I messed up."

Bill sat on the bed, cleaning the Glock. He paused to fiddle with the bullets in the magazine. Seventeen of them, 9mm. He would leave one in the chamber. With the safety on.

First, he had to put it back together.

"I'm home, Daddy!" cried Wendy, coming in the front door, her keys jingling against the charms on her keyring.

"Code," he shouted from the bedroom, reminding her to de-activate the alarm then re-activate the security system.

Bill hurried to assemble the Glock before she could find him.

Swinging into the open doorway, she gasped.

He didn't look up, kept after the assembly.

"It's a gun."

"A gun?" She was alarmed, then explained in an agitated voice how that's all they hear about America, how everybody has a gun. It's too dangerous. Don't go there. Even some students from China had gotten shot and killed while studying in America.

Bill agreed; he'd heard news reports over the years. The murders usually were by guys the girls had rejected, which was still no excuse. Not because they were Chinese. And there was that bombing at a marathon that killed several people, including a pair of Chinese college students who had stood at the finish line to cheer for a friend. But it was a rare occurrence. Now everything was different.

Finishing the assembly, he checked that the chamber was empty. He aimed at the wall by the bathroom, pulled the trigger. Click.

"Good." He had put it together correctly. "I was just cleaning it."

Wendy stood in the doorway, one hand on each side, filling the space, her face reflecting horror when he gazed at her. He waved her in, invited her to sit on the bed.

"Yes, I have a gun. More correctly, a pistol. Or handgun, some say. It was my father's. I inherited it when he died. I've never concerned myself with it, or the thought of having a gun, but now everything is different. I need to be ready."

Sitting beside her, he weighed the Glock in his hands, resting in his lap. She stared down at the pistol.

"You can touch it," he said. "It's unarmed. Won't hurt you."

She dared to poke it with her finger.

"Now I need you to listen carefully." He turned to be able to meet her eyes. "Today I went out for a little while. When I came home, there were two men in the house. They broke in somehow. Yes, even with the security system. I thought it was on. Maybe I turned it off, forgot to re-activate it. Anyway, they ran out. I chased them but they got away."

She was in shock, and he put his arm around her shoulders.

"This is not normal. This is not America. Not the real America. These thugs are targeting this house because they have some of the things, some knowledge about the family that lives here. Me—you—and Becky and Barb. Whatever they think, they think it's worth trying to rob. They stole Barb's car and they've been casing the place—looking around, right?"

She started to cry, pushing against his shoulder.

"Why they want come to here?"

"That's what I want to know. But don't worry. I have a plan." He didn't really have a plan, he knew, but it sounded comforting. "The most important thing is you. I will protect you. I must keep you safe. It's my responsibility. So I'm thinking of having you stay with a friend. A school colleague. One of your friends would be okay, too, I guess. Those thugs wouldn't know where that is. I'll stay here and wait for them. When they come back I'll be ready."

He held out the Glock, aiming it at the baseboard beside the chest of drawers, and pulled the trigger, hearing the click.

"I have to protect you. It's my duty."

She swept her arm up and hugged him, digging her teary face into his shoulder.

"I'm sorry," she mumbled repeatedly.

He kissed the top of her head.

"It's not your fault. It's America's."

20

THE NOVEMBER EVENING had begun when Bill delivered Wendy to the new house. Her classmate Jackie lived there. Bill knew the family, having taught six of the seven kids over the years. John Drexler, now an administrator in the district office, had been the principal when Bill first started teaching at Vista High.

Jackie came out immediately and cheered Wendy's arrival, taking her away to her temporary sleeping quarters as her mother greeted Bill standing in the doorway.

"Thank you, Jean." Bill forced a smile under grim circumstances. Wendy was already moving in, going to one of the bedrooms. Two of their kids were away in college but coming home for Thanksgiving, Jean had explained when Bill called.

"Oh, it's no problem, Bill. We love having your special guest stay with us a while. She's lovely! And I hear such good things about her at school. She's been helping Jackie with Calculus."

"I'm glad she won't be a bother. It's just for a few days. I hope."

"I know it's a stressful time for you."

"You don't know the half of it."

"We're glad to help out."

"Thanks again."

"Long as we're entertaining your exchange student, you might as well join us, too, for Thanksgiving dinner. We'll have some empty chairs. Jeff's going with his wife to visit her family this year, since they have the baby. And Fiona's going with her boyfriend. How time flies! We can put Nicky on the sofa for a few nights, she won't mind. A ten-year old still likes to camp out. Wendy can have her bed, share the room with Kelly. The other kids'll be here for the dinner but it's really no bother to add one more. You're welcome to join us for the dinner."

"Well, I'm not so sure what I have to be thankful for...."

"Then you come over for a good home-cooked meal." She put her hand to her face, shielding her mouth. "I mean American cooking. Not that there's anything wrong with Chinese food, mind you. It's just you probably've had enough of that by now, if she cooks as much as I hear. You might be gaining weight, Bill."

He patted his belly. "I lost some the first month after...after what happened. Then she took over the kitchen. Yep, she's a good cook. You probably didn't know it but her mother runs a lunch counter back in China. She helps her out when she can."

"She's such a kind girl."

"Yes, she is."

"So you'll be coming over on Thursday? About three. Early is fine, but then you'll have to help out. Late's not good. Then you may not get any food but dessert."

"All right, you talked me into it." He became sullen once more. "But first, I have some work to do."

"Of course." She smiled warmly, went to hold the door open for him. "You be careful now, Bill. We want you to be safe. And coming over for dinner."

"I'll be here, Jean, don't worry."

He stepped out the door, shifted his jacket collar up around his neck against the cold wind, and called back another thanks.

Bill was nervous as he drove home, wondering what he would find. He let the Escape roll past his house and continue down the street. He left the living room light on so it would appear someone was at home. But he debated with himself whether the light was actually a courtesy for would-be burglars, so they could find their way around without having to use a flashlight, avoiding irregular flickers that might call attention to a passing police car.

He reached the end of the block, paused, turned the Escape around in the intersection, and drove slowly back up the street, parking two houses down from his, in front of a neighbor's truck. He shut off the engine and lights, and sat there, watching his house.

After ten minutes' observation, he remembered what he'd forgotten to tell Wendy. He picked up his phone and typed a message about her laptop being dropped, probably needing repair, files retrieved from it. He would take care of it. He would buy her a new one if it couldn't be fixed.

Thank u so much Bill ! ! !

She texted back immediately, much to his surprise. Then another message came just as he was about to close the app.

Boy from school send me picture of penis ! ! ! ask me send picture of me with no clothes ☹ Do I have to do ? ? ?

Bill jumped on the tiny keyboard, punching with his index finger, cursing at the autocorrect changing his correctly spelled words into other words, but he got his reply out and clicked send.

NO! DO NOT SEND any pictures of yourself to anybody! He is wrong! It is a crime to send pictures of penis or any private area if you are under 18.

As his chest tightened, he contemplated his anger. He was being a parent. He was protecting her. He was the good guy, saving her from immoral America, from the bad boys.

Glancing up at his house, he hoped the light from his phone was not giving his location away.

Thanks Bill. I wont. I delete picture.

He sent a quick reply: Good girl. Respect yourself.

She continued to respond to his messages and before he realized it, a half-hour had passed, a lively conversation in text form. However, he wondered why she was free to text him. Wasn't she being welcomed and entertained by the Drexler family? Maybe she was sitting among them in the living room or at the dinner table and they were ignoring her. He feared asking.

Instead, he lectured her on the morals of America and how they had changed since he was her age. He had to protect her from anything that would harm her experience in America. As though the other things hadn't already. She'd seen her first gun up close, touched it. She was hiding out to avoid criminals. That was not the experience he wanted her to have.

Or, maybe, she liked that kind of excitement. He didn't like that kind of excitement. He stared at his house: the last of the sunset behind his rooftop illuminated the bare branches of the neighbor's trees, black fingers against the orange sky.

The house was too much. More than he needed. And it reminded him of Barb and Becky. Everything in it did. He should sell it. Maybe leave it furnished, or have everything hauled away. He would start over with new furniture in an apartment, like he was in his bachelor pad again at his first teaching position, a one-year contract to substitute for a teacher undergoing cancer treatment. She lived and he went off to Japan for a year.

Eventually he got out of the Escape, made sure it was locked up, and walked through the darkness to his house. He went in through the front door, the easiest way to get inside without anyone seeing. The garage door would make noise, be a big production. He remembered to punch the code on the wall pad to prevent the silent alarm going off. And when he opened the glass door and then the steel door, he held the Glock in his hand, the magazine inserted, one in the chamber, safety off—in case he found someone inside who shouldn't be there.

Except for the single recessed bulb above the fireplace, the house was dark and silent.

Suddenly he was filled with dread. This house would be his final resting place if he didn't move out. He froze at the intersection of the living room, kitchen, and hallway leading to the bedrooms. He looked down and saw other footprints in the carpet, the shoes of the first thief. This was a crime scene. He tried to step over it, to smash out the impressions. He did the same with the other thief's prints in the hallway, right in front of Wendy's room.

Becky's room. Oh, if his ladies had been home that afternoon! He was having a panic attack. He grabbed his chest, sucking air. Dropping to his knees, he fell over, coughing.

*   *   *

"I need to know for certain," said Bill to Detective Logan. He took the opportunity to ask his questions, having been called in and invited to identify his two burglars in their computer database. But he found none that matched. "When the time comes, I mean. What exactly can I do? I mean what I'm allowed to do by law. I don't want to have to stop and think of the legal ramifications of pulling a trigger."

Logan pursed his lips, sat back, raising a finger to scratch at his lip. Getting tired of this guy, Bill decided the detective must be thinking. Couldn't blame him.

"I mean, can I shoot a burglar? In my yard? How about if I'm in my yard but he's taken one step off my property after committing a crime on my property? How about inside my house? Has to be in my house or just me in my house and he's outside my house but still on my property? What if he's uninvited, unwelcomed? An intruder? Do I have to verbally warn him to get off my property, get out of my house, first? Have to fire a warning shot? At the ground? How close to his feet is that allowed? And if I hit him, which is better—for legal purposes—a leg or an arm? Or his front? Center mass? It's bad to shoot him in the back if he's fleeing, huh? We're supposed to let them run away, right? How close can I be? Is it better for my case if we're farther apart than, say, twice arm's length? What if I'm hurt? If he hurts me? Can I shoot him then? Do I have to let him shoot at me first? What if he threatened my daughter with violence? What if he already did the violence and is leaving? How many bullets can I put in him before it's considered excessive? Can I claim temporary insanity because I was enraged by what he did? How about if he—"

Logan held up his hands to stop Bill. "Hold on." He was shaking his head, a perturbed grin rattling dismissively back and forth. "Mister Masters, I can't tell you what to do. That's not my job. Besides, it depends entirely on the situation. You know, the circumstances at that moment. Which nobody can predict. Things can happen fast."

"I know. That's why I'm asking now. I want to be ready."

"Hey, you shouldn't plan to shoot anybody. It's a whole lot better if it's spontaneous."

"See? That's what I mean. That's what I need to know." He tried to breath easier. "I'll prepare, be ready, but I'll act spontaneously."

"But, you know, you coming in here to talk about shooting a home invader could be used against you. Proves you were planning it."

"I'm not planning to do it. I'm preparing to *be able* to do it."

"Judge may not see the difference."

"If they come back, I will do it. Go ahead. Tell the world. Let them know if they return, I will be ready."

"Just don't go chasing after them down the street, like, with your gun drawn. This ain't the wild West. That won't be good for you."

"So they step off my property, they're off scot-free?"

"Looks that way. Call our guys. We'll be there right away."

"In about thirty minutes, by my timing."

"Isn't a patrol car going by your place?"

"I haven't seen one. Not when I've been awake."

"I'll have'em send patrols by your address. Don't worry. I'm sure you scared them. Young punks like that seldom return to a place they got spooked by the owner."

Hannah crossed her legs, uncrossed them, recrossed them, balancing her notepad on her knees.

"You seem agitated," she spoke. "What's been going on with you?"

"Everything. But thanks for seeing me today. I know it's not our usual day."

"Thanksgiving always forces me to make adjustments."

"Me, too."

"So...you did not bring your exchange student, I see."

"I've sent her away to another family, but just for the week. She can't stay in my house."

"Why did you do that?"

He told her the story of the two punks in his house and his fears for her safety. The telling took most of the session, full of sensual details and speculative tangents, like he was planning a crime novel.

"That's commendable." she said, rare praise.

"I said before, I have to be sure she's safe. She came all the way here to experience the American life. But this isn't what she's supposed to experience, that's for sure."

"I'm sure she appreciates your effort."

"Yeah, efforts." He shook his head, then gazed out the window at a rainy afternoon, feeling his empty stomach complaining. "At least it keeps me busy. Too busy to notice my depression. It's like...now I don't even remember what happened, or why I'm feeling all this crap."

She adjusted her glasses.

"Depression is not an easy thing to pigeon-hole. It's not always the sorrowful experience. It's not just being sad. It can be acting normal while being more tired than usual. You can even have humor—as I see you sometimes display—while feeling empty inside. Feeling hopeless. It has some characteristics of PTSD. You know: Post-Traumatic Stress Disorder. And you've had trauma, make no mistake, even if you were not there. The main symptoms are the triggers—when something reminds you of the trauma. Also it's a catatonic state of immobility—unwilling or unable to do your normal daily activities because of fear or lack of motivation. In fact, I recently read an article which suggested a link between inflammation in the body and a reduction of a person's dopamine levels, which affects agency—the will to act, to get up and do something. Inflammation is often a result of excessive cortisol in the body, the fight-or-flight chemical, which comes from the trauma, and from how you respond to it. Stay in a stressful situation long enough and you draw out more of the stress hormone. Stress leads to cortisol which leads to inflammation which leads to low dopamine which leads to...immobility, loss of agency, and so on. It becomes a vicious cycle. We can give medication to block it but it's not something you want to be on very long. You need to get your body back to its normal function. You're here to try to understand what you're feeling, for the purpose of returning to a normal state."

She seemed to have finished, but Bill waited for more, turning his gaze to the wall behind where she sat.

"I'm going to move," he spoke after the silence had gone too long. "I want to get away from all the punks who want to break in. I also want to get away from everything that reminds me what happened." He regarded the doctor, chewing his lip and blinking a few times. "It's not that I want to forget them. I mean, how can I still sleep in the same bed I slept in with my wife the night before she was murdered? I do, but how can I? It took me three weeks to change the sheet—the one she slept on. I waited until it no longer had her scent. That's fair, isn't it?"

"I believe so."

"I need to figure out how to do the move so nobody knows where I move to, in case somebody's watching the house."

"You think someone is watching your house?" She made a note.

"I know someone is."

21

"AND PLEASE, DEAR LORD, bless Bill who has gone through so much," Mrs. Drexler spoke in a solemn voice, eyes closed, hands held up in praying position. "Help him find the strength within him to travel his journey and come to a place of calm. Help him find peace. Amen."

"Thanks, Jean," he whispered.

The others around the long table repeated the *Amen*. Bill heard the soft voice of the woman seated next to him. He was surprised Jennifer Claybourne, his fellow English teacher, had been invited, but it seemed the Drexlers were inviting all the single faculty. Across the table from him sat Wendy; she kept glancing at him, maybe for clues how to act or what to do. She offered him the grin he needed.

"It's good to see you," Jennifer had said, greeting him in the living room when he arrived, cleaned up and nicely dressed.

Then Wendy had appeared and was about to jump on him as she liked to do, but this time, held back at his hand signal.

"Hi, Daddy," she said in subdued tone.

Some of them chuckled at her playful greeting. Bill enjoyed her recognition. He glanced awkwardly at Mrs. Drexler. She stood behind Wendy, wearing an odd, disapproving scowl.

Mr. Drexler greeted Bill at the door, gave him a firm handshake and launched into introductions of the guests. Eventually, everyone sat down at the long table, expanded to handle the festive buffet. Bill saw the kids sitting at a card table, the 'kiddie table', just as he had once sat at when attending his grandparents' Thanksgiving dinner. That was a long time ago, he mused, accepting the chair Mrs. Drexler indicated. He pulled out the chair, about to sit, when Jennifer appeared beside him, her hand on the back of her chair.

"How're you doing, Bill?" She regarded him, sporting her famous half-smile, like she had come from the dentist, lips frozen.

"Hi, Jenn," he responded, startled to see her seated next to him. "Fine, thanks. Are they inviting all the single teachers?" He meant it as a joke so he added a laugh that fell to the floor between his shoes.

He thought to dress in school clothes for the occasion, then decided it would seem false. He chose instead a pair of nice jeans and a blue sweatshirt with the school mascot, an orange growling wildcat, on the front. He thought he looked appropriate.

Wendy, however, wore a lovely off-white blouse that had strings to tie the front V-neck and a wide collar that extended into a hood that lay about her shoulders. The shirt complemented her beige slacks. Her long, dark hair was brushed out, hanging full down her back. The best part of her outfit was her smile, white teeth on display, and the way her nose cinched up like a child's rebuke when she felt embarrassed or she reacted to a remark she didn't understand. He liked seeing her face wrinkle at his occasional sarcastic comments and just as quickly return to her perfect china doll façade.

Jennifer was dressed modestly in a blouse and cardigan, professional slacks, all in the shades of autumn, an ivory brooch pinned over her breast. Her short brown hair was fading into a lighter hue, the gray starting to infiltrate. She adjusted her glasses, grinning at Bill.

"They're such nice people," said Jennifer. "My third Thanksgiving with them."

Then Mrs. Drexler announced it was time for the saying of grace.

John Drexler gave a nod and everyone bowed their heads.

"And please give special blessing," said John, "to our new friend, Miss Wendy, coming all the way here from China. Help her have an excellent visit here in the United States, and then say good things about us when she returns home."

A few of the guests around the table chuckled.

"Amen."

"God bless Becky," Bill whispered, "and bless Barbara."

Sitting and settling into his position, Bill noticed Wendy directly opposite him. He grinned at her. She smiled back as she accepted the dish from her left, took a small sample, passed it on to her right.

"You're going to have to take more than that," he joked, "if you want to experience the real American Thanksgiving dinner. The goal is to eat more than you've ever eaten before, and have to undo your belt for the rest of the day."

"I don't wear belt," Wendy laughed.

Jennifer, next to Bill, also faced Wendy, her student in American Literature. It might be awkward for Wendy, he thought, but having everyone there together allowed for conversation with new people. He believed Jennifer was there for him, courtesy of Mrs. Drexler.

Jennifer passed the dish of mashed potatoes to Bill. He helped himself to a huge scoop. Next came the gravy boat. She held the boat patiently as he made an indentation in his potatoes.

"Must make a gravy pond, right, Bill?" she chuckled.

"You know the drill."

He watched Wendy talking with the young people on either side of her, the Drexler kids home from college. One of their daughters, Karla, tried some Mandarin on Wendy and she responded in kind. They had a conversation which caught everyone's attention for a few minutes, followed by applause for Karla's achievement. Jennifer was trying to pass the green bean casserole to Bill and finally got him to notice.

Eventually everyone had filled their plates and the eating began, prompting a lull in the conversation. Talking gradually resumed. Bill remained quiet, listening casually to five simultaneous conversations, catching bits and pieces. Everyone seemed to know which topics to avoid. Jennifer asked him questions and he responded politely but with little enthusiasm. He feigned the need to chew as a way to keep from engaging in serious chatting.

He didn't intend to be rude. He respected Jennifer as a teacher. That was the reason he recommended her for Wendy. But he felt awkward having her seated beside him, like it was Mrs. Drexler's plan to get them together. Sure, there was a good deed in introducing people to each other who had suffered similar fates, maybe get them to aid each other in recovery. But Jennifer had been dealing with her loss for five years, Bill only a few months.

He thought of last year's Thanksgiving, just him and Barb having a half-turkey, enough for a modest dinner and some sandwiches later. Becky had joined her friend Lily's family. He felt a deep pit open in his stomach. It couldn't be filled by the turkey, potatoes, vegetables, rolls, gravy, and pumpkin pie, no matter if he got seconds or thirds. He wanted to sit back from the table and examine his belt. It seemed more appropriate for him to starve, like he did the first couple weeks after the incident. Not pushing against his waistband yet.

He sipped iced tea from the glass beside his empty plate.

"Can I get you anything more?" asked Jennifer, waving her hand at the dishes in the center of the table.

"You need to eat, Bill," Mrs. Drexler scolded.

"Come on, Bill. Game'll be on soon," said John Drexler.

Then Wendy rose up, put a knee on her chair, and stretched over the bowl of mashed potatoes to plop a roll on his plate. It was a daring move for her, the angle causing one breast to scrap the potatoes. As she faced Bill, her cleavage was quite on display, fixing his eyes.

Jennifer noticed his gaze as Wendy dropped back onto her chair.

"Thank you," said Bill to acknowledge her sacrifice as she wiped off the potatoes from her shirt.

"Hey, Bill," called John, "who you like in the game tonight? I know you're a fan. You been following this season?"

"Thanks, but no," Bill responded, staring at the roll on his plate. "I...I just need some air."

He got up from the table rather brusquely, but he was careful to avoid bumping anyone as he scooted behind their chairs. With the roll from Wendy in his hand, he made his way to the front door. Opening it, he felt the cold air but ducked outside anyway without his coat.

They had included Wendy in their conversation, he was happy to see, asking obvious questions about what she thought of America and her American school, and many other topics, some awkward. She answered politely and graciously. She arrived in the aftermath of a mass casualty event, Bill could chide them now, standing on the front stoop, stuffing his hands into his jean pockets, rocking on his shoes on the porch. How's that for a first impression of America? Mrs. Drexler had piped up about some of Wendy's accomplishments and others added their compliments or mentioned other ways she had been an asset to Vista High. Jennifer had asked Wendy what her Christmas plans were, as if prompting her to consider going home.

He munched on the roll as he stared up at the sky.

"I want to see Mama," Wendy had replied. "I want to experience America Christmas, too." She had tossed a wink at him, so quick that he was caught with candied yam in his mouth and choked. "We have Mister Santa in China, and the flying deer, too, like here, but not a church story. No churches in China."

Mrs. Drexler had seemed disappointed. She offered an invitation to attend their church for the Christmas service. Then, thinking Wendy didn't know about the religious side of the holiday, she launched into the Nativity story for Wendy's benefit, until her husband cut her off, recognizing the girl's discomfort.

Maybe she does want to return home, Bill pondered as he gazed at the sky, the thick clouds hiding the moon but not its glow. With all that had happened, it would make sense. She came with the idea of staying the full year, but if she had enough after one semester, there was no rule against departing once classes were over.

And Jennifer kept leaning over to him, speaking under her breath, saying stupid comments about what others were saying, as though her remarks were supposed to be clever. Or flirtatious. She was a good teacher and, he guessed, had been a fine wife—and she was attractive for her age, which he guessed was about his, maybe a couple years older. But even if he was interested in dating, it was too soon. He needed another five years, minimum. Five years of living alone in a small apartment, a place where there was nothing to remind him of his former life.

If he'd known how things were going to go, he would've insisted Becky join her parents for Thanksgiving dinner. He would announce all the things he was thankful for and invite his ladies to do the same. Maybe Barb would say something about him welcoming her back after the past couple of years of discord. Maybe not. That would not be the point. The point would be to have the family together all at one time—like the Drexlers did.

If he had only known.... There were a lot of things he would've done differently. Or not. He was set in his ways, that's for sure. Trudging along through life, youth fading like an old TV set, gradually switching from being absorbed by his own accomplishments to being focused on Becky's life and what she was doing, taking pride not from what he did but from what she did. "I didn't amount to much," he might tell people, "but just look at my daughter and all the great things she's doing!" There were more great things coming. College. Career. Family. He would be a grandfather someday—

And it had all been cut short.

He felt moisture on his face, wiped his eye with his finger. It was not a tear, he discovered, but a snowflake. He gazed up and saw the stray flakes drifting on the breeze, scattering like...like so many lives cut short, spirits sent in random directions...like the well-meaning people inside the house, trying to help him regain a normal life? What would normal be from now on?

He studied the Drexlers' front yard, similar to his lawn, strewn with dried leaves, a gentle slope down to the street. The first winter Becky was in the house, he recalled, when the snow fell: a true blizzard, which only came by their new home in Oklahoma about once every three years and dumped six or eight inches before melting completely three days later. He'd pulled her out to teach her the fine art of making a snowman—snowperson, his little girl had insisted, picking up lessons from her second grade teacher, the hyper-feminist *Ms.* Frick who Bill never liked. But they'd made it anyway, a figure of snow which could've been neither male nor female, having no genitals. Becky was proud of their project, declaring to Barb that she wanted to embark on a career making snowpeople.

Bill smiled at the memory, holding out his hand to catch the flakes. He brought his hand to his face, studying them, watching them melt against his palm.... The meager measure of existence.... Melting. So why go on? Why fall from the sky if you know you will melt away? How about next year's Thanksgiving? How would he make it that far into the future? Even past that horrible August anniversary?

A tear hovered at the edge of his eye, then slid slowly down his cheek, an irritating tickle that he accepted, wouldn't wipe away, a deserved punishment.

He thought of other punishments he might deserve. He thought of the gun he had at home. It would be easy to recline on the bed and, as they do in the movies, put the barrel in his mouth and pull the trigger. The pillow would absorb the noise, collect the blood and brain matter.

But not until Wendy left. He wouldn't give her that memory to take home with her. No, he would hold it together until she had enough of America and departed with a bag full of good memories and souvenirs, not the horror he might offer. So he was good for now—

A hand weighed on his shoulder. He turned, found Jennifer beside him, holding his coat. He accepted it, pulled it on. She wore her coat but crossed her arms in front of herself. She noticed it was snowing and gazed up, smiling.

"It's beautiful," she spoke. "My favorite season."

"Mine, too." He counted snowflakes. "Hey, I'm sorry if I came off as rude. You understand, I'm sure, how it can be...being surrounded by so many people who have not experienced trauma."

"Yes, I completely understand." She gave him a grin. "And forgive me if I seemed too...I don't know, too cheery? They invited me a month ago. I didn't know you were coming. But it's good you did. Get you out of the house. No moping around on a social occasion."

"Yeah, social occasion. That's it, all right."

She asked how he had been occupying himself during the semester and he retorted that he was talking with Griffin's wife, the psychologist, and giving a lot of free assistance to the local police. She chuckled at his phraseology.

"I brought Wendy over here just for a few days," he said with more determination, "because our house is.... There's some punks trying to make it their playground. I didn't want her to be involved. I spent the past few days sitting inside, waiting for them to try to break in again—"

"Again? Oh my!"

"Or out in the backyard, in the dark, waiting for them to arrive. Then I'd..." He raised his hand like he held a pistol, then dropped his arm. "I would call the police, like any rational citizen."

"Oh, that's scary."

"I'm getting used to it. Always something to hassle with."

"I'm sorry, Bill. At least I never had that with Larry's accident."

"Well, the police—detectives—they have everything under control, they say. They're on top of things. But, you know, if it takes twenty-five minutes to arrive at my house after I call in a home invasion, then they are not quite on top of things. More like on the side."

Again she laughed, touching his arm. He noticed her gesture and she saw that he noticed. But she left her hand on his arm.

"I'm thinking of moving to an apartment. Something small and cheap. That nobody would think to break into because nothing of value would be there. I'll sell the house. Give everything away. Start a new life." He had to stop. "Like nothing ever hap—"

"Happened. I know what you mean. All the what-ifs...." She took his arm in hers, leaned against him like she was cold. "It's easy to want to try and pretend it never happened. But there are still memories we want. So we don't really want life to be as though nothing happened."

Bill gazed at her, saw a kind face staring back. "You're right."

"Those memories.... They continue to exist in you. You'll always have Becky doing her thing, and Barbara doing what she does. Don't give that up just to be without the pain."

"You're right," he mumbled, turning on the front stoop, ready to head inside. "I guess I'll go back in."

"And your guest. Wendy is so lovely. Smart, talented, pretty. It would be easy to become enamored by her."

Bill grabbed the door handle, opened the glass door, reached for the door knob of the wooden door, leaving Jennifer outside.

"Sorry," he called, pushing the glass door back open for her.

"Let's see what the others are doing."

Inside, the football game was on, noisy in the living room. John and the guys had set up the fan section. The women were clustered around the dining table, drinking and chatting. The younger guests were engaged in a board game. Wendy moved between the three groups. John was trying to explain the game of football to her. The kids were asking her to take a turn. The women were still posing a litany of questions. She saw Bill come in and rushed to him, hugged him.

"Are you ready to go home?" he asked her, setting her down.

She turned to the hostess, sitting at the dining table, giving her a big smile. "I enjoyed living with you, Missus Drexler. Thank you very much. And thank you, Mister Drexler. You are so kind to me. All of you. But I want to go my home now."

"At least wait till the game's over," John called.

"Oh, I don't know anything about football in American style," she replied, and laughed. She turned to Bill.

"You can stay longer, if you like." He regarded Mrs. Drexler. "I think the house is safe now. The police are on top of things, you know." He shared a wry grin with Jennifer. "Could be any day now the world's back in order."

"You're welcome to come for Christmas," added Mrs. Drexler. "Love to have you stay with us again, Wendy. And you're welcome to come for dinner, Bill."

"Thanks, Jean." Bill wondered if he wanted to endure a gathering like this again. But Wendy needed to go through the typical American Christmas morning. It had to be checked off her list.

Driving home, Wendy told about her visit with the Drexlers, describing the quirks of Mrs. and Mr. and each of the kids. With so much practice, her English was becoming more fluid. Bill laughed at her impressions of them, and it pulled him out of his funk.

As they approached the house, she fell silent.

Bill cleared his throat. "I think I'm going to move. Move into an apartment. Easier to manage. Away from this place. Away from all the memories. Away from the punks who are attracted to it."

He turned the Escape into the driveway, clicked the remote to open the garage door, rolled inside. Shutting off the engine, he clicked to close the door.

"I feel this is a turning point," he spoke, his voice wavering, after the silence became noticeable. The light in the garage automatically went off.

"Can we go inside, Bill?" asked his passenger.

He chuckled. "Yes, of course."

Once inside, Bill put the foil-wrapped dishes into the refrigerator, leftovers from the Thanksgiving dinner—enough for another meal for the two of them, according to Mrs. Drexler.

He sat at the kitchen table, glancing around the room as though recalling what occupied each cabinet, sorting the items in his memory, imagining the ghosts who moved back and forth doing their tasks. He could see Barb, in her morning smock, standing at the stove frying eggs. They would be overdone, dry. He could see Becky sitting across the table from him, scooping spoonfuls of cereal from a bowl, spilling the milk.

Then Wendy stepped into his field of view.

"Ah, I'm going to be an old man soon," he spoke up with a grunt. "Nobody to care for me. I need to simplify my life as much as possible from now on. Pack up everything, sell it or give it away. Just get out of this house."

"You're not old man," she said.

He gazed at her: standing with hands at her sides, face grim.

"So what are your Christmas plans? I didn't hear clearly what you said during dinner. Are you going back? I mention this apartment idea only because I might be living in a different place when you return. I could still drive you over to Vista High, so you can continue there."

She seemed to take his news badly, sniffling. "I don't know what to do. I'm sorry, Bill. If you move to new home, do I live with you again? Or live with other family?"

"Oh, Wendy. I didn't mean I was trying to get rid of you." He felt her worries. "I just wanted to warn you it would be an apartment rather than this house you would be coming back to." He looked harder at her, met her eyes. "If you are coming back."

She bowed her head, like she had done something wrong.

"I got ticket for flying home for New Year."

He regarded her, wanting to go and give her a hug, tell her there was nothing bad about wanting to go home. Home is where the heart is, right? She had her mother there. And an uncle, apparently.

"Ah, the big New Year's celebration." His face tensed. "But that's at the end of January, isn't it? The lunar New Year. What animal will it be this year? I'm sure you get days off in China, but we'll be having our classes then. Would you miss classes? Well, maybe a week or two wouldn't hurt."

He cleared his throat, getting a sense of the cold air affecting him. He shouldn't have been outside so long without a coat.

"Do you want to experience a typical American Christmas?"

That brightened her. "Oh, yes! I want to see Christmas life here. I want to make holiday tree and open presents." Then her smile faded. "Then I will go my home."

"You mean for the New Year's break?" He frowned. "Or forever?"

She pursed her lips, turned to the refrigerator after a moment, fetching her bottle of tea to give her a pause to think.

"Wendy," he spoke as gently as possible as she got a glass from the cabinet, "you're always welcome here, there, wherever I might be living. I didn't mean for you to think I wanted you to leave. I don't. Sure, I did try to set you up with another family when you first arrived, but that was because, well, I was a mess then, not a good host, from...well, you know what happened. But I like having you here. In fact...you saved me, Wendy."

He got up, intercepting her as she replaced the bottle in the fridge. As he went to give her a loving clasp of her shoulder, he nearly caused her to drop the glass she'd filled.

"Sorry," he said in alarm. "I mean, when you arrived, I had to get up from my mourning slouch and pull myself together. I had to at least pretend to act normal, for your sake. I didn't want you to have a bad impression of America from the way I was."

"It's okay, Bill," she said softly. "I like living here."

He returned to his chair and she took the chair at the end of the table, sipped from her glass.

"Having you here has kept me alive." He tried to meet her eyes down the table. "Helped me come back to life. Got me to see there's hope in the world. Honestly, I find myself waiting for you every day, happy when you come home. I enjoy passing you in the hall, hearing you in the next room. It's like I still have a family. There is someone here. Someone for me to be concerned about. To take care of. So I have to thank you for that, Wendy. I love you for that. For being here. For not being creeped out by this old man."

"You're not old," she said, halting the glass half-way to get the words out before finishing her drink. "Not too old."

"I just wanted to acknowledge the effect you've had on me. Your effect on my recovery. That's all." He smiled as warmly as he could at her; it wasn't difficult.

"You're welcome, Bill." She flashed a smile back at him, using all the muscles. "I like being here, too. You are easy to live with. No rules. Come and go as I want. Like you have trust for me. Mama has rules. Uncle has too many rules. If I don't obey I get punish. Here I can go with school friends. And this house is so big and comfortable. I like it.

And you are very kind to me. Always you say compliment about my cooking."

"Well, you are a good cook. I like everything you prepare."

"We have to eat." She grinned humbly.

"Yes, we do." He patted his belly. "And I have." Frowning, he studied her. "Didn't you eat anything at the Drexlers? You look as slim as before the big Thanksgiving dinner."

That made her laugh. She looked down. Her belly was not pushing out her shirt. He poked her belly with his finger, laughed. She lifted the hem of her shirt. Staring at her belly, he poked his finger again, felt the smoothness of her skin and slid his finger down to her waistband and lingered there.

"It is full," she murmured.

"Doesn't look like it."

22

HE WAS NOT THROWING OUT COMPLIMENTS just to be polite. He genuinely credited Wendy with reviving him, with giving him a reason to go on. But that was a temporary measure. She would leave soon and perhaps forever. And he would be back where he'd been when she called him from the airport.

Taking the pistol out of its carrying case in the event he needed to use it, he put it away in the top drawer of the chest. He realized how easy it would be to slip the gun into a coat pocket—or into a holster in the small of his back, if he purchased one. Nobody would notice. With cold weather arriving, people were wearing coats which could easily conceal a weapon. He thought of the shooter at the mall, wearing a raincoat in the heat of August, and nobody saw it as strange.

Wearing gray sweatpants and a faded Cowboys t-shirt, he climbed into bed, found a good sleeping position, always on his back to start, then on his side. The ceiling he stared at remain mottled. He thought of how the ceiling in a new home might look. It would be fresh, clean, free of memories. And he would be new and free, too, like he was a bachelor again, a young man starting his career, starting a new life in a new place, maybe finding a new partner, starting a new family, who knew?

The gentle knock on the door tore him from the edge of the abyss he was gazing into, ready to make the leap into sleep. The door opened and, of course, there was Wendy. He turned on the lamp. She wore something familiar: flannel pajamas, pale blue with white stripes.

"It's cold," she announced and stepped into the master bedroom. "Can I sleep here tonight?"

Bill sat up in the bed, rubbing his eyes.

"You okay?" he asked. "Nobody looking in the window?"

She shook her head. "The room is too cold."

"Oh." He hadn't yet used the furnace. Oklahoma didn't get cold by his standards until later in autumn, and the house retained warmth from the sun shining through the windows. He was comfortable. But he supposed he needed to make the house comfortable for her.

"Let me turn on the furnace." He got up from the bed and stumbled into the hallway, to the wall console.

He blinked, trying to focus on the little numbers on the screen that kept blinking off whenever he touched the pad to make changes. He cursed, then returned to the bedroom where she had already taken her place in the bed.

"I'll take care of it tomorrow." He told her about using a kerosene stove to heat his little apartment in Japan. At first, he didn't think it was safe, having no experience with a heating stove, and tried going without it at night. He soon bought an electric blanket; it sufficed to get him through the winter, but he suffered when he got up in the morning to a frigid home, heating the water, getting himself ready for school, riding a bike through the cold. She giggled as he told about Japan.

"We use stove in China," she shared. "Mama's home is very old so no heat pipes like modern homes."

"That's too bad," he replied, trying to imagine her there. He slipped his feet under the covers, pulled the sheet and blanket up.

"Are those pajamas Becky's?" he asked as she got up to straighten the covers on her side of the bed.

At his question, she got up and posed, showing the pajama set. "Yes. You said I can wear anything I like."

"Yes, I did. They fit you. They look good on you. And being flannel will keep you warm. But then you leave your feet uncovered."

She pulled her leg up, planted her foot on the bed. Her toenails were pink. "Never wear socks at night. We must let out sleeping spirits or we have bad dreams. Then we wake and feel like no sleep."

"Okay, I get it. But I need socks in the winter."

He switched off the lamp. She got into the bed and both of them lay on their backs a while, continuing to talk.

"Tomorrow is Black Friday," said Bill, his voice sleepy. "Over here, lots of people get up early for special deals at the stores. Before dawn. But not me. I don't like crowds. I don't like getting up early, either."

She didn't respond.

"You know about Black Friday?"

She yawned. "It's day for Black people?"

"Hah! Some would like to think so, but no. Actually it's a day for shopping for Christmas presents. The reason it's called Black Friday is because that's when stores go in the black on their profit/loss ledgers. You see, in the old days accountants used black ink on the pages to show profits." He spent ten minutes explaining the concepts of modern economics and retail customs. "So the day after Thanksgiving is the traditional start of the holiday shopping season. In fact, if you think about it, all American holidays are about either eating or shopping. Even for Labor Day. Some people have to work on Labor Day to handle the customers who're shopping because they're the ones who have the day off. It makes no sense."

"May first is Labor Day in China," she said. "We have parade and sing songs, wave flags."

"Sounds like a wonderful way to spend the day. Must get up and march, huh? So I guess nobody's allowed to sleep in."

"We don't want to sleep in anything. We want to celebrate."

"Yes, of course." He felt her hip bump against him. "Like for New Year's. Nobody invited me to any festive dinner there in Japan. But I was okay with that. I just went sightseeing."

She rolled on her side, facing him, her arms bent up, hands clasped between her cheek and the pillow. Like Barb had done before finally drifting off to sleep and turning over, away from him.

"I want to experience Black Friday shopping," she declared in a voice his tired ears almost did not hear.

"You do?" He struggled to pull himself up from the drowsy abyss. "All right. But not before dawn. We can go later. After the crowds thin out, okay?"

"Where we do it?" she asked, tugging on his sleeve after he yawned.

"I guess...we have to go to...the mall."

* * *

Another night as black as obsidian. Maybe it was good not to have any dreams. When Bill opened his eyes, flat on his back, he found Wendy laying against him, her arm bent over his chest, her face buried in his ribs. He hated to move, not wanting to disturb her. She usually arose before him and got herself ready for school but maybe the large dinner had affected her.

"It's Black Friday," he spoke softly. It was almost ten, he saw on the nightstand clock. "Are we going shopping?"

She stirred, rolled over, grinning. Her eyes remained closed as she stretched out her arms. Drawing them back to her chest, she cooed, "I sleep good last night," and smiled like a child in mother's arms.

Leaving her in bed, Bill went to the bathroom, checked himself in the mirror, a scruffy man who wanted to look younger. He began to shave, running the water until it was hot, splashing his face and applying shaving cream, cleaning the razor and starting the swipes across his cheeks.

"We must hurry or the crowds will be gone," he called out, thinking she'd gotten up and gone to her bathroom down the hall. But she was standing right behind him. He startled, almost nicked his face.

"I don't mind crowd," she said, laying a hand on his back, rubbing his spine. "May I watch you shave face?"

He grimaced. "There's nothing better on TV?"

"I like smooth face."

As he continued, she watched intently and asked questions about American holidays every few strokes. Finally he was done and washed his face, toweled it dry. Setting down the towel, he saw she was gone.

He shook his head, still not fully awake. Should have made coffee first. But now that she'd stepped out, he could complete his morning ritual. He stripped down and tossed his sleepwear out of the bathroom and onto the bed, then ran the shower. It was already hot so he stepped in and slid the glass door shut, realizing as he did that he hadn't closed the bathroom door.

After a few minutes, he heard the water running in the hallway bathroom, opposite side of the wall, and when his shower suddenly turned cooler, he knew she was taking her shower. He was finished anyway. He stepped out and took a towel briskly to his body. Standing before the mirror, he combed his hair, brushed his teeth. He looked decent. But still a man of forty-three.

"Are you ready?" she called from her bedroom.

He stood naked in the master bathroom, the door open, fearing she might enter and see him. He sucked in his gut, decided he didn't look bad. The 'dad bod' was working well: not too much paunch but not the slim, athletic body of his college days—

Stop. Just stop. What are you thinking?

It was going to be a day of shopping—pretending to shop. At least fighting through the crowds. Part of the American experience. Today was for her. It was for him, too. A return to the mall. A test.

"I'm ready," she declared, popping into the master bedroom and catching a side view of Bill in the bathroom.

He reached out and swung the door closed. "Be right there."

Waiting a minute, expecting her to leave the bedroom, he opened the door but she was sitting on the foot of the bed.

"You're still here?" he muttered, not intending to be gruff.

"I wait for you," she sang brightly.

She was ready to go, dressed in blue jeans and a Christmassy sweater of green with red trim over a cream-colored shirt, collar out.

"It's Becky's sweater," she explained at his stare.

Standing with his back to her, he wrapped a towel around his hips and entered the bedroom, going to the chest. Pretending it was Barb sitting there, he had nothing to be concerned with as he got his socks and shorts and dropped the towel to put them on. With his back to her, he slid into a pair of jeans, too. He turned, bare-chested, and strode across the room, past her sitting on the bed, over to the closet, ducked inside and selected a flannel shirt, blue and brown, and pulled it on, began buttoning it as he returned to her.

He grinned. "Don't worry," she had said as he bent over to step into the shorts, "I see Uncle before, no problem."

That didn't make him feel at ease. How much of this uncle did she know exactly? He began to overthink the situation, then decided it shouldn't matter. Not his concern. She would return to this uncle soon enough and he would be on his own again. That was the plan. That had always been the plan.

* * *

He opened the garage door and stepped outside, examining the lawn. The dusting of snow that fell the previous evening was already gone. The snowflakes barely touched the withered blades of grass and melted instantly, leaving no trace. He pondered that image. The snowflakes no longer existed, but they had existed long enough to be seen and appreciated. Like someone's life, he recognized. Someone had existed, and remained in his experience, made a memory—

"Are we going?" called Wendy, standing with the car door open.

Bill returned to the Escape. They backed out of the garage, then he paused on the driveway. He put the car in Park and opened his door.

"Just a minute," he said. "I want to double-check something."

He left the engine running as he went inside.

In the master bedroom, he slid open the top drawer of the chest and retrieved the Glock. He took the magazine out, checked that it was full, reinserted it. He checked that no bullet was in the chamber and the safety was on. He weighed it in his hand. With scarcely a second thought to the implications of carrying a gun into the mall, he slipped the Glock into his coat pocket, which was deep enough to hold it. The rough, brown canvas coat went to mid-thigh, heavy enough for the winters of Oklahoma. It was heavy enough that he worried it would be too hot wearing it in the mall.

But he could not enter that place unprepared. Not that he expected anything to happen there which would cause him to have to use the pistol, but—as his heart beat faster—he had to be ready. If something did happen and he was empty-handed, he could never forgive himself. If he'd been there with Barb and Becky that day, armed, they would still be alive. He thought of Wendy, the way she'd come up behind him in the bathroom, comfortable with him. She was his family now, and he had to protect her.

They grabbed a quick breakfast at Sonic on the way to the mall, pulling into a stall and ordering at the menu console beside the SUV. Wendy was impressed; nothing like that in Beijing. Lots of cars there but no drive-thrus. A server rolled out on skates with their food and Bill paid for his breakfast burrito and Wendy's egg and ham croissant sandwich. Coffee for Bill, O.J. for Wendy. She reminded him of the first

O.J. she ever drank in America, that first night, and laughed at his consternation as he apologized again.

He drove them down May Avenue to the far side of the Quail Run Mall, trying to avoid the main entrance and the traffic there. He parked far from the doors. There were closer spaces but he wanted to walk. It was a bright autumn day, the sky free of clouds, royal blue, and the sun a ball of gold. He paused beside the Escape, the door closed and locked, and stared up at the sky, felt the chilly breeze blow against his face. He remembered the last day that had been like this, a full year ago. Barb had gone to the mall early for the Black Friday sales. He'd gone to get her in the afternoon because her Lexus wouldn't hold the file cabinet she'd bought—

"You okay, Bill?"

He liked the way she said his name, with the *L* falling away so it sounded more like *B*, like the insects that buzz around the yard. Or maybe she was using only his initial, like when her school friends called her Double-U. He smiled; everything was going to be all right.

"Yes. Let's go."

As they walked down the parking lane, Bill kept his left hand in his coat pocket, making sure the Glock didn't fall out, fingering the safety lock. His other hand swung freely. Wendy skipped beside him, keeping up with his long strides.

Others were gathering at the northwest entrance, a crowd pushing through the four doors. Bill looked ahead, seeing if there was a metal detector there. Didn't seem to be. A plump security guard stood like a statue inside the doors, watching shoppers enter. Bill gazed at the guard but they didn't meet eyes.

"I hope you like crowds," he said as they passed through the double doors into the cavernous mall.

"Many people in Beijing," she laughed. "This crowd is small."

"I'll bet."

By going to this lesser entrance he hoped to avoid the crush of the main entrances. He would be at the opposite side of the mall from the store where the shooting happened. He knew he would go to that store, and stand there, maybe offer a prayer; that was part of his willingness to come to the mall. He had to face his fears, his regrets. It was part of his healing, a challenge to himself. But not as the first stop. He would work up to it. They would go around the rest of the mall first.

After quizzing Wendy about what she would like for Christmas, they went into one clothing store after another, browsing at leisure—like all women liked to do, Bill mused, happy to wait while she looked and looked. When she found things to try on he waited through that, his coat feeling heavier and hotter, but he had to keep it on, had to keep the pistol hidden.

"What you want for Christmas?" asked Wendy as they strolled from one store, two bags in her hand, over to the next one, a shoe store, where a pair of tan boots in the window display caught her eye.

"Well, my dear, frankly I don't really need anything." He was about to launch into his standard spiel about needing esoteric things that were not for sale in stores, the bigger things like world peace or ending pollution, but he stopped himself. "Maybe some books." That was the answer he gave Becky whenever she asked. Always books!

They were stacked up on every shelf in the house until Barb made him pack away the ones he'd read. He reminded her he didn't gamble away their money, nor did he spend money supporting a mistress, so she should be glad he only 'wasted' money on books—books he only read once, she liked to point out. So he started using the library and returning books. But still he browsed the bookstore and seldom left without a book or two.

"Okay, Bill," Wendy announced, raising her voice over the din, "I buy you book for Christmas. Where is bookstore?"

"Thanks, Wendy. It's way on the other side from here."

The crowd in front of them was shoulder to shoulder and he took her hand to keep together. His left hand remained in the coat pocket and Wendy held her bags in her right hand. Her left hand felt good in his right hand. He pulled her through the crowd, arriving like a baby being born out the other side with a plop into an empty space.

The Santa Claus House stood before them, with the fat guy on his throne, a screaming kid on his knee—long enough for pictures to be taken by the parents.

"Santa!" Wendy shouted. She turned to Bill. "Can I go there? Is it okay? I sit and take picture?"

"Well, you can see it's more for little kids." But as soon as he told her, a woman in her twenties took her turn posing while a boyfriend snapped a picture. "Or not."

They got in line and eventually, twenty minutes later, Wendy sat on Santa's lap and he took a couple pictures using her phone. She was delighted, mugging for the camera, playfully tugging on Santa's beard, and giving him a big hug before she hopped off and returned to Bill standing outside the little picket fence.

"It's great memory," she cheered, giving him a triumphant smile.

"Can you send me a copy of those?"

"Sure I can, Bill."

As they proceeded around the mall, Wendy tugged his arm every few shops to stop and have a look. He began to feel tired. He wanted to take off the coat but dared not. Maybe they could sit in the food court for a while. He didn't want to let Wendy go off on her own, not in this boisterous crowd, not with the gloom and doom hanging in the mall—although people around him seemed to have forgotten what happened here a few months earlier. Holiday cheer could shoo away anything, he grumbled.

They came to a set of movie posters on the huge columns holding up the mall's tent-like ceiling. Wendy pointed at one poster, saying she wanted to see it.

"Are you sure?" he asked dismissively.

The poster suggested a romantic comedy, the principal couple embraced in the center, lesser characters around them. They were dressed in some kind of space uniforms. There were spaceships in the background, flashing laser beams.

"Okay, might be interesting," he decided. Sci-fi romance he could put up with. It would be a good break from walking around. He could sit and relax. They headed to the theater entrance, down a set of escalators, beside the packed food court.

He swiped his card to buy tickets at the kiosk and they entered, a human tearing the tickets. Bill saw they had renovated the theater; he hadn't seen a movie there in more than a year, he realized. Everything was different. Flopping down in the reclining seats, he noted how some seats were designed for a couple to sit together—so they could snuggle during the film. He scoffed at that idea.

Sitting with Wendy felt odd, but when she scooted next to him, up against him as the trailers started, laying her head on his shoulder several times during the movie like they were on a date, it began to feel right. He pulled his arms out of his coat when they sat down, leaving the coat between his back and the faux leather seat, careful that the Glock rested in the pocket folded beside his thigh. He kept a hand on his thigh to make sure the pistol stayed close. His other arm rested around Wendy's shoulders—just as he'd done back when he was in high school, taking Karen or Mary or Sheila to movies on Saturday nights, followed by pizza or tacos.

But in those days no one would've thought to attack a theater. No one would've expected it or prepared for it. Not until that violent action movie came out which was so popular that some mentally unstable bastard tried to act it out, barging into the theater from an exit door, rifle blazing. He recalled the reports stating that, in the first minute, moviegoers thought the gunshots were sound effects from the film. Then they dove for cover or tried to run out.

Bill looked around the theater. He tried to twist sideways to get a look behind them. Sitting near the center, he had a good view in front but feared someone coming down the aisle behind him. He didn't pay much attention to the movie but constantly checked each side and behind him. He planned his escape route. He thought how he would push Wendy down to the floor if....

She got annoyed, sat up straight, giving him space to fidget.

I have to be ready. He thought of the swim meet, when that girl, the crazy one, approached Wendy and he freaked out that she might have a gun but she just wanted an autograph, or phone number, or whatever was written on her notebook. He felt silly. But the fear was real. He felt it with every breath sitting in the theater, walking in the mall. Everything looked different now. Every moment was a check of sight lines and escape plans. His cortisol was through the roof.

He hardly noticed when the movie ended. The rising music was his first clue, the scrolling credits his second. Wendy stretching her arms and smiling at him was third. She asked if he liked it and he had to say he did, even though he wasn't too sure what happened. Some space adventure, the guy trying to get his girl back from an alien species that had kidnapped her. She was a princess, he a space pirate. Wendy liked it and that was all that mattered.

Exiting the theater, she took his hand, swinging their arms in a lively arc, her sacks in her other hand. She talked about the movie, delighting in the experience. Her first American movie seen in a big theater! She could understand it easily, too. He let her be happy, and he also felt delight as he watched her pretty face slide through different emotions.

The food court was right there, he mentioned, and less crowded now, being two hours later, so he suggested they get something to eat. They strolled along the counters, seeing their choices. The Chinese food didn't look good, Wendy warned, wrinkling her nose the cute way she did. With an international menu, he suggested she should try something new and different. So they went to the Greek counter and ordered gyro plates.

A girl's voice cried out: "Wendy!"

She turned and saw a circle of girls from their school.

"Mister Masters!" called another girl. The noise made it hard to hear so everyone was speaking louder. "Haven't seen you since forever. How're you doing?"

Bill turned to the girls, realized he still held Wendy's hand. He let go and pulled out his wallet to pay for their lunches. He saw the girls' amusement at seeing him holding hands with a girl who was their age. Wendy said something to the others but he couldn't hear because of the din.

"May I sit with them, Bill?" she asked, coming up to him.

"Sure, go ahead."

He felt glad to be free for a few minutes, a chance to recompose himself and catch his breath. His fatigue came from the noise and the crowds, not from being with her. Let her go off with her friends for a while. They would get back together in a little while.

When the food was put on the counter, he gave one plate to Wendy and took his own to another table, sitting alone with her sacks. He could hear the loudest girl, the one initially addressing them, talking over the noise two tables behind him. Eating the pita folded around the gyro meat, Tajiki sauce dabbled on top, he listened to what snatches of conversation he could hear.

The girls seemed delighted, seeing Wendy holding hands with that old man. And her guardian essentially! Wasn't he? Her teacher, too, if things had been different. Wendy stuck up for him, though, saying they didn't want to get separated. Another girl made a joke about not being separated. The teasing increased. He expected she might leave them and join him to get away from it.

"It's daddy-daughter date," he heard Wendy boldly state.

The girls made jokes about that idea, their words running together.

"Yeah, if you're like ten years old. Twelve tops," said one girl.

Wendy was not deterred. "But I love him!"

That stopped all of them. She backed up and gave reasons for her announcement, but he couldn't make out the details. It was enough the girls seemed shocked by her declaration. He suspected she used the word to mean how family members love each other.

"So you have sex?" the loudmouth dared ask, making certain, he thought, that the whole food court could hear her.

"No," Wendy exclaimed. "We don't do it."

"But you slept with him, you said," one of the girls checked.

"Yes, sleep with him—"

The girls howled with derision. Eww! Mister Masters? How creepy!

"A burglar looked in window. I was scared," Wendy spoke. "I go sleep with Bill to be safe. It's not strange thing."

"Bill!" they roared with laughter.

"He keep me warm," she added, as though that information would resolve their concerns.

"Yeah, I bet he does," the loudmouth blurted out.

Good girl, he thought, feeling a warm glow form in his icy heart. She was absolutely right. They had been good. Nothing wrong with what they had done. Just too many gossips.

"In America 'sleep' means have sex," the loudmouth explained.

"Then what you say if you want to mean sleep?" asked Wendy.

The girls had no answer, then exploded into more teasing.

"Yeah, I can see that," was the next phrase he could understand.

"I guess he's okay. If you like older men," said another.

Something, something. About sex, it seemed.

"Older guys, they know what to do. Yeah, not like those fuckin' high school boys. Too shy or too grabby. Hate 'em."

"I hate rape culture!" barked one girl.

"Hey! He lost his wife, don't forget. And Becky. That's why he's not in school. He went crazy."

Something more about mental health.

"He needs some love and care."

"Wendy's good for that."

"A perfect China doll's what he needs."

"You *are* perfect, girl. But you can always show more skin. Work that cleavage, babe. Make him beg."

More of the girls' laughter.

He'd finished his lunch by then, trying to ignore the taunts. Mr. Masters was not creepy, he told himself. Just a regular guy. An angry, depressed man. Sure, he needs love and care. But he would need that even if he was a regular guy in a regular world. Like everyone.

Eventually they got up. Wendy took her tray to the trash as the other girls walked away, leaving theirs on the table. One girl, seeing her act, returned to the table and tossed her trash away, too, then ran to catch up with the others.

"They invite me for sleepover party tomorrow," said Wendy after coming to his table and sitting. "Can I go?"

"Another sleepover," he said with a chuckle. "What do you girls do at these sleepovers?"

"Most of all is talking." She didn't recognize his remark as joking. "I come back on Sunday. They will pick up me." She watched him gather up his trash and take it to the bin. "I need to go to pharmacy."

He looked at her, puzzled.

"Is it right word?" she asked.

"Yes, it is."

He sensed disappointment in her, like the day had been ruined.

Bill didn't take her hand again as they left the food court. Wendy seemed more serious, or tired.

They had two more stops. Then they could go home, Bill explained. First, the bookstore. He could browse for an hour easily, but for her sake he limited his browsing to his three favorite sections yet found nothing he wanted to buy. He found Wendy in the next aisle, looking over shelves of paperbacks.

"The trashy novels," said Bill with a sigh.

"It's not trashy," said Wendy, a fat paperback with a racy cover in her hands. "They all rich people. Not trashy."

"I'll get it for you, if you like. Then you'll learn about the American dream, for sure."

Remembering his book was going to be a gift from Wendy, he led her to the History section and examined the books about China. She leaned against him looking at the pictures in one book, adding her comments. She pointed to a black and white picture of peasants bent over working a barren field and told about her grandparents.

"They died in Culture Revolution," she said sadly. "I never meet them. Mama was only baby and cared by big sister."

"It was a tough time," he said, giving her a one-arm hug. "I know the basic history, but this book will teach me more."

"Maybe some things you don't want to learn," she said.

He frowned. "We must learn everything, good and bad."

Letting her carry the book over to the checkout, he watched her pay for it with the money she brought from China.

Spinning away from the cashier, she pressed the book to his chest, grinning like a Christmas morning kid.

"Merry Christmas!"

"Oh, no," he said, gently pushing the book back to her. "Not until Christmas morning. And it has to be wrapped, too."

He pointed to where a charity group was wrapping purchases for donations. She handed over the book and a woman in an ugly holiday sweater wrapped it, made it beautiful using gold paper and red ribbons. Bill slipped some dollars into the box.

It didn't take a map of the mall to know where he was. His heart was thumping; he could hear it over the cacophony of the shoppers' glee. He was getting close, putting it off as long as possible.

The store approached him like a menacing monster, stood before him, an unyielding monument, a mountain of granite. He couldn't go further. Wendy halted one step behind him, staring ahead.

It was boarded up, but in an attractive way, the same as when a store moves out and they block off the front while renovation goes on inside for the next tenant. He wondered if any other company had rented the space, planning to move in after the holidays. Or whether the space would forever be off-limits. They couldn't very well turn it into a memorial park. The pastel blue of the wall, with the mall's logo on each panel, made it seem like something good was happening inside. Soon a wonderful new shopping experience would appear.

"Are you okay?" asked Wendy softly, stepping up to him and taking his arm in her hands, the corded sack handles around her wrist.

He nodded, continuing to gaze ahead.

"This is the place?" she asked, voice rough. Either she was choked with emotion or she had strained her voice from talking over the noise in the food court.

Again he nodded, his hand feeling the pistol in his coat pocket.

"I'm sorry, Bill."

"Yeah.... Me, too."

He stepped toward the panels, placed his hand flat against one of them as though he expected to feel something, a vibe, a sensation, a voice....

Bowing his head, he mouthed a few words of prayer.

He opened his eyes and regarded the glow of daylight to his right: the mall entrance, one of the two main entrances, eight doors wide. Easy to enter, easy to exit. Good for a quick hit. No guards—well, there were two of them now for the holiday season. The first store inside, right on the corner after a short jog up the wide corridor from the doors. Outside he could see four concrete barriers designed to prevent a terrorist from crashing a vehicle through the doors. Like that would ever happen in Oklahoma! Truck parked next to a building, packed with explosives, sure, but not a generic ramming. Instead, a lone gunman had slipped between the barriers and did the damage, all the damage that could be done—

"Oh, by the way," he said, turning to Wendy with a cough. "Your laptop? They said it still runs fine. No damage from being dropped. Should be the same as when you last used it. Like it never happened."

23

FRIDAY EVENING turned into a bumpy country road, each trying to avoid the other, fearing a crash. Something had been said, maybe by her friends at the mall, he guessed, which might have made her rethink their relationship. He was comfortable sitting in the living room, trying to watch a football game on TV. It had been part of his routine before and he knew he had to get back to it if he was going to return to normal. He continued to contemplate what normal might mean and hardly paid attention to the game, giving an occasional glance at the gold-wrapped book on the coffee table.

Wendy was in her room. He didn't know what she was doing, which was how it should be. He didn't need to monitor her every minute. Becky had gotten to the point where she craved independence, too. Wendy said he had no rules for her, that she could come and go as she pleased, as though that was a good thing. However, then she asked his permission to go to the girls' sleepover, like she needed it. Perhaps she wanted him to say 'no' so she wouldn't have to go.

By the beeps and dings emanating from her bedroom, he guessed she was playing a video game again.

It was late when he was ready to go to bed, tired and drowsy. He got up from the couch and the floor creaked under his foot. The game noise had long ago ended.

"Are you coming to bed?" a voice called from his bedroom.

At first he thought it was his imagination. But as he entered, he saw that Wendy was in the bed, tucked in under the covers, a string-strap top visible above the covers as she leaned back against the headboard.

"You're sleeping here tonight?" he asked, repressing a yawn.

"It's cold in that room," she said, pointing.

"Okay.... Yeah, I still haven't fixed the furnace setting. Sorry." He let out a sigh which he thought she might take as a rebuke of her presence in his room. Too tired to argue, he stripped down to his shorts with no concern for her. If he appeared uncouth, so be it; she could leave if she wanted to, go sleep in her own bed. He didn't know which would be worse: her being there or her not being there.

In the bathroom, he swung the door closed but it did not shut tight. He did his bedtime routine, sitting so the pissing noise wouldn't wake Barb. He flushed, washed his hands and face, feeling whiskers. He brushed his teeth, staring in the mirror, wondering who the man was.

"Okay, let's sleep," he said, exiting the bathroom and going around to his side of the bed.

She reached out and grabbed the corner of the covers, flipped them back like opening the door for him, grinning all the while. He sat on the edge a moment, then swung himself up into the bed. He reached for the lamp on the nightstand.

In the darkness, he settled into his first position, flat on his back.

"Goodnight," he said in a sleepy voice.

"Goodnight," Wendy responded, then scooted up to kiss his cheek.

Waking in the morning, Bill found himself alone in the bed. Noises in the kitchen told him Wendy was already up. He smelled coffee.

Making himself presentable in the bathroom, he shuffled out to the kitchen in his robe, sat at the table, greeting her.

"Thanks for making breakfast," he said. "You are too good to me. I like having you here."

"You very warm person," she said with a soft chuckle, working the frying pan. "You heat bed like furnace."

"I heat up *the* bed like *a* furnace," he muttered.

Wendy laughed. "You do!"

"So you're saying I'm, mmm, hot?" He stood and came up behind her, laying his hands on her shoulders.

"Very warm. Like fry pan." She turned her head, wrinkling up her nose and puckering her mouth in her usual rebuke.

He returned to the table and she served the breakfast.

As they ate the eggs and diced ham, emptied a bowl of grapes, he suggested they go for a drive. They could look at apartments. As they arrived at the mall, he saw three new complexes standing on what used to be empty fields. He didn't want to be near the Quail Run Mall, but it would be convenient and they were new. He wanted to be the first one to live in the unit, free of anyone's presence, free of memories.

It was another sunny day, and Bill looked over at Wendy, expecting to see Barb pulling out her sunglasses.

As he parked in front of the office of the first complex, he wondered if Wendy should go in with him. With a blink and a bite of his lip, he decided he didn't care. Let them think whatever.

He talked with a sales girl who took his information and gave him a key on a tracking monitor, sent him to a vacant unit. Second floor, facing west. The unit would catch the afternoon heat. An upper floor would be safer. He could leave a window open without worrying that someone would climb up to get inside. He checked the siding on the outside to see if it had any secure footholds. The pipe that ran up the side could be grasped and a man could shimmy up it, he decided. The balcony could be accessed by a grappling hook and rope.

"What are you looking at?" asked Wendy.

"Safety," he replied.

They went inside. He stopped in the front entrance to survey the living room, the kitchen separated by a bar counter. The hallway back to the bedroom and bathroom started beside the kitchen. He walked straight back to the bedroom, checked it, then the bathroom. For a new place, it seemed rather plain. He could live there, sure. Enough for a bachelor who couldn't afford a nicer place, but he was worth more than that. He still wanted to be comfortable.

"What do you think?" he asked Wendy as he was ready to leave.

She made comparisons to the old place she shared with her mother in China. When she described it, he felt embarrassed to be showing off even this simple apartment with no fancy amenities. The uncle paid for their home after her father died. Bill began to understand.

"I live here, too?" she asked, waving her hand around.

"I know it's small. But, well, I'll be living here a long time while you'll be here for a semester. That is…if you return after New Year's." He left the last sentence hanging in the air. "So I really only need one bedroom and one bathroom. It's enough for me."

She pouted, turned away from him and he saw her hand go to her face, followed by a few sniffles. No matter what she might think of this apartment, or the house, it must have sounded like the only option she had was to return to China and deal with the creepy uncle. He wanted to encourage her; he thought to say, yes, she could live with him—which she would do if she returned after the break.

But then? After graduation in May? Where would she go?

They left Tuscany Gardens, which had Italian trappings but not much else, and drove across the street to the next property, Palomino Estates, which featured a Western theme: a pair of wagon wheels, a longhorn skull, and bunches of sage grass at the entrance.

Parked at the office, he surveyed the grounds and wondered if he was going insane, wanting to live within sight of the mall where his wife and daughter had been killed. He should be looking at apartments as far away from the mall as possible. Someplace like Yukon or El Reno, where it would take him an hour to drive to school, an hour of contemplation each day, each way, to clear his soul.

"If you lived here, it would be only a short walk over to the mall," he said, staring at the office through the windshield. "Maybe you could get a job at one of the stores." He thought a moment, realized his error. "Or maybe better not work there. You can do better."

He turned to her, sitting patiently in the seat beside him, an inch shorter than Barb. The girl's face was red from tears but otherwise so pretty. Like a doll—a perfect ceramic china doll, like her friends had said. Pure and pale…without wearing cosmetics, it seemed when he looked closer. She pouted and he unsquinted his eyes, leaned back.

"I get job here?" she asked. "Can I?"

"A student job, probably, with your visa. We'll have to check. But I…I was thinking also that…you could stay here. I mean in Oklahoma. And you could go to college here, study Engineering."

"Go to college?" She seemed surprised but not opposed to the idea.

"Yes." He took a deep breath. "Barb and I set up a college fund for Becky, so we would be able to afford it. Now it's…it's just going to sit there. One of the requirements is it can only be used for education, so I can't just claim it back and buy, for example, a sportscar." He studied her expression: mysterious, yes, but her eyes were bright, mouth firm, lips dry, a little rough. "You can have it. The college fund. I mean, if you really want to study here. In fact, there's a good university near the house. UCO—The University of Central Oklahoma. I'm sure they have an Engineering program. You could study there."

"And I live with you?" Her voice was hopeful.

"Yes, of course. That would make sense. If you want to, I mean. Or you can live on the campus, in a dormitory, with other students."

"It's good idea," she sang as he gestured to exit the vehicle.

"Think about it."

They entered the office, Wendy following behind Bill, and were greeted by a woman at a desk. The usual statements and questions. He handed over his identification in order to go look at a unit. Only half were occupied as it had just opened, he was glad to hear.

"Just for you?" asked the perky woman, Vicky on her name tag. She glanced at Wendy in the chair beside Bill.

He grinned. "Yes." He couldn't help turning and regarding Wendy, who smiled like they had a scheme in mind. "My daughter will be going to college, so I don't need a big house now. Thought I'd simplify my life. But she may visit sometimes...so maybe a two-bedroom unit. Is that all right? A single guy living in a two-bedroom?"

"We rent two-bedrooms to single people," Vicky responded with a grin and a wink. "It's the same rent. Some here are professionals who need an office. Or, like you said, some of our residents have children or grandchildren visiting."

Wendy reached out and lay her hand on his arm. Vicky caught that, gave a smirk. Lots of divorced dudes trying to sneak their gold-diggers in, her expression seemed to say. Bill pursed his lips, took a breath. There was nothing wrong with what he said or his intentions. He gave Wendy a smile, and took the key.

Inside the unit, empty and clean, smelling of fresh paint, he noted the attractive decorations of the place, the extra touches, the spacious modern kitchen, like it was a full home, not just a temporary pad. He could see the mall from the wide living room windows. Wendy stood in the doorway of the larger bedroom as though measuring the space, feeling the softness of the carpet after slipping off her Uggs by the front door. He remained in the living room, visualizing where each piece of furniture might go. New furniture.

They stood at arm's length, and when Bill reached behind himself as he faced the living room windows, he found Wendy's hand waiting for him. He tried to clasp her hand but it darted away, then returned to poke his hand, a game which continued another minute as they stood practically back to back, he on the living room's hardwood floors, she on the bedroom's plush carpet. He grabbed her hand, once and for all, and she struggled to pull away, so he let her. But her hand hooked two of his fingers. Using only their fingers, the tug-of-war continued, each trying to pull the other into one room or the other. Finally she won and he tripped backwards into her room.

"This is my room?" she asked in a voice so soft he had to ask her to repeat what she said. He stood with his back to hers, then turned half-way around, his fingers remaining hooked in hers.

"Like I said before, I'll be here a long time. You, only a semester."

"Or college?" Her voice turned silky.

"College would be another four years. Yes, you could live here for a few more years. That would be nice."

He liked the idea of this girl padding around his home, making it smell better, feel better, helping with the cooking, and greeting him with affectionate hugs. And he would help her, protect her, care for her. After a moment, he told her he liked the idea. Even if she chose to stay in a dormitory, she could visit him. They would see each other, have dinner, talk, and it would be like he still had a daughter.

He took her hand and she gave his hand a squeeze. He stepped up against her, facing her, gazing down at her.

"Wendy...." He was about to say something about needing to clarify their relationship. It was already too flirty. Too awkward. He didn't like her teasing, especially when he wasn't allowed to respond the way he wanted to. In fact, it just wasn't—

"I will share with you," she said, leaning forward against him, her hand still clasping his.

With her breasts brushing against his chest, she let go of his hand and raised her arms. She clasped his head between her palms and pulled him down to her. Halting in front of her face, their eyes met then closed as she drew him to her, and her lips pressed hard against his mouth.

He didn't stop to think about what was happening but let her soft mouth move against his, a ravenous kiss. Her hands slid down the sides of his face, over the day-old growth of whiskers, and rested on his shoulders while their lips remained locked, fumbling for the best position, refusing breaths, desiring the touch that had been missing for so long. His breathing stopped. The room stopped; he noticed only then that it had been spinning. The sun's rays through the windows froze and the world halted, then resumed its steady turning as they broke apart.

"I'm sorry," she sputtered, wiping her mouth with the back of her hand. "Very sorry."

"Don't be," he replied, sucking air. "That was nice."

Taking his words as a compliment, she threw herself at him, her arms around his neck, her head turned, cheek resting against his shoulder, a full hug. And he wrapped his arms around her as he held her off the floor.

They hadn't been home ten minutes when the girls arrived to pick up Wendy. Huddled in the doorway with her bag at her feet, she reached up to hug him, kissed his cheek in view of the carload of girls. He could hear their boisterous reaction, so he acted like he was annoyed by her attention. Secretly, he enjoyed having her hang on him.

Closing the door, he stepped back as he heard the car drive away, thinking *Shit, what am I doing?*

He sat on the couch staring at the TV, seeing in its blank screen the endless depths of the universe. Thoughts of Wendy filled his head, the kiss playing over and over. The one in the apartment. That one had opened his whole universe, made him want to explore, to go on an adventure. A kiss which switched on his desire. He felt his desire rise, like a Saturn V ready for lift-off, eager to blast into space.

Shaking his head, he stumbled down the hallway, crashing into the master bedroom and falling on the bed. He thought more about that kiss and his hand went to his crotch, considered masturbation to ease his frustration. He hadn't done that in months, since well before the incident at the mall. He had no place for it, no time to pull it off. It was like he was a teenager again, hiding it from his parents. But somehow he felt odd doing that with her as his muse.

He cursed, jumping up. The checklist remained in his head, the things to do in order to move on into his new life. He had to clear out Barb's office. The big desk would be the hardest part. So he changed clothes, wearing sweatpants and an old t-shirt, free to work up a good sweat hefting things. That would cure his excitement, bring him down to earth.

He surveyed the room, then went to work clearing everything off the shelves. He packed some items in boxes, a gift for Lexi who might need them. The knickknacks and mementoes on the shelves he set on the desk. He glanced at the little side desk, barely wide enough to set a laptop on with a stack of student papers beside it. Suddenly he hated that desk. He despised the way it was so small and pushed to the side, an afterthought in her business domain.

Putting all his effort into breaking down the side desk and carrying it out to the garage, the hard breathing and moisture running down his back was a sign he was a man. He regretted letting Barb treat him like she was the head of the family. He still got to write his stories, buy his books, go for a jog around the neighborhood. He got the Ford Escape to lift his status while she got the Lexus to fit her executive lifestyle. Sometimes she rewarded him with sex; it never seemed they had sex because of love. It was a reward for doing what she wanted him to do, he realized, standing in the garage, seeing his hands roughed up and bleeding from the wood of the little desk.

He returned to the office and moved the items he'd set on the top of the desk back to a shelf. The big desk was heirloom quality though not an heirloom, merely purchased from an expensive furniture store. It was a beautiful piece. So many days and nights she worked there, door closed, music playing in the background, working through documents of her business, which he never understood. In some ways he wanted to keep it; he would use it himself for his work. However, the logistics of moving it to an apartment—the second bedroom as his office?—was daunting. And those memories would remain to haunt him.

No, better to give it to Lexi. It would look good in the office there, lend an air of tradition. He would call Lexi on Monday and offer it to her. That meant he had to clean it out this weekend, and the day was going fast. Way too heavy to move, worse with the drawers full of paper. It had to be emptied.

He examined each pedestal, looked in each drawer, found them stuffed with papers and folders. Except the one on the lower right side, which was locked. He wasn't one to snoop around; he never thought there would be anything interesting enough to be worth the effort. Now he had to empty that drawer. He looked for the key in the drawer over the chair well, took out every pencil and paperclip and set them on the top of the desk. Cards and stamps and a couple flash drives. Scraps of papers and old sticky notes. No key. He sat back, thinking.

His eyes shifted to the items on the shelf, lingered on the vase with the fake flowers. He got up, went to it and picked up the vase. With a few shakes, he heard something clink inside. He removed the flowers and poured out a key into his hand.

Unlocking the drawer, he pulled it open. Stuffed full of papers and folders. The obvious question was why this drawer was locked and the others not, even though they seemed to contain the same kind of papers. He sifted through the top few inches of papers, then decided to heft them out wholesale and drop them on the top of the desk. The stack shifted, slid over half the desktop.

At the bottom of the drawer were a few smaller items, probably left there when the desk was new and the drawer empty. He picked up an envelope, saw '6k' written on it. Inside, as he dared to expect, was a bunch of cash. Hmm, thought Bill. Rainy day fund? Innocent enough. Runaway fund? Counting it, all hundreds, he found the mark to be correct. He had some money stashed away somewhere in the house, too, but only a few hundred. He thought where it might be.

Another envelope, unmarked, seemed to have a letter inside. He took out the letter and opened its tri-folded pages, straightened them, saw it was handwritten. Barb's handwriting.

Dear Bill, it began, and he stopped cold.

His heart rippled in fear. Did he really want to read this? What kind of letter was it? He suspected it was a farewell letter, back when they were having their problems.

He slumped in her executive chair, taking long breaths, and read slowly, searching for hidden meaning in every curve and loop of her handwriting. But the words he did not admire. She laid out the case for leaving him. She made it crystal clear what his short-comings were. It wasn't working out. She felt stifled, unable to enjoy her life. She explained methodically why it would be best for her and Becky to leave, to live their own lives. She no longer loved him, no longer wanted to live with him, and now, in fact, she'd also found someone she did love. They would be going away together. She wished him luck, ended with a compliment and a platitude about his valuable help with her thesis she had to write for her MBA degree.

Sincerely, Barbara

He realized his eyes were wet. Sincerely. At least she was being sincere, not phony. He started to wad up the letter, stopped, smoothed it out, re-examined certain passages. It was quite well-written. Nothing to mark. Yes, he never was exciting. He focused too much on himself, his pursuits, his interests. He wasn't good at keeping up the house or the yard.

Even his daughter, according to Barb, never felt a connection with him entering her teen years. Becky constantly complained about him getting in the way, asking too many questions, being a jerk in front of her friends. Always trying to make a joke. She hated him—even though he'd never done anything wrong, never acted improper, never cursed at her like many fathers did. In fact, he was always encouraging her.

His throat tightened. Even in her ghostly demise Barb could get to him, cut his heart. He reminded himself she wrote the letter three years earlier, before they reconciled. And she hadn't given it to him. But she hadn't tossed it away, either.

They had been a good family the past two years. Before, it was a bunch of misunderstandings and the desire to try something different. All marriages go through that, he considered. He ran down his list: no, he hadn't done anything she could use as a viable excuse to leave him. She simply wanted something different. But did she have to mention another guy? She didn't need to do that.

And if she had left him, taken Becky with her, and they lived separate lives, perhaps with him seeing Becky every other weekend, then.... And then? What if they had still gone to the mall that Saturday morning? Would he have been called? Would he drive down there, talk to a reporter before learning his two ladies were among the victims?

Would he have felt different?

Bill couldn't sleep that night, haunted by flashes of happier times. But they were all slightly askew, not quite as he remembered them. That was the curse of dreams. He got up several times to pee or get a drink. He found a couple bottles of beer in the back of the fridge, specialty brews Barb had been saving. He opened one, drank it slowly as he sat on the couch in the dark, staring at the dark walls, thinking how everything he had come to cherish was ready for the junkyard.

"It can all go," he grumbled. Get rid of everything. Sell the house. Run off to some forgotten land, live in a tent. Or a hole in the ground. He didn't care.

But what about the girl? He contemplated Wendy, the vixen he both wished to consume and hold away lest he be accused of things that would land him in jail. He'd already promised to wait until she was gone before he did anything—anything that would end everything. She was leaving soon. Over the Christmas break would be a good time. If she didn't return, fine. If she did, well, she wouldn't need to know all the gruesome details. She could live with the Drexlers. They seemed to get along. He would be gone, so nothing would matter to him.

Finishing the bottle, he had the urge to check the Glock, resting in the top drawer of the chest, fully loaded, waiting for an excuse.

He wondered who it was that caught Barb's eye. Someone from her office? He tried to conjure images of the people he saw when he visited a few times. Either an older executive or a young buck, someone who might model swimwear but work in the mail room. Mr. Henderson, her immediate boss...no, probably not. He would have a fling possibly but not run away with her. A guy named Ricky she mentioned once or twice, a younger colleague? He could see her running away with a guy like that.

With Ricky in his mind—based on what he remembered from those visits to Harding & Finch before Barb left the company to start her own business with Lexi—he eased himself from the couch and stumbled to the master bedroom. He stared at the bed, wondering if she ever brought him, whoever he was, to this room, into this bed. Or did she do the polite thing and go to a hotel?

He wanted to laugh but didn't have the strength.

That girl had been in the bed a few times. Was that his payback?

She had nudged against him, warming him, exciting him. Daring him to make a move. Or not. Perhaps she was exactly as innocent as she seemed. But the kiss....

She knew what the hell she was doing. Had she really expected him to do more? Didn't she know what was legal or illegal? Maybe, like many girls in school, she was testing her limits, seeing how far she could drive this man crazy without him being able to act. If he did act, then what? He could spend the rest of his life in a prison cell, forgotten by everyone he ever knew. That, actually, might not be a bad plan, he considered. One moment's ordinary pleasure—one that would give him a memory that lasted forever. Everything would be easy after that.

24

SHE RETURNED LATE in the afternoon, just before dinner, less perky than after the other sleepovers. Maybe she hadn't gotten much sleep, he thought, the way these sort of get-togethers tend to go.

He was in Barb's office when she returned, letting herself in with her key, then punching the code into the security box by the door. He heard it all. She called out to him, stepping warily down the hallway. He responded after a moment and she seemed to breathe a sigh of relief. Apparently, he'd gotten her to be afraid of this house.

He faced the window, his back to the open doorway, as he leaned over the desk to reach a stack of papers that had tipped over. The whole afternoon had been loose pages fluttering just out of his grasp or a bunch of papers collected in folders that seemed to scatter whenever he touched them. He'd picked up errant documents too many times, cursing as he gathered them into boxes.

"So how was the sleepover?" he asked, sensing her presence in the doorway but stretching for fleeing papers.

"Oh...." She was thinking how to describe it. "Not too bad."

"Well, that's better than bad. What happened?" He was just making conversation, not digging for information, as he brought some papers back onto the desktop. "Not much sleep?"

"Oh, we got sleep but too much talking," she said with a weary sigh. "They ask too many questions. Make me feeling uncomfortable. I try to answer best as I can say. They keep pushing me."

"Pushing you? Questions about what?" He straightened up as he checked the steadiness of the stacks of papers.

"About...you."

"Me?"

When he turned around she stood only an inch from him. He was sweaty, wearing an old t-shirt with several torn holes and ragged jogging shorts. He had dropped the sweatpants once his work became heated. With no concern, she swung her arms up around his neck. Her lips quivered as they came to his.

Grabbing her wrists, clasping them in his hands, he brought her arms down from his neck, holding them at her sides.

He gave her a reassuring smile. "You see how people can talk. They see something quite innocent and make up stories about what they see, turn it into something not so innocent."

"They asking too many questions about you," she said in a light voice which he took to mean she expected he would be happy with her answer, "and me."

"Of course." Bill took a deep breath, released one wrist so he could scratch his nose. She didn't struggle to get away but grimaced, a lovely expression that threatened to disarm him just when he'd loaded his words. "Listen, Wendy.... I think we have to understand some things. I don't know what you do over in China. Pretty much like in Japan, I'd guess. I expect you're more conservative than in America, even though you've modernized, gotten a lot of Western ideas tossed at you—the TV, internet, movies. But not everything is as it appears here. There are laws. Laws to curb emotion, human behavior." He gave a chuckle. "Kinda like in *Nineteen-Eighty-Four*. You read it?"

She shook her head.

"In that book love is forbidden."

She narrowed her eyes. "Why they do that?"

"So there are laws," he continued. "And I don't want to break any of them."

"What laws?" She frowned, wresting her other hand away from his grip. "I'm good girl."

She made another attempt to hug him which he blocked with his forearm, acting like he was reaching for something.

"Laws about what people can do with each other." He smiled to himself, the words coming together better than he'd practiced. "Laws that govern what a man of my age can do...with a girl of your age. Even if she says it's okay. You have to be eighteen to do what I...what I might want to do. Anything a man would want to be able to do, I mean. A normal man. So please...please stop flirting."

She looked angry. "Flirting?"

"Yes, flirting." He frowned at her surprised expression. "I like it. I like it too much. I like what you do when you're with me, but...you make it so hard...." He was master of his own rhetoric, he realized, shaking his head. "So hard to be with you. I mean, because you're so beautiful, and truly lovely, and.... It confuses me. So let's stop all the teasing and playing around. All right?"

She tore away from him, her face tense, and he heard the rush of tears, like a waterfall crashing down her stony cheeks. The door to Becky's room slammed shut, the echo lasting a minute. With Barb's office next to her room, he could hear sobbing.

He didn't hate her. She was a distraction, a beautiful distraction—a barricade that kept him from going to the edge of the abyss, the place he wanted to go, just to have a look, to stare down into the darkness and try to see if his alter ego looked back.

"It seems you are not yet finished with your journey to recovery," said Dr. Wisniewski, sitting opposite him, notebook poised.

"It's an endless loop," he said gruffly. "I believe 'recursive' is the term we like to use when we describe the writing process. Get an idea, organize, draft, revise, publish. But you might jump around between any of those steps before you're finished."

"Well put," said the doctor.

"It's kind of like what I tell my students when I give them a writing assignment. Tell me something personal, something you've actually experienced, not something made-up. But not too personal. I don't want to be shocked. I tell them what's written in English class stays in English class. Unless they confess to a serious crime. And I've had a few come very close."

The doctor smiled and he wondered what he'd said wrong.

"I don't know what I'd write about her." He took a breath. "For me, it's both easier and harder with her there. I mean, having her there, being in my life, coming and going. She's part angel, part devil. What do you call those female demons? Succubus? I think that's it. I always remember 'succubus' because they suck...uh, they suck out a man's soul. I didn't mean, like, a blowjob. Sorry."

The doctor nodded, pinched her lips. "Interesting." She made a note. "And do you have the urge for a blowjob?"

"You mean do I have any sexual frustration?"

"Yes, that's another way of putting it."

"Now I do. I confess. Before, I couldn't have cared less about sex. Too busy with all the grieving shit. Maybe that's part of the journey, too, huh? Wanting sex."

"Returning to everything you enjoyed before."

"I never enjoyed...." He looked away. "I never had so much sex *before* that I could say I'm returning to that kind of *before* again. Let's just say that Barb and I lived a cordial life the past two years."

"I see." The doctor scribbled for a minute.

Bill sat back with a sigh, rubbed his hands together. "So that's how our Thanksgiving break went. Loads of fun." He studied the ceiling, hoping to see an escape hatch. "Oh, and we stopped at CVS on the way home. That was *very* exciting. She needed to get something. Probably having her period. I waited in the car, let her go in and get what she needed. Like a good parent, a conscientious dad."

The doctor made a note, scratched out something, wrote more, then gazed patiently at him over the top of her glasses.

"And how did you feel about that?" he spoke for her. His tone was less sarcastic than usual. "About seeing the exact place where your family was murdered?" He rubbed his chin, raking his fingers through the start of a beard. "I felt nothing, which surprised me. I didn't cry. I didn't get choked up. I said a prayer but I doubt God was listening. It was boarded up so I couldn't see anything, anyway. Nothing to trigger me, like yellow crime scene tape, or...."

More notes. A grim smile.

"Eventually new experiences supplant the old," said Bill as he once more checked the molding along the top of the walls, "and you come to remember only the newer memories rather than the old ones. I think that's what happened. Being there with her was.... It was like I was young and dating again, and nothing happened to Barb and Becky because they.... It was like they were never in my life. Like they were someone else's family. And I just read about it in the newspaper."

"That, too, is a normal response along the journey."

"But then I see a report on TV. New developments in the case, you know. That kind of story. But they never called me. Didn't give me a heads-up on that. It could've been triggering. Well, it was triggering. I got triggered."

"What did you do to alleviate that triggering?"

"Nothing right then. But I went over there the next morning. That was Monday. I talked with the detectives, asked 'What gives?' They confirmed what the TV report said. They got the two guys that were terrorizing—they used that word on TV—survivors and their families. Burglaries, thief of personal effects, identity theft, fraud. The people who died lived on, it seemed, but their money belonged to strangers. Well, I've taken care of shutting down Barb's accounts, at least. And the two assholes who broke into my house? Got'em. They confessed to everything, the dumbshits."

"That's a good development. Isn't it? Less to worry about."

"Yes, indeed." He was grinning but suddenly lost it. "Fredrick John Singleton, the gunman, the shooter, ordered one of the hostages to gather everyone's personal effects, wallets, keys, phones. The one chosen to do that didn't get to finish because of the disruption by a woman who tried to protect her daughter from being raped behind the cashier stand. I call it rape, even though the forensics report didn't find any semen, just vaginal hemorrhaging. Like he used his fingers, they said. Robert James Kendall, the punk she rejected, once a classmate, got beat up for bothering her, so he wanted revenge, followed her into the store. He was the punk who was shot dead by the shooter when the S.W.A.T. team entered, thank God."

His chest was tight and he couldn't breathe.

"The guy that took everyone's things lived. A survivor, rah rah. Or, maybe better to say hah hah. And he took the bag with him. Then gave or sold things to his friends or other criminals, tipped off other thugs about who lives where, what they have in their homes, like that. Other survivors had the same trouble I've been having."

"Take a breath, Bill," she cautioned.

"I'm okay." He sucked air for a moment. "I'm all right. I'm fine."

He resumed normal breathing after a while.

The doctor refused to make more notes until he was calm again.

"It's good to have someone with you," she spoke gently, as though testing the waters of a very deep lake. "I would think.... No matter what kind of relationship you've negotiated, this girl has—as you previously indicated—distracted you from your grieving process. Perhaps that has been detrimental to your progress, keeping you from engaging in the process fully, as you need to do. She may ease your everyday grief but she prevents you from completing your journey."

"Journey, journey," he muttered. "Fucking journey." He regarded the doctor. "She's part of the journey. A test. I always think of her as my test. My second chance. Something meant to challenge me. And if I can do it—overcome her—I'll emerge on the other side, a better person ...some kind of superman, or a...an angel myself."

The doctor sat up. "That's a perfectly viable way of thinking of your situation. We create metaphors that stand in for the harsh realities we must deal with."

"And that, too, is a metaphor," he snickered in a dark tone. He stared at his shoes. "Everything is a metaphor. Life is a metaphor for death."

"Is it?" she asked after a moment.

He leaned forward, elbows on his knees, scratching his hand.

"Listen, Doctor Wisniewski, I'm wondering how long this needs to go on. I've reached a satisfactory position in time and space. I mean, I've gone through the journey, even doubled back on prior steps, and still come through it. I know my health insurance is covering all this, and I appreciate that. I appreciate getting to talk to you every week. It's helped. But...."

"But you think you don't need to continue? Is that it?"

"Yes, that's it." He tried to smile sincerely. "I don't mean I stopped enjoying it. I just think that.... Well, the semester is almost over. I'll be starting back in January. I don't know what I'll do over the break."

"The holidays are always a stressful time. Are you sure you don't want to continue through the winter break?"

"Because I can get lonely?" He squinted. "I've learned to handle it." He sensed she saw something in him that he was trying to hide, and regretted slumping his shoulders and pouting like a criminal. "I'll be okay."

"And your house guest will be leaving, as well. How does that make you feel?" She made a note. "Will she be returning?"

He hesitated, clearing his throat.

"She'll spend a so-called typical American Christmas with another family. Then she'll fly back to China. Given the experiences she's had in America, I wouldn't blame her if she stayed there. She certainly never expected what she got." He exhaled loudly. "And she has this uncle back there. I guess I told you before. Don't know much about him. I'm afraid to ask. I suspect he abuses her. She seemed glad to come to America partly to get away from him. That's what I like to think. But he calls her from time to time and she cries after every call. Probably he's cursing at her for coming here. I don't know."

"Is that why you haven't brought her here for me to meet her? Worried what she might say?"

"I'm worried what you might ask her."

"And what would that be?"

"Stuff like what we do in the dark. Like that."

"What would she say?"

Bill shook his head slowly. "I think she's being perfectly innocent. She seems to enjoy teasing me. But I'm not sure she understands how far she's pushing me, and what *some* men might do if they're pushed too far. Not me, though. I won't be a pervert. Or a criminal. I already told her to ratchet it down, to lay off the flirting. I like it, sure—I'm a man—but...I don't like it."

More notes. A lot of them.

"Really? This is note-worthy?"

"I don't wish to recall it incorrectly."

Bill rubbed his hands together until they felt hot. "Well, we've returned to our usual schedule now that Thanksgiving is done. I sleep in, she gets herself up, goes to school with a friend. Gets dropped off later. Some days it's late. I hardly see her. Maybe that's good. We 'broke up' kind of rough. Maybe she's glad to not see me. Couldn't blame her."

The doctor finished a new note, regarded him.

"Does she still sleep with you?"

He gazed up at the doctor, certain she was reporting back to some government agency about his behavior. He wondered what Wendy said to the exchange program representative who visited her at school each month to check on her. Probably she said nothing bad or he would've been hauled away by now.

"No, I put her off from that, I'm sure."

But he thought of that Sunday night when he was in bed, reading one of his stories. He found it while going through Barb's office and relished the chance to read it again. Not his best, but he was happy to have it in a magazine. He'd only gotten two pages in when the familiar knock on the door interrupted his escape into the fantasy tale. Wendy entered, sheepishly, like she'd done something bad and was seeking absolution. He looked over the top of the magazine at her, smiled, waved her in.

She climbed into bed beside him, like Becky had done when she was little. Her long nightgown was frilly, feminine, her hair brushed out and flowing around her face. She sat back against the headboard like him. What was he reading? A story he wrote years ago. She asked him to read it to her, and he did. Eventually, the human prince meets the elf princess. Two more pages and that prince has to kiss the elf princess to seal a treaty between their two realms. They had acted out the scene. With the kiss. He felt his boxers rise, prompting him to turn on his side, facing away from her. He could not fall asleep until he heard her soft purring.

"Something?" asked the doctor, seeing him lost in thought.

He broke from his trance, looked up. "No, nothing."

She glanced at her notes. "Will you bring your guest next time?"

"Hah hah, guest." He had a smirk.

The doctor adjusted her glasses. "What do you mean by that?"

"Well, you've heard of the guest who wouldn't leave?"

"Of course."

"She's the guest I don't want to leave."

25

DRIVING TO THE SWIM MEET the next Saturday, Bill thought about the previous day, when Wendy had caught him working in the master bedroom's closet, packing up Barb's clothes and accessories. Most of the closet was for her clothing, anyway. He found a box of neatly folded lingerie. Looking through the skimpy outfits, he tried to remember the times she'd worn them. It seemed she only wore each of them once, whenever she felt in the mood and he deserved a treat, and never shown a second time. He wondered if he should toss them out or donate them. Did people want used lingerie?

But Wendy had seen them. He had a black negligée in his hands when she walked in. He had to explain that his wife hadn't been a dance hall girl. It was just for their private fun. The short garment was so expensive yet had so little fabric, he laughed as he handed it over to his curious house guest.

She held up the chemise, studying it, then put it against her body and regarded herself, seeing how it fit. A bit large. But the idea of see-through sleepwear was interesting.

"I believe this style is called 'baby doll'," he said with a snicker.

"Baby...? doll...?"

"Don't ask me why." He held up another sexy sample from the box. "This one-piece is called a 'teddy'."

"Like bear?"

"Yes, exactly," he responded, grinning.

"But doesn't look like bear."

He grinned. "Use your imagination."

"May I have this?" asked Wendy, folding the short, see-through nightgown over her arm.

He wanted to laugh. "You sure?"

"It's pretty," she said.

"If you want it, go ahead."

He watched her carry it proudly out of the closet, with her baggy lounge pants swaying as she went. He was amused by her curiosity. Surely they had sexy garments in China. What did wives wear to get their husbands excited?

"How does it look?" she asked, suddenly reappearing in the closet doorway, wearing the black baby doll nightie like it was as normal to wear as a winter coat in December. He could see her white bra and panties through the black mesh, breasts cradled in the lacey cups, satin straps crisscrossing her lithe body, the filmy skirt flapping against her hips.

"Whoa!" He spun away. "I don't think you're supposed to wear underwear with that." But gradually he snuck a peek.

She gazed down at herself. "It's not for show off?"

"You wear just the negligée, without bra or panties."

She seemed puzzled. "You don't like?"

"You really shouldn't wear that." He sounded like he was scolding her and dialed it back. "Remember our agreement? No more teasing? This is big time teasing. Besides, that kind of garment is for a woman who has a lover she wants to excite. That's all it's for. Waste of money. I mean, I only want...."

He couldn't take his words back but pretended he had nothing to say. In all his years, he'd never been a prude. Now he felt a strange obligation to be modest, to instruct his guest on the house rules. Again. Something wasn't right.

"What do you want?" she asked, not dissuaded.

"I want you..." He stopped, had to think. "...to change back to the lounge pants and that bulky sweater. That's what's appropriate now."

"Okay, Bill."

He sensed she was upset but when he turned she was gone.

The image stayed with Bill as he pulled into the parking lot, went around to the aquatic center and parked. He felt restriction in his jeans as he shut off the engine. He wished he could shut off his desires, too. Let the world go on without provoking him like a horny teenager. That life was done. He had things to do.

No football game on this Saturday so the parking lot wasn't full for the final swim meet of the year. Following the line of fans, he stepped up the bleachers and took his usual seat, then sat back to wait. Wendy had been picked up earlier by her friends and he'd slept in.

The humidity of the place soon got to him. He hoped it was warm enough down at poolside. He'd warned Wendy to make sure her hair was dry before going out in the cold air. Feeling uncomfortably warm, he took off his coat and folded it on the seat beside him, careful the Glock didn't fall out of the pocket. He knew it was illegal, carrying it with him, especially on school grounds, but he felt better having it with him.

"Hey, Bill!" someone called, startling him. It was George Griffin, principal of Vista High, climbing the bleachers in a full winter coat to meet him. "How ya doing?"

They shook hands, Bill sitting and George standing. Then George took a seat next to him, the opposite side from Bill's coat. George inquired again about his health, his on-going therapy. Bill explained in his usual laconic style exactly how he was. George frowned. Bill joked how he should already know everything from Hannah, but George repeated the doctor-patient confidentiality mantra and that was the end of that line of joking.

"I'm going to sell the house and move into an apartment," said Bill, turning to watch the pool area below. "Get rid of those memories."

"Oh, you don't want to get rid of memories," George responded. "But, yeah, I can see you wanting to simplify your life."

"Simplify.... It's a start."

"So is your guest going to live there, too?"

Bill was surprised by the question, turned and squinted at him.

"What?" He shook his head. "My guest? You mean Wendy Wang? I don't even know if she's coming back after winter break. I think she's had enough of the American experience. Can't blame her."

"Really?" George seemed disappointed, like America had failed. "Sorry to hear that. Haven't heard anything from the program rep."

"I've looked at a few apartments. I told her I would be moving, so if...when...she returns, she might be living with another family. She stayed with John Drexler's family over Thanksgiving week and that seemed to work out. They got along well. She and Jackie are the same age. Only problem is when their older kids come home from college on the weekends."

"Yeah, could be tight." George was surveying the pool area below.

"She knows what to expect if...when...she returns."

A pang of regret rumbled through his gut. He realized, perhaps for the first time, the truth of his statement. She might not return. Then what would he do? He told himself he was moving, starting over, alone. But she was the last spot of glue holding him together.

"Anyway, that's reality. Things happen."

"Yeah, about those things happening." George lowered his voice until the din of the aquatic center threatened to cover his words. "You know how high school students can be. Just thought you should know. There's some gossip going around the school I heard. Others reported it to me. Just gossip. Talking about you and your exchange student. About your relationship."

"Our relationship?" Bill *tsk*ed, shook his head. "I'm not even in school now. What can they be thinking?"

"Well, you two do live together," said George. "That's enough to get some of them chatting it up. I don't pay no mind. I only wanted you to know it's going on. I wouldn't want that kind of scuttlebutt to cause any difficulty when you return."

"Thanks," Bill responded flatly, glancing at George. "You know I tried to get another family for her when she first arrived. I was in no condition to be any kind of host. But it's worked out, I guess. We hardly see each other. I sleep late and she gets herself ready and rides to school with Casey Turner or some other girl on the swim team. And a ride home, sometimes late. No, I'm probably not the strictest parent these days, but what're you gonna do, huh?"

"Yeah, Casey's a good young lady. Good role model for Wendy."

"Well, I wouldn't call Casey a role model. She can be rather...what's the right word? A tease?"

George laughed. "Tease is the right word. But it's all for show."

"Probably started when we went to the mall on Black Friday," said Bill. "Yes, the Quail Run Mall. Yes, I dared myself to go. I wanted her to experience the madness of Black Friday. But not until the afternoon. Not so crazy then."

"Yes, I heard about that."

"You heard?"

"The girls were talking."

"Okay, so we held hands in the mall—in a crowded mall. Didn't want her to get lost. And we saw a movie, too. She was thankful and gave me a hug when we came out. A daughterly hug. And, well, a peck on my cheek, too. Right then a group of her friends saw us. But all perfectly innocent. Father and daughter stuff. That's all."

"I get it. Kids'll talk." He clapped his hand on Bill's shoulder. "Hey, just checking on you, buddy, not being the school gossip. Making sure you're going to be all right to return in January."

"I'm looking forward to it." Bill grinned. "Too much time sitting on my hands at home. Or helping police track down criminals. You know, like a superhero but without a cape."

George laughed. "You and your stories!" He got up.

"Also, for your information, the class-action is going forward. You know, families suing the store chain and the mall for lax security. The usual. I might have to go sit in court some days next semester. Thought you should know."

"Right," said George with a hefty groan. "Well, you do whatever you gotta do. Take it easy, Bill."

"Good to see you, too," said Bill with a wave of his hand. "And say 'hi' to Hannah."

He watched George stumble down the bleachers and realized his chest had gotten tight. He hadn't lied. He simply didn't divulge quite everything. The girls couldn't have seen everything. There was not enough evidence to make a case against him. But Wendy had the sleepover. Was she grilled about their home life? Was she pushed to reveal more than would be wise? He could argue they'd done nothing wrong. There were moments someone might consider inappropriate, but he had set the rules again.

Despite his ranging thoughts, he tried to watch the meet. It wasn't always easy to understand what was going on below. The announcer was not good at informing the crowd of every detail, but Bill could see. The girls and boys teams walked out in lines, took their seats. When it was time, they got up and dove in and swam down and back, churning the water like a swarm of sharks in a movie. Wendy got second place in breaststroke but last in freestyle. They had to help her climb out of the pool. Looked like she was hurt.

He remained patient as they helped her limp into the locker room. Later, after the meet ended and everyone left, he went around to the locker room's outside doors, standing in the cold with the afternoon sun not quite able to warm him. Finally the girls came out.

Wendy was standing on her own but taking a step made her wince.

"Hurt my leg," she told him, making a face.

"Oh no," he mugged, then saw she genuinely hurt.

He offered to drive the Escape up to the doors so she wouldn't have to walk so far. But she wanted to walk, saying it would loosen the tight muscle on the back of her thigh. Her coach came out, greeted Bill, and told him in more detail what happened. Even with her out for one race and wounded for another, they had managed to win the tournament.

"Go Vista!" Wendy and a few girls cheered.

At home, Bill helped Wendy from the garage into the kitchen, his arm around her waist, her arm on his shoulder. He sat her down on the couch in the living room, suggesting she get a hot bath and let her sore leg soak. She agreed, so he ran the water in the bathroom, fingering the water until it was hot, as hot as he could stand.

"Your ba*h*th is drawn, Madame," he said, bowing and waving his arm like a servant.

"It's not funny," she said, pouting and wrinkling her nose.

He helped her down the hallway, bumbling like they were in a three-legged race, and on into the bathroom. He sat her down on the toilet seat.

"It's very hot," he warned, pointing to the steam rising from the other side of the shower curtain. "Can you get yourself undressed?"

She nodded and he stepped out, closing the door, then paused.

"Let me get you your robe," he called back.

He went to her room and retrieved the robe she used for going to and from the bathroom. On the desk was the CVS bag and he could see a box inside, thinking it must be tampons she'd needed so desperately. He was a good dad. He took her robe to the bathroom and reached around the door to hang the robe on the hook on the back of the door, then closed the door.

"Call if you need anything."

"Okay, Bill."

While Wendy soaked, Bill put a dinner together. Pasta and sausage, marinara sauce, green beans. It didn't look too bad. He called down the hallway to Wendy and heard her reply from the bathroom. He listened as the door opened and the limp-thuds proceeded down the hallway and into the bedroom. Then, a couple minutes later, she appeared, almost hopping on one foot into the kitchen.

"Oh, my goodness. I should've brought you dinner, let you eat in your room instead of having you walk all this way."

"Coach said I should try to walk," she responded, then winced.

He helped her up onto the chair at the table. He served her a plate of food, got a glass of water.

"Let me know anything you need."

She took a few bites. "I got exam on Monday. Literature."

"What's it over?"

"Everything."

When she'd finished as much as she cared to eat, Bill took the dishes away and helped her back to her room, lowered her onto the bed. He gave her the books from her bag that she needed and moved the laptop around so she could see her notes.

"All set?" he asked. "Call if you need anything."

"Okay, Bill. I will."

26

HE FELL ASLEEP on the couch, watching an old movie but most of the time thinking of the future. The people in the movie had a difficult time but by the end everything worked out. Then he got himself up and went to bed, noting the light was already out in Wendy's room. It was a good sign, he thought with his last flicker of consciousness, feeling for his bed in the dark. The new rules were working.

In the morning, he awoke and heard her tinkering in the kitchen. He got up immediately to intercept her, not wanting her to have to move her injured leg. She needed to stay off that leg. He worried how she would handle school on Monday.

"I'm okay," she said. "Don't worry." She leaned against the counter, her weight on the good leg.

He helped her to the table, served the eggs, bacon, and toast she had prepared. She was so Westernized now.

"When can we have pancakes?" she asked with a sly smile.

He brought her a glass of O.J., a mug of coffee for himself.

"I have to pick you up from the airport," he replied. "That's the rule. I promise to do it right next time." But she would need to leave in order to arrive at the airport again, and the thought made his stomach tight. "When you return...."

He wondered whether he had misspoken, suggesting she fly home rather than stay through the winter break. He didn't want to push her to leave. In fact, he wished she would stay, if only to make breakfast, if only so he could watch her stand or sit or sleep, to see her lovely smile each day.

"That's special, isn't it? Pancakes? A good reason to return."

"I know you pick up me okay next time," she said with a wide grin, her teeth so white.

He tried to help her move after breakfast but she waved him off and hobbled back to her room. He offered to clean the kitchen. Padding around in his robe, he thought of what else needed to be done. He decided packing up the boxes of papers he'd taken out to the garage would be good, making them easier to load into Lexi's Mercedes when she stopped by the next day. He got a big roll of tape and went to work.

"You doing okay?" he called as he passed her room, seeing her stretched out on the bed studying.

"I'm okay, Bill."

Everything was going to work out, he thought as he soaped himself and rinsed off. Nothing like a hot shower and the rub of a brisk towel to make you feel alive. He wore the towel around his hips going into the master bedroom to put on fresh clothes. What else for today? He considered going for a drive, the bright afternoon sun so inviting, maybe check other apartments. Or just look at the bare trees. There was a nice park not far away. He recalled going to a park during his grad school days just to sit and read.

"Hey, Wendy," he called, going to her open door.

She rested on the bed, on her belly, wearing a long, white t-shirt that might have once been his but somehow got into her room. The shirttail went just over her bottom as she reclined on the bed. She had tucked her elbows under herself, shoulders raised, with her bare legs extended toward the door, feet in fuzzy green ankle socks. An open book rested beside one shoulder, a notebook by her elbow.

She looked back over her shoulder. "What, Bill?"

He felt the warmth of the room. "I guess the furnace is working fine now, huh?"

"It got too hot," she responded, waving her hand through the air.

Seeing her legs stretching down the bed, a hint of pink underwear beneath the hem of her t-shirt, he forgot what he was going to ask her. Instead, he scanned the books stacked on the desk.

"So you read *I Know Why The Caged Bird Sings*? And *A House on*

Mango Street, too, hmm. Missus Claybourne has a tough reading list for American Lit. I don't envy you."

"We had to read. All assigned." She looked up from the book before her. "Next we read *Joy Luck Club*, but I read already in Chinese. And 'Killing Mockingbird Too.'" She looked up, wrinkling her nose at him. "Missus Claybourne always complain nobody read books but I like to read books."

Bill smiled. "You are almost perfect, Wendy."

"Yeah, hah!" She narrowed her eyes at him. "Almost?"

"Well, uh...." Words caught in his throat. "Uh, what are you reading there?"

Lifting the book and turning it over, she showed the cover.

"Oh, *The Sun Also Rises*. Hemingway. Any good?"

"Yeah, it's good. Easy to read in English. But they are in Spain. Fighting bulls."

"The bullfighter dies at the end."

"Shh! Don't spoiler!" She slapped the mattress.

"A good counterweight for *The Awakening*. Can't imagine Kate Chopin writing about bull fighting." He tried to corral more words as they stampeded for the gate. "So...Wendy...I was thinking...."

She returned to her work, then looked up. "Yes, Bill...?"

His eyes were on her legs, a bit more on the one with the strained muscle.

"How's the leg?" he asked before he knew he was speaking.

"It hurts," and she made a face, a mask of pain.

"You want me to massage it?" he asked, completely sober. "Barb said I'm kinda good at loosening muscles. She always had me help when she ran." He winked. "She never finished her half-marathons."

"If you want to," Wendy responded, returning to the book.

"So that's a yes?" he asked, his hands hovering over the back of her thigh like a mad scientist. He could see tension there as her leg was extended. Pain saw his hands coming.

"Uh-huh," she grunted. "Please make stop hurting."

He placed his hands on her thigh, gently at first, amazed how soft her skin was. He focused on the muscle, testing its limits. She sucked in air when he pressed too much in one spot. Again at another spot. He worked his fingers along the line of the muscle, feeling the tight areas and coaxing them to loosen. Back and forth with steady, even strokes using the heel of his hands.

"It hurts," she moaned, giving up studying. She rested her chin on the open book.

He dug his fingers deeper. "Say it in Chinese."

"*Tòng! ...Hǎo tòng!*"

He tried to repeat after her but she laughed.

His hands became more sensitive; he understood the muscle's complaint, found the key to unlocking the pain, making it soar away like a frightened bird. He should've become a masseur instead of a teacher. Focus on the muscle, soothe the nerves, ease the tension. Bring peace.

"How's that?"

"It feel good," she said.

"Looser now?"

"Oh, yes."

"This muscle is what we call the hamstring."

"Ham...string...?" She giggled. "Like pig?"

"It connects to the ham, yes." He gave her butt a playful tap. He didn't know why he did it. The way that small mound of flesh jiggled intrigued him. "I can guess how much this muscle comes into play when you're kicking during swimming."

He worked his hands around her thigh, pressing his thumbs into the muscle, feeling it relax. His hands worked high on her thigh then down into the softer corner of the thigh, inside, and sweeping back to the outside like a pro.

"Ooo, feel good now." She was breathing slower, her body limp on the bed. Burying her face in the bed covers, her arms lay straight along her body.

"Does it?" he asked, making prattle like a good masseur.

She moaned as though what he was doing was just right.

"*Bùyào tíng xiàlái,*" she groaned.

"What's that? Boo-yow ting-zhee-lie?"

"It mean 'don't stop'."

"Okay, I won't."

He continued but after a while slowed his strokes and let up on the pressure. He finished with lighter *shiatsu* strokes like he experienced in Japan. Prone on the bed, she remained limp, ready to sleep. When he stopped and raised his hands from her leg, a sigh escaped, like the pain had evaporated. When he'd had massages before, he wanted to lay there and sleep instead of get up and get dressed, and leave.

"Anyway, I'm glad it feels better now."

Instead of remaining on her belly and sleeping, she turned over, her bottom pushing the sheet aside, pressing it into a clump along the wall. Her long t-shirt rode up, the hem rolling up. A swath of belly showed between the hem of her shirt and the top of her pink panties.

There, before his eyes, a dark image beneath her pink panties, a delicate triangle that stopped his heart.

"Uh...." He shifted his eyes to her face.

Her face was somber, serious as she gazed back at him.

Kneeling beside the bed on one knee, his hands rested on the edge of the bed beside her leg. Now it was her good leg closest to him. Did she mean for him to massage that leg, too? That might be her intention by turning over.

"Are you all right?" he asked softly.

His eyes reverted to the dark triangle showing through the panties.

He couldn't take his eyes off it.

He kept staring.

"Bill...."

The way she said his name sent a storm of tingles down his spine. He was staring at the triangle, studying the way a simple weave of fabric curled so dramatically down between her thighs, like the falling of water over a cliff, as she said his name again and slid her hands over her belly to her waist, letting her fingers slip inside the waistband.

"Want to look?"

He was entranced. Unable to move.

"No." Something exploded in his head. "I mean, yes.... Uh, I'm sure it's...attractive, but...it's not...appropriate. It's not okay for me to look at...."

She seemed reticent. "If I say it's okay, it's okay."

All he could do was stare—as her fingers lifted the waistband off her belly and pushed it down towards him.

"I shouldn't be seeing that."

His breath grew heavy. His neck weakened and his flushed face bent closer.

She wriggled the panties over her hips.

"It's okay." She reached for him, placing one hand on the top of his head. Her fingers dug through his hair. "I know you want to look."

He couldn't speak as she lifted her bottom off the bed and slipped the panties off. Now it could slide down her legs without hindrance, and she did—as far as her hands could reach—until his fingers assisted her, hooking the top edge, where the panties became rolled around each thigh, and pulled further.

Unsure what was happening, or what might be about to happen, Bill sprang up from beside the bed and dashed out of the room. He bumbled into the master bedroom, shutting the door firmly behind him but moderating the sound so she wouldn't think he was angry.

Oh God! What just happened?

He was so swollen, raging with desire, like nothing he had felt in years. He was afraid of what he wanted to do and used all his strength to pull himself away. How easy it was for something innocent to be transformed into perversion! He was only trying to ease her pain, a charitable act, but she turned it upside-down and inside-out, letting it become seduction. He was certain she knew what she was doing this time. No doubt. There could be no feigning a lack of understanding of foreign customs as an excuse.

He wanted to finish it, to let out his frustration in a fountain of joy, yet with her so close, he dared not. To calm himself, he entered the bathroom, making sure to close the door tight, and ran a cold shower. He stepped in and nearly cried out at the icy welcome. He regained his composure, turned the temperature up little by little.

When he opened the bathroom door, there she was: sitting on the side of the bed, facing the bathroom, wearing the same t-shirt and the panties returned to its proper position. Her long, dark hair lay down her front, covering her chest, and her face wore a strange fusion of a lingerie model's smugness and a school girl's irrevocable purity.

With his clothes draped over his arm, he spun around to hide from her view although his rear end was now on stage. He reached for the robe hanging on the door hook. Dropping the old clothes at his feet, he pulled on the robe, then picked up the clothes and tossed them into the laundry basket.

An awkward grin. Noticing his robe was open, he pulled it tight and fixed the cloth belt around his waist.

Her face displayed worry, as though awaiting punishment. He didn't know what to say, but something needed to be said. Her eyes followed him as he moved to the bed and sat beside her, shoulder to shoulder.

"I'm sorry, Wendy." His voice sounded rough even though he tried to make it gentle. "That was.... I don't know what to say. I...I didn't intend for that to happen."

"For what?" she said, pouting like a child.

"We shouldn't do...*that*." He quickly composed an excuse. "We really shouldn't. Shouldn't act that way. Like we are lovers. Not like men and women who are married. Or, well, planning to marry. Or, okay, when couples enjoy being together, like a lot of people do these days. Not like that."

He recognized his parents' voices echoing in his head and knew he was reciting a script from long ago.

"You mean sex?" Her voice was tiny, as though she was only six, and that made him feel more guilty.

"Yes."

Her shoulder rested against his arm, her hands folded neatly in her lap, directly over the pink panties, as though she knew to cover the dark triangle that excited him. She pursed her lips.

"Uncle always want to look," she spoke after a moment. "He always say I'm beautiful girl. He like to put fingers there and I have to make sounds. He tell me what sounds to make. I pretend I like it."

"That's awful." He wanted to put his arm around her but decided it might not be best.

"Uncle always say my mama and papa want to kill me before I'm born so she can try for boy. Only one child in China. Now it's two. But already too late for Mama, too old for other baby. Uncle say only one thing girl is for. He says I'm beautiful. So he want sex." Her voice was so light he strained to hear. "Mama say I better keep Uncle happy. So we can have good home. Uncle pay for everything. But then I got scholarship and I join exchange program."

"I see." He let out a long sigh. "I'm sorry you had to experience that. And now I've been a creep—"

"Uncle does not like me here. He call me and send messages always angry. He call me bad things. I'm bad girl for going away. He say I forget Mama. And she is crying all day. He does not—"

"I would do anything, Wendy," he said in a rush, "to keep you safe and make a good life for you here. Anything to keep you safe."

Then he had a thought, seeing the uncle in his mind, an angry man expecting this girl to finish being groomed and become his plaything.

"Is this about what I mentioned before? About Becky's college fund? Going to college here? Is that why you...why that happened just now?"

She shook her head, still bowed, as a few tears dropped onto her bare legs and her hand quickly wiped them away.

He turned to her, reached out to lift her chin with his finger.

"Wendy, you don't have to do anything—nothing like that—for me. Certainly not because I'll pay for your college if you stay here. I'm not like that. I'm not like your uncle. I offered it because—well, right now, you are my family. You are the only person who can use it. And you don't have to do anything sexual for it."

A pair of tears slipped out of her eyes. She gazed at Bill.

"Uncle like to touch me." Her hand went to her breast. "Here. And here." She pushed her hand between her thighs. "Make him happy. Then he is kind to Mama and me. Uncle get angry if I don't want it. If I don't let him, or I say don't want it, he hits Mama. Sometimes he hit me, too." She wiped her eyes.

"I am so sorry," he mumbled, taking her in his arms, kissing her head. "Men are jerks. Some men are." He shook his head. "I am so stupid. Why couldn't I figure that out?"

"You not jerk, Bill." She moved her hand up to his shoulder.

"Well, you are beautiful. I mean in a sexy way." He took a breath. "I mean...'sexy' means that when men look at you, your appearance makes them want to have sex with you. It shouldn't be that way, I know, but it is—"

"I know what it mean."

"Some girls like it. Some girls hate it. Either is okay, as far as I'm concerned. Well, as long as she gives her consent. And he doesn't hurt her, of course. And consent includes her being old enough to know the difference."

She pursed her lips. "I'm old enough. I know difference."

"Do you?" He took a deep breath. "I believe you do."

She straightened up, her face red and wet with tears.

"Please don't push me away." She paused to gather strength. "Becky write email and told me about you. About you and Missus. Not get along together. Becky said I will like you because you like Asian girls. She said I must be kind to you and you do anything for me." She let out a strained laugh. "I know it's crazy. She write bad things about you. But not true. You are very kind man, and take care me, and always buy food, and watch house while I sleep, and never hurt me. That is important. Becky was wrong. She told me things her mother say about you. But she say you will like me." She wiped her eyes. "You do like me, don't you?"

"Oh, yes—definitely." He hugged her. "But there's a big difference between like and love."

She pouted. "I know."

"We must be careful. People will talk. They'll see something sweet and perfectly innocent, and they'll spin it into some lurid erotic tale. Something that never occurred."

She moistened her lips. "Like your princess story?"

"Kinda." He stared at the wall, seeing a play unfolding on its surface, faint shadows of him and his lover in silhouette, lit by a fire in a cave.

She took his hand in hers. "Bill...."

"I see a lot of that stuff, versions of it, at school." Too many stories, in fact, but he couldn't tell her. "High school is a strange world."

"There are boys call to me, good and bad," she said, "but—"

"Yes, I hear a lot about relationships between students. Most is hyperbole—exaggeration—to build themselves up. I get it. I was a kid once. But kids can be cruel. I see boys groping girls. I see lots of PDA. You know what that is? Public Displays of Affection. Like kissing and hugging in the halls. Sometimes it gets rather risqué and if I see it I have to stop it. Teacher's duty."

"Bill...?"

He recalled some of the naughtier acts he'd heard about.

"Bill...."

"School is not the place for that kind of activity. Everyone should be able to go there without worrying about that kind of behavior. It's a workplace, after all. Do we do such things in an office? And students aren't the right age, anyway. And don't get me started on boys using cell phones to snap pics under the girls' skirts. That's not only against school rules, it's criminal. If they did it in a public place, they could be arrested."

She took his face in her hands, gazing into his eyes.

"That's how serious it is," he continued.

"Listen, *Bill*," she said in serious tone, imitating the way he always got her attention. She pressed her hands against his cheeks. "I am not your student. Not now. I am not your daughter. Not really. I am not your wife, too. I am me. Only me."

His chin dropped to his chest, unable to look into her eyes. What did she want? Comfort? Love? Something to boast about with her girlfriends?

"Yes, of course I want you," he spoke, voice choked. "I want you so badly I'm almost okay with going to prison for that one great moment of ecstasy with you. Just for the memory. But I—"

"We can be together." She stared into his eyes.

He flashed a smile, more resignation than hopefulness. "We are together." Then he shook his head. "In a really weird arrangement. I get it. Is this real or is it just fantasy? Hah, it's a role playing game! Are we free to do whatever we want, or will higher powers condemn us for wanting, for needing, to find comfort together, comfort in each other? We are together, sure. No denying it. But...only until you have to leave. Until you go home. You have to go home eventually."

"I don't want to go," she whimpered, wrapping her arms around him, hugging him tight.

He closed his eyes. Reality was growing brighter, blinding him.

"I don't know what I'll do then. When you leave."

She continued to hold him in her arms.

"Can we be lovers?" she spoke into his ear. "Until I have to go?"

He glanced up at the ceiling, gray in the meager light, and inhaled deeply. The air, blown through the furnace, was too dry.

"Lovers." He smiled pensively. "That sounds so good."

"It's good," she whispered. Her hands pried the two sides of his robe apart and caressed his chest.

He lay back on the bed with a sigh. "Even for a moment."

"Wait for a moment," she whispered.

She popped up from the bed, catching her balance, then prancing in her teenage glory out of the bedroom and across the hall. Returning with a hobble, like her muscle was tight again, she tossed a small box to Bill. It hit the bed beside him, bouncing, but he caught it.

He regarded the box of condoms.

"Ah, the CVS store," he said with a snort. "I thought you just needed tampons. Why did you get this?"

She flashed a smirk.

"What were you thinking?" He seemed confused. "What *are* you thinking?"

"Girl friends...they say I better be prepared for you."

He grimaced. "For me?"

She dropped beside him on the bed.

"They tease about you and me in bed. They say sleeping means sex. I tell them we never do sex. But they laugh at me. They say men get crazy. So if you get crazy I should use this." She pointed to the box. "If I can't run and hide from you, they said use this. But I don't want to run and hide. Not now. Not any time from you, Bill."

He regarded the box of condoms in his hand, turning it over and over as though reading the instructions.

"You are so lovely," he said, the words catching in his throat.

"If you get whorey, I should be ready, they say."

"You mean 'horny'?"

"Horny...?"

"Like the horns on a bull. It means 'aroused'. Turned on. Sure, I want to be turned on. I like it. I want that. But there is a right time and place for that. And the right person."

"I'm right person." She put her hand on his leg, high on his thigh. The robe fell open. "I want to turn on you."

He gently lifted her hand off his leg. "I don't want you to turn on me, hah. Or turn *me on*, either. I'm not a strong man. I would be easy, too easy, and that wouldn't be good for you or me."

"But my girl friends say if I turn on you—"

"It's 'if you turn me on'—"

"If I turn you on then you can be horny. Then you are happy. But must use this." She picked up the box. "I know what it is. I know about sex. I'm not *a* little girl. I'm *a* woman."

"Yes.... That's all true, but...."

His breath filled his chest but wouldn't leave. Staring ahead, he saw the shower cubicle where he had a cold shower which obviously didn't take. He chewed his lip, wondering if she had any prior experience—welcomed or not. Perhaps with the uncle? He couldn't ask her that question. And he didn't want to be the bad guy in her life, not like the uncle seemed to be.

"But you know a moment's pleasure doesn't last," he said instead. "It gets twisted over time, becomes a caricature of a comic book meme that's sharp as a knife and cuts you every day. At least that's how I imagine the rest of my life if I gave in to you just now. And someone found out what I did. Even if you say it's okay."

She put her hand on his knee. "What we did."

"No, it's me. My responsibility. There can be no forgiveness. There are laws. It would be the end of my life if we did anything more than...than what we did. And that's too much already."

"It's okay, Bill." She sat back on the bed, braced on her elbows. "I can be silent. Never tell anybody."

"It's not just that, it's—"

She tried to swing her legs onto the bed but winced as the pain returned.

"Hurts again?" He wanted to take her leg in his hands, massage it, anything to break the tension of negotiating a new relationship. He was losing, anyway.

She lay on the bed, her legs hanging off the edge. "It hurts." She made a face. "*Hăo tòng.*"

He was glad to change the subject. "Shall I help?"

Her face flashed through several emotions, settled on an impish grin. "Yes, please."

He wasn't sure by her tone whether she was just acting or she really felt pain. Maybe it didn't matter.

"Massaging sore muscles I can do. That's allowed. But I promise to be more careful."

Scooting further over the bed, her t-shirt rode up. Frustrated, she paused, sat up, her abdomen tightening, and pulled the shirt off over her head, dropping it on the bed. Her pink bra matched her panties. He liked the way her breasts filled the lacey cups, jiggling as she lay back. The pink panties with its shadow remained in view.

She placed her hand on the upper part of her thigh. Her good leg.

"Can you rub here?"

Bill took a breath, wondering if she actually felt pain or was teasing him once more. It didn't matter; he would not shirk his duty. He placed his hand on the spot she indicated and began moving his fingers gently against her skin, working the muscle beneath.

She breathed deeper as he massaged.

"Here," she said after a moment, moving his hand higher.

Her thigh was softer there, more pliable.

"Now here," she said with a loud exhale.

His fingers went deeper, rubbing what he knew was forbidden to him. She had a plan, he figured. She needed to get him hooked, so he would do anything for her. But the joke was on her: he already was hooked. He couldn't stop. His fingers went further, pressing through the cloth. He withdrew his fingers when they became wet.

She moaned like a grown woman, and slid her hands between her thighs, clenching her legs together.

"I love you, Bill."

He lost it. "Oh, Wendy, I don't want you to ever leave."

"I want to stay with you always," she said, breathing hard.

"What can we do?"

"I must take care Mama. If I don't go back Unclc will hurt her."

"Then bring her here."

The words just slipped out, but hearing them echo off her ears he decided he liked the way they sounded. It only took a heartbeat to know it was the right thing to do. Meeting her eyes, he focused until they were both on the same thought.

"Can we?" she asked, reaching for him.

She wrapped her arms around him, and he held her tight—so lithe, so light.

"She can come here. Bring her back with you." He kissed her cheek. "I won't sell the house. There's plenty of room for her. And you can study here, get your degree, have a great career. And we'll be together forever. All of us."

She smothered him with kisses. "I always make you happy, Bill. Always! Promise."

And they kissed fully, without regard for the world. Like lovers.

27

"I AM GOING STRAIGHT TO HELL," said Bill to the strange man reflected in the frosty glass door he had wiped clean. He pulled it shut against the cold December wind thinking how Wendy had hobbled out the door on her sore leg to catch her ride to school with Casey only to return a few seconds later to give him one final kiss before darting out again—and he not yet completely awakened despite two cups of coffee, which should have been enough. But now that he was getting up the same time as her—after asserting their right to sleep together without the world needing to know their business, beginning in each other's arms and awakening the next morning with their backs pressed together—they would take a few minutes for cuddling before he got up and refreshed himself, then went to make breakfast as she got herself ready for school, dressing for the cold, and ate the breakfast he prepared. A big farewell hug and kiss like they were already a married couple, and off to school she went while he turned to face himself in the glass door before resigning himself to mope about the house the rest of the day, seeing Barbara and Becky in every spare shadow or random glint of light, following him around, excoriating him for what he was doing. He had no response, choosing to simply take it, take their arguments as white noise, letting their words prick him like arrows, bruise him like slings, pretending nothing hurt and anything they might say was likely a lie: Wendy had shown him the emails Becky sent her, full of lies, criticism of everything he did as a teacher, father, and husband—with no consideration that he might've been doing the best he could, because what is a man but an automaton packed full of the rules, standards, and procedures programmed into him by other men down through the ages, trying his best to be both an ideal husband and father no matter how the wife and child might fight against his better judgement: because trying is all he has to offer, the effort of trying, the attempt to make himself better in any way he can, even at the risk to his soul, to his manhood, to his existence in the world. Indeed, even if it meant becoming lovers with a temptress from the other side of the world, lovers in name only—although he did use his fingers to tease her and often brought her to a pleasurable height before letting her down easy, then holding her in his arms, kissing her goodnight, wiping his fingers against his lips before closing his eyes for the night, daring to dream of the future: wherever that exotic destination might be, there behind his eyelids, a glimmer of hope glowing like wildfire just above a dark horizon.

He filled the days scrambling to get information on bringing her mother to the United States. Getting a visa would take some time, he learned, the way the Chinese authorities had to approve her first, and then the Americans. It couldn't be accomplished by the time Wendy would return in January. But her mother would come eventually. If she could endure the uncle a little longer. Maybe get her away from the uncle first, he suggested, hide her somewhere.

And he feared for Wendy going back there to face the ire of the uncle, maybe be forced into awful situations. In his nightmares, he saw her being raped by the uncle, to get what he believed was his. Then she might not return—might not be able to leave, or not want to, choosing to give in to her lot in order to keep the uncle satisfied for the sake of her mother. He tried not to dwell on those scenarios, but his mind insisted on reviewing them constantly while he tried to sleep or in his idle daytime hours.

Wendy showed him a picture of her mother, then got upset when he described her as 'handsome'.

"Handsome is for boy," she said in an angry tone.

He explained the full range of descriptive terms for females.

"No," he told her, "she is pretty...for a woman her age. So the word 'handsome' is appropriate. Because she's about my age, we can use 'handsome', and it's not an insult."

"My mama is beautiful," she insisted.

The picture on her phone showed a cheerful woman close to 40, black hair cut short yet stylish, garbed in working clothes, ready to cook and serve lunches at her counter. She had a lovely smile, good teeth, and because of her hard work, her forehead glistened from the steam and the heat of the kitchen.

He found himself gazing at the picture, wondering how she would like living in America, and feeling grateful for birthing Wendy. Strange how people meet, fall in love, make a baby, quite at random, it often seemed. He wondered how Wendy might feel about having a baby.

"You want to marry her?" Wendy growled. "Or me?"

He didn't know how to answer her; one of them would be insulted no matter his choice.

"I could see myself being her husband," he said, teasing her, "but I really don't know her. I'm sure she would be a good wife. But what would we talk about? So I would have to pick you, of course. Not *have to*—want to! You and I already have a lot of connections. But is it too awkward? Me having a mother-in-law who's my age?" He laughed and insisted he was actually younger than he appeared. "And a wife young enough to be my daughter? Maybe I should marry your mother."

She slapped his arm. "No, not Mama. Me!"

"Okay, you." He picked up her hand, gave it a kiss, romantic style. "Only my princess."

"Yeah, I'm your precious princess!"

He laughed. "Your Highness, your wish is my command."

"Then I command you to..."

...do all kinds of things, it turned out, and he was happy to comply.

He started going to a fitness center each day around noon, and adding a jog around the neighborhood later. He watched his meal portions. And he took his hygiene seriously, a lot more than before she arrived, or during that month when he hated her for coming into his life and pushing Barb and Becky out. That seemed so long ago.

Meanwhile, Wendy was focused on final exams. She did well and was praised by her teachers. He boasted about her scores to Dr. Wisniewski and to anyone else whenever the topic came up, like the Drexler family—who offered her the Christmas experience, eve and morning, with a couple gifts; the only night they weren't together—as well as the Johnsons, the Lees, and the Timmons—as proud as if she were his own true daughter. Then he would stop and remind himself she was a lot more.

"If only you had been born sooner," he lamented at night, feeling her soft body beside him, arm around her, sorry for the hair on his chest and down his belly which tickled her skin. How could the world care so much about calendars? He knew younger people who were more mature than him, and older people who were so childish in their behavior. Back in high school, his friend Lance had boasted of all the sex he and his girlfriend Cindy were having, both sixteen. They actually married three months before graduation, becoming the only married students in the high school—and she wasn't even pregnant.

Sometimes when they were undressed and an embrace was not enough, he would pull her onto him as he reclined on the bed, and she would get him breathing hard, groan happily, maybe release onto his belly. Or he would urge her to scoot up his body so he could kiss between her legs. She liked that, sometimes initiated it. But as much as she wanted to do it—the 'big deal' he called it—he insisted on holding off until an official date could arrive.

With a 6:15 a.m. departure, Bill suggested they go to bed early. It was difficult to fall asleep, so they talked about the future. As Wendy reminded him through her words and deeds, she wasn't his daughter, not his wife either; and not his student. She asked him who would know what they did. The walls have ears, he murmured, like they needed to be quiet. However, she insisted more with each gentle kiss: cheeks, lips, throat, down his chest. His heart beat faster as he waited for the knock on the door, expecting to see flashing lights through the window curtains. Yet she climbed over him, lowered herself carefully, and gently rocked back and forth, her breasts taunting him, until she lay exhausted beside him, both of them grinning.

A couple hours later, he drove her up to the curb at the terminal, got out like a celebrity's chauffer, carried her pink suitcase inside, up to the check-in counter, waited to make sure she was all set, then escorted her over to the security checkpoint. The line was short at that early hour, half the people yawning while they waited. At the last moment, they embraced like lovers who wouldn't see each other again for a long time. He kissed her, ignoring the other travelers. And she kissed him back. He stepped away when it was her turn to have her passport examined. Then she was going through the big machine, her Uggs off and hands up, then recomposing herself and waving at him, walking down the corridor out of sight.

He hurried back to the Escape parked alongside the curb with its blinkers on and found a ticket tucked under the wiper blade. Parked too long, he guessed, but he didn't care. He was doing the right thing seeing her through the airport protocol. Sitting inside the SUV, he checked his phone for messages. Nothing. He drove away from the terminal, paused by the long-term lot to check again. Nothing. Perhaps there was a weak signal. She had the phone he'd gotten for her, right? Maybe she was using her Chinese phone to call her mother. Or the uncle. Someone to pick her up in Beijing.

She would call him soon. Relax.

He drove on home, sat at the kitchen table waiting for the phone to buzz or a message to ping. Nothing. He checked the battery, the signal, that he had the latest update of the app. He stopped fiddling with his phone, setting it out of reach. He knew a watched phone didn't ring. By then she was probably on the plane and had to turn off her phone. She would call when she got to San Francisco, before boarding the flight to Beijing.

His nap was short, dropping into sleep for a few minutes only to pop awake thinking he heard the phone do something. Checking the time, he guessed she was over the Pacific. When she landed in Beijing, maybe she would call or text him, maybe using her Chinese phone. So he had about ten more hours, he figured. Then she would let him know she arrived safely.

Maybe she didn't arrive safely was his theme the next day.

Perhaps she had enough of America, he considered for two days.

When he finally decided to try calling her, he found the phone he'd given her buzzing on the desk in her room.

It was possible she wasn't coming back, he realized.

"I was stupid," he cursed, Dr. Wisniewski taking notes. "I don't even have a picture of her. Oh, I took pictures of her—with her phone. She was supposed to send copies to my phone. So I could transfer them to the computer and save them. To look at them. And remember.... But she didn't. I only have her in my mind's eye."

"And how does that make you feel?" asked the doctor.

He hated the question. "Like maybe it wasn't real. Never happened. Just a strange dream."

"What do you think it means?"

"Like it's Christmas and the diamond I thought I had is actually a lump of coal. Yeah, a moment's joy then...nothing."

He saw her tuck a smirk in the corner of her mouth.

"I do have some concern," she spoke cautiously, "that you may be relying on this young lady too much, expecting her to be, shall we say, your anchor in stormy seas."

A dull ache formed in his gut. "No, she's not." He shook his head. "She's important to me, but not...not my goddamn anchor. I'm fine. Even if she doesn't return, I'll be fine."

"I would like you to examine your feelings for her. Be sure you are not using her to stabilize your new life. That is not fair to her. And it does not enable you to complete your journey."

He rubbed his hands together. "Yes, well, fuck my journey."

Days passed with no call or message and the winter gloom consumed him. No longer expecting a call or message, he reverted to his pre-Wendy lifestyle: sleeping a lot, drinking too much, eating too little, and staring for hours at her bed. She had taken everything she'd brought, he noticed—in case she didn't or couldn't return? That was smart. But was that her plan?

He got angry. What was her plan? And did she have it all along? Or did he present himself as such a fool that she quickly invented a plan? It didn't help that he gave her money to buy her mother's ticket to America. He thought it was the polite thing to do; now he wondered. She showed him the emails: Becky told her exactly how to manipulate him. And that was exactly how she had, he realized.

His mind was racing through all kinds of bizarre scenarios, each a deck of cards, flipping faster than he could shout "Stop!" But knowing it was all mindplay and getting it to stop were two different things. He drank a bottle of whiskey over a couple days, purchased solely to stop his head from conspiracy-mongering. A case of beer followed. Over-the-counter sleep meds. Late at night, when the shadows were deepest and the mind tricks cruelest, he wanted to talk to Dr. Wisniewski, to share his horrors with someone, to prove to himself they were real, that he was not simply going crazy. But he already had his session for the week. And he dared state that he thought he was done, didn't need it anymore. That he was fine now, ready to go out on his own.

A week of nights seemed like a year of despair.

Only that Chinese girl could alleviate his ills. If she were real.

The phone was buzzing and he rushed to answer it.

"Hello," he responded in a weak voice to Jennifer Claybourne's strident "Hi, Bill." It was not the call he wanted.

A minute of pleasantries that hurt.

"I was calling because, well, I thought maybe you'd like to come over for dinner. Call it a late New Year's dinner. Nothing formal. Just us. I thought maybe you'd like some home cooking. I sure can't make a full meal for just myself, right? So we might as well eat together. I'm thinking of roast beef with all the trimmings."

"All right," he said, coughing back disappointment. "Sounds good."

As he drove over to Jennifer's house, the same place where she lived before her husband died, apparently not haunted by memories of him there, Bill gazed at the granite sky, felt the cold wind pushing his SUV, and suddenly he saw his future, as ephemeral yet real as the snowflakes that drifted across the windshield.

He would end up marrying Jennifer, wholly for convenience, for tax purposes, for companionship, like they were just playing house, sharing their English-related stuff, reading poetry to each other in the gloamings, and sitting down to holiday dinners with no children or grandchildren to count between them. It would be safe, comfortable, yet devoid of passion or love. She was nice, but nice did not excite him. Then he pondered whether he deserved excitement. Then again, he'd had his fifteen minutes of excitement. He got his memory.

And Wendy would return home to Beijing, be compelled to stay, uncle or not, and she would meet a boy her age. They would fall in love, and he liked to think he had taught her how to love, something to pat his back for. And one day in the future she would return to him. He would answer the door and find an older Wendy standing there, a child beside each leg. She would look gorgeous, and wrinkle up her nose at him when he smiled. But his strained smile would quickly melt—like snowflakes on his palm—and she would step forward to give him a hug, like she did years before. And he wouldn't know what to do. She might come back even later, when he was old, to hold his hand as he took his final breaths, comforting him, letting him believe she really did love him and that it wasn't just a game.

"Classes begin tomorrow," Bill spoke into the frigid air, a cloud of syllables forming as he stared down at the twin monuments for Barb and Becky. "I'm not sure how I'll manage. Got the usual schedule so I can use lesson plans from last spring. But my heart's not in it. Not yet. I've been away too long, can't feel the vibe." He sniffled. "What does it matter, anyway?"

The day was cold and gray, the cemetery lawn dusted with snow, withered grasses poking through. Bill gazed up the slope, the stately trees with empty branches, stray leaves, dull red or crumbling brown, scattered among the graves or balanced on tombstones. He let the wind scrape his freshly-shaved face, breathed in the cold air, let it burn his throat—as he deserved.

"I miss you guys," he said, quieter this time.

He knelt before the two tombstones, facing the words on them, names and dates, *Rest In Peace* over each. The granite looked good, proper. As it should be. Like everything should be—should've been. If he'd done this or not forgotten that. If he'd gone with them, or if they hadn't needed to go to the mall on that day because the Chinese girl, Wu Ting Wang, the exchange student, wasn't coming.

"I've made a lot of mistakes," he spoke to the stones. "I know. I admit. Can't fix them now, though. Just trying to do better. As best I can. Or maybe don't try, just give up. Call it quits. Like I was meant to do right after your funeral. But there was too much to do, things that needed to be done. Stuff I had to do. But I don't want to have to do anything. Not then. And not ever again. I'm just too damn tired. Tired of everything."

He burped up the taste of roast beef, which at that moment seemed both nasty and delicious. He coughed, spit.

Jennifer had been correct. She got him to confess. He was in love with Wendy. She understood, could see it in his eyes, the way he reacted to her. She was willing to comfort him, help him through his loss—meaning Wendy's departure. She flirted until he had to get up and leave, apologizing but not stopping at the door.

"Can you see me?" he asked the tombstones. "Are you looking down on me? Do you even want to see me?"

He thought of the times he called to Barb, something he thought important to tell her, but she ignored him, focusing on her own business. He wanted to share his excitement over his story being published and she patted his back like he had made a decent cup of coffee. Or when he tried to get Becky interested in playing soccer in the backyard but she preferred to stay in her room and play video games where animated kids kicked soccer balls. He asked about homework not to check on her diligence but to open the door to helping her with it, to show he loved her.

He stood in the living room of his mind, seeing them sitting on the couch, gazing up at him, their expressions confused. Outside, he knew Wendy was somewhere he couldn't be, in another world, lost to him forever, only a pleasant memory. But memories went away when the brain's neurons stopped firing.

Reaching into the pocket of his coat, he pulled out the Glock, let it rest in his hand. He had emptied the magazine, left the bullets at home in the bottom drawer. Except one. Only one bullet remained, seated in the chamber, ready for an excuse.

He spread his knees to steady himself, then raised the pistol to his face, trying to find a good angle. Upside-down seemed the best. Both hands on the handle, barrel positioned, mouth open wide as though he might miss, finger on the trigger.

A series of breaths.

Then a big breath, shutting his eyes tight.

A faint ping seemed to echo off the tombstones.

He stopped, lowered the gun, looking around. No one anywhere in sight. He checked the Glock.

The phone vibrated in his pocket.

He set the gun down on the snowy ground between his knees and grabbed the phone.

Leave San Fran soon. you pick up me?

He stared at the phone a couple minutes, not believing.

"Pick *me* up," he mumbled, holding the phone before his teary eyes.

Ripples of emotion coursed through him and he laughed wildly, uncontrollably. He tried to stand but his knees were stiff. He tripped, spilling to the snow. Righting himself, he got to his feet, head dizzy, and brushed himself off.

The Glock remained at his feet, resting on the margin between the two plots. He reached down, picked it up, and in one smooth motion spun on his heel, pointing at the nearest tree, squeezing the trigger and hearing the bullet hit the bark, crack it, burrow into the wood—safely away from his thoughts, an excuse no more.

28

"WELCOME BACK, BILL," his colleagues called as he strolled down the long corridor in coat and tie, school bag swinging on his shoulder. He waved at each of them as he passed.

Arriving at his room, Bill glanced through the small window in the door, saw the desks in perfect alignment, lights off, like it had not been used the previous semester. He pulled the key from his trouser pocket and opened the door, flicked on the lights, and went to his desk at the head of the room. A few students loitering in the hallway came in after him, took seats, too sleepy to chat.

"Are you Mister Masters?" asked one dark-haired boy, slumping in a front row seat, wearing t-shirt and jeans despite the January cold outside. Maybe he'd put his coat in his locker, thought Bill. The boy had no books or bag with him but he did have a phone, resting on the desktop.

"Yep," Bill responded, looking down as he put his bag's contents away in the desk drawers. "And you are...?"

"Albert."

Bill looked up. "Albert, huh? ...Got a last name?"

The kid grinned like he'd been interrogated many times before.

"Perryman." He wore a smug expression, a challenge.

"Nope," said Bill, shaking his head, continuing to prepare his desk. "Doesn't ring a bell."

A joke. He felt he was ready to lighten up, back to his usual humor.

Life was looking up. He thought of the way Wendy had run to him in the baggage claim area, leaping onto him, half-crushing the bouquet of flowers he brought; the way they embraced, like a big reunion in a movie, kissing with wild abandon as other travelers gawked; the way she said "I miss you so much!" and he responded with "I miss*ed* you so much" and she countered with "Me, too!"

They had gone straight home, undressed and showered together. Laying in each other's arms, he thought over their conversation driving home when he asked about her mother. They sold the lunch counter, Wendy told him. There was a competitor always wanting to buy her out so it was easy.

"I told her we got to leave from café and not go home," Wendy explained. "Uncle was coming soon, so I got my school friend to take Mama to subway and go around on three lines, out to Hebei province and back again. I went different way with my old classmate. So Uncle chased me instead of Mama! He shouted cursing at me. I saw his friend also chasing us. But we got to train station, run out from taxi, then get on line to Beijing. Then we can be safe, but we never can go to home again. So we had to go shopping for new clothes, and went to salon, too, change hairstyle, and Mama was so happy."

"You're a brave girl. That would make a good movie."

"Sure I'm brave girl!" She grinned proudly. "I come back to you. And living in America."

"Everything's okay now," he sighed.

"Now Mama stay with my friend's family, waiting for interview. She was crying a lot to be going to America. Worry about guns. I told her it's finished. It's safe now. I told her about you. How you take care me. I said we got security at home and you protect us. Everything is safe now. She can relax."

"Yes, I think so." He'd breathed deeply, wanting to believe it was true.

"And thank you for money to help us, Bill. I spent carefully."

"That's okay. I want to help you. Both of you." He was glad to get rid of that envelope of cash Barb had been saving for a rainy day. "It's the right thing to do."

Although they stayed up most of the night, Bill felt energized and ready for anything the next morning. He didn't need the two cups of coffee—with Wendy sitting across the kitchen table from him in her lovely pink sweater over white blouse, dark hair in long braids hanging down from under a pink knit cap, a big smile letting him know she was happy to be home—nor the large coffee from the drive-thru on the way to school.

They shared a grin, sitting in the Escape before the front doors. After a moment's hesitation, she leaned over and kissed him, then got out and he drove around to the faculty parking lot—

"Bell doesn't ring for ten more minutes," a student popped up.

Breaking from his thoughts, Bill glanced up at the clock, still not changed from when daylight savings ended in the fall. More students came into the room, some looking around like they didn't recognize it. A few sniffed, and he smelled the locked up room's musty scent, too. He had to admit it didn't feel like the same room, but it was just as he left it the previous June.

He stood before his desk, sizing up the four walls, a row of windows to his right, the hallway to his left, the only door being by his desk, a closet at the back, bookshelves along the back wall. One entrance, one exit, he noted. The windows could be opened but the gap was too small for most kids to slip through.

Taking a deep breath, arms folded over his chest, he leaned back against the front of his desk, practically sitting on the old wooden contraption. More students filed in and took their seats. Then came the final rush as the bell rang.

When the students had settled down, he welcomed them, wrote his name on the whiteboard behind his desk, started talking about writing, the subject of this first period class. Advanced Composition was an AP class, he warned them, so they would be doing serious writing.

"How're you doing?" asked Laureline Richards, one of the more conscientious students at Vista High who volunteered for everything.

"I'm doing well," said Bill. "Thanks for asking."

"Doing well?" asked a blond boy behind her. The roll sheet was going around the room.

"You don't know?" Laureline asked, turning around to him.

"His wife was killed," said a redhead girl across the aisle from the boy. Her name, he recalled, was either Trisha or Teresa.

"And Becky," said a different boy with no hair, head shaved clean.

Was it a statement or cancer? Bill couldn't decide.

"She was killed, too," said Laureline to the red-haired girl.

"They were *murdered*," spoke Albert in ominous tone, like he had come fresh from a horror movie. The kid probably didn't know who Vincent Price was but imitated him very well.

"Shut up, Albert," growled the bald boy.

"Geez, Al, give the man a break," said Tiffany, sitting behind Albert.

"Yeah, don't be so insensitive," Debi Garza chastised.

"Hey, I can say it," the boy retorted, an edge in his voice. "My mom got murdered by my dad. He's in prison now, so *you* shut up."

"Oh, now I see. That's why you live with your grandma," said Laureline.

Several students voiced their sympathy to Albert.

One more to Bill for his situation.

He pursed his lips as images flashed through his mind. He tried not to let the talk bother him. He knew it would come up, especially with Becky being a student at the school. Students had known her, cared about her. Others would talk; he would simply have to ignore the talk. He would hope the students' short attention spans would gloss over what happened back in August and concentrate on January.

Besides, he had someone new in his life. And students were already talking about that, it seemed, like it was an urban legend: a teacher sleeping with a student. Could it be true? Mister Masters? That old fuddy-duddy? Well, he wasn't a fuddy-duddy any longer! He was hot stuff. A smile crossed his face. He was daddy to her baby doll.

It took all his energy to follow through with the lesson plan for each class and by lunch he felt exhausted. He took a cup of coffee in the faculty lounge but it did not perk him up much. A couple teachers greeted him, welcomed him back, asked how he was doing, and he responded politely. He was getting by, figuring out how to move forward. He didn't mention that he checked escape routes everywhere he went. Or that he carried a gun in a holster at the small of his back, hidden under his sportcoat.

At the end of the day, he waited patiently for Wendy, standing by the front doors chatting with George Griffin.

Finally, she and her friends sauntered up the hallway.

"I'm ready, Bill," she called to him, like she'd earned the right to address him so casually. Her friends cackled at that. George had a smirk. A flurry of goodbyes among the girls, then he and Wendy were out the doors and driving home.

To celebrate the start of a new semester, he proposed they have dinner out on Friday. Like a date. She loved the idea. Although they continued to enjoy her cooking at home—they bought a rice cooker and a bag of rice—he insisted there weren't any good Chinese restaurants in Oklahoma City. Maybe her mother could open one.

He suggested they try a Mexican place not far from the house.

"...and your daughter," said the cheerful waitress, not much older than Wendy. The words grated on his ears. She was not his daughter, he wanted to explain. She was his...girlfriend? fiancée? muse?

After the dinner, because it was across the parking lot, they walked over to Andy's Frozen Yogurt for dessert. Other nights, they would pick up a pint at the drive-thru and take it home. Often Wendy would sit in Bill's lap in the living room as they shared spoonfuls.

"I gain one more kilogram," she complained.

"But what's that?" He pressed his hand flat against her soft belly. "About two pounds? I don't see it."

A few times they swung by the local sushi restaurant for dinner and Bill talked her through the Japanese names and customs.

"We have this in Beijing," Wendy laughed.

"But do you have Oklahoma roll there?" Bill countered.

One weekend they got dressed up and drove downtown to have dinner in an expensive restaurant next to the art museum. They tried bison and rattlesnake, Oklahoma delicacies. In an elegant blue gown, her hair up, she was a precious princess to his aged king. She was particularly careful not to spill anything, especially not down the low-cut V of her dress, her breasts like the Arbuckle Mountains in southern Oklahoma. Other diners snuck glances at his beautiful date. Proud daddy, they must have thought. Or what a dirty old pervert! He didn't care any longer.

He promised more dating. Doing things that were fun. But he was a museum and gallery type of guy. She liked more active adventures. They compromised. He took her to the Cowboy and Western Heritage Museum to learn about the settling of the West and of Oklahoma. He bought her a cowboy hat as a souvenir which she wore the rest of the day and often to school. Then he took her to a stable to ride a horse for the first time ever. They traveled south to visit the Chickasaw Cultural Center one Saturday, learning about Native culture, the history of the Trail of Tears, and he saw her get teary-eyed. Another weekend they stayed at the Artesian Hotel Resort and enjoyed the mineral baths. Another weekend they tried their hand at the Riverwind Casino. Only Bill was allowed to gamble, but he let Wendy call the dice or the cards. Lost all their money but they had fun. And they saw movies, a ballet, and a country music concert, and always had great dinners—the full Oklahoma experience. And every night at home they enjoyed a period of affection before going to sleep.

They discussed plans for Spring Break, a week off from school in late March, right after mid-term exams. Bill thought of driving up to Kansas City and showing Wendy the places of his childhood. He was born there and grew up there, graduating from high school and college there. Plenty to show her.

"That's where I fell in love with my first Asian girl," he offered as they lay together in bed one night. He held her in his arms. "She was Thai, actually, but born in the U.S., spoke like an American but was kinda shy. I still remember her name: Panjarat Muangnakin. Beautiful name. No idea what it meant. Everyone called her Goi, just Goi. We were fourteen. I met her at a summer camp for journalism. Can you believe that? I wanted to be a journalist? She had the most amazing brown skin and silky black hair, a tiny button nose and such big, warm eyes. Like you."

"I don't have brown skin," said Wendy. "But I get tan if you like."

"No, you're perfect the way you are."

"But you like Thai girl."

"And Korean." He laughed, then confirmed what Becky had told her about the woman he was dating when he first met Barb: another graduate student named So-Young who was an English teacher in Korea. More of a study partner than girlfriend.

"All Asian girls," Wendy giggled.

"No, I dated Western girls, too. Blondes mostly, and a redhead. My school was very white, so when I first saw Goi, I was intrigued. I went out with a few Japanese, too, when I lived there. The Art teacher at one of my schools. And English teachers at different schools. Not at the same time, hah."

"You are very popular!"

He laughed. "Not at all."

"I first fall in love with boy named Zhou," she countered, poking his belly, then sliding her hand down. "But we were too young then, so we only walk around holding our hands together. He pay for my noodles sometime. We drink from same straw, so its like kissing, but we didn't kiss. Too shy."

"I only kissed Goi twice. Once at the end of a so-called date during that camp—we had pizza at a place on campus—the other when the camp ended and we had to leave. I swore I'd write to her. She lived in Denver, me in Kansas City. But you know how those long-distance relationships can go: you exchange letters for a while but then they become fewer and further between until nothing."

"We never exchange anything. He stop calling me." She withdrew her hand from below; he was too engaged with their stories. "And I stop calling him. We see each other at school but he always look away. I don't know what I did make him not like me."

He squeezed her against his shoulder and kissed her forehead.

"Foolish boy. How could anyone not like you, huh?"

Bill leaned against the long counter in the faculty lounge where the well-used coffee machine sat, nearly empty by mid-afternoon.

"God, I'm gonna die," Bill moaned within earshot of George Griffin.

"Trouble at home?" the principal mugged.

Bill caught his amused expression. "No, no troubles. I'm just not used to the full day routine, the weekly regimen. That's all."

"Pace yourself. Take a day off if you need it. I know it's a struggle putting together the pieces of a new life."

"You sound like Hannah."

George chuckled. "I guess I pick up some of the lingo."

"Talking with her was helpful. I think I told her that. Now I have to learn to get myself going, do what needs to be done, and finally move on. The road continues—always; I was merely pausing in a rest area, emptying my bladder." He took a long sip of coffee.

"Interesting metaphor. That's what it's called, correct?"

"Correct. A riddle wrapped in a dream."

He thought of the dream he once had: seeing Becky graduate, the cap and gown, the accolades, the hope for the future. It was so hard, but he had to let that dream go—or transfer it over to his fiancée. In May he would see Wendy walk across the stage and receive her diploma. It would feel about the same, he decided. He'd heard that Becky would receive an honorary diploma.

Then Wendy's mother would arrive and they would all live happily together in the house on Forest Drive. Her mother spoke no English, Wendy cautioned, but she would translate for Bai Li.

"Hmm, Bai Li," Bill pondered. "'Buy Lee'. Her English name could be Bailey. It's a little uncommon but not weird. I could get used to calling her Bailey. Ma Bailey." He laughed and she slapped his arm.

"*Ma* means 'horse' in Chinese," she said with a growl. "You got to be nice to my mama."

"I will. I must thank her for having you."

"Thank you for welcome her to America and living in this house," said Wendy. "She will like to be called Bailey, I'm sure."

However, before that day, there were so many things to do.

Bill offered to teach Wendy how to drive. They spent Sunday mornings cruising the mall parking lot. The Escape was too big for her to manage at first, but she got used to it and could drive in a straight line and make three-point turns adequately.

While Bill dropped off the electric bill at the office on Main Street, Wendy saw a sign on a storefront offering a job. It was an ice cream shop. With his encouragement, she went in and asked about the job. She would've gotten it but for her visa status which didn't allow her to work. Bill talked to the owner of the small shop, the father of one of his students, and they came to an arrangement. Bill would pay her wage— it was just for extra help on the weekend—so she could have the experience of working in America. She could take orders, make change, and so on, gain a sense of accomplishment.

As February turned into March, the senior pictures period arrived. For young ladies of the school, it was a big deal. Hiring professional photographers to make a full package of photos, a portfolio suitable for starting a fashion modeling career. When Wendy went to the studio for her photos, the guy was too complimentary.

"Your face is so pretty, so cute, like a little girl," the photog called as she posed, "yet your body is so fricking awesome, with your big tits and those long legs. Really fantastic. Love to see a nude of you."

Bill frowned, sitting to the side. "This is how you talk to high school girls coming for senior pics?"

"If she's hot, like her, then yeah."

"And you're the one the school recommends?"

The photog held the camera, snapping pics, circling Wendy.

"Yeah," he said with a laugh. He looked up from the camera, gave Bill a grin. "I also do glamour photography, if that appeals to you." He put his eye to the camera again. "Got to get'em young if they're gonna have a decent career. You know, before they get too old and their looks are gone."

Bill clapped his hands. "I think we're done here."

"Hey, man. I'm still taking her senior pics. They're all rated G, I assure you."

"Finish up."

"Besides, when she's eighteen she can decide for herself. She'll be out of your control. How soon's that?"

Wendy was flattered, but Bill was not amused. When they went to outdoor locations to take pictures, part of the package, she dressed in lighter clothing despite the cool weather, sleeveless and low cut tops and leg-baring shorts. The photog was further impressed, inviting her to his studio to make a portfolio that would get her into magazine modeling—if she was willing to do semi-nude.

Bill declined for her, telling him to lay off high school girls.

"Of course I mean after she turns eighteen," said the photog. "Then she can sign her own contracts. Otherwise, age of consent is sixteen in Oklahoma. But you knew that already, I bet."

Bill wanted to punch the guy, wanted to boast Wendy was with him as a lover. *They* were together. She had chosen him.

But for how long? The thought exploded in his head. She could leave him at any time, fly home to China, and he would be alone again.

Sure, he thought as they drove home, he was a hypocrite. He knew they were doing things which many people would consider improper. But it was love. The great alibi. Anything for love. He never forced her to do anything. Besides, he also protected her.

"That guy's a perv," he muttered. "Stay away from guys like that."

"Okay, Bill. Thank you," said Wendy, hugging his arm in the SUV. "Only for you. Only you, Bill."

His heart warmed and a smile spread across his face.

The rhythms of the school year never ceased, Bill cursed, forgetting the stressful life he had before.

The senior prom was coming and registration had begun. Voting for the Prom King and Queen was updated to the Prom Royal Couple. Bill was worried who might ask Wendy to the Prom. He knew she'd caught the eye of several young men. Boys were talking to her at school, showing up at the house.

"I have boyfriend at home," she would tell them, not explaining that home meant the very house she was living in with Mr. Masters. The boys would never understand that.

But they showed up as the mild winter rolled into an early spring. One time two boys offered to mow the lawn for her 'dad' just to hang out with her. She sat on the deck in her short shorts and pink top, drinking lemon tea. She would let them do the mowing because she knew how much Bill hated mowing the yard. But she always told Bill how she loved the sight of him with his shirt off, sweating under the sun, arm and shoulder muscles flexing, working the machine like a medieval battle weapon, slaying the lawn dragon.

"Anything for you, my precious princess," he declared.

The swim meets continued, and Wendy advanced up the leader board each event, finally winning the breaststroke race. He would stroke those breasts at night. He mused how he'd cup his hands over them, or let them be pillows for his face. And he continued to massage her legs and back whenever she needed relief.

As for the Prom, Bill had skipped his own as a senior, although he had the distinction of going with a senior girl to her prom when he was a sophomore lad. For Vista High's Prom, it could be awkward. If he volunteered as chaperone and Wendy went solo, they could be together at the big dance. He might even dust off his dancing shoes and strut his stuff while Wendy cheered him on.

Then final exams and graduation. And life itself.

It all seemed so easy.

29

VALENTINE'S DAY was a big deal at Vista High. Some students swore off the occasion, not being in couplehood, calling it an evil holiday and triggering for singletons, going rogue with black greeting cards on the lockers of those they had crushes on but which were not reciprocated. Administration cautioned students against these 'microaggressions'. Bill only got involved by being asked to check the spelling on some of the poems the students wrote.

"Good sonnet," he praised Fiona Hansen, the goth girl who was the best poet in school.

"That's not actually a tanka," he cautioned James Langley, the son of his colleague in Biology. "It's five-seven-five, like a haiku, then two more lines of seven. Try again."

"Going for slant rhyme, I see," he said to Meghan Tipton in his Creative Writing class, who seemed to change her hair color depending on the day of the week.

Wendy had gotten a box of chocolates for him, possibly purchased with money she earned scooping ice cream on weekends. There was a gift shop next door. She came into his classroom to hand the red box to him right before his 2:00 p.m. American Lit class started, and the students who were already in their seats had shouted and teased him for her kind gesture.

"Suck up," called one boy from the back of the room.

She didn't seem to care what students thought.

He was surprised and asked her about the custom in China. Not popular, she told him. Love wasn't something worth celebrating, he surmised, too anti-Party. So he mentioned the custom in Japan when he taught there, partly to explain why he didn't have chocolate for her. Only the boys gave chocolates to the girls on Valentine's Day. Then in March the girls return the favor by giving white chocolate to the boys, perhaps white to symbolize the purity of their love. He wasn't clear on that; he simply liked getting chocolate. Because she was giving him chocolate in February, he would return the favor in March.

"Kiss him," shouted a girl, and Wendy pecked his cheek.

Bill had accepted the box of chocolates from her, adding a little Japanese bow. A few laughed while others clapped, and one gave a whistle. He worried they could see how much in love he was—

March, mid-term exams the previous week, a dead week, then on to spring break.

He texted Wendy to come by his room before his 10:00 World Lit class. He didn't tell her he was going to give her the box of chocolates he owed her to complete the ritual. She texted back that her mother had finally been granted an interview for the visa.

He smiled at the news. Everything was going to work out. With a glance at the cute red box on his desk, he turned to the students who had already arrived.

"Everyone read today's story?" A few students were trying to quickly read it. "A couple extra minutes probably won't do it, if you haven't. Mister Chekhov will not be pleased."

"That story is so gay," said one girl sitting by the windows.

"How can it be gay?" asked a boy across the aisle from her. "It's about a man and woman having an affair."

"I thought it was about a lady and her dog," said another student, clueless.

"No, she's got a dog when he first sees her. That's page one."

"But it had no ending," said a boy at the back. "They just keep on meeting. And planning how to keep having their affair."

"No clear ending is what's different about it," Cherise chastised her classmate. "You gotta figure it out yourself. How do you want it to end? Do you want them to be together? What do you think will happen after the end? I want them to be together. After all they've gone through, they deserve it."

"Very good, Cherise," said Mr. Masters with a wry grin. "I'll let you teach the class today. You seem ready."

"Are we gonna get our mid-terms back today?" asked Michael.

"No, not today. Maybe Friday," Mr. Masters replied. "I ran out of red ink."

"But my family's leaving town for spring break on Friday."

"Not my problem."

He regarded the open door, expecting his Love to appear at any second. She was well-known in school now, even nominated for the Royal Court. Her presence in the classroom wasn't unusual. Everyone knew she lived with Mr. Masters. Some kids gossiped they were more than housemates.

At the edge of his peripheral vision sat a scraggly boy in the front corner desk. No book or notebook. He shivered in his winter coat. Kevin something. Never spoke in class, hadn't turned in any papers. Absent often. He fidgeted.

"You need to go to the restroom?" asked Mr. Masters.

"No, I don't need to go to the restroom," sneered the kid.

"Suit yourself."

He looked at the wall clock. The bell would ring any minute. Then Wendy would be late to her class, so he prepared a hall pass.

She arrived, out of breath like she'd been speed-walking.

"Hi," she said with the biggest grin, straightening the hem of her pink sweater over her baby blue slacks.

"I have something for you," he said, reaching around behind him as he leaned back against the desk.

Instead of grabbing the box, he found it was just out of reach so his fingers only managed to push it further away. He stood up from the desk, turned to grab the box—

A girl screamed. Then others screamed.

Bill spun around to see the fidgeting boy standing beside the door. The kid held a revolver, his arm extended, swinging the gun around at the students in the classroom. He stood by the door, now closed and probably locked by him.

"*What?*" Bill exclaimed. More words stuck in his throat.

"Kevin!" Jayla Meadows cried out. "What're you doing?"

"Shut up!" the kid shouted. "All of you, up against the windows."

Students started to get up from their desks and move to the wall with the bank of windows, spreading out along them.

"What *are* you doing?" asked Mr. Masters, catching his breath, trying to remain calm. He stood with hands on his hips, facing the boy. His heart was beating fast.

"I'm acting out," the kid grumbled, pointing the gun at him. "Isn't that what it's called?"

"No, I mean.... That pistol...." Mr. Masters waved Wendy to step aside, move to his right, out of the line of fire. "What is it? A Sig Sauer? Or Smith and Wesson?"

"Does it matter?" the kid challenged. He looked at the pistol. "I dunno. One of my dad's guns. A thirty-eight special."

"Kevin, please put the gun down," called Jayla, hands out, begging. "You don't have to do this."

"Shut up!" He spun around like a Western gunslinger, outstretched arm pointing in Jayla's direction. The gun went off and the kid seemed surprised. The bullet caught another girl, Emily Carter, in the upper arm and continued on to pierce the safety-glass window behind her. The girl screamed in pain and others froze.

"Stop! Put the gun down," said Mr. Masters in a tightly-controlled voice. "It's not too late. Give it up. Set it on the floor. Now."

Emily's arm bled. The girl standing next to her, Rachel Kim, had gotten blood sprayed on her, but seeing the continuing flow, pulled off her gray Vista High sweatshirt and wrapped it around Emily's arm, leaving Rachel wearing only a black sports bra.

"That's it," said the kid, reasserting his authority. "That looks good. So how about all you girls take your tops off?"

Suddenly the alarms sounded in the school—the same as if there was a tornado but a different pattern, Bill noticed. That was new. He held his hands up as if holding back the kid's anger.

The intercom buzzed. A robotic voice announced: *"The school is now on lockdown. Follow lockdown procedures. Police are on the way."*

The message repeated. It was loud and with each repetition became more annoying. The sound of the gunshot triggered the emergency system, Bill guessed.

"Make it stop," shouted the kid.

"I don't have any control over that," said Mr. Masters. "It'll stop soon. Just put the gun down. It will go a lot easier for you if you stop this now."

"But I don't wanna stop now!" shouted the kid, his face red.

Bill took a breath. He was the teacher. He had to be strong. He had to protect his students.

"So what's your gripe? Or is it you just want to feel powerful? I get that. We all feel small sometimes. Like the world is ignoring us. We want some attention. I get it."

The kid gave a smirk, returning his focus to the other students in the room. He waved his gun at them. "Go on. All you girls take your tops off. Do it." One started to unbutton her blouse but the others hesitated. "Do it. Now." He looked over the line of students. "Not you fatties. Not you, ugly girl." He saw Wendy out of the corner of his eye, posed a little to the front of Bill. "You, Asian chick. Come here."

She threw a look at Bill, seeking instruction.

A flood of thoughts crashed through his mind and he tried to sort them, find the right response. Before he could say or do anything, the kid grabbed her arm and spun her into the grasp of his free arm, her shoulder locked in his armpit, his arm extending across her chest. She squirmed against his grip and he held her tighter.

"Let her go," cried Jayla. "Please. She didn't do anything. You don't have to do this."

"Yeah, I do. This is for Derek."

"Derek?" asked Mr. Masters. He stepped back, felt the edge of the teacher's desk against his rear. "Who's Derek?"

"Derek Martin. My step-brother." He sneered at Mr. Masters. "You know him. He drives an orange car...?"

"Who?" Bill knew then Orange Car Guy was related to this kid with the gun. "Wasn't he arrested? For burglary or something?"

"Exactly. Arrested for nothing. Nothing to do with nothing. I heard you got him arrested."

"Didn't he graduate from here? About three years ago?"

"Four—"

"Then got in with some ring of thieves?"

"No, he was just making a living."

"Okay, I see this is really between you and me," spoke Mr. Masters. "So how about letting her go, huh? Letting everyone go, okay?"

"Not this one. She's the one you wanna save. I know about the mall thing. Now it's a school thing. And somebody's gotta die today. So how about you and your slutty girlfriend here?"

"Why?" Bill met the kid's frightened gaze. "Why does anyone need to die today? It's so easy to let everything go—to let go of everything that bothers us. Your brother will be out of jail soon. He'll get on the right path, find a job, be a good citizen. Life goes on."

The girls in the class had shed their tops. One had worn no bra so she crossed her arms over her chest. Others stood with an assortment of bras on display. Kevin noticed they had complied. Holding Wendy in his arm, he waved the gun at the girls.

"Now take the rest of your clothes off." He chuckled. "You guys close your eyes. Now!" Again hesitation, then unsnapping of pants, loosening of belts, slipping off shoes and boots. Unzipping of a dress. The dropping of a skirt. But they were too slow. "Do it now!"

"Don't," Mr. Masters countermanded. "Don't do it."

"What? Are you insane? You don't talk back to me!"

The kid whirled around and fired the gun.

Bill cried out as the bullet struck the meat of his hip. He fell against the desk, sprawling over it. Wendy had jerked away as he pulled the trigger, or else the bullet might have hit him in a more vital place. He wasn't sure what the damage was—

"See? I mean business." The kid faced the girls once more, checking that they were obeying. "Not you fat girls and you, the ugly one. I don't wanna see what you got. Guys, close your fuckin' eyes. And get on your knees, hands behind your head. This is only for me to see."

Wendy was crying, squirming in his grasp.

"You wanna go to him, don't you? You wanna comfort him, yeah? Like you do all night? Because you're a slut. Ain't that right? My step-dad fought in Vietnam. Lotta sluts over there, he said."

"Stop this right now," Mr. Masters grunted through clenched teeth, holding his left hip. He had fallen across the desk on his right side, on top of his right arm. Blood wet his trousers, stained his left hand. "You've done enough to show you're a man, now give it up."

"You taught us that," said the kid, shifting Wendy into a tight hold.

"Or Mister Chekhov did. If there's a gun on the mantelpiece in the first act you better fuckin' shoot it by the third act. Ain't that right?" He laughed. "Is this the third act, Mister Masters?"

"I don't know about any third acts," Bill muttered, grimacing. He took a breath. "Is this about dramatic form? Or about good and evil? The perpetual war. And we take up different sides? On any given day a good person, like you, Kevin, can be lured into an evil act. Why do you feel the need to do this? Nobody knows. Maybe you don't know, either. On any given day a person who usually acts bad can show compassion. Even a person committing an immoral act just might save the world, while the purist soul might do something even accidently that destroys something precious—"

"What a load of bullshit!" The kid kept the gun on Mr. Masters.

Pounding on the classroom door caused the kid to twist and check who was there through the door's small window.

"It's here," said whoever was outside in the hall. It sounded like Principal Griffin or Coach Bufford. "Police are here," the man outside shouted through the door. "Put down the gun." The door handle rattled but the door remained locked.

Bill's right arm was under his body. His hand dug into the small of his back, under his sportcoat, unsnapped the strap.

"Sometimes the gun doesn't need to be fired," said Mr. Masters. "Its mere presence is enough to impact the scene. Ever think of that?"

He worked the pistol into his hand. The man at the gun range told him there was no reason to carry if he kept the safety on and had to load the first round when the need came. He flipped off the safety; a bullet was already in the chamber.

"We can all sit down and still have our lesson." He rolled onto his belly to free his right arm, then rolled back as he continued speaking. "We'll send Emily to the nurse's office. As for me, I think I can tough it out through the lesson. Then I'll go for treatment. Just a flesh wound. We can get some help for you, too. You didn't mean to do it, I'm sure."

"Sure I did!" shouted the kid, aiming in earnest.

Bill swung his right arm up, the Glock poised in his hand.

"*You* got a gun?" The kid was surprised but held his ground.

Trying to steady his aim, Bill looked down the sights. He could see Wendy in the kid's grasp, her eyes closed tight, her face wet from tears, her mouth whimpering. She tried to pull away, to Bill's right, but was held back by the kid's arm.

"What're you gonna do? Shoot me?" He seemed nervous behind his shield of bravura. "Teachers don't shoot students. Not happening. That's not your story, Mister Masters."

Bill aimed, controlled his breathing, centering the target.

"You see? The mere presence of the gun is enough to impact the scene," Bill spoke. "I don't need to shoot it." He held his aim steady.

"Go on," the kid growled. "Do it."

Should he aim for a leg? Disable the kid? Maybe he'd still be able to fire back—or shoot at one of the students. And Wendy was in his grasp. The S.W.A.T. team had to be in the building. If he could wait a little longer. Delay. Keep him talking.

"You see I have a gun so you have to rethink your plan. You decide to put your gun down, because if I have a gun, I must know how to use it, and you have no chance—"

The kid squeezed the trigger, sending a bullet into Mr. Masters' thigh, just below where the first shot had struck him. He rolled back, grimacing against the pain, glaring at the kid, and squeezed the trigger.

Wendy tore out of his arm hold, stumbling and falling to the floor on her hands and knees in front of the desk.

The kid froze where he stood. His grip loosened, arm dropping to his side, the pistol hooked on his trigger finger, as pounding on the door covered the echo of the shots.

If only I had waited a few more seconds....

The kid crashed to his knees and tumbled over on his face. The splash on the wall behind him and the blood pumping from his throat signaled the end of the incident.

"Wendy?" Bill called from the desktop down to her. "You okay?"

She got up, crying, hands to her face.

He flicked the safety on and laid the Glock on the desktop.

"Unlock the door."

A team of police burst in as the girls scrambled to put their clothes on and the boys got up from their knees.

Wendy started to throw herself over him but hesitated, looking over his injuries, distraught, unable to decide what to do. She took his face in her hands as tears ran, and kissed him.

"Could someone please call an ambulance? Take Emily first."

He rolled onto his back.

"Got one right outside, sir," said a man in uniform, looking down at him. Another was checking his hip and thigh.

"Oh, Bill," cried Wendy, hovering. "Bill, my lovely Bill."

He took her hand, pulled it away from his face.

"If I don't make it, Wendy, be a good girl. All right? Make someone else happy. Okay? Promise me."

"No, Bill! I make *you* happy!" She tried to smile. "I'm gonna marry you, Bill. Nobody else. I'm your precious princess!"

A few students lingered by the desk as others were ushered out by officers. Some stood in shock and had to be led out by their arms.

"Let's clear the room, people," called an officer.

"See? I told you," said one boy, filing by the desk.

"Leave'em alone," said the girl behind him.

"I knew they were together."

Wendy clasped Bill's hand, his eyes closed, as a paramedic put an oxygen mask over his face.

"Ma'am, you have to go," said an officer.

"Take care, Mister Masters," called a boy.

Some students clapped their hands.

He flashed a thumbs-up as they moved him onto the gurney.

"We got you," George Griffin told him, hand on Bill's shoulder as they rolled him down the corridor, Wendy running after. "You're going to be okay. Don't you worry about a thing. We got this under control."

30

THE FIRST PROM BILL ATTENDED since he was fifteen was several steps up from the event cast in his small town's small community center. He surveyed the ballroom of the resort hotel, noting the elegant décor and the thematic elements of God and Country, the red, white, and blue of patriotism, almost as though it was a 4th of July dance. But the kids were happy, dressed in their colorful tuxedos and ball gowns. The band was good, too.

And there was his fiancée, Wendy Wang, in her bright red gown, dark hair put up, gold ear rings catching the light, her lovely white shoulders and arms bare as she tried shaking a move in the unsteady high heels with a tall boy he thought was Freddy Kent, one of the swim team members. In his Prom debut, he might have taken to the floor all of three times—slow dances where he could simply hold his partner in his arms and turn around like a decoration on a wedding cake.

A parent chaperone sidled up to Bill as he leaned on his wooden cane beside the refreshments table. He lifted a plastic cup of red punch to his lips, thinking of the days when someone would have spiked the bowl. Not tonight. Tasted right.

"Sam Sullivan," said the man, extending his hand to shake.

Bill shook his hand, said his name. They both wore black tuxedos with black bow ties. Sam asked him how he was doing, like it was common knowledge, and Bill responded plainly yet politely. He didn't know this man.

"Oh, sorry. I'm a sergeant with the Oklahoma Highway Patrol," he explained. "Heard about your school episode. Wanted to shake your hand is all." He grimaced like he hated to say what he said. "Helluva shot. So I heard. Under the chin, right through the spine. Amazing. You were in the military?"

Bill frowned. "National Guard way back when."

He was not proud. He didn't want to shoot anyone for any reason. But the moment came and he could not do nothing. He told Sam the same thing but in more elevated language, constantly looking away to hide a lone tear that always threatened to drop. Sam understood.

"As a parent and a first responder, I know we can't be too careful," said Sam. "Wish I'da been on the team responding that day. Never good to go to your own kids' school for something like that. Or any school. I was working near Guthrie that day."

"Who are your kids?" asked Bill, turning to regard the man.

"Lucy Sullivan. Know her? And you probably had Luke, too. They already graduated."

"Oh, the twins. Right. I remember them."

"My youngest is graduating this year. Alex?"

Bill had to think. "Alex...?"

"Alex*andra*," said Sam, pointing to the crowd of dancers. "That's her in the purple dress."

Bill recognized the girl: one of the students in his World Lit class, the class that had the 'incident'. She'd been standing on the opposite side of Emily from Rachel, who lent her shirt. Alex could just as easily have been the one shot.

"She wants to go Marines, like her old man," said Sam, pride in his voice. "I wanted to thank you personally for giving her that chance."

Bill swallowed. "I didn't want to do that."

The words bounced around in his head and with each repetition sounded more like what he should say in a courtroom. But there was the gun, the kid putting it to his girlfriend's head, and he would fail again to protect his ladies if he did nothing, so he gave up all thoughts and let his finger take command.

The music played on, students dancing.

"It shouldn't have happened," Bill continued. "Need to catch them before it gets that far."

"But it did happen, and I'm glad someone was there who could take care of it." The man scanned the room. "I'm working security here." He opened his tuxedo a bit to show his holstered sidearm.

"Never can be too careful," said Bill, wishing he didn't have to be careful, that he could be careless and still not have anything to worry about, because the world was safe and everyone was in love, respecting each other, like some kind of pain-free paradise.

They took the conversation away from the shooting, mostly on the basketball playoffs and the Thunder's chances, but circled back to it, watching the kids have their fun.

"I just hope the judge goes easy on you. Clear case of self-defense. Anybody can see that. You saved them. Lucky you were armed, even without a concealed-carry permit. We're cheering for you. The laws are ambiguous, at best. And the situation...well, you had to act or more lives could've been lost."

"Thanks," said Bill. "Thanks for your concern. And don't forget the Martin family's lawsuit for wrongful death."

"Yeah, well, that's bullshit," Sam growled. "Parents gotta keep their guns locked up."

"Even if I go to prison, at least my family will be safe."

"Helluva shot," Sam mumbled. "If you hadn't fired, who knows? Could've been that girl who got it."

"Which girl...? The exchange student?"

"Yeah, that one. The hostage. Anyway, good luck."

He nodded his goodbye as he stepped away.

A group of kids led by Wendy arrived at the table.

"You are okay?" she asked, stretching up to hug him.

"Doing okay." He winced at the bump to his hip. "Now you have almost completed the American high school experience." He already told her of his one time at Prom, long ago when life was tougher. Had to hike uphill through the snow to get to the Prom. She laughed but hugged him all the same.

The boy shook his hand. "I wanna thank you for what you did," said Freddy. He'd been in the classroom, sitting at the back, playing a game on his phone, when the kid at the front stood up with the gun. Freddy pissed his pants. Nothing to be embarrassed about. Bill heard that he had previously experienced an armed robbery.

"Thanks," said Bill. He had been shaking hands all night.

A sturdy cane, presented to him by students of the woodworking class, didn't alleviate the pain, now merely discomfort, in his wounded hip. Doctors were able to stitch him up but the marks would likely last forever. The bullet had gone through the meat of his hip and lodged in the wall plaster under the whiteboard. He was lucky, doctors said. The bullet in his thigh was close to an artery. If his pelvis shattered he would be a long time in recovery.

"I want to dance with you, Bill," said Wendy, faking a sorrowful face, like an anime character.

"Frankly, my dear, I'd love to," he said with a chuckle. "But I can only dance horizontally." He gave a wink which Freddy didn't see. "I promise to dance with you at the wedding."

"You will be okay to pick up Mama from airport?" she asked him, a serious expression on her face.

Freddy caught that. "I can help, if you need somebody."

"I'll be fine. I can lift suitcases. It's just dancing that hurts." He tossed back the last of his punch. "Actually it's just my excuse for not having to dance. I've been planning this for weeks."

"No, you didn't!" Wendy snorted, patting his arm.

She was becoming so American.

"Don't worry. I'll be ready. Every mother should get to attend her daughter's graduation. I'll be sure to load up on pain meds."

Soon graduation would arrive, the commencement ceremony in the big auditorium, where Wendy would receive her American diploma. Cap and gown were already ordered. By then, he would meet Bai Li—Ma Bailey, he always said and got a playful slap to his arm or shoulder.

It all seemed so easy.

Wendy swirled around the ballroom in her flowing gown, queen of the Royal Court. Well, okay, he recalled, she was only a 'member' of the Royal Court since there weren't supposed to be any gender-implied roles. No more king and queen, just Royal A and Royal B. But at home, he was king of the castle and she his princess bride.

He was lost in thought when Jennifer Claybourne approached him. She gave him a cordial hug, remarked how handsome he looked all dressed up. She added her condolences, how it was so awful that what happened had to happen. He agreed.

George Griffin arrived in his bright teal tuxedo, sparkling sequins covering the jacket and slacks. As though rescuing him from awkward conversation, he clapped Bill's shoulder, greeted them.

"You take care now, Bill," said Jennifer, excusing herself.

"I will, Jenn. And thank you. For everything."

"Doing okay?" George adjusted his teal bow tie, which matched his tuxedo. Students were amused by his colorful style.

"Really?" asked Bill, glaring at the sparkly tux.

George held out his hands. "What? It's a big hit. I wore this last year, too. And the year before."

"Good thing I skipped them. Smart move."

"So how're you doing?" George asked, turning serious.

"As well as can be expected," Bill replied, glancing down at himself, as though looking for flaws.

"You'll be out there dancing it up by Homecoming, I know."

"Have to take some lessons first."

"So do it." He tapped his temple. "And Hannah said she's pleased you two are getting hitched. Makes you respectable."

"May I remind you Miss Wang turned eighteen already?" Bill gave a wink. "But you're invited to the wedding, of course."

"Thanks." George scanned the crowd. "How's she doing, anyway?"

Bill watched the crowd of students undulating to the music as he leaned on his cane. "She's fine. The counseling is helpful. She likes talking to Hannah."

"Good, good."

"She'll be going to UCO in the fall to study Engineering."

"That's great."

They focused on Wendy, dancing with a different boy, grinning in delight, being young and having a great time, the future full of promise but put on pause for an evening.

Principal Griffin refilled his cup and returned his gaze to the crowd of students dancing the night away. Like it was an ordinary semester. Like nothing had happened.

"You're a lucky man, Bill."

Acknowledgements

Although a few places are mentioned by name in the novel and other places have had the names altered, no disrespect is intended, nor is any suggestion made of actual impropriety in or by these entities; they are used fictitiously. Some geographical locations as well as police jurisdictions have been compressed or merged for the sake of the story. My appreciation goes to the cities of Oklahoma City and Edmond and the state of Oklahoma where I have made my home for lo these many years. Nothing bad has ever happened to me here.

I always use music to assist my imagination. For this novel, I listened to the music of Italian pianist/composer Ludovico Einaudi (albums: *Divenire*, *Eden Roc*, *Elements*, *Seven Days Walking (Day 1)*, *In a time lapse*, and *Una Mattina*). This body of work was supplemented by the music of British pianist/composer Helen Jane Long (albums: *Embers*, *Identity*, *Intervention*, *Perspective*, and *Porcelain*). A work by Ólafur Arnalds (*For Now I Am Winter*) also contributed to feeding the muse. Many thanks for the great creativity and musical sensitivity.

About the Author

Stephen Swartz grew up in the Kansas City, Missouri area, where he dreamed of traveling the world. His writing usually includes exotic locations, foreign characters, and smatterings of other languages—the trope of strangers in strange lands, which he has often been for much of his life, traveling extensively, and living in Japan for several years.

After studying music early on, including the composition of a symphony, Swartz planned to become a music teacher before deciding to exchange his musical chops for a new typewriter and write fiction. After years of struggling with his craft, his catalog finally took off with his first published literary novel *After Ilium*, followed by several more books.

Not counting trips to China to teach summer classes, Swartz spends his days teaching at a university in Oklahoma while continuing to write late at night. His stories have appeared in anthologies and literary journals. *Exchange* is his twelfth novel.

Also by Stephen Swartz

Contemporary Literary Fiction

After Ilium

Aiko

A Beautiful Chill

A Girl Called Wolf

Fantasy & Science Fiction

The Stefan Székely Vampire Trilogy

I. A Dry Patch of Skin

II. Sunrise

III. Sunset

*Epic Fantasy *With Dragons*

The Dream Land Trilogy

I. Long Distance Voyager

II. Dreams of Future's Past

III. Diaspora

www.ingramcontent.com/pod-product-compliance
Lightning Source LLC
Chambersburg PA
CBHW071111250626
47159CB00002B/701